The Tzaddik

a novel

Michael D. Doochin

PUBLISHED BY WESTVIEW, INC.

Nashville, Tennessee

ISBN Perfect bound 978-1-935271-40-6, Dust jacket 978-1-935271-41-3

First edition, January 2010

Cover photo and design by Esther Villalobos

Printed in the United States of America on acid free paper.

PUBLISHED BY WESTVIEW, INC.
P.O. Box 210183
Nashville, Tennessee 37221
www.publishedbywestview.com

For Linda,
Jonathan,
Arielle,
and Jeremy

Preface

More than a decade ago, I began the study of kabbalah with Rabbi Yitzchok Tiechtel of Nashville, Tennessee. We began by learning the *Tanya* each Shabbat, each Saturday afternoon, that we were both in town. The *Tanya*, first published in 1796, by Rabbi Schneur Zalman, today remains the "Bible" of the Chabad-Lubavitch school of Chassidic thought, which descends from the teachings of the Bal Shem Tov. It is a compilation of Hebrew Scriptures, Talmud, and esoteric wisdom, or kabbalah. The *Tanya* is not a text that one can read in a few sittings, nor is it a work that one can ever say he has completed; rather than learning a chapter at a time, the reader is more likely to read a few pages or perhaps only a line or two. The layman who reads a translation will not only encounter a language barrier, but will find it necessary to span a stretch of thought extending more than 200 years, and then beyond. Yet, what is most difficult about the *Tanya* is that in relatively condensed wording, it speaks of spiritual concepts and metaphors, which because of their connection to G-d, possess an infinite nature and cannot easily be described in our physical and finite world. Indeed, learning *Tanya* is not a dispassionate intellectual exercise whereby at each sitting one carries away a simple concept or opinion. It is a personal journey, a crossing, and a true journey is one that takes a person to a place that he could never imagine before he started. It is more akin to working a personal holistic puzzle over a period of time, because the message of the text is spiritual and therefore individually tailored for each soul. Because it speaks eloquently of the truths of human nature and of the specific reasons for our souls incarnating on this earth, the reader must wrestle with the material. As the reader engages that material he metamorphoses, so that his original perceptions of the text change, creating a continuing process that engenders more personal transformation. This is why the *Tanya* is best learned over a lengthy period of time. The reality of our existence is veiled and not easily accessible and there is no simple definition of truth. However, this must not dissuade a person from attaining an understanding of self that is essential to one's mission on this planet.

From the beginning, the *Tanya* spoke to me and its metaphors stirred my soul. I was returning to my spiritual home and I looked for a means to pass this gift to others. Initially, I was encouraged to write a text explaining the *Tanya* from a layman's point of view, as a way to introduce and distill its truths to those who could not take the time to fully read and understand it. I wrote a preface and first chapter and was encouraged to continue. But discussing intellectual concepts, by breaking them into more digestible pieces, could not convey the full feeling, the full understanding, of the *Tanya* journey. It would be necessary to tell a story, so that it could be better absorbed and comprehended by readers on emotional and spiritual levels. But what story should I tell that would impart the essential nature of such an important reference? Attending an ice hockey game one night, I glimpsed a small understanding of what a tzaddik might encounter in this world. So from the chochmah, or epiphany, of that hockey game, portrayed at the beginning of chapter three, I knew much of the message I wished to convey. The tzaddik, while perhaps a more interesting character on a macro scale for a tale, nevertheless, as any human soul, must confront the same issues and choices regarding his mission as all of us.

I cannot take credit for the creation of this novel, other than being a willing vessel to receive it. All creativity is G-d given. And as I wrote, usually in the middle of the night, when the reception from the universe is best, I was often surprised by what would appear in various scenes. Always wishing this novel to be completely realistic—and I believe it is—even though it is couched in the form of a tale— because I believe that we create our own tales in our lives just as the protagonist does—I was initially concerned about what I had transcribed. I consoled myself that it was indeed a work of fiction and that I certainly had the license as the author, but I was not totally at ease. Then while this work sat for a number of years and I had dozens of readers give me their reactions, my wife Linda and I began to do energy work and I learned that all that I had questioned was actually indeed "true", with scientific evidence to support it. The energy work indeed paralleled kabbalah and merely connected dots from a slightly different perspective.

Actually, I have continued to learn much more. Seemingly accidental names or situations introduced into the book have turned out to be significant to the story as more knowledge was revealed to me afterward. In that sense, this book, as are all projects for each of us in our lives, has been a journey for me. Its development has been a microcosm of what I set out to convey from the beginning in this novel: that of Divine providence—that nothing we do is accidental or insignificant. And these revelations for me have most often come about through the observations and assistance of others, in the same way that the characters in the novel reach their new understandings. In that sense, my readers are co-creators in this project; I have only helped to bring it to a certain stage, but they will elevate it to a higher understanding throughout the universe, which is the purpose of writing this book. We are a vast community of incredible human souls and when we unite, we break through our perceived limitations.

I am grateful to all of my teachers in this life. As words here remain inadequate to describe those who have aided me in my growth or supported me in bringing this project to fruition, I hope that I have thanked you all in person.

And I hope that you will find part of what you seek in this book. There is a **glossary** in the back to assist you with some of the concepts. Hopefully you will learn much of the vocabulary from the context of the story, as was intended.

Michael D. Doochin
December 2009

The Tzaddik

Prologue

The man quickly turned the corner and entered the bedroom. "Well, well," he said. "I see you've made a lot of progress. Down to one box now. Your mother will be pleased."

"This one's not mine grandfather," the boy said. "Maybe you can tell what it is."

The man studied the box for a minute. It was different from the others. It was not just older, almost decayed now, but of a totally different material, a vintage he rarely remembered seeing. "What's in it?"

"A bunch of strange stuff," the boy said. "Like this. I've never seen anything like this before."

The man laughed. "That's what they used to call a picture. Before we could project and store the representation of a person in real space, all they had was this two dimensional image. Not the same at all, is it?"

"No. But who is it?"

The man took the picture into his hands and studied it while slowly squatting to sit. His eyes became distant and his body became still in a way the boy had never seen. In response, the boy's posture stiffened in the long silence and he refrained from even clearing his throat.

"It's funny you should come upon this now, right before your Bar Mitzvah," the man finally said. "This is your namesake. Let me tell you a story:"

1

Once upon a time, a long time ago, there existed a world very different from the one we live in today. Our story begins in that world, at the turn of the third millennium, that is the year 2000 in the old Christian calendar you learned about in school, which corresponded to 5760 on our Hebrew calendar.

Now the world was full of darkness and evil at that time. There were righteous people living then, as there are at all times, but little respect was accorded to them. The face of G-d was hidden, in exile, because most humans put Him there. Rather than bow down only to G-d, they worshipped the false idols of money, vanity, and ego. Everything seemed to revolve around the satisfaction of personal pleasure. In the name of personal pleasure, people hurt others and pillaged the great resources of our planet. Worst of all was the perversion of truth. In order to get what they wanted, those in power used money and the media to drown out those who stood up for decency and honesty. While the misuse of power was nothing new, the new use of communications beginning in the twentieth century was. You see, there had never been so much power to convince people that they thought a certain way. Convincing the people to think absurdly was the only way the powerful in a democracy could continue to commit completely irrational acts. The state of things was becoming so bad, particularly the devastation of the land, air, and sea, that it was not clear if humans could continue to reproduce and live on the earth.

Though G-d was in exile, because of human choice, G-d's hand remained apparent in all creation. Nothing could continue to exist without G-d's ongoing creation each minute, not the seat I sit in, nor this conversation, if G-d did not Will it. And though G-d allowed the humans to have this choice, G-d was determined to assist the righteous in setting everything right, as G-d always is. But human souls would have to physically rise up and perform this service in the name of G-d. G-d would assist, but not do. G-d would preordain the possibility and the choice, but humans would have to make it happen.

By the year 2000, or 5760, the world had reached a feverish pitch. Those in power proclaimed that everything was okay. And it was true that some had never lived better. Others, who had tasted of the material fruits of everything they could imagine, but were still unhappy, tried to turn inward, seeking spiritual guidance—often false—from others through many different means. Others starved, living a hopeless existence. All of this was expected and known by G-d before it even happened. Even though it happened through human choice, G-d was aware of what that choice would be. Because G-d is infinite and all knowing, the boundaries of time mean nothing to the Almighty.

As the world approached the end of the sixth Hebrew millennium, it was in G-d's Plan that humans would repent, reverse their course, and move toward a Messianic world. The end of the sixth millennium—as did the specific years 2000 and 5760—held special spiritual significance. Certainly, religious Jews, Kabbalists, and righteous Gentiles knew this and had tried to live their lives accordingly. But it would be necessary to convince those in control of the most powerful governments, so that fundamental changes would occur in the societies.

So this is what took place in our heavens. The conversation here can only be imagined, and I must beg forgiveness for portraying G-d in this manner, since we know that G-d really speaks through revelation and not in the way that we will record it here for our finite human understanding.

"Ein Sof, Infinite One, you have summoned us," the Angels said.

"Yes, I am in search of a proper neshamah, soul, to take the oath and enter the revealed world of medeber, humans."

"And what will be his charge, Ein Sof?"

"If he accepts his charge, he shall have the possibility of becoming a tzaddik, not just a righteous person, but also a Lamed-Vov, one of the thirty-six Just Men who hold up the world."

"And what will be his place in society?"

"He shall be born to great wealth and station."

"And his learning and family background?"

"The learning of course is crucial, but it will come later. First, it is critical that his family have unparalleled wealth and power."

The Angels gasped. "But, there are few very wealthy Jewish families of great learning and observance suitable to raise this child for the role of Lamed-Vov."

"That will be My concern, not yours, how I will elevate his soul to a tzaddik and Lamed-Vov in a nonobservant family. But it shall be necessary in this case."

"Yes, the Almighty will of course do what is best. But Ein Sof, why must his soul now enter the household of a nonobservant Jewish family, when so many other worthy and learned families are available to educate this child?"

"Before this century, the human power often resided with those with the moral authority to lead the community. In the Jewish communities, the Rabbi usually made the decisions. This is where I sent the older, highly developed neshamahs to lead the Jewish people. But now, the power of choice no longer resides with the

Rabbis, with righteous clergy, or learned people. So, in order to continue to give the people the choice to change their society late in the sixth millennium—and we must continue to give them the choice to make a Messianic world—we must choose wealth. It will be a person of money that can make a difference."

"But Ein Sof, of course, You are all knowing, so how can we question you with our limited understanding, but still we have observed how money corrupts even the best that you have sent to earth, and it would be a most unusual human soul that could live with the temptations that he will undoubtedly face. And then he will do this without sufficient religious training and knowledge of halachah? How are we to understand this? Is it not sure failure? And who will accept this charge, with the likelihood of such pain and isolation in their earthly existence?"

"Only one of My exceptional souls. Only one who need not return to earth in order to elevate his soul, because he has already performed his G-dly service on earth well. That soul will do it without question, as he, like the patriarchs, has earned the status of "chariot of G-d". His great hidden love for Me will carry him through the ordeal, though it is true he will face great pain."

"Will he be the Moshiach, the Messiah, if he is able to fulfill his mission?"

"As always, that depends on the Jews and all My other peoples as well. They must make that determination. Will they stand behind this Lamed-Vov, and choose the righteous path, or will they oppose him?"

2

The angels were even more aghast when they saw the actual family to which the Lamed-Vov would be born. Not only was the family not observant, which was bad enough, but it had only a tenuous connection to Judaism. Not even the surname, Reed, gave any inkling that they were Jews. The grandfather of the parents of the child had changed it to the most Christian one he could imagine, in an attempt to flee his heritage, after he came to the New World and began the family's path to great wealth. But the irony remained, as it did in so many families. Even though there was little Jewish connection, the family had apparently chosen not to convert to another religion, though it would have aided their social rise. Though choosing for the most part not to observe, and not to associate with any religious Jews—in fact they were embarrassed by them—they remained secretly proud of their ancestry and heritage. And as in so many Jewish families that were assimilating, this tiny hidden spark and love of other Jews kept their knowledge of who they were, alive from generation to generation, preserving the choice of Judaism for their children. And if called upon to defend fellow Jews against anti-Semitism, even to lay down their lives in defense of G-d, rather than bow down to someone else's rule, they would more often than not have chosen to do so, though they refused to recognize this hidden attribution in themselves, and thankfully had not been tested on it in America, as they had been repeatedly in the nineteenth century in Europe, and continually throughout other times of the Diaspora.

Because the chain of Judaism had not been broken, surprisingly not even disrupted by intermarriage, the uncle of the new tzaddik soul to enter this world, unmarried though he was, had become a bit of B'al Teshuvah, a returnee to Judaism. Apparently being more of a spiritual nature, he had chosen much to his family's chagrin and unlike his brother, the father of the new potential tzaddik, to walk away from active administration of the business empire. His interest in Judaism only served to magnify his black sheep status in the Reed family.

The parents of the new child to be born were certainly nice enough in a conventional sense, but the advocates for the child among the angels felt that they were sending the poor soul, distinguished though he be, behind enemy lines, where he had not the faintest possibility to survive. Certainly, almost as worthy of souls had previously failed the test between good and evil in even less adverse circumstances. But after a while, the angels realized that there was true purpose in G-d's intentions, because only by this soul going to the source of the evil in the society, and trying to change that evil, and make it worthy of uplifting to G-d, could G-d begin to achieve His purpose of setting the stage for a Messianic age. Thus, the taking of the oath by the new soul prior to his birth, and the breathing of life and soul into his body at birth, was the most widely anticipated event at that time in the heavens.

On the subject of wealth, the Reed family of San Francisco was certainly what the Ein Sof had decreed. They were by far the richest Jewish family in America and were estimated to have a net worth in excess of $50 billion, all controlled by the new soul's father, since his brother, and only sibling, was content to let his brother vote his stock shares. Moreover, not only was the family rich, but it was continuing to rise in the business world. While the original patriarch had built old wealth with old line industry, the father of the new child had successfully invested in new technology related to health and the internet. While the child's father was not what one would call a good observant Jew, he was a shrewd businessman with unusual foresight.

Being the first child and only expected heir of the Reed couple, the eminent birth of the new child was just as anticipated and celebrated in the revealed world as it was in the hidden heavenly worlds. As was true of so many of the couples of that age, the Reeds had not even married until they were past thirty. And then it had not occurred to them when they might have a child. Being of a generation that tended to consider itself first, the couple was more concerned with climbing social ladders, travel, and entertainment—that is when Mr. Reed was not engaged in business endeavors. Not until the early deaths of Mr. Reed's parents jarred them, did they think about producing an heir. By that time, the Reeds were well past forty and unable to do this by themselves. The resulting ongoing attempts at in vitro fertilization and their failures were highly humiliating, but quite instructive, to a couple that was used to ordering up whatever it wanted in this world. They learned that only G-d grants life in this world. And thus, they were exceedingly grateful to the Ein Sof, when Mrs. Reed succeeded in getting pregnant on the sixth and final attempt before adoption. So, just as the soul came to be granted to unusual parents, he was also the first tzaddik to be conceived in a test tube.

The new soul was born to a body that was both perfect in form and a grand sight to behold. As their son developed the Reeds were in awe; while neither of them was particularly bad looking, this child seemed to possess traits which could only be traced to generations past. G-d seemed to have gathered all the most beautiful recessive genes to make this blond, athletically built child, that their doctor predicted would be at least 6'4" —a very tall person for that time—before parents were able to order the body size they wanted. After the short period of time of a few months, it was also obvious to all observers that the child was extremely intelligent. His motor skills and first words came extraordinarily early. With his natural physical and mental gifts, and with his great monetary inheritance—being the sole heir—it seemed that a prince had truly been born. And so "Prince" was actually the nickname, and soon the only appellation, which the young boy came to be called, among the circle of friends and colleagues that surrounded the Reeds.

The earliest years of Prince's life were experienced in the Reed's grand lifestyle and the boy continued to learn and then to perform for the Reed's social contemporaries beyond even their greatly rising expectations. The child was reading by the time he turned three and could discuss with adults articles he had read on contemporary events at five. By that age, with relatively few music lessons, he also was playing sophisticated pieces for violin. He had become the marvel entertainment at the Reed's legendary parties and the greatest source of pride of his parents. Moreover, Prince had won all of the track and swimming events for small children into which his parents had entered him; he had not just won them, but had bested his contemporaries by huge margins and one room of the Reed mansion outside San Francisco had already been plastered with winning medals. Several newspaper articles had been written about this child prodigy.

But in his earliest years, what was most unusual about Prince was the spirit that seemed to shine from his soul. He seemed to have an eternal smile on his face, and displayed no concern about his own personal daily reversals. Ultimately, this is what made the child so attractive to all those who surrounded him. Moreover, if he had gloated in his triumphs or had been a showoff, then all would have eventually tired of him. In such a case, the Reeds' house attendants and Mr. Reed's workers would have surely continued to be overly solicitous to the young boy, considering his status, but they would not have had such a genuine affection for the child.

The apex of this glorious world of Prince's earliest years was around the age of five, when he had multiple conversations with adults. Many of them occurred in the natural course of his daily affairs with his nanny/tutor figure.

"Well, Master Prince, how are you doing this morning?"

"I'm fine, Nan. What do I have to worry about anyway? I have everything I need. It's a beautiful day outside, isn't it?"

Nan pointed over to the table. "I see you won several more swimming trophies this weekend. Where did you go this time and how bad did you beat them?"

"It was just some State practice meet for kids five to eight—that's why they had such a big competitive age group. I thought that it might be hard to beat the older ones. But I'm afraid I won by at least several body lengths, and that was against the second place finisher, who was quite good. So, I'm a good swimmer, I admit it, but that doesn't mean that I'm any better person."

"Master Prince, always minimizing your good characteristics!" She sat down for a minute at the table to examine the trophies.

"But we've talked enough about those. What's on your mind right now, Nan?"

"Oh, nothing. Really nothing new."

"That's not true," he said. "You're staring out into space. Look at your eyes. You've been crying, haven't you?"

"How in the world, do you know these things? That was last night, and I've got a load of makeup on this morning," she said.

Prince laughed. "Well, that's one of the ways I noticed. You don't usually wear nearly that much, so that got me to looking more closely at your face. Then I saw your eyes, and they're so sad."

"Eyes sad? But eyes don't change. We've talked about that. They stay the same, as a person ages—don't they?"

"That's what the painter who's doing Mom's portrait said, of course," Prince said. "But I think that the light that shines through them changes. I can see a difference. It allows me to tell a lot about the person. I've seen something mentioning Divine Light. Do you think that's what that is?"

"So you're saying that you could tell that much about me by looking at my eyes?"

"Absolutely, I can read your eyes. I don't know why, but I can," he said.

"What else...what else can you see?"

"Your hands. Look at the way they are folded," he said. "Look at the way your feet are crossed. Those are expressions of your energy, and it's not the same as it usually is. And your posture is different."

Nan looked down at her hands and then slowly at her feet. She sighed. "How do you know this, Master Prince, at your age? I've never seen you wrong on anything." She paused. "Really, I've enjoyed you so much, but you will require someone special to teach you. Already, you are way beyond me."

"You are special," he said. "Everyone is special. And all the things I've done—well, I've been very lucky."

"Lucky? What do you mean? You're brilliant."

"That's right. I'm lucky to be brilliant. But so what? It doesn't make me better than others," he said. "In fact, I'm not as good. What have I done for anyone today? I'm just sitting in this castle, but there are people struggling out there. This family hasn't done anything about it. That's why you'd be doing me a big favor by letting me help you. It's Phil, isn't it?"

"Yes, it is," she said. "I'm thinking that I will leave him. Do you think that's wrong?"

"It all depends on what your goals and motives are. I think that it's very good that you are finally thinking about what you should do."

And so the conversation proceeded. Those who didn't know Prince well often approached him as a social curiosity, but frequently, given just a few accidental minutes alone with him, found him so intelligent and engaging that they were consulting him for advice. They were embarrassed later to admit that they had asked a five year-old his opinion on anything serious, much more so a facet that pertained to some critical personal matter in their lives. Thus, it became an open secret among those that associated with the Reeds, that in addition to his worldly accomplishments, Prince was an excellent source of advice. It was an open secret because it was potentially a great source of embarrassment to the important figures who associated with the Reeds and had sought the advice; and those figures also did not want to in any way offend the Reeds by their interaction with their son.

These earliest years of Prince were also the subject of much discussion in the heavens. Of course, because of the spiritual metaphysics, the actions of those on earth would determine spiritual reactions in the hidden worlds. But, it must be admitted that there was a lot of additional discussion, gabbing and speculation, something that might be related to lashon hara, or evil speech on earth, but not quite the same in our understanding. That's because the hidden worlds had a level of purity, not commonly found on earth. The G-dly force was not so veiled by the kelipah, or the shell, in the heavenly worlds. Nevertheless, there was wagering on the outcome of the potential tzaddik, called Prince in the earthly realms.

The mainstream body of angels that had been certain that Prince would never survive in such a G-dless setting had dwindled significantly, as they had watched the way he interacted with people. Some of the angels had watched his personal and physical qualities, as well as his clearly triumphant ways in the sports arena, and decided that G-d had given him not only the means to survive, but the persuasive abilities to permanently change the world. Others, also impressed by Prince, argued that G-d might have given this potential tzaddik certain abilities, to be sure, but there was no way that G-d would guarantee an outcome, since the human society must ultimately choose between good and evil. That was the whole purpose in human souls residing on earth, where G-dliness was hidden, and the choice of good was not so easy and simple, but instead required faith and sacrifice.

A camp, totally opposed in viewpoint to the two above, stuck by their original viewpoint that the potential tzaddik would fail. They noted that Prince, while a very worthy soul, had not really been tested in the outside world; the world was so corrupted by that point that no one alone could make that much difference. Eventually, the world would figuratively chew him up and spit him out. And in any case, they pointed out that the child was only five, had experienced only the greatest material advantages in the world, and had been relatively infrequently in the company of other children. In fact, Prince had become such an adult curiosity that his time had been virtually monopolized in social situations by those at least thirty years-old, not even to mention that there were several adult people in the Reed household workers assigned around the clock to satisfy his every wish. This adult "supervision" in Prince's early life had been much preferred by the Reeds to the screening of questionable child companions whom he might befriend; the Reed's position had been bolstered by their developed belief that no child could match the ability of their own, so that no real purpose could be served by wasting his time with other children. This situation, this camp of angels argued, would prove to be very troublesome for the child when he entered school.

This last camp of angels proved to be correct in their sense of something potentially wrong. But they did not totally understand the cause of the conflict that would now invade Prince's soul. At least in his early school years, the corruption of the outside world did not cause Prince to be corrupted himself. And if, as his school years progressed, Prince continued to be isolated from his peers, it was not because of his initial isolation, but rather because he consciously chose to be separate.

Perhaps the changing psychology of Prince might be noticed in his earlier conversation with his adult companion, Nan, because this is about the time that Prince slowly began evolving from a child that supported the status quo of his parents' world into one that spiritually opposed it. At first, his parents were much too involved in their own lives to notice. If Prince was starting to decline to talk to friends of his parents, or to "perform" at parties, in order to demonstrate to the world that he was a genius, then perhaps he was having a bad day. And if his former incredibly social behavior seemed to be veering onto the asocial side, then maybe he was just adjusting to beginning school, which soon became necessary for him to leave. At least this modicum of disagreeableness gave his parents some common ground about which they could joke among friends with similarly aged children, since outwardly at first, Prince's behavioral contrariness merely seemed to resemble those of other children. The Reeds were most disturbed when he started declining to compete in athletic events, since they knew that he could easily win. What a pity—when you could win! And since Prince's athletic prowess had been followed by so many people, this was something that embarrassed them most. How could they explain to the world his unwillingness to compete?

But it did not stop there. All parents are subject to the type of difficulties above. But when the pendulum began to swing for Prince, it went from one extreme to the other. As incredibly fortunate and proud as the Reeds had felt with the arrival of their son, that was how distraught and upset by his presence they later became, until they wondered if G-d had cursed them, rather than blessed them—not that they had ever considered G-d very much. This is what one would have expected from them, because they had never stopped thinking about themselves and their needs, even after their son's birth. It never occurred to them to examine their son's soul and consider that G-d had special plans for him, and figure out how they might assist those plans, even after observing his most unusual gifts. But we can't fault them too much. So many of us are like them, totally oblivious in the revealed world to the spiritual elements around us, even when they hit us in the face. G-d knew that Prince's parents would oppose his destiny and this became part of his test, and the world's test.

As the Reeds' problems with their son worsened, they began to seek advice. Paranoid about publicity and with no affiliation with any religious congregations, they sought out the advice of psychiatrists. Going from one to another, they heard different theories, but there was no consensus. One of the earlier conversations occurred after Prince left his school and began self-instruction.

"Since this is our first visit, I want to hear in your own words, what you consider the problem to be with your son," the psychiatrist said.

"Our son is brilliant. He has an IQ of over 200. He is an incredible athlete..." Mrs. Reed said.

"Yes, I've heard tale of that. There was a newspaper article, wasn't there? You must be very proud of that," the psychiatrist said.

"But he's very disturbed," Mr. Reed said.

"You say disturbed. In what way?"

"He's completely antisocial. He was the most social child when he was younger. He'd walk up to people at a party and start a conversation on any subject. Everyone loved him," Mr. Reed said.

"And now?"

"Well, to start out, when we have people over now, he stays in his room. Doesn't come out," Mr. Reed said.

"That's not so unusual. As the child develops, it's not unusual for a child to sometimes avoid his parents entirely or their friends," the psychiatrist said.

"With all due respect, doctor, he's only seven. He's not a teenager. But when he finally comes out to eat a snack and runs into one of our friends, he questions them on their business and lectures them on their shortcomings," Mr. Reed said.

"What do you mean?"

"I mean it's everything," Mr. Reed said. "First of all, what are the labor conditions of our friend's business, is he polluting, has he considered alternative energy sources, and did he give to charity that day? And following on the personal front, is he spending enough time with his daughter, who needs his attention?"

There was complete silence in the room while the doctor stopped. It seemed that he couldn't find any words to express his thoughts, perhaps a new phenomenon for him. Finally, he said, "Let's get this straight. You are telling me that you have a seven year-old who does this? I...I don't think...I don't think that anything like this has ever been documented clinically. I'm not even sure what the problem is here, though I can see why you're aggravated. It does sound highly unusual, even for a brilliant child."

Mrs. Reed's face looked as if it were going to explode. "Look doctor, he's brilliant. I told you that when we walked in. I was proud of it. But I just want relief now. Let's cut to some of the real stuff here. He's not just antisocial; it's a lot worse. I just cannot handle his vomiting."

"Vomiting? When does he vomit?"

"All the time," Mrs. Reed said. "Could surprise us with that at any time." She sarcastically threw her hands out and tilted her head to emphasize her point.

"Is he doing this to prove a point or make you do something? Can you correlate it with anything?"

"We've tried," Mr. Reed said. "The best we can figure is when he doesn't like something."

"Give me an example."

"A number of times it's when he's watching the news. And I don't think he's trying to be difficult, because he always says he's sorry and can't help it," Mr. Reed said.

"Do you remember what was happening on the news before he vomited?"

"Yeah, I remember," Mrs. Reed said. "How could I forget, when we have to stop dinner and call in our help? It was about some rain forest being cut down. He couldn't stand it I guess. There are so many things he can't stand. Life is hard for us all. Why does he have to be so special?"

"Have you ever actually asked him why he vomits?"

"We tried, once. And actually, after that, he seemed relieved that we asked. And after that conversation, the frequency of his vomiting seemed to lessen for a few days," Mr. Reed said. "But I simply don't have time to keep asking why he's vomiting. No other parents would put up with this. That's why I'm here. It's your job. Hopefully you can stop this stupidity."

"Okay. But what did he say?"

"I don't know exactly. It was a fifteen minute speech on the evils of the world. Seemed like he mentioned how upset he gets when he sees injustice and misery, when mankind can do something about it. He was upset not just about people, but the condition of the earth. The boy can't stand to even see a tree cut. If we drive by such a scene, he wants to get out to convince the tree cutters to stop, and if it's already cut down, we have to shield his eyes to keep him from vomiting all over the car." Mr. Reed then let out a loud sigh and slumped motionless in his seat.

"Well, our session's about up. I'd have to meet with him, to try to figure anything out. Would you consider drugs to help calm him down?"

"We'd consider anything, for some relief," Mrs. Reed said. "Boarding school, but who's going to take him, crazy like he is, and already reading philosophy and doing algebra? I don't think he'd come to meet with you and he'd certainly not take drugs. He's completely opposed to that."

"With all due respect, Mrs. Reed, he's only seven. You're in charge here, not him."

"With all due respect to you, doctor, he's in charge," Mrs. Reed said. "You've never met anyone like this before. I know he's not an unkind person and means very well—actually he's probably the kindest person I know—but I just can't live with him. I know I wanted him, but I didn't know what I was getting into. What in the world did G-d do this to me for?"

3

Later that week, the Reeds brought Prince to an ice hockey game. They sat in the Reeds' traditional box seats.

"This is the first game that you've been to," Mrs. Reed said. "You're not going to vomit all over us, are you? Don't make me sorry we brought you!"

"I'm sorry. I can't determine that," Prince said. "Do you think I like to vomit? Do you think that it's fun?"

"Well it must be something. Everyone else can contain their urges," Mrs. Reed said.

Prince gave his mother a stare only a teenager could usually manage. He sat in silence and said nothing until the game began. "Is that all these guys are going to do—just skate around on the ice and try to hit that puck into the goal."

"Yeah," Mr. Reed said. "That doesn't suit you either? Going to complain about this too?"

"Well, it's violent. What's the point, anyway? Why not do something constructive?

"What do you think is constructive?" Mr. Reed said.

"Doing something for someone. This just looks like a way to bash someone's teeth in," Prince said.

"Okay, I got it," Mr. Reed said. "But can't we just watch the game for a while? Do you have to drain all the enjoyment completely out of it? Remember, others just aren't as great as you. They'd rather watch the game."

"I'm not great. I just don't see the point," Prince said.

When one of the opposing team players raised his stick and forced one of the home team into the side of the rink causing a loud bang, Prince's mouth dropped open. "That's the third time he's done that? Isn't the ref going to do something?"

This time the player took matters into his own hands. As soon as he completed the bounce off the rink he turned around to slug the offender and a fight started. The two refs stood by and allowed it to develop. The crowd roared with encouragement. "Get him!" "Take him down!" "Show him who's boss here!"

The roar reached a joyous crescendo as the home player began to connect with his fists into the other player's head. Still, the referees stood idle, choosing not to break up the fight. Prince jumped out of his seat. "What is this? The refs are doing nothing? I can't believe it."

The Reeds said nothing. They were wrapped up in the high drama. "Someone's got to do something." Prince said. He climbed up on the railing and cupped his mouth with his hands and screamed "Boooo" as loud as he could. His left hand grasped the railing tightly to support his body while the right one flailed angrily in the air. "This is wrong. Stop it now. Boooooo."

The Reeds turned to watch Prince in embarrassment. Fortunately for them, no one noticed. Everyone else was cheering as the home player's jabs finally took the opposing player down on the ice. Both were now being hauled off to the penalty box. Everyone seemed happiest just at that moment and quickly quieted down as the game resumed.

"Another activity we can't bring you to do with us, young man!" Mr. Reed said. "You are a constant source of anxiety and irritation!"

"You just think I try to do this, don't you?" Prince said. "I want to like what you do. But how can anyone watch this and not be appalled? Animals are nicer to each other. The news media, parents, everyone preaches nonviolence, but then watch the news on television and in the paper tomorrow. They'll be reporting this game as if nothing extraordinary happened. These same people wonder why people are shot and wives are abused every day. They'll be the first to say we need to educate people on the subject. Let them come here and see the examples set. All this cheering of violence reminds me of the Romans. Seems their society collapsed after years of this junk."

"I see you've got to Roman history in that world history book you've been reading," Mr. Reed said. "I can't say it's going to do you any good if you can't get along with the people around you."

"What's the point of getting along with these people anyway? If this is all there is, if this is what getting along with people is about, I don't want it," Prince said.

A few weeks later all three Reeds were out early Saturday morning on an excursion in San Francisco. It was unusual for the senior Reeds to spend semi-structured time with their son, especially on a weekend, but they were feeling in the mood to take him on their jaunts. Occasionally, the tension between parents and child lessened in the Reed household, causing the Reeds to think that their son might be returning to his much more agreeable past. Though this never really happened for any lengthy period, it was easy for the Reeds—as all parents are prone to do—to delude themselves into thinking that there was hope.

"Our driver must have gotten lost," Mr. Reed said.

"This would have never happened with Ralph. I hope he recovers fast from his surgery," Mrs. Reed said.

"Let's walk over to the museum and we'll telephone him and tell him to meet us over there after we're finished," Mr. Reed said. "Now Prince, I think we've run out of all of our change and small bills. Can we dispense with giving to every beggar on the way over there?"

"He hasn't vomited all morning," Mrs. Reed said.

"No, he hasn't," Mr. Reed said. "But he looks scared as all getout. Prince, what are you scared about?"

"I don't know," Prince said. "Maybe I'm just sad, or ill at ease. When I see the way people live, the way they are treated around here, I just feel bad. Look at their faces. I see such distressed souls and I feel as if I must help them. Why don't you feel that way when you see these people too?"

"Now Prince," Mrs. Reed said. "These people probably live this way because they have chosen to do that. No one forced them."

"Chosen to do this? That's an interesting concept. What's choice in this world anyhow?" Prince said.

Suddenly it began to pour. Without any umbrellas, and anxious to reach the inside of a building, they followed Mr. Reed. It was too early for most of the retail establishments to have opened, but the large, open, double doors of a synagogue drawing in worshippers, beckoned.

The Orthodox service was just starting. The senior Reeds shook themselves dry in the large entrance. Prince ignored his parents lead and instead walked slowly into the service while staring at the high ceiling. All the anxiety had left his face. His body relaxed and he smiled. Prince rarely smiled any more, but when he did, he reflected an inner light, almost the soft glow of a celestial body. Many of the congregation turned to watch his presence and one of the males on the lower floor offered him a kippah, or head covering. He politely thanked the gentlemen and placed it on his head. Another gentleman smiled at him and opened a prayer book to the place in the service. Delighted, Prince listened to the sounds of Hebrew being intoned around him. Those prayers which he heard several times he was able to repeat in part.

The senior Reeds paid no attention for several minutes. Finally, after they had dried off, the storm had stopped, and they wanted to quickly leave, they looked for Prince, realizing only then that he had disappeared into part of the service. "Well, I'll be...," Mr. Reed said.

"You'll have to go in there and get him," Mrs. Reed said. "They're not going to let me in there with the men."

"You don't expect me to go in there with those people, do you?" Mr. Reed said.

"What do you expect me to do? Go up to the balcony with the women and wave at him?" Mrs. Reed said. "Now that would be a sight!"

"Well, I refuse to walk in there and get him. We'll just stand out here and wait as long as it takes," Mr. Reed said.

"Probably another couple of hours. I hope you like the sermon," Mrs. Reed said.

As the service proceeded, they could see the back side of their son. No one would guess that he had never been in an Orthodox service, even less so in a synagogue. After conferring with the gabbai, or service assistant and organizer, he was invited to assist in the service. That was the first time the Reeds could see their son's face.

"I'm not believing this," Mrs. Reed said. "His face—I've never seen such a look of contentment before. As a mother, I'm glad, at least for now, but it just figures. He would only like things we despise. Why? If G-d is really in this place, maybe he can tell me why. Why do I have a son who must oppose everything I am?"

Prince had now again turned his back to his parents and was again facing the bimah, or pulpit. His body was swaying with the chanting of the prayer and Mrs. Reed could imagine that his eyes were closed. It seemed that he might levitate over the congregation at any moment. Toward the end of the service, during the aleinu, or adoration, she watched him bow down. "It's amazing. I've never seen him do such a thing. He gives no deference to others like that."

"Well, I guess he must do it before G-d," Mr. Reed said. "But I just wish that G-d would arrange to finish this now. Enough already."

When the service was finished, Prince stayed to chat. He was in no hurry to leave and both Reeds declined to go into the sanctuary to retrieve him, lest they have to say hello and mix with those strange people, explain themselves, and their absence from their son during the service. They remained outside gritting their teeth. Prince was as sociable as they ever remembered him from earlier years, shaking hands and conversing in the excellent and charming manner of which he was so capable. Because of his large size for his age and the intellect apparent in his conversation, his fellow worshippers probably mistook him for a relatively small child who was approaching Bar Mitzvah age.

Prince remained talking until the last person left. Then he walked out in a relaxed way, greeting his parents with a big smile.

"Just what did you think you were doing, young man?" Mr. Reed said.

"Praying, of course," Prince said.

"And you didn't have the courtesy to come out. You're with us. We decided to bring you today and you go off and do your own thing. Typical stuff. I can assure you that this will never happen again," Mr. Reed said. His face became very red when he felt that he had been thwarted.

Prince smiled sweetly at his father. "You didn't notice when I went in. I was near the aisle where you could see me. Why didn't you just come in and get me? No laws against it, you know." He made sure that he caught his father's eye once more and broke into another smile.

Mr. Reed acted as if he hadn't heard the question. "I'm surprised they welcomed you like that. How did you get them to do that? That's an Orthodox congregation and they don't just let anyone in. You're a stranger to them you know."

"Maybe I'm a stranger," Prince said, "but they welcome strangers, especially Jews."

"How did you know you were Jewish?" Mr. Reed said. "We've never talked about that? It is not a part of our lives."

"And how did you know you were Jewish?" Prince said. "Did anyone tell you that you were Jewish?"

Mr. Reed stopped walking to directly face his son. "I don't know Prince. I can't tell you why I knew, because my parents never talked about it."

"I can't tell you when I knew either. But when I walked in there today, I knew something big time. I felt as if I was there in this world that I used to know a long time ago, a special world that G-d provides to us on this earth."

"You know I despise those people—I mean the way they pray," Mr. Reed said.

"I know," Prince said.

"You know I'm not bringing you back to a synagogue, ever" Mr. Reed said. "That's something your uncle does that I'll never understand."

"I know, even though you know that is what I need and want," Prince said. A sad river of pain was temporarily cast over his joyous face.

Prince's beautiful glowing face and the agreeable personality found in that synagogue that day lasted only one week. Like a candle running out of fuel, it faded by the next Saturday. The senior Reeds were pleasantly surprised by the turn in their relations with their son that week and then distraught with their sudden reversal. But they never associated their good fortune for one week with the prayer in that synagogue. As time transpired, Prince remembered only that he was Jewish; he lost the special meaning that he had felt that Shabbat in synagogue. What was left was a big hole of suffering.

4

As the next few years passed, it seemed to many of the angels in the heavens that the only real opportunity for Prince to pursue his destiny had been lost. G-d of course works in mysterious ways that are often completely unfathomable to humans, but not one of the angels could write a script, could anticipate in any way, how this soul could fulfill the special role for which he had been sent to earth. Not only that, but the situation with Prince only seemed to be worsening. As a result, there was great consternation among the heavenly beings.

While the boy was undeniably brilliant, and continued to read voraciously, he continued to withdraw into himself. Since he had been so far ahead of his fellow students in school, and from the point of view of his parents had been unable to get along socially with his classmates—or for that matter with anyone else—they had somehow arranged for him to be privately tested and then certified by the school system. In that manner, Prince achieved his GED when he turned ten. But such isolation from the school system had meant that Prince had experienced very little contact with children his own age; in fact, most of his social contact revolved around Nan and those servants who ran the Reed household.

The Reeds had long ago surrendered their hopes of actually "helping" their son and then ultimately their dreams that he would be a suitable heir to them and the Reed fortune of whom they could be proud. They still sought out the aid of psychiatrists, however, for advice on how to handle their son, and for words of consolation during their parental struggles. Generally, the doctors they saw gave them advice which proved to be useless since very few seemed to grasp the entirety of the problem and since Prince had refused to visit any of them for evaluation. Shortly after he qualified for the GED, he surprisingly agreed to visit one of them with his parents.

"Your parents tell me that you have never before visited a psychiatrist," the psychiatrist said. "I appreciate your coming today. Can I start out by asking why you have come today after all this time? Of course, if there's something you would like to say before that, we can begin there."

"I know that this seems a big surprise to my parents and you, but the reason why I've never come before is that I knew that it would do no good. It wasn't because I was trying to give them a hard way to go. Believe it or not, I have tried to follow what my parents want, but I knew that it would be totally worthless."

"Okay," the psychiatrist said. He jolted out of his seat and began pacing around the room as he mulled over Prince's answer. "That raises a bunch of questions. First, so why are you here today?"

"You're different?"

"And how did you determine that?"

"Well, I've always listened to what they have to say—I mean when they try to get me to come to these things. They think that I ignore them," Prince said looking squarely at his parents. "But I judged in this particular case that it might be worth a try."

"And what did you sense about me?"

"That maybe you're honest," Prince said. "I mean no one's completely honest with themselves, but you seemed to be trying."

"And you think that all the others weren't honest?"

"No," Prince said. He pointed over to his parents across the room. "They've been to a dozen or more of these guys and I would say that the rest of them are not honest. They're not doing their jobs in a professional manner and really don't have my interests or my parents' interests at heart—"

"—So, you in your know-it-all role presume to tell us that all those qualified doctors, with national reputations, some who've written well known articles and have been on talk shows, don't know what they're doing?" Mr. Reed said.

"Wait a minute," the psychiatrist said. "We've finally got him here. Now, let's let him speak. Prince, let me understand what you're saying. Why aren't those guys honest and why do you suddenly think that I might be."

"I know this might seem strange to you doctor, but I see things. I see people's souls. I know their character. I've tried to not see these things, believe me. It's not that I want to be so strange. But I can't help it. And these perceptions won't leave me alone."

"But surely all those doctors can't be so bad," the psychiatrist said. "Prince, you haven't even met these people, either. How can you comment on them if you haven't talked to them?"

"I don't have to meet them in person. When my parents talk about them, I have visions of their personalities. It's like I can suddenly focus in on them and perceive their souls. As for all of them being so bad, you'd think it wouldn't be so, but it is. It's hard to believe that the world is so messed up, isn't it?" Prince said.

"We told you about his view of the world," Mr. Reed said nodding his head in the direction of the doctor. "You would have thought that we made it all up, but we didn't."

"Let's stay on the point," the psychiatrist said. "Prince, what makes those doctors so bad?"

"The fact that they wouldn't even ask me the questions that you are doing here. They'd jump to conclusions. For example, many of them told my parents right off that I was having delusions, since I have these visions about things, but I know that it's not the case," Prince said. "Then, based on that, they'd trot out some drug program. Seems that most of them only know how to prescribe drugs, and that, not very well."

"Well Prince, some people do have delusions and perhaps they're paranoid or something else," the psychiatrist said.

"Fair enough, but at least they ought to consider the possibility of something else, especially before they meet me. You see, what it is with those people, is that after all their training, they have big egos, and don't want to admit it when they run across something they have never seen before, which they don't understand. So they try to pigeonhole everything. 'It must this, since it can't be that.' You know, I admit I don't care for most psychiatrists, but I'm not trying to pick on them. The problem of ego is everywhere. It is the source of most of the world's problems. Ego is behind most of the wars going on in the world today."

"That's right," Mr. Reed said. "You've never discriminated solely against psychiatrists. You're an equal opportunity criticizer."

"Mr. Reed, please let's refrain. I just want to establish the facts," the psychiatrist said. He paused from his pacing and sat down to write a note to himself. Then he looked up from his pad. "Prince, what makes a person honest and what did you see in me to decide to come today?"

"It starts with an ability to see oneself, as others and G-d see you, and then to assess and deal with others in a manner that's not motivated by personal desire or need. Most people can never be honest with themselves, and as a result are dishonest with others as well, because they are filling some inner need," Prince said.

"Hmmm, you seem to have a kind of handle on life," the psychiatrist said. "So, why did you come today?"

"Because, if I'm honest with myself," Prince said, "I know that I have a problem. My parents are right about that, but they have all the wrong reasons for getting me here. They were trying to make me be like them, not allow me to be happy in my own right. And I'm very different from them. Not that I relish that, but I am. I see the world very differently. Because of their selfish desires, they never looked for the right people to help me. They just happened to accidentally stumble over you. And that's after they ran out of other names."

"I'll tell you who's selfish here," Mrs. Reed said. She turned to stare defiantly at her son.

Prince stared back. "What's a matter?" he said. "Did you have to break up that tennis club match and party today to come here? Or was it the nails or hair you weren't able to do?" Then he turned to his father. "Have you ever missed a business deal to be with me?"

The expression on Mr. Reed's face totally changed. "Prince," he said, "I...I didn't know that you cared. What...what did you want me to do?"

"Just be my father occasionally. Put yourself in my shoes. Try to understand what I see, instead of mocking it," Prince said. He lowered his gaze to the ground to avoid his parents' countenances.

"Prince, you're so smart. What was there to do or say to you?" Mr. Reed said. "It wasn't like I could have taken you to a ball game. I tried to take you to a hockey game and look what happened. You don't appreciate our friends."

"No, that's all true. I was a big pain. But instead of trying to understand me, you gave up so fast. You were only interested in what was good for your name, reputation, and place in the world. You never tried to understand why I was different and allow me to be who I was. I know I might have embarrassed you, but you could have at least tried to appreciate me for who I was, and help me get to where I'm going in life, where ever that is."

"It's true," Mrs. Reed said. "You're very smart, and we haven't figured out how you'll use it."

"No, Mom, let's admit it. I'll use my smarts all right, but I've got to find my purpose first," Prince said. "Why am I on this earth?"

Mrs. Reed laughed. "Haven't your father and I asked this question over and over?" Turning to the doctor, she said, "What do you think about all this?"

"Mrs. Reed, I'm not in the habit of diagnosing conditions on the spot, as I told you in our consultation meeting, but I can say with assurance that your son doesn't fit any kind of mold, and frankly, no one should use the word 'sick' here. Honestly, I'd say that I'm not the person for your son. What he needs is some spiritual guidance to use his great talents in this world." Looking at Prince, the psychiatrist said, "I'm also told that once you were an athlete. Seems that you have a lot to contribute, but are at a loss to find a way to do so."

"It's called finding a path," Prince said.

After this session, even the senior Reeds had debated whether to seek spiritual guidance with a Rabbi, though Mr. Reed was still loathe to do so. Still, during those days, the tenor of the Reed household changed once again. Finally, there was dialogue and hope. The angels rejoiced in heaven; it looked as if there would be a dramatic change for Prince after all. Of course, the heavenly beings had been wrong, they told themselves. G-d does cause miracles. Why had they ever doubted Ein Sof?

Then ten days after the session, the senior Reeds were flying back from a political conference in a bad thunderstorm in their private jet and were lost on the radar shortly before they were to land. The plane had lost its bearings in the fog and dived into the ground. There were no survivors.

Prince's uncle, now Prince's guardian, as well as custodian of all the Reed worldly assets, arrived at the Prince household late that night to find Prince. Upon reaching the entrance of the house, he spoke to the bewildered Reed servants who quickly gathered around him. "G-d speaks to humans in unfathomable ways. He gives and He takes away. Though it is hard to understand, my brother and sister-in-law have evidently served their purpose in this life."

5

Though Prince's uncle had become the black sheep of the Reed family, after choosing during his early adult years to become religiously observant, he was not from our view point some crazy, unbalanced person. He had merely evaluated his limited spiritual existence growing up and determined that he wished to deepen it; the path of his Jewish forefathers seemed to him to be something that he should explore first. His initial learning had led him to search much deeper.

Moreover, Prince's uncle was apparently just as gifted as his brother in matters of business. But he had been in no hurry to demonstrate that gift. Wishing to structure his life to become fully observant in Judaism, he chose to leave work early on Friday afternoons to observe Shabbat and to miss work on other Jewish holidays. Thus, he was glad to allow his brother to fully run the day to day affairs of the business, though he continued to sit on the company's board and to run one of its large departments. Because Prince's uncle had become very spiritual and insightful, he also judged that it would be counterproductive for him to serve in the business as an equal to his brother. He had observed his brother's ego and wisely concluded, that in order for the family business to function smoothly, there should only be one head honcho.

Though Prince's father had privately sneered at his brother's choice to not only affiliate with Judaism but to become fully observant, or Shomer Shabbas, and to further step away from the day to day affairs of the business, he knew that his brother was a completely rational person capable of stepping into his shoes, should something unexpected occur. Though he would never admit it to himself, he was also secretly proud as a Jew that his brother had chosen his religious path. Not only that, but after his brother had chosen Jewish principles to be guideposts in his life, Prince's father knew that regarding matters of stability, conscience, morality, and truthfulness, he could count on Prince's uncle, as he could most observant Jews, to be straight as an arrow. Though Prince's father may have seemed at times to have selfishly ignored his son's interests, when it came to conducting business on an ethical basis, he was beyond reproach. He often approached Prince's uncle for advice regarding moral issues that arose in the business. Given this history, it was not at all surprising that Prince's father had designated his brother to be trustee over Prince's share of the business and legal guardian of Prince.

Once Prince's uncle had secured the reins of the business by conducting inventories, reviewing the status of the company's various high level managers, and initiating further long range planning, and had additionally settled many of the Reed estate issues, he turned his full attention to his nephew. Though he had watched Prince's unusual story unfold, and was fully aware of the issues surrounding the boy, he was nevertheless at a loss of how he should best act. During the better part of a year that it took Prince's uncle to fully evaluate and take control of the Reed empire, Prince had begun a steady descent.

Certainly, an observer could never claim that Prince had been close to his parents; yet, Prince's parents had been one of his few tenuous holds on the outside world. Whatever their faults as parents, the senior Reeds had claimed him as their own. If they had tried to change him, even for selfish reasons, at least Prince knew that they cared—not of course the way he would have wished they had—but at least at some level. While they had been alive, there had still been hope that they would come around and support him in what all three of them had agreed would be unusual and difficult choices in his life. It had seemed that all that might finally begin to happen after Prince had visited the psychiatrist with his parents and a beachhead of dialogue had finally been attained, but then his parents' plane had crashed. Though Prince had attained an extremely high level of intellectual achievement for his age, and as a result appeared to those around him better able to handle his parents' death, the reality was that it is often hard for any person to handle one parent's death, even harder when both parents suddenly die, and even harder when additionally the survivor is a mere ten years-old. Though a wise, old soul did indeed inhabit Prince's body, it still required the years of childhood to develop emotionally. To make matters so much worse, because of the unusual circumstances of his childhood, Prince possessed no childhood friends or parents of friends, and no school, community, or religious structures that might support him and help him heal from his parents' deaths.

Prince's uncle now began the first attempts to provide structures in Prince's daily life that he hoped might help him eventually lead a fairly normal and happy existence. He enrolled Prince in several college courses, entered him in community athletic events, and sent him to overnight summer camp with boys his own age. Finally, he arranged for him to learn about Judaism. Unfortunately, it was too little too late.

Of all those activities, perhaps an outside observer could say that at least the college courses superficially served the purpose for which they were intended. Prince continued to greatly expand his intellectual horizons and grew in his ability to understand the world. He easily aced the courses, but as a pre-teen sitting among late adolescents, he developed no real human connections. To the contrary, he was usually viewed by smart aleck students as some kind of wunderkind. Because of his obvious great intelligence, he was viewed as an extremely fortunate phenomenon who did not share their burden of working very hard to do well; as the word got around that great monetary fortune was wedded to such intelligence, many ironically believed that this child was on easy street. Once again, Prince felt himself to be in a situation in which he could not be seen as the distinct individual person and soul he was. So, in a very real way, the courses only served to emphasize and increase Prince's sense of isolation.

The athletic events had much the same effect regarding Prince's development as the college courses. They taught Prince about competing with his peers and gave him a chance to excel. They allowed him to continue to train his body in swimming and track events, events he continued to win handily, but they hardly allowed him to establish social contact with his opponents. Rather, he became feared. No one could hope to win against his effort, so all contenders, particularly the serious ones training to compete and place in future regional and national competitions, tried to avoid him in their competitions. Repeatedly, Prince and his uncle could overhear the dialogue of parents and children when he would arrive at the field or pool; comments such as, "Not that guy, again," or "Why doesn't he trip and break a leg,", or "It's not fair that my son has to compete with a guy like that. My son trains every day after school, struggling to make each improvement, and because of his hard work, was always the best until that outsider came along and won effortlessly. He never loses. Who does he think he is?" were said loudly at the most opportune times for overhearing. After a while, it seemed that a union of competitors had been formed for the explicit purpose of chasing Prince away. The comments became coordinated among the participants, who would try to rattle Prince before each competition. Winning became painful for Prince. The only surviving message for Prince from these events was that human contact and competition should once again be avoided.

As for Prince's camp experience, it can only be described as something incredible, rather unbelievable, from not only Prince's standpoint, but from all those in attendance at the camp. Although Prince's uncle was an Orthodox Jew, he knew that his brother would have abhorred his son attending a camp that was observant in Judaism; though he had decided to educate his nephew as a Jew, he still wished to honor what he knew would have been his brother's wishes on this matter. Besides, Prince's uncle himself had been raised with no knowledge of Judaism whatsoever, and the camp that he had attended had been a totally secular one in northern Wisconsin; though the composition of its campers had been almost 100 percent Jewish—primarily because of socio-economic issues, some involving discrimination against Jews at the time, and also because the owners were Jewish—there still had been absolutely no Jewish observance. One of the few continuing friendships that Prince's uncle maintained as a result of those camp experiences was with a former camper who, after making a considerable sum of money on the sale of his business, purchased the camp to begin a new job and life. Prince's uncle felt that he could trust Rusty with his nephew. Months after the camp session ended, and Rusty visited San Francisco to see old campers and recruit new ones, he visited Prince's uncle again.

"I appreciated your telephoning me last summer about Prince," Prince's uncle said. "I know you tried to take good care of him, and I appreciate that. But I know it was not easy. I'm really sorry about that."

"I didn't want to make you feel bad over the phone," Rusty said, "but it was a lot worse than I let on. I really tried not to tell you what was really going on, while it was happening. I figured that he was there and I'd try not to send him home. I've thankfully avoided that with almost every difficult camper."

"Okay," Prince's uncle said. He suddenly let out a big sigh. "Obviously, I need to get into it. What did he do?"

"Well, I don't want you to get upset when I tell you this. But we've always been absolutely forthright with each other, and you need to know. You know I've seen a lot of campers in my time, between being at that camp as a camper, employee, and owner—I'd say several thousand at least. And I've seen some really weird ones. I've also seen sand in the weirdest places and plenty of treachery, drugs back in the late sixties..."

"Come on, just jump in," Prince's uncle said.

"I've never seen anyone cause a revolution," Rusty said.

"A revolution?"

"Yes, a revolution. My camp was in revolt because of your nephew."

"But I thought that people would pick on him," Prince's uncle said. "How could he cause a revolt?"

"Oh, they picked on him all right. Mercilessly. Usually that kind of thing is restricted to a cabin, maybe a little bit to the division the camper's in. But I had campers several years older joining the fray." Rusty shook his head as if he still couldn't believe what he was saying.

"What did they say?"

"Things I couldn't believe, like he didn't deserve to live. Honestly, it was complete warfare."

"But why?"

"I've thought about that a lot, believe me. I think it's because he upset all their assumptions about life. You see, at camp, it's like the rest of society. There's the weak and there's the strong. Everyone kind of knows his place in the pecking order. Every year the order gets worked out, the first day for the most part. But the minute, it got worked out, Prince was in there upsetting it."

"And how did he do that?"

"First of all, your nephew has a very strong presence. I think he can look at somebody and they feel as if he is looking through them. I never thought I would say such a thing, but I think that he can actually see their secrets, their inner thoughts, and they absolutely hate that, particularly the devious ones, who have something to hide. You must have observed that about him."

"Yes, I'd say I have. But did everyone feel that way about him—I mean objecting to his looking through them—that kind of thing?"

"No, that's what was so interesting. It seemed to be only the nasty campers. The ones you'd call purer souls seemed content, some delighted that he could read their minds."

"Keep going," Prince's uncle said after pausing to mull over the information.

"Well, another thing that many of these guys really didn't like is that Prince was not a weakling that they could pick on. He didn't cower when they went after him. I mean the bullies/alpha males. I shouldn't talk about bullies at my camp because it's not good salesmanship, but you know a few exist everywhere. They are used to picking on weak guys. When there's the inevitable division between the in guys and out guys, a strong guy—you know, someone who's considered attractive, a good athlete, a good joker or conversationalist, etc. —usually goes over to the alpha male side; even if he's not a bully, or into dominance, like a few of the others, he's not going to stick his head out and oppose the bullies. It simply takes too much energy and the company seems much better over there. No one wants to be left out and made fun of. No respectable guy wants to associate with the weak. At least that was the paradigm until I ran into your nephew."

"So they were mad at him for associating with the weaker guys?"

"No, no—it was much more than that. Of course the alpha males got mad when they'd see him over there with those they'd made fun of in previous years. That arrangement didn't play by the rules. If he could have been on the strong guy, inside guy, side and didn't choose to do that, then there must have been something wrong with him from their point of view. But your nephew went a lot further than that." Then Rusty's tone changed for a minute. "I mean why should he stop there, when you could create a really novel social situation? But why did it have to be my camp? I'm still hearing from a lot of parents about last summer."

"I'm really sorry. I don't know what to say."

"Like I said, he didn't stop there. Oh no. He started to organize the weak guys. And I have to admit, as much trouble as this whole thing gave me, I did think that this social experiment was interesting. You see, all of a sudden, these weak guys became empowered. When one of the alpha males or bullies—the other strong guys who weren't bullies weren't interested in fighting, just initially in socializing with the strong, so it was only the bullies—when one of the bullies confronted a weak guy, Prince would walk between them.

"By confrontation on the part of the bully, I often mean body language. Often there's been no verbal communication, just a show of deference by the weak guy to the bully, like getting out of the bully's way, or letting him go first, when he felt like it, whether that's first for a hot dog, a shower, or at baseball. Or it may be having to hear a crude comment about yourself and just smiling meekly through it. If you weren't watching the situation carefully, you'd hardly know most of the time that a guy is a bully, or being mean, because most of the cues pass quickly between the guys and the weak guy has always conceded to the strong guy without any resistance. That's why before your nephew arrived, camp always looked peaceful, at least on the surface."

"And then what?" Prince's uncle's mouth had dropped open.

"Well, he'd tell the bully that the weak guy didn't have to take his stuff, in so many words. Politely, as your nephew assuredly is, but firmly. The bully'd get the message. He'd take one look at Prince and that athletic body, and those muscles—and I have to admit he looks as if he could fend off a counselor—"

"—I assure you he doesn't get them from lifting weights, either. That's what is so incredible."

"Anyway, he'd step between the two campers, and darn it, if the bully didn't end up backing off. Well, that meant the bully had lost face and had to somehow regain it. Otherwise, he was going to lose his pecking position. So he'd try to up the ante. You know, like double or nothing. He'd maintain the fiction that he had backed away only to really get back, when Prince was least expecting it. But the bully was really scared. He'd never had anyone do that to him before. So he tried to enlist the support of the other bullies, if not some of the other strong guys, to trap Prince and really give him a blow. But a lot of the other bullies or strong guys weren't buying. They felt as if Prince had eyes in the back of his head—you know the way I said he could look through you.

"And then, some of the strong guys, who'd never liked the bullies in the first place, began to associate with Prince and his crew. And it didn't stop there with the campers, you know. I never realized how wrapped up the counselors are in the social dynamics of the campers. Evidently, some of them thrive on the pecking order as well. Some of the immature counselors associate with the strong campers, if not some of the bullies. So, when all this social order got disturbed, they didn't know how to react. Many of them decided to shun Prince. Believe it or not, there was a very heated staff meeting on this topic."

"Did Prince refuse to do anything he was supposed to do at your camp?"

"No, he was a model camper in that respect."

"You were saying a while back that Prince empowered the weak guys and then we seemed to get sidetracked."

"Yes, Prince actually organized the so called less desirable guys in athletic events. Darn, if he couldn't almost win some of those events all by himself. And by the time he got the others on his team so excited that they performed better than they or anyone could ever imagine they could, and then recruited a few of the campers who came over from the strong side, they were able to win most events. That shattered the invincibility of what was previously the strong side of the aisle."

Then after a pause, Rusty said, "You implied before Prince came to camp that you thought that he would stand off from the other campers. And I could see that could certainly be the case. Yet, when he got around my campers, he almost took a leadership role, if you could call it that."

"I'll bet that with all his actions, he still isolated himself—I mean stood back from the crowd and didn't socialize with them. Maybe he organized them," Prince's uncle said, "but I'll bet that he didn't mix with them the way other campers did. There was probably little unnecessary contact between him and anyone, whether camper or counselor."

"That's true," Rusty said. "I hadn't thought about it quite in that vein."

"Another thing," Prince's uncle said. "He may have been capable of temporarily extending himself in order to assist the weak and stand up to the strong, but it's not a permanent situation. Others would gain confidence in their abilities and would feel stronger and more proud when they could move a situation like he did at your camp, but not Prince. They would become emboldened. Their egos would be inflated. But with Prince, it's just the opposite. The experiences at your camp were confidence busters for him. Now, I suppose it's my turn to make you feel bad, only you shouldn't, because there's nothing you could have done to prevent all this. Experiences such as this have always caused him to turn inward, not outward as most of us naturally would."

"I wonder why," Rusty said.

"I think it's because he feels the pain around him. He doesn't relish putting down or even getting even with that bully. 'He can see the worth in that person, though he can't relate to him the way we do."

"He always did seem humble, even when he totally had the upper hand," Rusty said. "And strangely, he did seem very upset when he used his own power. Boy, is he different from anyone I've seen."

"You bet," Prince's uncle said. "And because he's not feeding on everyone else's energy, for example to inflate his own ego, but instead is solely using his own inner resources to give to others, he feels very drained. The only way he can recharge is to withdraw from the world around him and seek that inner source of peace and energy within him. He's told me about this a bit. You know, he's not even a teenager yet. Maybe he can learn to manage that energy drain."

Prince's uncle had also chosen to expose him to Judaism. In this matter, he clearly chose to oppose the earlier wishes of his brother. Insisting on religion, he still might have chosen Reform Judaism or some other more liberal branch of the religion for his nephew of course, since this would have been the philosophy closest to his brother's. But since he had chosen to completely break from the family history concerning religion, he chose Orthodox Judaism, with which he was now most comfortable. As Prince approached the Bar Mitzvah age of thirteen, his uncle arranged for him to meet with a teacher at the synagogue for training. Finally, he would learn about the religion of his forefathers that had so entranced him that day in synagogue when he was seven.

The training went quite well from the viewpoint of his mastery of Hebrew and the Torah readings. Prince also learned Talmud and quickly reached a point at which he could argue issues with the best Rabbinic minds. The Bar Mitzvah he would experience at thirteen would now be only a formality to mark a learning process that had already far exceeded what many scholars reached in a lifetime. His uncle beamed with pride in the weeks before the big event. It seemed that the prophecy in heaven would finally begin to be born out, though Prince's soul had seemingly taken a most delayed route to that destiny. Then Prince approached his uncle to talk.

"Sit down Prince. What's on your mind?"

"Well uncle, I've been a lot of trouble to you," Prince said. "You didn't sign up for me."

"No, no. It's been all right. Our souls were meant to engage each other in this life. I've rather enjoyed it," Prince's uncle said. His smile as he spoke to his nephew quickly evaporated. He had never seen Prince with such a strange mixture of determination and consternation on his face. His glassy eyes indicated that his thoughts were distant.

"I say that," Prince said, "because I'm going to cause you to come to more grief, more than you've ever known with me."

"What is it Prince? Did you do something?"

"No, uncle. It's what I'm about to do. It will cause us both pain."

"Well, just stop. You don't have to do it."

"Yes, I do. I have to do it," Prince said. "This is one of those things that I don't have a choice in. I'm being compelled. Do you think that I like this?"

"To do what?" Prince's uncle's mouth hung open with that last word.

"To leave this house."

"Leave? Leave, but where?"

"I don't know."

"Am I hearing this right? You're saying that you have to leave, but you don't know where? And how long will this be for?

"I don't know. Probably years. But I know you will see me back. Just not sure when."

"Whoa." Prince's uncle held his head in his hands and sighed deeply. Then he bent his body forward in the chair, supporting his torso with his elbows on his thighs. "Prince, you know I've tried to give you every opportunity to develop in the manner that you needed. You know it hasn't been necessary for you to do the usual thing with me, as your parents would have wanted. But truly this is preposterous. Your Bar Mitzvah's coming up. You've trained for it. What purpose could leaving possibly serve? Anyway, you're just turning thirteen. You can't just leave. People your age don't just walk out on the street. I'm responsible for you. You'd never make it out there, not to mention that I'd be abandoning a child."

"You know you can't keep me here Uncle. I'm leaving because I have to, not because I'm thwarting you. This is not about you or me. It's about something else much more powerful in the universe."

"Prince, I know it's been tough growing up and maybe I haven't helped with some of the things I've suggested for you. But I really thought that we were finally on the path with some Jewish things. It wasn't just that you had done so well in training for your Bar Mitzvah. I actually thought that you were enjoying the way we observed Shabbat and spending time with friends in our traditional community. Isn't that the kind of thing that you enjoy?"

"Yes," Prince said. He smiled ruefully. "Yes, I have so much appreciated the warm, traditional, and close feeling, and you've been so kind to me, but this is not about what I enjoy. Even more so now that I know about being a Jew, I realize that there is Divine service. There's all the hidden world that supports us. What I think is not very important in the universe."

"Prince, there is Divine service, and we all have our part to play in that, but your home is here. G-d always wants us to do the right thing. That's why we're here. G-d placed you here."

"Yes, that's right. And the Jewish path you've shown me is right. I don't quarrel with that at all. In fact, I believe in it. But as quickly as I have received it and understood it, I've got to leave it. It's almost as if I've got to throw it away right now. Uncle, have you ever felt compelled to do something that you logically know is crazy?"

"That's been a way of life with you, hasn't it Prince? Prince, tell me, where is this all leading? I know that your abilities give you some insight into that. Just tell me what you do know now."

"What I know is that I have to leave and that sometime I will be back. What I also know is that G-d will take care of me, so you needn't worry. But where I'm going is unspeakable. Am I compelled to do this because G-d commands me, or am I some kind of crazy lunatic who chooses evil over good, falsehood over truth, chaos over the strength and family and stability that you've offered me? I don't know. And if G-d truly commands me to do this, if this is my destiny, how is it that G-d would want me to do this? If I believe the voices I've heard, that I should go—go where ever I'm going—then I'd be some kind of special soul, singled out up there, and I simply can't believe that. I suppose that's the only thing separating me from schizophrenia right now, my logic analyzing my illogic, though there's no psychiatrist out there who wouldn't commit me right this moment. Yet I'm compelled to go."

"Go? Go, just like that, but not knowing where?"

"Tonight, Uncle. Tonight! In a few hours, as soon as I pack a few things. Enough for my back pack. My parents departed this world, so that you would have charge of me, teach me Judaism, and then permit me to go."

"Prince, you know that I couldn't handle it if something happened."

"I know. Don't worry."

A long silence ensued. Both were trying to hold back their tears. Neither one of them could look at the other for fear that they would break down. Finally, Prince's uncle slowly said, "Prince, I know I shouldn't ask where you are going, not that you know now. And when you get to these places, it's not that I have to know where you are...exactly. In fact, you can hide that from me, particularly if it's embarrassing to you, but it is important that I know that you're okay. You've got to signal me somehow, by mail, e-mail, telephone, maybe mental telepathy, if it's in your powers. Just make sure the universe sends me a message somehow. Would you please do that? For both of us? And you will let me know if you need my help, won't you— you won't come to grief because you can't contact me, will you?"

Prince smiled. "Yes, Uncle, I'll be able to do that. Believe it or not, G-d doesn't want you to suffer any more than is necessary here. You'll know I'm doing fine. Uncle, one more thing. Will you give me your blessing to go, not just your agreement?"

"Yes, I'm a crazy old fool, but you have my blessing to go." His voice cracked at that point.

"Thank you, Uncle. Now, will you bless me as your son, with the priestly blessing that all of the Reed ancestors used to bless the Jewish people?"

"Yes, I will."

When Prince had packed and given his final farewell to his uncle, he quickly moved a hundred feet from the Reed house. He sat down on the concrete by the side of the road in the dark, wet night and cried from the deep recesses of his heart, as he had never cried before. It was thirty minutes before the big, strong boy could raise himself and go forward. His uncle sat teary eyed by the inside of the doorway, restraining himself from following his nephew. In the heavens, there seemed to be only despair. While all actions on earth cause reactions in the hidden worlds, this one spoke the loudest for some time. Some even voiced their doubt of G-d's intentions, the kind of doubt about G-d that was heard so frequently on earth at that time.

6

G-d will scatter you amongst all the peoples from one end of the earth to the other, and there you shall serve other gods, from wood and stone, whom neither you nor your ancestors have experienced. Yet even amongst those nations you will find no peace, nor will you find a place to rest. G-d will give you there an anguished heart and eyes that pine and a despondent spirit. The life that you face shall be uncertain; you shall be in terror, night and day, with no assurance of survival.

Deuteronomy Ch. 28, vs. 64-66

Prince had entered the darkness without any idea of where he was going. Like a modern day Abram, being told to go forth from his native land and his father's house, to a land which G-d would show him, Prince's only thought had been that he must leave where he was. But whether Prince had faith, like Abraham, that G-d would eventually lead him to the appropriate place, to the promised land, we can not be sure. It would be nice to believe that this old soul did indeed put his faith in G-d at this point, but such faith would not in the end be necessary for him to act as he did. The predominant truth here was that Prince was in great pain and all of us go into exile from ourselves and our world to avoid such pain. The immediate result was that Prince turned his face away from G-d, so that G-d was forced to hide His face from Prince.

Prince was very large for his age, approaching six feet, as he turned thirteen. He still continued to exhibit many boyish attributes which might give away his age to roving figures of authority, but his powers over his mind and body allowed him to reflect an air of maturity that convinced most that he was much older. Even at that point, he could easily pass for sixteen, and with the fake identification card with its social security number and the driver's license, that he had quickly made up, he could play a young eighteen, the age when he was eligible for any kind of employment on the farm or in a manufacturing plant—when they still had manufacturing plants in America. No one was inclined to question such an earnest face.

Prince's first motivation had been to move as far as he could, spiritually and geographically, from where he had been. During the first few months, when he had still been fairly close to his former home, he had worked in the California migrant fields picking vegetables and fruit. This had suited his need to earn quick cash, and because the expected length of the jobs was naturally so short and the quality of the workers always questionable, it was less likely that questions would be asked by the employers when hiring. Plus, the practice of meeting different employers and learning their needs and the questions that they were likely to ask, was good training for him before he ventured further afield. Prince had a strong back and could carry a heavy load for hours without tiring; his work was efficient, focused, and directed in a manner that had rarely been seen in a migrant setting; several work supervisors had observed his work habits and offered him permanent employment, a highly unusual offer and one usually very much sought after.

But he was determined to keep going. Like a fugitive, always fleeing, only in this case fleeing himself, he kept moving, always moving with the wind. When a dust devil would go by, he would be gone in its midst. The other migrants would look up and ask where Prince was, thinking that they had only missed him for a short time, but he would be gone, disappearing into that large landscape. For most people fleeing, that wide open space would have been enough to drown their sorrow, to escape themselves. But the hole in Prince's heart was too big to fill, the isolation too great to bridge; he was always looking for a place in time and space that would possibly do it better.

When the migrant work did not fill his needs, he decided he must go even further. He then became a merchant marine. Working odd shifts and walking the ports in strange lands had seemed to fit him for a while. He would be thrown in with various crews while in transit from one port to another. He was content to stay virtually invisible among them, doing his work, saying little, and trying to mind his own business. He was considered strange company on the boat, but then there were certainly others, though generally rare cases, who had been observed to isolate themselves. Still there were times when Prince became engaged, or injected himself, into the social dynamics of the group.

Jen looked up from his large poker game. "What are you doing? I've told you to stay out of this area, haven't I?"

"Jen, how can I. You took my paycheck, borrowed one of my shirts," George said.

"Ain't nothing over here that's yours."

"I saw you with it on when I was on duty on the bridge a few hours ago."

"You calling me a liar?"

"No, I just want to look for it. Just want it back. Got to have my money."

"Well, I don't know where that is, you hear me." Then he smiled and said, "But you don't make as much as I do."

George began frantically searching through Jen's bunk. Jen's bulk quickly rose, turned around, grabbed George by the neck, and drew a switch blade. "I told you to stay out of here, that there's nothing that's any of yours here."

Everyone froze and there was complete silence just before Prince walked in the room. "Drop that knife, Jen." Moving closer, Prince said, "I said, drop that knife."

Jen looked around in surprise. "I've got a knife on him punk, and there's nothing you can do about it. What are you going to do? You can't make me drop that knife." He greeted Prince with his practiced sneer.

"No, I can't make you drop the knife. But you have two choices, eventually. You're going to have to wound him, maybe even kill him, or let him go, as I said. If it's the first choice, I'm going to be waiting for you. You're not going to get away. I'd suggest that you drop that knife now and return his things."

Jen still had the sneer. "Did you hear that boys? This little boy over here wants me to drop my knife. What are you going to do to me little boy?" No one moved or said anything. All waited, entranced. Jen had not been challenged in anyone's memory, probably because he appeared to weigh more than 300 pounds. The fact that he faced a young challenger that could not have exceeded 150 was intriguing.

Prince remained in his same position, arms folded across his chest, calm and silent, not willing to make even a conciliatory statement that might appeal to Jen and enable him to save face. The sneer disappeared and Jen's tone changed. "Listen boy, it's between me and him here. It don't have nothing to do with you and you shouldn't make it your business. You hear."

"Oh, but it does have to do with me. You're not going to prey on the weak around here. He's done absolutely nothing to you. He tried to mind his own business. But you just couldn't leave him alone. Couldn't leave alone someone who wouldn't associate with you. Now take that knife and put it away, give him his things back, and leave him alone, and I'll have nothing more to say." With that, several mouths fell open in amazement. Now that it was clear that a major fight would ensue, one guy close to the hallway went up on deck to find an officer. But no one else moved or even spoke, to try to restrain the two.

Jen remained still for several more seconds and then he quickly released his hold on George. He turned around and swung wildly at Prince with his knife. Prince picked up a chair and began dancing around the room. Jen came after him at every turn, missing widely and heading for the wall. Every time Jen would bump into something, Prince would give him a powerful kick, just like a soccer ball. Jen would scramble, eventually picking himself up, but in the process he became wounded, by his own knife. When the knife eventually went flying across the room, and was secured by the witnesses, Jen took his powerful frame and leaped onto Prince. They tussled in the air for a moment until Prince went down under Jen's weight. By this point, the noise in the room was deafening. Grown men were screaming, though they didn't realize it. For several seconds, Prince appeared to be pinned and the fight seemed to be as much as over. Then Prince suddenly pushed Jen off of him. Jen lay on the floor wriggling in agony, while Prince got up and walked away.

"What did he do to him?"

"He got him. He ain't going to be doing any business when we get to port tonight."

Neither Prince nor Jen was doing any business with the marine merchant when they reached port. Both were confined until they reached land, warned never to apply in the industry again, and then summarily left. For Jen this was a disaster, as he had no means to return home. For Prince, it posed little problem. He was still growing and maturing. He grew a beard, long hair, and once again changed his identification papers.

Some time later, once again in the merchant marine, Prince found himself involved in more subtle conflicts. Once he had been sitting at the dinner table minding his own business while several of the guys next to him had been shooting the bull.

"The way I got it figured, when we get to port, we ought to grab chow and then link up with Estelle and her friends," Arnold said.

Lester broke out into a loud laugh, which was then echoed by unanimous laughter, almost like an amen. The expression of Prince's face remained unchanged, as if he hadn't heard anything.

"I mean I liked the one in the pink dress." John said. Again, they laughed in unity, this time in a somewhat more sinister way, with their eyes twinkling. Again, Prince tried to ignore them.

Suddenly Arnold turned toward Prince. "What's with you man? Ain't you ever had feelings for a woman before?"

"Look," Prince said, "I'm not part of this, okay?"

"Yes you is too. If you're not, why are you sitting over here with us?" Arnold said.

"I'm just trying to mind my own business and eat," Prince said.

"As far as I'm concerned, you can eat out on the deck. No need to sit here in judgment on us," Arnold said.

"I'm not judging you," Prince said.

"Yes, you is," Arnold said. "You always sit over there by yourself. Never having a conversation with anyone. You looking down on all of us. We all sees you reading, whatever that stuff is. You're strange, not like us." His face had become beet red.

"I don't mean you any harm." Prince had hardly shifted in his seat and his still relaxed face reflected his calm demeanor.

Arnold rose out of his seat, stretched across the table, and put his fist in Prince's face. "What I say hasn't even concerned you, has it? You ain't even human. Who are you? Let's just go upstairs and settle this matter, man to man."

Lester rose and wrapped his arm around Arnold's outstretched torso. "Arnold, this isn't a good idea. It'll get you thrown off and besides you don't want to fight him." Then he whispered into Arnold's ear, "Arnold I've seen him lift that freight out there. He may not be as heavy as you, but I assure you, he'll whip you good. Believe me, he ain't worth it to you. Let him be. I admit he's strange, not good company for us, but he's not after you."

With that, the conflict was defused. But when they reached port the next day, Prince quit anyway. It was time to move on. Prince always had a sense when things were getting a little too dangerous, a little too close for comfort, when those around him were beginning to ask too many questions, questions about who he was and why a guy like him was there. At all costs, he must preserve anonymity and never admit or be who he was.

After a while, Prince left the merchant marine. He had tired of moving from one port to another and chose to stay on land. Having learned Spanish from his migrant work and in his days on the sea, he first worked in several farm settings in South America and Central America. Then he moved back to the States. Now he felt secure enough to take jobs of longer duration. Perhaps this is because he looked quite a bit older now and easily passed for eighteen.

It was easy for Prince to secure a job when he arrived at each city. Usually he arrived by rail or bus—he had the funds now for a car but was afraid it might be traced—and scanned the listings on the internet screen in the terminals; the companies sponsoring the internet service offered rides to their places of employment. And now that Prince had shaved off his beard and groomed his hair, he was much more than presentable to any potential employer.

By his mid-teens Prince was approaching 6'6", and weighed only about two hundred pounds. His frame fit into a man's 46 jacket and his arms and legs were pure sinew. His hair, which would have normally retained its naturally sandy blond color from childhood, had bleached to a golden color during his work in the fields. His eyes were of a light blue shade, and when they looked directly at you, they could pierce your inner being. People were said to have commented on his beauty, such an incredible human specimen, only to gasp when he turned around to look at them. The closest physical analogy might be to say that he surprised his observers as much as a needle unexpectedly piercing their skin. His magnetism was so great, the physical attraction so overwhelming, that whole towns, even cities, would talk about this stranger. He would begin to draw crowds that observed his behavior and newspapers—the kind they had back then—would be sent to try to interview him. The local TV nightly news would be heard asking, "Does the stranger, who has reportedly excited this area with his presence, exist? Follow our reporter in when she interviews those who say they have seen him. Find out what his neighbors and coworkers say he's really like."

Then Prince knew that it was time to move on, lest he in some way be discovered. Still, as the word passed from one point to another about this person, and stories became embellished about his potential intelligence and his powers, powers he had been loathe to demonstrate in any way, people began to look for him in various places near where he had been sighted, and he was forced to quickly increase the radius of his movement. Even so, word began to spread over a regional and multi-state area, so that Prince began to be asked if he was the reputed youth by several potential employers he encountered. Then once again Prince felt as if he were going to suffocate. Physically reacting to his predicament, his neck would actually develop red marks. Or when he felt as if he were trapped, his eyes would squinch to reflect the light as would an animal snared. As had been the case so many other times, there seemed to be no escape from his being.

Only then did Prince turn to his yetzer hara, or evil inclination, for relief. Up to this point Prince had merely fled his own person. Though he had avoided Jewish observance, he had nevertheless otherwise scrupulously always done the proper thing. In cases where he could do a mitzvah, or a good deed, could defend a weak person, he had always and unquestionably done so. It wasn't that he was proving anything to himself, or trying to uphold some standard, Jewish or otherwise, because he set no standards for the person he denied. Rather, he fell into doing the right thing naturally. His soul couldn't have chosen otherwise. And now, when he turned toward his yetzer hara, it wasn't the way you or I would turn toward our yetzer hara. You see, Prince still had all his powers of intellect and emotion and when he turned toward his yetzer hara, he did it in a way that he wouldn't hurt anyone. To the contrary, the wrong actions he took, though they may have involved his fellow person, he "knew" were ultimately supportive of that person. The people with whom he sinned, he hoped would only come away from him as better people for their contact with him; and in fact, it was true that they could only love him afterward with feelings that strengthened them for the remainder of their lives. Feeling that these lost souls were on the same crossed path of life that he was, Prince had great compassion for them.

No, it wasn't the people around him that he wished to hurt. It was G-d with whom he had the quarrel. G-d had put him in this predicament, set him down on this earth, and forced him to be some kind of stooge from the beginning. G-d had given him this great intelligence, body, and money, and expected that he do something great with it. But G-d hadn't supported him. It had only been painful, absolutely nonsensical. And then when he had tried to escape, just mind his own business, he had been reminded of it all once again, then again, then again. Where ever he went, he saw it. He began to hate the reflection of his face in the mirror and wished that he could wear a hood. At least when they had rounded up his ancestors during the Crusades, pogroms, and the Shoah, or Holocaust, there had been quick death, and if there wasn't, there were others in the same predicament. But Prince felt all alone.

It would be too facile to commit suicide. That would be giving up too easily. He knew that. The way to get back at G-d was to completely disobey Him, to attempt to destroy the part of him that was G-d. He would drag his soul, his G-dly inheritance, through the soiled and disgusting world, the kelipah, in which G-d had placed him. He would descend through forty-nine of the world's fifty levels of kelipah, just as the Jewish people had done in their captivity in Egypt before their redemption by G-d. He would block out his Divine soul and operate through his animal soul. He would no longer serve G-d, but attempt to remedy the wrongs of the world in the way he sought fit. Prince looked up at the heavens and shook his fist in defiance. "I refuse to live like this," he yelled.

To spite G-d, he sought out women. It was not necessary to solicit anyone. Prince merely abstained from turning them away. And so it went for a while. Each person was different. But he never gained anything from the experiences, nor did he gain any psychic energy from his deeds. And because he did what he did solely to defy G-d, he spent a tremendous amount of energy. And with the wall he had erected between G-d and himself, there was no Divine Light to recharge him. Like a candle that was burning at both ends, his soul was gradually getting eaten away at his core. Before, his great attraction to all those around him had occurred naturally, as he allowed part of G-d's Light to shine through him. But now, he had to work increasingly harder to make his presence attractive to others; now only the small residue of G-d's dwindling presence in him manifested itself to others. Like a light bulb, powered by a weak battery, he was forced to shut down for increasingly greater periods of time in order to conserve his energy. During those hours when he physically shut down, his countenance had changed to something dark and sinister, truly unrecognizable to those who saw him during public appearances. His face appeared to reflect light in the manner of a nugget of coal; the dim shine of his apparition was all that was left of the Divine energy in it. The few that observed him in his unguarded moments—he had many of those moments now that his powers were waning—said that they were looking into an infinite void, a shell, a dying star. To see him in that state was to see a semi-comatose individual, whose Divine soul wished to divorce itself from its animal soul, and return to G-d, its Maker. Prince was dying and those who looked down into the hole that was sucking the energy from his soul, were repulsed and fled. They could not stomach the great evil they perceived.

Ironically, Prince's severely failing health was of some relief for him. When he finally realized that he no longer had the powers to defy G-d, and when he also sensed that his misery would not—in fact could not—go on forever, his burden was somewhat mitigated. Prince was relieved to know that G-d had provided constraints, or Gevurah, to his behavior; if he was subject to rules like everyone else, it meant that G-d cared. He wasn't alone. It meant that his choices were meaningful, that they had consequences. If he was subject to the laws of the universe, he must therefore have some relationship to the order of the universe.

So he decided to make a turn, to give up his defiance. Not that he was returning home or wished to give up a lifestyle that would guarantee his anonymousness. He was still in pain and fleeing, but he would seek out a more permanent situation, one that he hoped would help him avoid the publicity that had begun to surround his personage. At that time he moved from the Mississippi Delta area westward to Texas. He had heard in a little eatery that they were hiring several field hands at a very large ranch, and with his athletic build, he had been hired as soon as he arrived. There the land seemed endless and there was simple housing for the workers. This is all he required.

7

He had decided to go under the alias of Joseph at the ranch. He did the farming chores that were assigned to him well, with intelligence and strength, and when the assistant superintendent had left the ranch after a few weeks, the chief superintendent had asked him to take his place. Though he had not realized it then, he had been noticed by Judy and John Jones, the owners of the ranch. Within several months he could perform all of the key functions of the ranch and was suggesting improvements that might be made. No one had asked him any more questions about himself; no one seemed to suspect his background or inclinations. He was content to look at the wide vistas and watch the clouds move slowly across the sky.

One morning, following the previous day's instructions from the chief superintendent, Prince had risen early to inspect the fence line several miles from the ranch homestead. He received a page to immediately return to the staging area for the workers, where he was greeted by a gentleman he thought was probably the Jones' personal secretary.

"Are you Joseph Reed?" the gentleman said.

"Yes," Prince said.

"Mr. and Mrs. Jones want to see you in their living room right away."

When Prince arrived, Mr. Jones was sitting, writing at what appeared to be his personal desk, a huge platform supported by a couple of large pieces of wood. He did not pause from his activity and in fact then proceeded to call one of his assistants on the telephone to give them instructions. He was dressed casually and appeared to be in his late thirties with a bit of a paunch.

Mrs. Jones smiled at Prince and walked across the room to shake his hand. "You're Joseph, aren't you? Please have a seat." She motioned him to a corner of the large room away from her husband. She was tall, and at almost six feet, appeared to be taller than her husband. He guessed that she was quite a bit younger than her husband, perhaps in her early twenties. She wore a buckskin top and her brown hair fell to halfway across her back in a large mass of tightly wound curls. Her blue eyes were clear and her face was unlined and untroubled. He immediately noticed her energy and her friendliness.

After a few minutes, Mr. Jones hung up the phone and motioned Prince over to the worn leather chair beside his desk. "They tell me that you are Joseph Reed."

"Yes sir, I am."

"You may not be aware of it yet, but Helmsley, your direct supervisor and the chief superintendent of this ranch, died during the night of a heart attack," Mr. Jones said.

"No," Prince said. "I'm sorry about that." He wondered if he might have known about it earlier, if he had previously focused his thought on Helmsley.

"That's okay," Mr. Jones said. He had no time for casual conversation at this point. "Look, the point I'm trying to get to is that we'll be needing a manager of this ranch right away. Normally, we'd go out and get someone who's had a history of this, check references, that kind of thing. I mean this ranch is one of the biggest in the Lone Star State. Normally, I wouldn't even look at someone like yourself. No offense to you, but you're just a stranger to me, and I need someone I can really rely on. But in this case, we've lost our superintendent and his previous assistant in a very short period of time. I just don't have that luxury."

Prince nodded but said nothing and there was silence in the room for a moment. Then Mr. Jones resumed. "There's another factor here. And that's Judy over here, my wife." He motioned with his hand over to her. "She's an excellent judge of people, better than I am. She's been observing you and she says that you are very capable. What do you say about that?"

Prince shrugged. "I'm pretty good."

"She says that you been at the cutting edge of breeding those animals, that Helmsley relied on you, because he really didn't understand that new genetic technology. Is that true?" Mr. Jones said. "I mean I was told that it's so new that only a few places in the world know about it yet and have started to put it into practice."

"Yes, it's definitely cutting edge," Prince said.

"Well, how do you know about it? I paid a lot to get access to it," Mr. Jones said. "Did you study it somewhere?"

"No," Prince said. "I just read about it. It seemed very logical and when I saw you trying to practice it here, I thought I could help."

"But, you could only have read about it in scientific journals at this point," Mrs. Jones said.

"Yes," Prince said, "I did read about it in several scientific journals."

Mr. Jones paused to consume what he had just heard. He squinted at Prince's large frame. "I just don't get this. I'm not sure who you are..." He stopped himself. "Another thing—my wife is what you'd call a spiritual person. I mean she just knows things about people. And she picked you out of that crowd before you ever started to demonstrate any of these talents. She watched you. She says that G-d is with you and that G-d lends success to everything that you touch, everything that you undertake. She says that if you manage this place that G-d will bless us." He then realized what he had just said and shifted nervously with embarrassment. "You know I rely on my wife for guidance in certain matters, but the main thing I need here is a manager. Can you do it?"

Prince moved his focus from Mr. Jones to his wife. She was staring boldly and confidently at him. She had no doubts about her convictions. He felt that her vision was piercing his mind. He had never felt anyone do that before. He sensed that it was the same feeling that people had had about him when he "looked through them". He smiled. "Yes, I can do it. But I will need to know what your expectation levels are. You will tell me the specific things I need to get done for you personally, besides the day to day managing of the ranch?"

"Oh yes," Mr. Jones said. "You can manage people all right, can't you?"

"Oh yes," Prince said. He smiled again. "That will not be any problem."

And so it had started, the relationship between the three of them. Prince had reported to them formally for several weeks. By then, Mr. Jones realized that Prince was not only quite capable of managing the ranch as well as it had been done previously, but that his wife had truly been extraordinarily perceptive about Prince's abilities. But even Mrs. Jones could not have imagined the dramatic and positive changes that he would implement. As time progressed, the tenor of the labor force had changed under his direction, both through morale improvements and the hiring of better laborers, which Prince was able to attract by virtue of his efforts and his charisma. The breeding program began to yield such results in a short period of time that it became nationally known; Prince had been requested by several research departments at universities to coauthor a number of scientific articles. And the ranch became extremely profitable as the Joneses sold the animals that were bred, as well as Prince's consulting services.

The Joneses could not begin to believe their good fortune and they were not oblivious to the reasons for it. Mr. Jones had purchased the ranch with some inherited wealth and now it looked as if he would earn another huge fortune. Naturally, he wanted to find out more about this strange manager, who had no stated background, and who had mysteriously arrived out of nowhere. Not understanding Prince's motivation, he was afraid of losing him as quickly as he had found him. Obviously, Prince could have been successful at any place. That is why

Mr. Jones had so wisely resisted his temptation to question Prince's background in the initial meeting; if he had, perhaps Prince would have bolted from the room right then. But Prince had been meant to stay at the Jones' ranch, and so by Divine Providence Mr. Jones hadn't followed his usual inclination.

With Mrs. Jones, it was a different matter. She had no question that Prince would stay, at least for the time being. She knew that whatever conditions of the universe had brought Prince there had not changed yet. There was some purpose in his being there—she knew that. Whatever that purpose was would be manifested at some appropriate time. It was no use her getting concerned about it, since it would surely happen the way that G-d had intended. What was fun for her was watching Prince in action. She knew he was a supernatural. It was as if she were attending a movie or play about some incredible event and reacting as the plot unfolded.

Both the Jones' motivations led them to want to spend more time with Prince, outside of his regular duties as their employee. This was unusual for them and unusual in the world of employment at that time. Employers were not known to socialize with their employees. The social classes were more distinct than we know them in our world now and there had not been as much cultural fertilization between ethnic groups as we have today. Managers of day laborers were maybe a step above day laborers, but still a full step behind their employers. First the Joneses had invited Prince to join them for a working lunch. But that lunch had quickly veered into personal matters of the Joneses; they hoped to draw Prince out, have him reciprocate by talking about his personal background, but he never did. Still, the Joneses were charmed by Prince, in much the same way that he had attracted those around him in his very earliest years with his smile and his natural gifts. They began to see him as an individual and as a friend, a very unusual one at that, but not as a total stranger. He offered them serious advice on their lives and empathized with their struggles. They were attracted to his beauty. Now that he no longer shut G-d out of his soul—though he still did not embrace Him—and had recovered from his physical slide, he once again became a magnet to those around him.

So, working lunch had progressed rapidly to just a friendly lunch for its own sake, then to invitations for dinner, then time spent on holidays, then as a companion on short trips, and then as just a true friend with whom to spend time. They became a threesome. He was told to call them John and Judy. They came to rely on Prince for everything that they did. John put him in charge of his household, placing in his hands all that he owned. And from that time, G-d did indeed bless the Jones' house for Prince's sake, continuing to multiply the profits and health of the ranch. And when the Joneses saw that, when they saw how successful he was, they offered him a room in their house.

Prince's relationship grew separately with each of them. With John he would play chess after a meal, always winning, even if he tried to lose. He was capable of discussing real estate, financial investments, hunting, guns, sports—both of the Joneses wondered how Prince could know so much about the art of competing in swimming and track. It was an equal relationship with John, even if they retained unequal abilities.

With Judy, it was quite different. She ran the show. He had none of his usual powers over her, nor did he want them. Rather, it was she who led their relationship. She was the first person who had powers over him. She would point to a magazine article that she had retrieved over the internet. They would spend time in the library—it was all her books, not John's—perusing books on various subjects. Back then they had many of the kind of bound books that are so rare today. They would argue philosophy and compare readings. She would make a point and then each would meet the other's gaze, wondering if the other was thinking the same thing. But nothing further was ever said. Each banished the thought.

They didn't have to familiarize each other with their thoughts. Each could complete a sentence the other started. They both understood the other's thoughts on spirituality without any explanation. On these matters, that they had only surmised about the universe, and had not discussed with another living soul, they were in complete agreement. Prince, who had never consulted another person's opinion, never relied on the wisdom of another, never really depended on another since his earliest years, depended upon Judy. He really liked being supported. He began to wonder who she was, as much as she wondered about him. Come to think of it, he knew a lot about John's background before his purchase of the ranch; he had originally thought that he knew a lot about her too, since she had been so open with him about her current life, but now he realized he knew virtually nothing about her past.

Each of them began to have a series of dreams during their sleep at night. They dreamt as they had never dreamt before. Each would interpret the dreams of the other in sessions after breakfast. The dreams were "real" dreams, the kind from which you awake realizing that you have personally experienced something consequential. These dreams would repeat, or manifest themselves in a series of related subjects, one night after another; G-d was telling them they were significant. Of course, Prince, with his personal powers, would have normally understood more in his dreams than he did then, but he found his powers curbed when he was around Judy. Somehow, she seemed to compensate for his loss of powers, or maybe he had merely lent them to her for the time being, so that she could use them, and provide him with the objectivity of an outside friend, that he had never possessed.

One morning, Prince repeated three dreams that he had experienced. "Actually," he said, "they seemed more like visions than dreams."

"What do you mean, Joseph?"

"They had the same feeling as dreams that I've had at night while sleeping, but one actually occurred yesterday afternoon, while I—well at least I thought I was awake. The other two...you could say happened at night, and perhaps I was sleeping. But it seemed more like I had woken up to see what I was experiencing in these dreams. And another thing—I seemed to be completely aware of my entity while I experienced these 'dreams', or visions. It was more like watching a movie that stars yourself. I wasn't so immersed in the movie that it seemed to be total reality to me, the way we experience most dreams; yet, I wasn't controlling what happened in the movie either."

Judy smiled. "Maybe you're supposed to examine the script then, and see if you need to change it, I mean rewrite it." She fastened her gaze on him until his eyes met hers. Then she knew that he knew what she was thinking.

Prince caught his breath and proceeded. "There were three visions. The first one was much longer than the second, and the second was much longer than the third."

"I'll bet that the first one is more general and sets the stage for the next one, which in turn is more general than the last. Probably each succeeding one has more specific detail about your life, and the choices facing you now," she said.

I had a vision, Prince started. *I was in a beautiful hollow. At the base of this ravine was a stream, its shallow waters flowing quietly and gently, but steadfastly through the hollow. The water was clear and the bedrock underneath was well defined. The passage of time was not important here. Though the water that passed through was replaced by new water, I could not discern any change. Only the stones seemed well worn. Turtles and fish swam through the waters and large trees on the side drank its fluid and sheltered it. It was good.*

I knew that I was part of that stream, that somehow the source of the water in the stream was the same fluid that was flowing through me. I was one with it all and I felt content to stay there—forever. Everything that I could ever imagine desiring could be found there. But I could not remain. I felt this desire, this absolute necessity to begin to climb the ravine around this stream.

The ravine was extremely steep with thick, lush vegetation throughout the path I chose. And with each step that I took I often fell back much of the way. My feet became trapped in mud and roots and many of the plants scratched or stung my body. I could not see far in front of me, nor did I have any idea where I was going or how far I would travel. Yet, I was drawn up, up, up, even as I tired greatly and had to stop frequently to regain my strength.

My course up the ravine was under a dark canopy of trees. I was afraid—afraid of the dark and the unknown and afraid of what I would touch. I was afraid of reaching for support, and failing to get it, and then falling down all of the distance I had traveled. Yet, every time I reached for support through that darkness, it magically seemed to be present. If I put out my arm to grasp a rock, root, or branch, it was there and it supported me and propelled me forward. As well, in spite of the darkness, I was able to see quite well the forms around me. The vegetation was lush, almost ethereal, and if I had not been so scared, I would have actually found it quite comforting. There was always food, beauty, and sustenance for my spirit. This I vaguely understood when I would relax, my mind would expand, and I would permit myself to understand and accept my surroundings and be part of them. But most of the time, I caused this stimulating and comforting environment to be a distant reality outside myself, as I continued to worry where I might end up and argue rationally with myself whether I should return to the stream, whose world I thought I at least knew. Several times I turned around and took the first steps back down the ravine, but that always led to a great confusion. My spirit knew that I must eventually get to the top of the slope, if I was to achieve any understanding of my purpose here at all.

So I struggled on for much time. Gradually, I became comfortable with the assumption that I would be able to continue the climb physically and survive. But my heart ached and I remained scared. And now I felt in addition, a great loneliness, except when I would drift in and out of reveries and imagine that I was speaking to a tree or that a hawk had landed on my chest to deliver a message from above. Actually, with great happiness I imagined much more, even miracles that do not happen, but I would always cruelly awake to realize that nothing of the sort could have happened to me and that I had deceived myself with stupid dreams. And then I would vow that in the future I would not waste my time with such useless wanderings of the mind. And then a great terror would descend upon me and I would cry out, but I was alone, very much alone, and no one was listening. This cycle would repeat over and over, always starting with great happiness as I imagined great beauty and the presence of G-d around and through me, and then suddenly descending into great anguish, as I denied the existence of all of this imagined world, which I knew was preposterous.

After many times at this useless cycle, and feeling strongly that nothing would ever come of it, nor would it ever end, I felt the ravine side become even steeper. The vegetation was no longer lush and it seemed more open, drier, more defined, but with each step, I fell back more often. Now, I wavered in my step and I no longer seemed sure of my ability to continue. The terror and fear was partially replaced by fatigue. My body ached. I fell more often and did not recover so easily. Now, too, I was a bit bitter and looked back on this long journey with disgust. If only I had stayed where I was comfortable at the stream. I could not see that the path I had taken would be very useful for others, nor could I see any other purpose in these travails. Yet, I continued onward, needing to explain to myself a reason for this journey and hoping to finally find it somewhere at its end.

One day, as I was sure that I could continue no longer, I saw a totally unfamiliar sight. Instead of the monotonous vegetation, I saw a glimmer of light up the ravine through the trees. As I propelled myself forward, more light appeared. This light seemed to trigger a distant memory from a happier time, though I could not place the memory. Now, the presence of the light was strong and I was drawn to it, even more so than I had been drawn up the ravine. My former bitter feelings about my journey seemed to fade and become trite in comparison. I felt a strong, outside force drawing me in and channeling me. I forgot my physical fatigue as I was caught up in this draft. As I drew closer to this attractive force, I saw what appeared to be a *field with tall grass, but then the light was so intense, especially after the dark woods I had experienced for many years, that I was forced to shield my eyes. The waves of light energy swelled around and through me and my body burned with its powerful touch, but I experienced a great sense of well-being which overwhelmed any bodily discomfort.*

As I entered the field, I continued to rise above it. Despite being blinded, I could look back at the woods and see the entire path that I had traversed. The water at the base of the ravine was still flowing evenly, as it had been a long time ago, and the darkness provided by the trees was still present as always. Only my feelings about the forest had suddenly changed and the love that I had occasionally felt in my dreams along the journey, or as I passed from sleep to wakefulness, had magnified many times. And I realized that I had never been alone and that many were now traveling the same path that I had cut through the vegetation, just as I had followed others' paths, and that I was connected with them. I yearned to go back to those still on the path and tell them not to worry, that their journey would be worthwhile, meaningful, and would ultimately lead to this beautiful field. With my fear now gone, I yearned to re-experience the forest environment, hug the trees and kiss the birds. But I also yearned to stay in this beautiful, heavenly place.

"That's the first one," Prince said. "Want to stop now and comment, or go on?"

She smiled. "I've got my ideas already. But we shouldn't jump to conclusions yet. Let's hear the other two first."

Then I had another vision, Prince began again. I was in a field of grass so high past my head that I could not see in any direction. Not knowing where I was or how to escape I felt a great sense of panic. My stomach and limb muscles knotted up, and I became so tense that I could hardly move. As I struggled a few steps in one direction, the stalks of grass began to harden and tighten around me in contorted shapes. I became very angry and resolved to free myself in any way possible. But the more I struggled, the harder I became bound by the grass. Nevertheless, I struggled on, until extremely tired, I could not move any more, and the grass bound me tighter than ever. I cried out to no avail. It was then that I finally realized that I could never expect to free myself. But instead of the fear and anger I thought I would feel more than ever, the realization that I could no longer change my fate brought me an unexpected sense of relief. I no longer needed to struggle, but to calmly await what must inevitably happen. It was then that a beam of light from straight above me shone down on me like a great searchlight. It enveloped me and flooded me with a sense of peace and security. Then the grass that had gripped me so hard and cut off my blood circulation, ever so subtly began to relax, until it lost its contorted form. It wound itself backward, as deliberately as it had grabbed me, until it again stood upright. And then after a pause, the grass began swaying beautifully and rhythmically in the wind from side to side, its green shoots gently caressing my body. And I began moving with it in a sensuous dance. Then as the grass continued to move, its shoots parted in front of me, leading me away.

For a few seconds, there was complete silence, and then Prince said, *Finally, I had a third vision. This time I was under water, too far to swim to land. The water was clear and beautiful and multicolored fish swam through beds of coral and sea grass. But my eyes could not adjust to the flickering light and my body could not swim for very long. Worst of all, I gasped for breath, needing to come up to the surface constantly for air. But when I came up, I was blinded by the sunlight and extremely disoriented.*

"It is as I thought," Judy said. "The first one is most general. It was intended for you, but it is a vision that might be relayed to many people. The other two dreams are one and the same message, and they are more specific to you.

"The first one is metaphorically your life, from birth to death. We start in a very beautiful place before birth and we don't wish to be pushed down into this world. Of course, the light that you see at the end of the journey is the place of your death, when you are able to look back on your life."

"Okay," Prince said, "but why did I have this dream? This dream could have occurred to anyone."

"Very true, Joseph, very true." She laughed deeply and freely. When he heard her laugh like that, he thought that he would do anything for her. "Joseph, you are obviously a very special soul. I thought it from the beginning. Now G-d is confirming it for both of us."

"Why do you say that?" he said.

"Joseph, for a brilliant person, you haven't seen, or don't choose to see, the obvious about yourself. Look, it's like this. All of us go through this journey in life. We're all afraid of that darkness in those woods. G-d is always there to support us, but because we can't see that source of support, and because we can't see where we are going, and what the purpose is, we're scared. Those reveries of hawks and trees talking to you in your vision—you thought they were just your cruel imagination—but they were the real thing. Your cruel imagination was in your denial of miracles and all the possibilities around you. You said no one was listening, but when the universe responded, you not only failed to acknowledge it, but you denied it outright."

Prince said nothing, so she continued. "Look, not many of us get a chance to hear from G-d about this kind of stuff."

"What does G-d want me to know about this?" His voice was trembling.

"He wants you to know that you're not alone down here. That these travails you're experiencing along your path in the woods, when they're all over, you'll look back and know that it was a good thing, a very good thing. Look Joseph, G-d has blessed you with this understanding, so that during your sojourn here you will lose your fear and see the beauty of your soul and existence, and know that G-d is ever present and protecting you. Above all, G-d doesn't want you acting in this life out of fear."

"And the other two visions?"

"They are more specific messages to your situation. The second vision is a warning. If you persist in your fear, you shall knot up in a thousand contractions and live life as in a prison. You shall have all psychological space of existing in a pit, or any other confined space."

She paused and then continued. "Whatever great struggles you have endured in not accepting your fate in this world, have made it only harder for you to move freely. They, like the grass, have bound you tighter and tighter. It is only when you accept your fate, your destiny, that you will feel relief. Then the world will support you and 'the grass will caress your body' as you are drawn to your destination."

"And the third?" His voice cracked and he could barely get the words out.

"The third is the most graphic," she said. "The point is being made emphatically; the club is being waved at you." She waved her fist above her head to make a point. "Here you are in this beautiful world, but you cannot breathe. Joseph, you know that breathing is not only a physical necessity, but a spiritual one as well. G-d breathes a part of His soul into our bodies right before our first breath. You've taught me that. So, you have been starving yourself spiritually. But your assumption is that you can just suddenly rise above the surface of the water and breathe in that spirituality. And you can't. Spirituality is strong medicine. Without practice, without taking small amounts in on a regular basis, you will be blinded. Even more important, without accepting who you are, and your destiny, you will be unable to stand that strong light. Without accepting your fate, that light will burn you, because your spiritual receptacle will be too small to absorb it and hold it."

She sighed. "Here you are in this vision, in such a beautiful spot in the world, and yet you are unable to be part of it. You are exiled from G-d's world, the beautiful world around you. But your exile Joseph is your own doing, not G-d's. You're the one who's constructed the wall that separates you from G-d. You've confined your own space to such a degree that you're suffocating. When you're willing to break down that barrier, G-d will be waiting."

8

And so it had gone on for many mornings, the interpretation of dreams. And when there had been no dreams to discuss, there was repartee on various issues; sometimes the discussion had turned to their own desires and needs, but they had been so careful not to cross a line of concurrence, an understood demarcation between what constituted each individual in the relationship and what could have been the merging of those individuals into something very different.

One morning Prince had spent an hour with John in the field showing him the latest results of the breeding program. Then John had left the ranch on a business trip for several days. On one worker's radio in the field, Prince heard a program announcing and explaining Rosh Hashanah, the Jewish New Year. He had studiously avoided the observance of Judaism since he had left his uncle in California; many times he had run across his heritage and thought little about it, but for some inexplicable reason he had paused this time to reflect on it. Perhaps it was the oddity of hearing this announcement in rural Texas, or the spiritual discussions that he had recently experienced with Judy. Whatever the reason, he had stopped for the first time that day to reflect on the cooler temperatures and lower angle of the sun that had come with the coincident beginning of fall.

When he had arrived back at the main house, he had been greeted by Judy's personal secretary. She had had what he thought was a different look on her face as she greeted him. "Joseph, Judy says that she will be in the first room upstairs and that you are to knock loudly, wait for about ten seconds, and then enter." He had briefly thought that instruction was a little bit unusual—since he had never met Judy there before—but Judy had always been the master of novel situations.

Each old wooden step he had climbed protested the weight of his large frame. When a knock elicited no reaction, he entered the room. It was unoccupied and possessed an eerie, undisturbed calm. He squinted at the bright midday light coming through the large windows, and then he heard her voice call him from an adjacent room.

"Is that you, Joseph?"

"Yes," he said softly, almost whispering, lest he break the silence.

"Come on in."

He first followed her voice. Then he decided he should go no further and turned around.

She emerged from the room. "Joseph, please..." She began to weep. It was deep and sorrowful; he had never seen her upset before.

After a moment, she continued. "Joseph, I know that you'll be leaving soon, and I'm sorry for that. But could you please just talk to me for a while before you do leave? Make this our afternoon together...for old time sake." He nodded his head, but did not look at her.

"I'm really sorry," she said. Then she broke into another series of loud sobs. "I know this is my fault—it's my fault that you'll leave now, but you know I couldn't help it." Then swallowing hard, she regained her composure and looked directly at him until he was forced to meet her gaze. "Look Joseph, it's another one of those things with the universe. It's happening for a reason. I'm just its agent. You came here for a reason, and now that that reason is behind you, you're leaving for a reason."

He shook his head back and forth but still said nothing. Then he finally said, "Judy, there's one thing I do want to say. I've never told this to anyone else. I love you, but..."

"...But it wasn't going to work", she said, nodding.

There was a short silence. Then she moved around to directly face him. "Joseph, what is your real name?"

He looked up with surprise. "What do you mean?"

"You know what I mean. Your name is not really Joseph, is it?"

He smiled, the way one does when he's been caught at something. "How do you know these things?"

"I just do. Joseph, I couldn't know you any better, if I were married to you. I know what you're going to do, even the tiniest thing, before you do it."

"Judy, we are partners in every way. We've been married in other lives and our souls are joined spiritually in this one, just not in physical marriage. We are two halves of the same soul. Naturally that makes us yearn for each other. It makes us both suffer."

"Yes, it's true. I'm guilty of trying to join the physical with the spiritual today. But now, you're not going to get off the hook so easily. What is your real name?"

He laughed. His whole body shook as the tension, that had been created to hold his secret, began to dissipate. "Well, that's an interesting answer. I lived in California until about the time I was thirteen and went by the name of Prince."

She nodded. "But that wasn't your given name, was it?"

"No, no one ever called me by my given name—that I could ever remember—except you. You see, my given name was Joseph."

"In your travels, did you ever use that name anywhere else?"

"No. Among other names, I used Pierce for a while, when I came back to the States, after leaving the merchant marine. It had its own irony. It was not only close to the name Prince, but seemed to suggest my ability to pierce people's consciousness."

"You did that to me too. That's why I first noticed you," she said.

"I felt that you did it to me. You're the first person that's done it to me," he said.

"I can give as well as I get in this relationship," she said. "So why did you decide to use your real name here?"

"I don't know. But names are significant. It's never an accidental thing."

"Joseph, who are you?"

"What do you mean?"

"I mean all this wandering around the world," she said. "I don't even know the fourth of it. I mean who is this person inside that you are running away from?"

He bit his lip.

"Joseph, I told you I can figure out a lot about you. Why don't you just tell me?" She paused. "Joseph, you're a Jew, aren't you?"

"Why would you think a thing like that? A Jew? What possible relationship would I have with that?" he said.

"Joseph, look at me. After what we are to each other, you're not going to sit there and lie to me, are you?"

"No," he said very quietly. "How did you know it?"

"You look so scared now, like a little boy. You know Joseph, you can't run away from it forever," she said. "At some point you have to face it."

"But how did you know? I thought..."

"You thought that no one could see it. You thought that if you ran far enough away from it, in this vast world, that you could avoid it. But that was silly. You can't. You can't avoid it because it's inside of you. It's what you are."

"But how did you— "

"—Know it? My friend, it's written all over you. It literally oozes out of you. It's those eyes searching for justice, and the way you have defended those around here that are dispossessed. It's the way you are hunched over in fear when you think no one is looking. No one fears G-d like a Jew. It was your insistence on charity. It was the stranger in you."

"Stranger? There's nothing but strangers coming to this ranch," he said. "How was I different?"

"Sure, they come here as strangers. Most of them leave as strangers," she said. "But they are only strangers in the sense that they come from the outside and stay on the outside, so that I never get to know them. Never find out who they are. But you—you are the real stranger. The stranger's inside of you. You insisted on staying a stranger to me, even after you came inside this house, and even after I got to know you well and could predict each little thing about you. There was something there, a barrier, a wall, a world where I could never go. I was never permitted to go to that core. I was never permitted to join you in that place. You haven't even permitted yourself to go to that place."

She watched his expression and waited to see if he would respond. Then she continued. "You see, if I had gotten to know one of them as well as I know you and he had stayed in my house, as you have done, it wouldn't have been long before he became presumptuous enough to feel as if he owned part of the place. At least he would have felt as if he were right at home. But not you, Joseph, even though John and I offered you everything we had. The Jew in you held back. Your people have always lived at the margins. Never had a real home. Just like you, even in the best of times, the G-d fearing ones were afraid to move to the center in any society, afraid to take what was rightfully theirs, for fear they would lose it, for fear that they didn't deserve G-d's goodness and mercy. The Jewish people would have withdrawal symptoms if their great historical suffering ended. They really wouldn't know how to handle it. Isn't that your story too, Joseph? The Jew in you has denied yourself so many of G-d's gifts, including me today."

"Wait a minute," he said. He began pacing around the room. "You think I like suffering? You think I like the way I feel? Better to say that the world would have withdrawal symptoms if they couldn't pick on us." Then he sat down, as if he was calculating something in his head. He stared at her for a short time, and then said, "It's your people too, isn't it? How could I miss it? You're Jewish too, aren't you?"

She blushed a deep purple.

"Now it's my turn to deduce what I should have already observed," Prince said.

"How did..."

"It takes one to know one," Prince said. "I should have spotted you a mile off. If I'm really Jewish, if I ooze my Judaism, then how is it that I'm so attracted to you, or vice versa? How is it that our souls are so intertwined on such a deep level? That's the sheer logic part, but now I also feel it. I couldn't explain it to myself before. But you know, once you admit to yourself more of who you are, once you stop totally denying yourself, you can see others more clearly too." He paused and smiled knowingly. "Besides," he said, "only a Jewish person is going to perceive the dispossessed part of me the way you do."

She bowed her head. It was only the second time he had ever seen her shameful, both times that afternoon. "Joseph, I wasn't really trying to deceive you, any more than you were trying to deceive me," she said. "My mother was Jewish, and what little exposure I had, I walked away from several years ago. I never thought of my Judaism. And I never thought of myself as Jewish until I met you. And then, this afternoon, I don't know what came over me. It was an outburst."

"It was your Chochmah, your connection to G-d. That connection is going to stay there whether you want it or not—it's like breathing automatically," he said. "It's the same thing that makes even a nonobservant Jew give up his life, rather than submit to those who deny G-d, and be parted from G-d. Without that connection, none of us would exist and G-d's creation would disintegrate."

"Yes," she said. She smiled at him in what he thought was such a most beautiful way.

"Thank you, so much for everything," he said. "Judy, now that I have to leave, now that I have to go back out there to that prison of an outside world, what was the purpose of my coming here to the Jones' ranch? Of course, most would think that this place is the prison, being isolated as it is, but it's the only place I've felt even partially comfortable, and now I have to leave it."

"Ah," she said. Her smile had broadened. "Now that's what makes life exciting. The answer to your question will surely be revealed to you, if you are sensitive and spiritual enough to perceive it, which you will surely be. G-d will not leave you out there on a limb."

"What do you think?"

"I think where you are going, Joseph, that you will do unusual service for G-d in this world. And there were certain things that you needed to know and experience before you went there."

"Like possibly what?"

"Like the feeling of love, that only a woman that understands you, can give you."

"That love will carry me always," he said. "It's like an old friend, old song, that I've been reintroduced to. It's always been there."

"It will always be there, for eternity," she said. "Joseph, when you feel that emptiness out there, when you're all alone, doing battles with the world, for the sake of G-d—and you will be—remember this love. Remember it not just in the past. Remember that just like G-d's creation, it's ongoing, it's continuing. That even though I'm not physically there with you in the same spot, that I still love you. Remember that G-d has given me the powers on this earth in this lifetime to help you. I will know where you are, even though you're far away, and I will see and experience the same pain that you feel. You will feel my love through many miles and many barriers and some of that great burden, that great pain that you have, will be relieved. I will be with you always Joseph."

At that late afternoon hour, he had proceeded to wrap up a few ongoing details on the ranch. He had made sure his assistant could make the transition to manager as smoothly as possible and said good-byes. Late that evening he was finally packing the few meager possessions he had carried with him in this world. He would be leaving early the next morning.

"What are you doing, Joseph?" He heard John's voice behind him. His voice had no surprise in it, just resignation and sadness.

Prince turned around to face him. "I thought you were going to be away for a few days."

"I thought so," John said. "But Judy called to tell me. I just had them turn the plane around, you know."

"Oh, you didn't have to do that."

"No, I couldn't see doing it any other way," John said. "Here, Judy gave me this to give to you. She thought you'd want it back."

It was a chain that went around his neck, fastened to a small, multifaceted and colored memento from his parents. It was the only thing that he had kept that reminded him of his childhood. "Thank you," Prince said. "But that's strange. I don't remember ever taking this off. I've never taken this off since I left California."

"Well, you must have taken it off your neck. It doesn't come off any other way," John said.

"The only reason I'd take this off...or the only reason this could have been taken off of me is..."

"There isn't a good reason, is there? —except if..." John said. He looked directly at Prince.

"Look John, I don't know why Judy told you I'm leaving, but it's okay with me. Whatever she says, is okay."

"Well either you have something to hide here, or you don't," John said. "And Joseph, if you don't, then I don't know why you're leaving."

"I'm leaving John because I have to now. It won't work any longer here. The universe is pushing me out."

"Look Joseph, it may surprise you to know that Judy refused to even talk to me about your leaving. She just told me you're going. She's never been so close mouthed on anything else."

"So you want me to fill in the blanks."

"Yeah, I'm your friend! I have a stake in this too," John said. "Joseph, I thought we had a deal, an understanding, and now it's suddenly gone."

Prince sat down on the bed. His voice became sorrowful. "Yeah, you do have a stake. You're right. I'm really sorry about this." There was an uncomfortable silence.

"Joseph, if you've been involved with my wife, or something else happened, you can tell me."

"No, it's not that."

"Then why are you leaving?"

"Because of my feelings about your wife."

"That's no sin, you know."

"How can I walk around here like that? Not to mention that it demeans Judy and it demeans you."

"Joseph, you are everything here. You're not only my best friend, but you made this ranch, put it on the map, and made me a wealthy man many times over. And now you're leaving just like that. There's nothing for your efforts—for your intelligence."

"That's the way it's always been with me. It'll just have to be that way again, won't it?" Another silence ensued.

"Joseph, I wouldn't blame Judy for her relationship with you."

"Thanks John. But you know that can't continue to work as it has. I think we've all been a bit naïve, because we wanted to be. For my part, John, I apologize. I'm very sorry."

"Apologize? For what exactly?"

"John, we think in this culture if we don't cross certain lines, that whatever else we do is perfectly all right. I mean, we're encouraged to take risks and go right to the brink, pursue, woo, chase, flirt, whatever, but as long as we don't actually do any more, it's considered okay. But it's not. G-d considers our motives. He knows what we're thinking. Sharing someone's soul, someone's inner being has real meaning. Considering where I've been with Judy, I shouldn't stay any longer."

Then Prince walked over and put his arm around John. "John, I love you too. And it's because of my love for you, separate from the kind of special love I feel for Judy, that I'm leaving. You see, the bonds between Judy and me are something from a different realm. I was drawn to this ranch because of her. Now, it has taken all my might to refrain and to leave. But it is the right decision. I am wise enough to know that my role here is finished. All three of us will have important functions to play in the future and mine is not here. My destiny lies somewhere else."

When Prince left the next morning, an unexpected storm blew in from the southwest to propel him onward. Its winds were unusually strong in intensity, with gusts that slapped walkers in the face and forced them to take immediate shelter behind whatever immovable object lay in their proximity, lest they be blown some distance. Some of the weather forecasters said it had to do with a hurricane in the Gulf of Mexico. Others tagged it to the change in weather that always comes with the fall; they said that it was just an unusually strong wet/warm front rushing to meet a cold front descending from the Canadian Rockies. Still others pointed to its vehemence as a sign of the climatic change caused by the green house effect. But all who watched it were surprised by its occurrence and failed to predict it.

The angels in heaven knew otherwise. The winds were the angels' audible sighs in heaven as they reacted to the events of earth. In a series of action/reaction/action, like a ping pong ball being hit back and forth between heaven and earth, the events of those few hours on the Jones' ranch in Texas had reverberated first to heaven and then back to earth, straight to the vicinity where it had all begun. It wasn't just the weather that was affected either; there were many subtle changes in people's moods and daily activities, only, as always, they failed to be recorded and correlated with each other in the media on earth, because very few people believed in that kind of thing. Judy Jones knew and she fasted and prayed that day, for the first time as a conscious Jew, in remembrance of Prince.

In many angels' view, Prince had once again moved from a situation that had some promise of fulfilling his soul's destiny to ground level zero. They still could not understand the intentions of G-d in putting this soul on this earth in this environment. Their gasps, leading to the dangerous winds in Texas, were caused by their great despair, despair in watching such a great old soul, who needn't have returned to earth at all to serve G-d, be not only in such pain, but in needless distress; they saw no purpose in his wanderings and certainly no meaning in his lack of observance of his religion. In an ordinary soul, the pain would have only minimally impacted the heavens, but the capacity of Prince's spiritual soul to carry pain and suffering was extraordinarily great and the effect of that huge reservoir of his soul overflowing on earth, as it had in those few last hours on the Jones' ranch, meant that the usual heavenly routine of the angels was disrupted. Many of the angels who had previously tried to forget their anxiety in watching the drama around Prince unfold on earth, who had tried to ignore those earthly events in the way a person watches a horror movie with hands over his eyes, were now forced once again to confront the stark reality of what was happening on earth. There was renewed fear about the future of the potential tzaddik.

A very small, but vocal minority of the angels, felt differently. They could not understand what G-d was doing, but their intuition told them that finally something could be happening. No, it had been a bitter experience for Prince to have to leave his soul mate, but at least he had finally understood human love. And for once, Prince had seemed to be in control of a situation; he had managed it, determined it, rather than merely reacting to it.

Regardless of their point of view, all of the heavenly forces were now riveted by the anticipation of future events on earth surrounding Prince. Perhaps it was the Jewish New Year, Rosh Hashanah, that created an air of expectation, or maybe it was the angels' faith that G-d would not make any individual continue to suffer as much as Prince had, or maybe it was the influence of superstitious forces on earth that had reached the angels, or maybe it was the subtle way that the heavenly environment was affected before major changes occurred on earth—like the feeling a person gets in their gut before a lighting storm—but many intuited that there might be a future transformation in the works on earth.

9

Return, Israel, unto G-d your G-d, for you have fallen in your sins. Take words with you and return to G-d, say to Him, "May you forgive all sins and accept good intentions, and let our lips (prayer) substitute for the bulls (sacrifices)."

Hosea, Chapter 14, vs. 2-3

He left the Jones' ranch the way he came—in the flatbed of a dump truck. This time there was the driving rain. He left with no more than with what he came. The driver had asked him where he was going. He answered where ever the driver was pointed. He had never bothered to find out where that was.

For a while, he remembered Judy. He kept saying to himself that less than a day earlier he had been able to see and feel her. For a while it was a consolation.

Then he had become numb. All the feeling had been drained from him. He was unable to focus. He saw nothing but a landscape of endless plains going up and down with the truck.

After a while his soul was one big sore festering with pus. There was pain, terrific pain. With the pain, came the return of his former powers of perception, the ones he seemed to lose in the comfort of Judy's presence, but he no longer had any interest in their use. He was alone, alone once again. He could not move, he could not think, he could not bear to act. His ashen face was expressionless; his hands were frozen, half clenched in space. His companions in the back of the truck whispered that he was the living dead.

He had been dropped somewhere north of the ranch. It seemed to be many miles away, but he didn't know and he didn't care. He had no object, no goal, not even a thought of surviving. He saw no purpose. He had no hopes, no volition, not even a desire. He felt nothing physically. He forgot to eat. He didn't remember sleeping. Time became an abstraction. He neither cared for day nor night.

He had no boundaries. The space inside of him was disintegrating, being reabsorbed into the world around him. He made no claims on his soul. Because he refused to possess it, it had emptied out of his body and spread its form throughout the area. What was left inside of him was bleakness, a desertedness, a vacuum. His face flashed nonresidence; his body was that of a darkened and abandoned house, with broken windows through which the wind whistled. His inanition sucked the energy out of those around him. Those who observed him in that state said they were afraid that they would plummet into his hollowness, from which they could never climb out. Prince was dying once again. This time he didn't know if he could be reborn, didn't even care.

When he reached Oklahoma City, dawn was just breaking. He had been dropped off by a road crew. He had not intended to go specifically where they went; they had just happened to stop where he had sat and had offered him a ride. That option seemed as senseless as any other, so he took it.

Upon arrival, he had walked through the city, with no destination, not the simplest calculation of the future. The storm had moved through, and in place of its insistence, there was extraordinarily still air. The storm's fury had almost seemed to drop him there, like a boat in a patch of dead sea. There was a coolness to the air, just the hint of fall. The city was silent and anticipative. During those ten days between Rosh Hashanah and Yom Kippur, the Jewish New Year and the Day of Atonement, you could feel there the fate of the world hanging in the balance. Humans could remain oblivious to it, ignore it, but each bit of nature knew. Every tree knew whether it would bud out next spring and whether it would live through the next growing season. Every squirrel had figured its prospects. Every acorn falling and breaking the silence was a bid for immortality.

When he reached a quiet area with small buildings adjacent to the downtown, the bright sun had warmed the earth enough to make him seek out the more ample shadows of a corner structure. He sat on its steps and looked across the short street at the sign. "Vacancy, rooms by the day, week, or month," it read. He didn't know why he decided to enter.

He knocked at the large, dark, wooden plank door, and when no one responded, he pushed it open. The door barely cleared the floor and moved slowly, creaking as it went. When he shut it, the light was dim and dusty, seemingly undisturbed and unoccupied for some time. He waited for his eyes to adjust, and then failing to see a desk or an attendant adjacent to the entrance, he walked further in. At first he saw nothing at all. Then he perceived that he was in a very long hall bounded by tall walls. The hall was lit only by the small windows near its ceiling. He could hear his feet slicking on the concrete and sandy floor as he proceeded. He guessed that he had come more than seventy-five feet.

"Come in. We've been expecting you."

"I said, come on in. We've been expecting you. We thought you'd be here by now."

Prince had kept walking. He hadn't responded right away, because he still could not see the speaker.

"It would be courteous if you could at least respond."

"Yes...ah...yes, but I don't know with whom I'm speaking. I can't even see you yet."

"Keep coming. You're almost there."

Three men sat on a stage at the end of the hall. It must have been an old theater, Prince thought, maybe even a former vaudeville venue.

"Can you see us now?"

"Yes, I believe I can," Prince said. The three men sat at an oak library desk, strewn with many books, in the middle of the stage, about twenty feet in front of him. It was the middle one who spoke. He wore a dark suit and a kippah, or skull cap, and had a long dark beard streaked with white. Prince guessed that he was a Hasidic man somewhere between his early forties and fifties.

"Well, it's time that we met each other and got down to business," the middle man said.

"I'm sorry," Prince said, "but I don't believe I'm in the right place."

"Oh, but I think that you are," the middle man said.

"The sign out there said that this place was for rent, that you had some rooms, but I must have come in the wrong building," Prince said. "The sign must have been for another building."

"You read the sign correctly, and you are in the right building. As I said, we've been expecting you," the middle man said.

"Well, perhaps you could describe the rooms you have available. And perhaps you're looking for someone else, because I don't have an appointment here with you. I didn't call ahead for anyone to meet me," Prince said.

The middle man smiled while his companions sat relaxed, and alert, but otherwise expressionless. "Yes, you do have an appointment," he said. "Just because you didn't call ahead, doesn't mean that you don't have an appointment."

"I'm a little confused. Maybe you could tell me why I'm here," Prince said.

"No, the purpose of this visit is for you to tell us why you're here," the middle man said. "After all, you're the one who has come here. We've just waited for you."

"I don't get what you mean," Prince said.

"Well, we didn't come here for nothing," the middle man said.

"Did someone tell you to come here? I certainly didn't," Prince said.

"I believe that you are so wrapped up in your pain, so self-centered after what has happened to you, that you are unable, or should I say refuse, to see the world around you," the middle man said.

"With all due respect, I cannot follow this," Prince said.

"You cannot follow it because you don't wish to follow it," the middle man said. "With all due respect to you young man, we are here today because G-d has heard your cries."

"I don't believe..."

"But yes, if I am not wrong, you have repeatedly complained to G-d about your anguish. You have spent years running away from it and yourself," the middle man said.

"What do you know about my anguish?"

The countenance of the middle man turned a bit rueful. "I know about despair. That's why I'm here today. I came to help."

"You know about me? You know about my anguish?"

"Yes, I know something about your heart, because my heart was once there where yours resides now," the middle man said.

"If you're here to help me...I'm a little puzzled about this..." Prince was shaking his head.

"If you're puzzled, it's because you've refused to use the powers given to you by the Ein Sof," the middle man said.

"But help like this?"

"Well, what would you wish for? Do you expect G-d Himself to swoop down and pick you up? Surely, G-d works through normal channels of the natural world. Any closer exposure to the light of G-d, and I believe that we would all be nullified by His presence. I do apologize if He sent mere mortals here to assist in this process. Actually I would say that my colleagues sitting on my right and left are quite distinguished. I rather doubt if you could have done much better."

Prince was still standing in the same spot where his conversation had started minutes earlier. He paused to recollect, to try to fathom the meaning of this sudden and peculiar rendezvous. A lengthy silence followed. None of the men seemed concerned about the time. They waited patiently, each one searching Prince's face for his next response. These men seemed no more absurd to him than the environment outside the building from which he had entered. His spiritual soul had emptied out of him; with no more will of his own, he was receptive to them in the way a very young child looks to a parent for direction. "If you are here to help, then how do we go about that?"

"Now then," the middle man said smiling, "let's address your problems. I believe that you've spent almost your entire life running from the soul you are. The last few years you've added the physical dimension to your spiritual flight."

Prince cocked his head. "Who are you?"

"That is not the appropriate question at this time," the middle man said. "The question is 'who are you?'"

"Well, I walk in here and I have three men sitting in front of me whom I have never seen before, and they are offering me advice. I think it would be proper if you told me who you are and why you think that you can offer me advice."

"This is not about us. It is about you," the middle man said. As he spoke, Prince noticed the profundity of his eyes, as if their blue portals had suddenly opened for viewing. He glimpsed a slice of a vast knowing universe. Then he was aware. He was aware of the presence in the room of something much more important—much more significant than his own thoughts. He quickly turned his gaze.

"You think that you are the only one who has felt pain in this life? There are others," the middle man said.

"What is the purpose of this pain?"

"There is more than one answer, as there is more than one purpose," the middle man said. "We do not know all G-d's reasons for pain in this revealed world. There is a purpose in the hidden world, olam disgolai. We do know that 'In every sadness there will be profit.'"

"So there is purpose to my sadness?"

The middle man laughed. "Yes, of course. Everything has a purpose, nothing is by accident, and there is Divine Providence in everything that happens. So there is a purpose for everyone's sadness, but especially yours. But I would have to say that when you erect a wall and do not permit the light of the Ein Sof to enter, you will feel sadness, great sadness, because He is your only support. Just as all energy on this earth originates from the sun, whether it be directly, or indirectly through wind, hydroelectric power, or fossil fuels, all our inspiration, creativity, and energy comes from G-d. "

"How do I stop this great sadness?"

"By allowing G-d's energy to flow through you. By fulfilling your destiny. By allowing your soul to achieve its purpose on this earth. When you put your hand into the proper size glove, it fits. When you try to fit it into the wrong size, or what's worse, leave it out of the glove to face the cold, it is painful," the middle man said. "When it's outside the proper glove, that hand will always be trying to find its way. It will never be content where it's at. Thus your great wandering around this earth."

"My destiny? Look at my destiny!" Prince held up his arm to demonstrate his recently torn and dirty sleeves. Then he moved his arms out to his sides with his palms turned upward, to emphasize the rest of his body. "Some destiny this is. This is a fine destiny. Yesiree, this really does it."

The middle man took one of the large books within his reach and dropped it hard onto the table. "I will not have you waste our time any more with your insolence. This has been your choice. Do not degrade G-d with your insinuations that you have been forced to live like some kind of skunk out there. G-d doesn't force anyone to do that. G-d always allows us to choose. You have chosen poorly. Yet, ironically there is Divine Providence in your choice, as it too has its purpose."

"I chose nothing about this existence," Prince said.

"Oh, but you did. You took the oath in heaven before you descended to this world," the middle man said.

"An oath?"

"An oath to 'be righteous and be not wicked; and even if the whole world tells you that you are righteous, regard yourself as wicked,'" the middle man said.

"And what does an oath have to do with my destiny?"

"Everything," the middle man said. "First of all, it was your choice to come to this world. G-d did not force you to be here. And the whole purpose of coming to this existence was to act righteously."

"Let us say for argument sake that you are right about our purpose here in this world. But there is nothing in that purpose that applies specifically to my destiny," Prince said.

The face of the middle man had become exasperated. He stood up from his seat and gestured with his right arm. "Considering your intelligence and your soul, you know better than that. Why must you persist in denying what you know? You scream to the universe for help, but you will not open your spiritual receptacle even the slightest bit to take our assistance here.

"Now you listen to me, because your opportunity to make a turning in your life now is coming to a close. We are in the days of awe between Rosh Hashanah and Yom Kippur and soon, in a couple of days, as Yom Kippur ends, your fate will be sealed by G-d, and then human intervention here will do you no good. G-d has laid out the choice before you to do good or to do evil. That choice is before you now, as it has been before you all along in your life. It will be before you in the future; G-d always welcomes the true repentance of sinners. But, if you do not make a turning back toward G-d now, you will have made a fateful choice in this particular life. There will be no turning back and you will live your life, if you can call it life—I call it death—in great misery, much in the same way you have persisted in living it till this point. The gift of your life will be wasted. You will violate the purpose of your existence here in this world now and you will have violated your own agreement with G-d, made in the hidden worlds. This is why all of us are here in this room today. All souls are given repeated opportunities to do the righteous action, but very few are given so much assistance in doing so. In this life, G-d has granted you many gifts to guide you, including dreams, a soul mate, and three wise men here today, not to mention your original gifts of intelligence, perception, and might."

Prince again saw the immensity of the middle man's soul as reflected through his intense blue pupils and he again felt this awareness, a vast spiritual intelligence. He quivered. He could not bear to meet the middle man's gaze for more than a few seconds. "But how, if I may ask, does this oath of righteousness apply specifically to my destiny?"

"Because," the middle man said, "what is righteous is specific for each individual. Surely, G-d doesn't expect the same of one with simple intelligence and capability, as he expects of one with a greater capacity. Moses was reprimanded by G-d for merely striking a rock in anger and could not enter the Promised Land. Each individual descends to this world with his own spiritual mission. Each of us is given the capacity, the power, to fulfill that mission. The idea of being righteous is that you will take the power given explicitly to you, with which you are invested, and recognize that you should use it in the proper manner. Denying that you have that power, not participating in the test of life, as you have insisted on doing, is both cowardly and evil. There is no apathetic middle ground."

Then the man on the middle man's right spoke. He appeared to be about the same age as the middle man and was dressed casually. His hair was neatly cropped and his face was clean shaven. "This is not just about you. This is about the universe. We are tied together on this earth in a web of interconnecting relationships, like a textile which threads are woven together to make the fabric of life. Without your choosing to fulfill your destiny, playing your role, others will be denied their full choices here. There will be a hole in the garment. And those who have interacted with you will have acted in vain." He paused. "I believe you know well to whom I refer in that regard."

Prince fell down onto his knees.

The middle man sat down in his seat again. "You think that we have made this up? You think that this is unique to you? You are a unique soul, but others have traveled on the path before you. They know the way. Do you insist on being proud and arrogant, turning away from G-d, and denying your own powers, so that you can struggle through a briar patch and bleed from the thorns? Must you tread through a geography of despair? Will you insist on exile when the goodly alternative exists? Or will you finally embrace your tradition so that you can climb up the mountain to G-d?"

"I'm sorry," Prince said. "I suppose that it is very clear to you how you should act. The choices haven't seemed so clear cut to me. I am not that good. I have lost my way." He bowed his head down.

"We must be hard on ourselves," the middle man said, "so that we do the right thing. But we must not be too hard. G-d does not wish us to suffer for the mere sake of suffering. It is not necessary for you to put yourself down; the only necessary thing is repentance, true repentance in which the heart yearns to cleave to G-d.

"The truth is that the three of us here can see your situation much more clearly than we can see ourselves and our own lives. You see, our egos cloud our ability to see ourselves. Even though we may try to be humble and minimize our egos, the fact that we think at all, and the fact that we perceive ourselves to be separate entities from other parts of the universe, including heaven forbid G-d Himself, means that we must have an ego. Because our egos cloud our thoughts, keep us from being truly objective, it is only natural that we feel some confusion about our lives. But that is why we must put our trust in G-d. G-d is the only true and objective part of the universe. G-d is real, and our lives are often an illusion."

"Now, may I find out who you are?" Prince said. "How can I know if this is all true and sent from G-d, or a completely surreal experience? I don't know any more. I don't even know how I arrived here."

"The Ein Sof, Himself brought you here," the middle man said. "You may know the answer to who we are, once we know who you are. First, identify who you are. Find where you are. Find yourself. Find the center of your being and its purpose. Stand before G-d. Admit who you are and surrender to Him. Then, we will know who we are relative to you. We cannot define ourselves before you, until you define yourself."

Prince began to whimper softly. He remained bowed, on his knees.

"There comes a time," the middle man said, "when we are all faced with this dilemma, this decision. You see, it's clear cut in heaven. There's nothing ambiguous about the light of the Ein Sof there. That's why we're sent down here, to this darkness. We are challenged in this world to make the right decision when the light of the Ein Sof is hidden, and it's often not clear what we should do.

"Most of the time we go along down here on automatic pilot. We think that what we're doing is not important. But everything's important. It's all Divine Providence. But I think there are key decision points, key points in time, when we're given a specific opportunity to fulfill our destiny. Everything that our souls have previously experienced, even though it might have seemed trivial at the time, is important in helping us reach that decision. We may have other opportunities to do the right thing, maybe in other lives, but in this life sometimes it just boils down to that particular moment—with everything leading up to that moment—when we stand in front of G-d, when we must decide whether to follow our oath. Your time has arrived here today."

Prince began to weep. It was a deep sorrow. "But I have committed every evil in the book. I am not worthy. There are better ones than I in this matter."

"That is not for you to decide. Only G-d may decide the worthiness of a soul to fill a certain role here on this earth," the middle man said. "Besides, your reluctance is only an excuse. As you know, you may choose, with some effort, to make your soul worthy of its destiny, its role, at any time."

"Why was I given so much assistance, so many repeated opportunities to choose this destiny?"

"Because G-d gives us the opportunity to repent repeatedly," the middle man said. "In your case, G-d has apparently been more insistent than usual. G-d always gives us the means to fulfill our destiny. He never sends us down here unprepared. We are never given something we cannot handle, if we really try. Our lives may be extremely challenging—yes, but it is within our power to do the right thing, to choose good over evil. The love and fear of G-d 'is very near to you…in your mouth and…heart, that you may do it.' If G-d has given you repeated opportunities, then it is a reflection of His love. It is also a reflection that your role may in fact be very difficult, that it may not be easy for you to overcome your pain and accept your fate. And perhaps it reflects the importance of the oath that you took. G-d cares. He cares about what you do here. He has shown that in every way, even sending us here today. Will you now turn away from G-d at this moment of decision?"

Prince began to wail. Finally, he said, "But I don't want this. I never wanted this. Let someone else do it. G-d has many souls to choose from. The burden is too great for me."

"This is the service of G-d that is needed," the middle man said. "This is the manner in which you may make an apartment, a dwelling place, for G-d on this earth. This is the purpose of your existence here. G-d will assist you with the burden, but you must have faith in Him. You must place your trust in Him, for that to happen."

Then the third man spoke. He sat on the middle man's left side, was also clean shaven, and was dressed in a business suit. Prince guessed his age to be similar to the other two. "If your heart truly desires repentance, then it is only necessary now to begin the process. This is certainly not something that can be completed quickly. We will be here with you what ever time is necessary."

"What will it take?"

"It will take a complete transformation of the heart," the middle man said. "This is a physical process. It can only be done by completely expelling evil from your heart. What do you say? Will you serve G-d?"

Prince lifted his head up and explored each of their faces. His sigh bounced from one end of the large room to the other. "Yes…it appears that I have no other choice," he said as he shook his head in a kind of surrender.

"You have a choice," the middle man said.

"A choice? What kind of choice? A choice between life and death, good and evil? The choice is obvious, isn't it? 'Its ways are ways of pleasantness, and all its paths are peace.' That's what is said about the Torah. Who could feel that he wanted to turn that down?"

The middle man smiled. "I'm glad that you still remember."

"But the choice is obvious enough, isn't it?" Prince said. "So why call it a choice? Why not call it a demand? G-d is demanding that I assume this role. Otherwise, I will continue to live in great distress. I will continue to wander—rootless, hearing voices, dreaming, having visions. Could we not say that G-d is selfish in this matter?"

The middle man's eyes grew distant and sad. "If it is not a choice, then why do so many people turn down the option of fulfilling their own destinies? Why do so many people persist in living in such distress on this earth?"

"Maybe because they weren't given such ample opportunities to change as I have been," Prince said. "They weren't given the opportunity to see what I've seen."

The middle man's sad eyes had turned painful. "No, so many of the world live that way because their animal souls leave no room in their hearts for their Divine souls. They actually enjoy the material pleasures of this earth, the gluttony, greed, and sex, which overwhelm their Divine souls. Their Divine souls live in exile in their bodies. But for you, Joseph, that wasn't the problem. You turned down the material pleasures. The problem was the enormity of your Divine soul fitting into this finite body of yours. You've struggled with that continually."

"How did you know my name was Joseph?"

"I believe that you haven't gone under that name for most of your time on this earth, but that is your name, whether on this earth or in the heavenly realms," the middle man said.

"But how did you know? Have you...can you..."

"Joseph, my colleagues and I here are mortal human beings, but there are some things that we are permitted to see, if we maintain our spiritual state in this life."

Prince began to whimper softly once again.

"Joseph, look at me, so that you may feel what I am feeling," the middle man said. "I told you that my heart was once where yours resides now. I do think that I know how you feel. None of us starts out wishing to be a slave to his destiny. We all prefer to start with a clean slate. But the fact is that we don't. Our souls have a history and we are part of a Divine Plan. And there's something else. I was the same way. I didn't want the burden of serving G-d. I rebelled against the thought that I was an ox pulling G-d's cart."

"So, how did you resolve that?"

"I was guided by someone, like I hope to guide you. Never underestimate the power of human relationships and their ability to assist G-d in transforming us. Now, I want you to look at me, just a moment, so that you can see into my heart, understand my intentions," the middle man said.

For the third time, Prince saw the spiritual vastness of the soul of the middle man through the blue openings in his forehead. This time he didn't avert his vision. It reminded him of a time long ago, when he had been in some beautiful place of no longing. That place had no coordinates in time or geography, but seemed to extend around him and through him in an endless stream of light and energy. Prince's anger dissolved, as a knotted rope falls limp, when pulled in the proper direction. His large frame shivered and fell limp. Then a wave of love surged through him, then another, then another.

"The kelipah in your heart is dissolving, isn't it? Now, you can feel G-d's love, can't you? There is nothing, no wall, that keeps G-d's Light in exile in your body, that keeps your Divine soul from infusing your entire system," the middle man said.

Prince nodded.

"If you could feel this love all the time—and G-d has benevolently given you that potential power, should you choose to develop it—would you now feel as if you were being forced into this choice?" the middle man said.

"No."

"But now it is a choice, isn't it?" the middle man said. "Only now, it's not quite like you phrased it before. It's a real choice. When someone loves you as much as G-d loves us all, then we really do want to serve that person. What you said before is true—that the choice, the decision, is obvious. There's not a question what to do. But it's not as if you have to do it, that you're being forced to do it. Now you want to do it, don't you? There's a difference."

"Yes, right now, I want to do it," Prince said. "I feel as if I am part of something much larger and important. But how long can I count on that feeling lasting? I've felt it a few times before, but it's never lasted for long, and it seemed that the things that could cause it to last, have always been denied or taken away from me."

The middle man smiled. "The feeling that you feel now, is the feeling that a person achieves in true supplication or prayer, or in the study of Torah, when he is in touch with his Divine soul. Only you haven't done much of that, have you? But the lofty level that your particular soul may achieve in this life in this world, if you so choose, is to achieve that feeling permanently, whether engaged in the study of Torah at that particular time or not. No more emptiness. No more wandering. No more exile. Now you may return home. You may find this vast sea of love. What do you say? Will you serve G-d?"

"Yes. Yes, I will do teshuvah. I will return to G-d."

"I didn't say that it would be easy," the middle man said. "It will be neither easy nor simple for you to perform either the teshuvah or your subsequent role on this earth. But despite your struggles, your soul will be at peace."

"No, it will not be easy," Prince said ruefully. "But then I suppose that's why I was given these powers of perception and intelligence, this charm—if I want to use it, and this powerful body."

"Yes," the middle man said.

"Whew," Prince said. He sighed. "I'm suddenly very tired. But now, would it be possible if I ask a few questions, that would help me understand a little bit more about all of this."

"Yes, that's possible and quite understandable now," the middle man said.

"Who has G-d sent to me here today to turn me toward Him?"

"I am a Hasidic Rabbi," the middle man said. "My colleague on my right is a medical doctor and on my left is a business executive. I didn't wish to seem unhelpful before, but I think that you can understand why we wouldn't wish to discuss ourselves until you had committed yourself to our purpose here. First of all, it is hard to define a relationship with someone who doesn't know who he is; a person who is not honest with himself can hardly be truly honest with others. Until that person's self is anchored firmly to a spiritual core, anyone who deals with him must tread a slippery slope of deceit and treachery. So our relationship with you could not begin to possess true substance and reality until you defined who you are.

"There's a second point. While all three of us are known for certain roles in our public lives, our major spiritual purposes here on this earth must remain hidden. Otherwise, we would be unable to continue to achieve those purposes. If our spiritual identities were to be exposed to the outside world, great forces of the yetzer hara, or evil impulse, would rise up in opposition to our efforts. Just like in physics, each spiritual force can have an equal and opposite reaction. Occasionally, it may become necessary for one of us to manifest some spiritual ability in our public lives, to alleviate a special situation. This can not only neutralize our future spiritual powers in a certain situation, but can be personally dangerous. Then we would be forced to begin a new life incognito in some other place. You, yourself, have already unconsciously understood the concept of 'concealment'. When your special powers or abilities began to come to light in your wanderings, you tried to hide them. When you return to the public life, for the purpose of achieving your destiny, you will be better equipped to obscure, or veil, your abilities, so that they may be properly and discretely used when needed in specific situations."

"Hm...You're kind of like secret agents. Are you Lamed-Vov's?"

"I cannot answer that. That's something that perhaps only G-d knows. I would not presume anything, about my soul. That is not a power granted to me." the Hasidic Rabbi said.

"Why are there three of you here?"

"At least several reasons," the Hasidic Rabbi said. "The most important is that three of us received separate instructions from the universe to be here. But three is an important number. It takes three witnesses to witness a divorce proceeding, so you shall have three witnesses for your repentance and the transformation of your heart. And there are three columns of sefirot, the attributes, or windows onto G-d. Those three columns lead to balance. You must have the proper mixture of both the left and right side, Chochmah, or wisdom, and Binah, or understanding, for example. Or Chesed, which is kindness, and Gevurah, which is severity. The three of us together may provide that balance."

"And the purpose of your training and public occupations? Is there a purpose here?"

The Hasidic Rabbi smiled. "As I said, with Divine Providence, there is always a purpose. We are all here for your spiritual needs, of course. But I will be providing the bulk of your Jewish training and counseling regarding your repentance and the transformation of your heart, so we will be spending considerable time together. Our business person on my left will be making contact with your uncle so that you may reenter the material and public world you left several years ago. It will be necessary for you to do that as promptly as possible to fulfill your earthly purpose. He will be also taking care of your future arrangements for schooling. And my colleague on my right will be your health consultant during this period. I told you that this is a physical process. You will be expelling the evil out of your system, so that you may become a righteous person. This will make you very sick, since all that impurity must first come to the surface, in order to be expelled from your system. Most righteous people have never experienced such kelipah, so their process of purification is much simpler."

"But why did I spend all those years in that kelipah? I know it was my choice, but you said there was a purpose. What could have been the point in my contact with all that evil? And if there was a purpose to all of this, why didn't G-d tell me, at least let me know, that there was a reason? Why did I have to suffer so before I knew?"

"Perhaps, we should answer the last question first," the Hasidic Rabbi said. "A discourse in human suffering and depression would take too long at this time, but we humans do suffer here because we see only the manifest material world and fail to see the hidden spiritual world which underlies and maintains our true existence here. It was certainly not G-d's purpose to make you suffer in this world, but if G-d had initially made His purpose aware to you, then you would not have faced a true choice in the manner in which you conducted your life. We can all be good in heaven, when G-d's intent is crystal clear, but choosing to be righteous and good here on earth is another matter.

"As to the first part of your question, God wished for you to be different. First, he wished for you to understand evil, so that you could ultimately confront it, modify it, and banish it from His realm on earth. Only a person with intimate experience with evil among mankind would have been wise enough to realize its source and been able to fight it. Words from learned men and tzaddiks in the past have roused the choir, but ultimately have been unable to change the underlying reality of the world's condition. Again, if you had understood the reason for your exposure to evil, then you would have avoided certain temptations, and consequently, you would have lacked the understanding of those enchantments and seductions.

"You see, G-d wished for you to be a bridge, a connection between the holy life you will now lead and the evil world, which you now understand, as a result of your past experience. In order for you to link these worlds, He has not consigned you to a strictly religious life, but has ordained that you should work in the mundane world and carry your spirituality to that world. It was Divine Providence that you ultimately ran away from your uncle when you were completing your Bar Mitzvah training; if you had stayed, you would surely have loved your religious study in a way that might have prohibited your participation in a larger business world. G-d has given you the 'might' spoken of in the V'ahavta part of the Sh'ma, which commands you to 'love the L-rd your G-d with all your heart, with all your soul, and with all your might'. 'Might' refers to your great financial resources.

"There is another very important reason for your passage through evil. Some great men are born with lofty souls which never fall. But the Brachot Talmud says that the greatest credit in the heavens is given to those who are B'al Teshuvah, those who have repented and returned to G-d. 'The place that a B'al Teshuvah can stand at times even a complete tzaddik cannot stand.' The B'al Teshuvah are the ones that have taken the hard steps for their love of G-d. They are the ones who have risen from the evil to do G-d's Will. Theirs choices to serve G-d in this world are not as obvious as the choice presented to the complete tzaddik.

"Finally, perhaps your journey through evil was a test of your spiritual capacity to face the future. Since G-d doesn't ask any of us to undertake missions that we cannot complete with our own personal resources, perhaps G-d was measuring yours here. And in your case, since your mission is so critical to the balance of the spiritual world, it was absolutely essential that G-d examine whether you were spiritually fit to fulfill your destined role. A failure on your part was not just a lost opportunity for you and the world, but could easily retard, or even reverse, the course of the world's spiritual development. You've already survived great pain with the integrity of your soul essentially intact. But the temptations that you will soon face will be all the greater."

10

It was of course no accident that Prince's leaving the Jones' ranch and his subsequent meeting with the three wise men had occurred during the Ten "Days of Awe" between Rosh Hashanah and Yom Kippur. Those ten days, and the prior month of Elul on the Hebrew calendar, represented the time when the "King was in the field," that is to say when G-d is accessible to human souls in a special way that does not exist during the rest of the year. G-d made Himself closer, more reachable, so that with some spiritual discipline and effort—perhaps metaphorically a trip to the field where the King would travel at that time of year on His way to His castle—even the common person could behold Him and penetrate through the spiritual layers surrounding Him.

While Elul represented a month of spiritual preparation prior to the Ten "Days of Awe", the ten days represented the big spiritual event itself. "On Rosh Hashanah it is written, on Yom Kippur it is sealed; how many shall pass on, how many shall come to be; who shall live and who shall die..." It was the one time of year when human choice and Divine Providence would interact, creating a new spiritual compound that would power human activity for the remainder of the Hebrew year. To most of the humans, it seemed that G-d had all the power to determine their fates. But in reality, G-d waited patiently, His hands figuratively tied, for the human response to His offer. G-d could make Himself available, could set up office hours, but it was strictly human choice to approach Him in supplication.

And so G-d waited during those fateful days for Prince to approach Him in repentance, just as he waited for all Jews, and all of His other subjects, to come before Him. G-d's "Countenance", the inner quality of His Supernal Will and His Desire, the desire to dispense life to all who belong to the realm of holiness, was attainable to all those who chose to be close to Him, and renounce the "other gods" found in kelipah. If Prince had suffered so much, it was because he had previously turned away from G-d's Countenance and looked for sustenance from kelipot, which derived their vitality from the "hinder-part" of G-d's Will. The minute measure of light and life which the kelipot derived from the hinder-part of G-d's Will could sustain the kelipot's belief that they existed as independent beings separate from G-d, but was extremely poor sustentation for human souls. For a soul as vast as that of Prince's, his exile from the support of G-d had left a huge void and had been very painful.

By Divine Providence, Prince's dialogue with the three men had ended at dusk. As the three men broke through the wall of kelipot, with which Prince had surrounded himself in a kind of self-defeating defense, and connected with Prince's Divine soul, a protective shadow had first gathered around the spot in the vast room that Prince had occupied. As the darkness gathered strength throughout the balance of the space, the middle man led his companions in bringing out a meal from one of the building's chambers. They set it out on the oak desk. Then they said the blessing over the food. "You must eat well now," the middle man said to Prince. "You must always fortify your body, so that you may serve G-d, and it is especially critical now, in this night, in this darkness, before the light comes—for the light will bring new challenges in your new life."

Prince did as he was told. He was suddenly very hungry. He ate a multiple portion, even for his large frame, and then as soon as the blessings after the meal were sung, quickly fell into a deep sleep. As he did, the crescent moon of the new month, set in the western sky, and the night became very dark.

He awoke in bed abruptly—as if to meet the anticipated challenge of a new day—around five in the morning, just before the light of the morning began its ascension. An inner voice rose within his head, his consciousness, and he felt the Divine Presence with him, moving throughout and around him—as if the form of his body had no bearing or position. It was both filling him and surrounding him, comforting him, and assuring him. He knew when the light came he would never be the same. Then It was gone, as if a spiritual blanket had been removed, just before the light of day began to enter the room.

The sunlight struck his bed first, just as the protective shadow had enveloped him first the previous evening. Within a minute, he had covered his eyes and screamed for help.

The Rabbi and doctor rushed into the room. "What's the problem?" the doctor said.

"My eyes...they began to burn terribly the minute the sunlight touched me. And now...now...I can't see. I can't see any more!"

"Let me take a look," the doctor said.

"You will not see any difference," the Rabbi said. "No use looking my friend."

"Oh," the doctor said. He drew away from Prince. "I see. I should have surmised that this would happen."

"What happen? What is happening to me?" Prince's hands frantically groped for the frame of the bed and the wall next to it.

"It's okay, Joseph," the Rabbi said. "I know that you cannot see. Your eyesight will surely return—within a few days. You must wait."

"Wait? Wait for what? Ouch! Now, my fingers are burning too. My whole body is hot. I have this metallic taste in my mouth and the room smells like manure."

"I told you that you would be sick," the Rabbi said. And then with a twinkle in his blue eyes, which he was happy Prince could not see, he said, "You know, we smell the manure too. That is a real smell to us, as well. And it's not the cows in the farms nearby. It happens to be your smell today, as you metabolize that filthy kelipah and we have to put up with it, because we are taking care of you. No feeling sorry for yourself here."

"But I didn't know I'd be blind. Do you know what it's like to be blind, not to have your eyes?"

"It's happened to us all. Spiritually, it's been happening all your life, Joseph," the Rabbi said. "You've had those eyes, but you haven't really bothered to see through them. The eyes are centered in the head for a reason, and it's not just to have a short path for the optic nerve. It's because our brains are the principal locations in our bodies from which our souls are drawn and revealed. Thus the eyes' location—spiritually they want and need to be near the brain. Without the spirituality behind those eyes, they're nothing but a camera lens, without a discerning photographer to direct them."

"Okay, I know you're right, Rabbi, but will you tell me what's happening physically here for the next few days. I still need my eyesight back."

"Joseph, you're like a puppy just born. There's nothing wrong with your eyes. That sunlight didn't blind you this morning any more than it's done any other morning. In fact, your eyes are capable of seeing a lot more today than they've ever seen before. And therein lies the problem. It's the connection between the brain and the eyes."

"What do you mean?" Prince said.

"You see kelipah comes in layers," the Rabbi said, "like the physical garments that surround your soul. We peeled many of those layers back yesterday. Like the outer layer of thick, dead skin being removed, it left the inner layers of alive skin a little raw, and a little unprepared to suddenly assume their new role of facing the world.

"There's a bit more," the Rabbi said. "With the kelipah going away, your sensitivity to your environment increased dramatically. Your soul is capable of perceiving much more of G-d's revelation than most around you. But your optic nerve, is unable to process that information, without some physical transformation."

"It's like the blind fish in the cave," the doctor said. "They can no longer process light to see, as other fish outside the cave do. They've lost that capacity permanently because they have not used it and have no need for it. Only in your case, the difference is that your system is human. It's adaptable, to handle many physical, and especially spiritual, situations. G-d has separated the four levels of existence, from the inanimate, to vegetative, to the animal, and finally the medeber, man, who speaks, and whom G-d has given the spiritual capacity of choice."

"As soon as you chose to do right and began to remove the kelipah yesterday, G-d started the mystical adaptation of your physical system so that it would be compatible with your higher level of spirituality," the Rabbi said. "Now, if you will place your trust in G-d, as you proceed from this point in life, G-d will surely provide the physical transformation, the physical position in life, your physical needs, that you require to do His work."

"Okay," Prince said. "But why, if G-d is capable of doing this for me, must I be blind now? Surely, G-d is capable of taking care of my eyesight now, rather than having me suffer."

"Ah," the Rabbi said. His eyes twinkled again, and he slowly stroked his beard, while he formulated his answer. "Joseph, G-d doesn't really wish for you to suffer. But this is the world we live in, where G-d is manifest to us in very limited ways. The revelation of his light is restricted in this world, so that we may have a physical presence here. Without the restricted light, which is limited as a result of the contractions used to create this world, our identities as individuals would be subsumed in G-d's presence, because, as you know, G-d is everywhere, inside of us and outside of us, and the boundary of your body means nothing in the spiritual world. In the spiritual world, which is hidden to us here on earth, the choice to do right is obvious. We come to this mundane world to make choices which are not so obvious to us, between right and wrong.

"So in this context, I have several answers to your question. First, G-d's manifestation must be limited in this world for us to have choices and function as we should spiritually here in this realm. That's why you don't usually perceive G-d flashing His powers, as He did for us at the Red Sea. Not only that, but if G-d had given your eyesight immediately to you this morning, you would have taken all of this for granted. Your physical transformation, to match your ongoing spiritual change, would have gone unnoticed. We would not be having this conversation. It really is a miracle that this is happening. But, just as it is a miracle that we live now and that your bed here in front of us does not collapse beneath you and descend into chaos, we would not have labeled it as such. Better that we are witnessing G-d's power in the face of your hopelessness, because I'll bet that your eyesight would be tops on your list of physical qualities that you value most. Furthermore, miracles seem to happen most often through normal means. G-d has already provided through the natural world, as He always does. There is no need to speed this change in your eyes up and change the world merely for your sake. You are here to serve G-d, not the other way around.

"In addition, once again, my friend, you are being tested. Your faith is being tested here, and it will continue to be tested, in part to prepare you for the future. In the future, much of the world will seem to turn against you, but you will have the fortitude to know that G-d still resides with you and will protect you, no matter what will be done against you. Now you are amongst friends, who will help you understand those trials of faith and prepare psychologically for them.

"Finally, it will be useful for you to miss your eyesight for a while. It will help you sharpen and develop your other senses, not just your physical ones, but the whole range of your spiritual senses—the subtle ones that we fail to use because we are literally blinded by the light. We hardly know about these senses, and only have vague words to describe them, such as 'intuition', 'foreboding', 'weird feeling', 'other worldly sense', etc., but they are more real than the physical world we take for granted."

"A rebbe will use these senses above all, to protect the Jewish people," the doctor said. He smiled wryly. "Of course, many will say that followers of a rebbe will obediently heed his instructions, even though his directions are irrational and that this proves that his people cannot think for themselves. The reality is though, that a rebbe sees things, sees future events that others not at his spiritual level cannot possibly perceive. He may not be able to put into words what he sees, nor does he always deem it advisable to do so. That's because whatever he says is easily misinterpreted by those with less spiritual capacity. And of course, when a rebbe speaks his reasons, he invites the yetzer hara to oppose him. So, just as G-d moves the world on a hidden plane, the rebbe—who is closest in our mundane world to G-d's spiritual world—tries to do the same."

"A rebbe—this is what you think that I will be after all of this? A rebbe?" Prince said. "I'm not complaining about it. I just want to get this straight." He was still furiously groping around the bed. Now that his eyesight was unavailable to watch their faces, he felt at a distinct disadvantage in the conversation.

"You will be what you will be, and only G-d knows that, though His people will certainly have a choice in this matter. Neither one of us said you'd be a rebbe. We certainly don't have the power of the Creator to know that," the Rabbi said. "By the way, if you'd stop fidgeting over there, you'd start to pick up on some cues from us. I know that you think that all you can pick up from us, or "hear", is words, so that you are somewhat clueless as we converse. But that's not true." When Prince frowned, the Rabbi laughed. "What I'm saying is that you can begin to read my thoughts, just as I just read yours."

"You've been looking at my countenance, but I'm unable to look at yours," Prince said.

"True enough," the Rabbi said. "The point is well made and I see that we will have spirited discussions during this period and that I will learn much from you. But there are many cues you are still not noticing, even in your blindness, or should I say because of your blindness, because it is the spiritual blindness that prevents you from perceiving them. Consider this idea for example. G-d shows us His Countenance every day as long as we follow His holy path. That Countenance is for the most part hidden in a conventional sense—that is we don't physically see G-d's face. Yet we can know that It's there. How do we know this if we cannot see It?"

When they left the room, Prince lay in the same kind of darkness in which he had awoke only a few hours earlier. After a short time, he was unable to move. His body seemed to become as stiff as a board. The burning sensation grew intense throughout his body, until he felt that a huge flame had engulfed him. Then, as if it had consumed its contents, the flame died out, and he felt an intense cold, then an emptiness, a total void inside him. The doctor had entered the room only to put a blanket over him, but he had been unable to respond. After that, he no longer tasted or smelled anything. Only his hearing and thoughts remained.

But he heard nothing audible. It seemed that his companions or teachers, or whoever they were, were no longer there, and that he was completely alone. After a time, the silence was no longer quiet. The longer he was immersed in this world which he thought lacked sound, the greater the volume of the silence. It was as if there had always been this background volume, this baseline of sound, but he had never been aware before of its existence. His ears had always been tuned to the much higher decibel level of daily life; now the cilia in his ears unfolded to grasp the more subtle dimension. As some undefined time went by—he had no idea of time's nature any more either—and the background volume grew insistently more intense, he realized that he was hearing the universe. Or was he "hearing" it, he wondered? Rather, perhaps he had begun to sense the universe's energy, the creative intelligence that G-d had provided that underlay all life. Which one of his senses was picking that up?

As some more time went by—he knew not whether it was day or night—he entered a deep and very long meditation. This was not by choice, for he had no control over his body, but as a result of the natural course of his sickness, since his mind could now neither shut out nor refuse to receive what was presented to him. Neither could he seek out some alternative outside stimulation to replace what he might have chosen to ignore. This lack of control forced him—and then after a while ultimately taught and disciplined him—to accept and submit to powers greater than his own. He finally accepted emotionally and psychologically what he had only previously known intellectually.

Before, his brain, his reasoning powers of Chochmah, Binah, and Daas, or wisdom, understanding, and knowledge, had told him that he could not control and dominate in a field of kelipah. He "knew" in his head that he had no dominion over the evil affairs of man. But the left side of his heart—where the blood is pumped throughout the body—was full of evil. It had argued with his brain, and caused the conflict that had threatened to strangle his Divine soul. His heart, influenced—and diseased—by the presence of kelipot, had told him that he did not deserve his destiny and had caused him to quarrel with G-d about his plight. It was as stupid as if he had come to a great banquet hosted gratis by the King himself and had foolishly complained about the circumstances under which he had been invited. And then he had subsequently wondered why the King seemed to him to want to have nothing to do with him. In order to avoid dealing with the conflict between his brain and heart, between the intellectual and emotional parts of his being—which should have been in great harmony—Prince did what so many other people do with conflict. He sublimated it. He tried to hide it away in the deep recesses of his being from his own consciousness. But, by denying the truth, and reality of his existence, he had placed his Divine soul, and thus G-d, in exile. When G-d is in exile in the body, then the Divine soul—which must be nourished by G-d, as all things are—wants to separate from the body and return to its source, G-d. Disease and pain result when the Divine soul and the body, or the animating or animal soul, are in conflict and cannot live in the same house together.

Though Prince had not wanted the material pleasures of the world to which he had ironically been born, his soul had nevertheless had to deal with the yetzer hara. The great size of his Divine soul meant that he was confronted with an enormous yetzer hara to match his soul. If a person was going to wrestle with the yetzer hara, then he would have to do it in the proper weight class. G-d had given Prince a choice to fulfill his oath, just like everyone else. Only his choice was more difficult and more monumental.

The kelipot in Prince's heart, in his blood—which was the essence of his bodily flesh—derived their sustenance from G-d, as do all beings. But they could only remain separate, independent entities by residing in an environment of exile from G-d and receiving their energy from G-d's hinder most parts. That is to say that they did not receive the energy allowing them to exist directly from the Divine Light, or G-d's Countenance, but by parasitically feeding on exiled light, light that had been previously separated from the Divine force and been trapped in Prince's heart as a result of his ego, arrogance, and lack of humility. That ego sought to separate itself from G-d, rather than surrender to Him. In that sense, Prince had violated the second of the Ten Commandments, which commands us not to have any idols.

Locked as usual in the dark evil of Prince's heart, the existence of the kelipot was supported quite well. As with all evil components, they cared little about where they would dwell, as long as their basic survival needs were met. In fact, they could be moved where ever any human power pushed them. But in the Divine Light, the kelipot could no longer maintain a separate existence. They would dissolve like minerals in water, evaporate into the air, snap like a knot in a rope unraveling, their remaining components becoming only subtle physical remnants, which would then recombine with other elements. In the bright light of G-d, in the end, the kelipot would revert to molecules essentially no different than the constituents of a person's body. When Prince lay almost lifeless, with his energy levels at the minimum needed to maintain the union of his Divine soul with his body, he was unable to direct his thoughts, unable to control, restrict, or constrain the Divine energy that effused through his soul, beginning in his brain, so that he became dependent at that time upon the direct, pure, and unadulterated Divine Light for his momentary existence. That Divine Light entered into the left part of his heart and nullified the kelipot, annihilating the evil residing in Prince's body and creating the potential physical conditions necessary for a true tzaddik.

Of course, one could say that G-d had done this for Prince; G-d had chosen Prince and had expelled the evil from his heart. It had not been Prince's doing, so that nothing particularly special was achieved here. But that would be ignoring the fact that none of us may fulfill his destiny without the assistance of G-d. Not one of us has the strength to surmount evil and do G-d's Will without His help. The very thought that we might have the strength, separate from G-d—even though nothing is separate from G-d—creates the exiled energy which nourishes the kelipot in this world. It allows us to pursue all the material and spiritual idols of our world that ignore G-d. But G-d cannot help us unless we first surrender to Him, and that surrender in this world is dependent upon our faith in Him. With that faith, we are able to face the trials of a life in service to Him. In the case of Prince, a lesser person would never have taken the oath in heaven, nor finally agreed to take the painful course of becoming a potential tzaddik. And a lesser person would have agreed to death in that room in Oklahoma City, rather than the stream of fire or the purgatory of snow which Prince now endured. G-d knew that he had chosen a special soul in Prince and He was not disappointed at that time.

During this process, Prince never lost consciousness. But his hold on the physical life that we know on earth was so tenuous that he was unsure whether his body was alive or dead. His consciousness hovered above his body and in it, as well as split between his body and some of the space in the room. The angels in heaven watched in awe. Events such as the transformation of a tzaddik's heart not only were rare enough—with each having its own unique circumstances—but this one had a greater potential power to change the world. This occurrence between Rosh Hashanah and Yom Kipper had restarted the angelic debate over whether Prince had a fighting chance to fulfill his destiny of making the world a better place; some of the angels even doubted whether the transformation in Prince's heart would be complete enough to make him a potential tzaddik.

Meanwhile, as the heavens watched Prince's consciousness hover around his body, Prince slowly began the return to the existence of this world. He vaguely remembered the Rabbi and the doctor finally returning to his room and holding a bagel into his mouth. "If it worked for the sages, it will work here. Have him bite on this," the Rabbi said, "so that he will not be nullified by the Divine Light and leave us. G-d wishes him to return to this world to perform his service."

After the Rabbi and doctor had assisted him in biting into the bagel—they had actually moved his jaw back and forth—Prince began to very slowly feel obscure sensations in his skin and then in patches in his limbs. As the feeling returned to his organs, he had the indefinable feeling of a shifting in his internal system. Almost like a fluid, something had been removed and something had flowed to take its place. It seemed that everything was adjusting. "It is important that you do not move right away," the doctor said. "Your eyesight was the first to leave and it will be the last to return. That's in part your body's way of getting you to slow down at this time."

"This will be the last time you get any rest," the Rabbi said. "You're going out in the big world now, and we have a lot of training to do. So enjoy it while you can." The Rabbi smiled, knowing that after this time Prince would be in full control of his earthly powers and would be able to respond verbally to him, giving him back as much in argument and good natured ribbing as he gave Prince.

Prince's eyesight returned slowly. After a day or so he had thought that it had completely returned. But then it seemed that the world around him kept becoming increasingly sharper, with more brilliant colors than he had ever remembered. "Am I seeing that much more than I did before, or has my perception changed? And if my perception has changed, is it because of my temporary blindness, or is because of my repentance, or possibly the fact that my system has ridded itself of some of kelipot?" he asked.

"Don't know," the Rabbi said. "This is the first one of this kind that I've watched. You're probably going to go away from here with more questions than answers. A learned man has more questions than answers. The more he learns, the more he realizes what he doesn't know. That is, if he's humble as he should be, and if he's not humble, well then he's not really a learned man in my sense of the word.

"So, if you thought you had uncertainty in your life before, you haven't seen anything yet. In fact, the amount of uncertainty we experience in life I think is directly correlated with the magnitude of the Divine service we undertake. But not to worry. The difference is that when you have faith in G-d, you weather the uncertainty.

"How does your heart feel now, Joseph?" the Rabbi said. "I mean how do you feel about things in general?"

Prince smiled. "It's a funny feeling. For one thing, it's a rebirth. It's like waking up to a world that's familiar to you, that is you know how it all works and you weren't born yesterday, but you feel completely differently about it all."

"And how's that?" the Rabbi said.

"There's acceptance of this world first of all. None of this rationalization of why something should be, or anger that it isn't," Prince said. "It's such a relief to have the anger gone."

"That oversized ego in your left ventricle has disappeared," the Rabbi said. He smiled. "Your ego doesn't require all this maintenance. It's not pulling all this energy away from your mind. The fact that your mind and your heart are finally starting to work together, and your mind doesn't feel as if it's getting cheated by your heart, is enough in itself to stop the anger."

"I also feel as if I see things so much more clearly," Prince said. "When my heart wanted something, it tried to get my mind to decide to do it by justifying it to my mind. Like the yetzer hara arguing for something wrong, it made for a lot of cloudy, fuzzy thinking. My head stayed confused a lot, even though my intellect was fully functioning."

"Very true," the Rabbi said, "and well said. Your intellect is of course Divinely inspired and given and is purely objective. But previously, your intellect operated through the lens of the subjectivity of your heart. Your ego prevented you from seeing the world in objective terms. Now that your heart is operating in unity with your mind, you are no longer observing and interpreting the world through the maze of wants and desires in your heart. Our sages have said that only tzaddikim have control over their hearts. Hopefully, the subjectivity of your experience will soon become as objective as a human's can be. Of course, the only true objective source in the universe is G-d, who is both the knower and the known. By knowing Himself, G-d knows all created entities, since He is the source of their existence. He is the source of everything."

After a brief pause, the Rabbi continued. "And how do you view your mission in this life?"

"That's a good question," Prince said. He laughed long and hard, releasing a latent energy. "My mission before all this was not to do my mission."

"I know," the Rabbi said. "Now that would have been a real waste, wouldn't it?"

"Well, yes I have to admit to that now," Prince said. "It doesn't even make sense to me though. I know it was just a matter of days ago that I was fleeing as fast as I could. How could we be talking about the same person? I don't even understand that person, any more. It's the same body and soul. How could this be?"

"Pretty miraculous," the Rabbi said. "The pain is even gone from your face. It's not even the same face and those who knew you before will have difficulty identifying you now. Repentance does it. True repentance is complete turning. It's facing the same situation and temptation once again and making a different choice. And it just demonstrates what a difference a choice and intention makes. You see you're not the same person, at all. I'm delighted to hear you say that you feel so different, because it means that the transformation is real. There will be no turning back now."

"To tell you the truth," Prince said, "I don't feel as if anything's tugging at my heart any more. I feel emptied and cleansed. Not much desire there at the moment. I'm kind of just experiencing the moment, not worried about the past or present, not planning or calculating anything." His whole body lay relaxed in a manner he did not recall ever experiencing.

"And how do you feel about G-d?" the Rabbi said.

"G-d? I feel good about G-d. Whatever G-d wants, I want. Let G-d direct me. Let me be his agent on this earth, as he intended. I have no other agenda now."

"You will be a 'chariot' for G-d," the Rabbi said.

Then the Rabbi got up from his chair and took several steps back from the bed. His mood became more serious as he paced around the room. "Joseph," he said, "we will be coming back to the issues that we've been discussing many times in more depth. We are not finished with them by any means, but now it is necessary to discuss other matters. Everything fits together here. I did not want to discuss your specific future without knowing for sure that the transformation of your heart had indeed occurred. What I have to say now would otherwise be gravely misinterpreted by you. But you are now a humble man, and my words will go to your intellect, not your heart.

"Your uncle has been told that you have been found and that you are well. The business of your family is quite good. G-d has certainly looked after that. It is now the largest and most powerful company in the world and you are its sole heir. You will head this company when your secular education is completed." He shook his head in disbelief. "To think now that a religious Jew, a humble man, who wishes to do right in the world, will soon head the most important commercial enterprise in the world just boggles my mind. We spent two thousand years in helplessness. Then Israel came along, and the gathering of the exiles there. Now this. Surely, the Messiah is not far away." As he said the last line, his eyes examined Prince with a ferocity, causing Prince to shrink back in his bed.

"Are you still agreeing with this mission, with what you've heard? I know that I am throwing a lot at you, but time is of the essence here. We have no time, when the Messianic Age is at hand. But you can still turn this mission down at this point."

"No," Prince said. His voice belted out across the room. Now he had startled the Rabbi. "I will do as I was intended to do. Praise G-d." Then after a pause, he said, "Rabbi, how is my uncle? It pains me that I left him the way I did. He must have been very worried about me all these years."

"Quite well, actually. My colleague spoke to him in a long conversation and he will fill you in shortly. Don't worry about your uncle. He's no dummy when it comes to spiritual matters, and he had figured out that something was up with you and the universe. Come on, Joseph. You weren't the most usual kid in the world.

"You are going to be a very learned man," the Rabbi continued. "Many of us in the observant religious community will recognize you as a rebbe and a tzaddik." He smiled. "It will be the first time in our history that we will recognize a businessman, running an empire, as a tzaddik. But not everyone will recognize you as such. You will have many detractors. For some it will be that they do not like change. For some of my religious colleagues, they will not like sharing religious sanctity with a businessman. And then there will also be the yetzer hara. You will have a lot of power and the yetzer hara will oppose your noble wishes.

"And that's just the Jews. We haven't even talked about the Christian and secular responses. Some Christians, Moslems, and others will be adamantly opposed to you, because you will be a Jew with power. But you will attract many others because of the nobility of your aims and because many of them share our beliefs in a Messianic World. That's because they have already been heavily influenced by us."

"If some of the Jews will see me as a tzaddik, how will other followers view me?" Prince said.

"To the Hindu world you will be an individual who has attained a higher state of consciousness. They might say that you had attained cosmic consciousness. Of course, the Buddhist followers might see you in the tradition of Buddha. The Christian response is likely to be more complicated. There are many Judeophiles among the Christians.

"But having followers from other religions will cause you trouble with other Jews. Even though your message will be undeniably and specifically Jewish, some Jews will become suspicious when they find that you have Christian followers. But though G-d made us the chosen people, he never intended to discriminate. Your Christian following will be every bit as genuine as your Jewish one. I cannot predict the future except to say that your path through these groups will be torturous. You will be gravely misinterpreted and you will experience much pain. G-d will be testing all of us, to see if we can get along. After all, the Messianic Age is not just brought to us by G-d. We the humans must create it with G-d's help."

"I know who I am now," Prince said. "Yes, I will experience pain, perhaps great sadness, but that pain will only be earthly. My soul will be anchored in G-d. The pain will be nothing like the spiritual exile that I felt."

"You know, even if we are successful, my friend, and there's no guarantee of that," the Rabbi said, "there will be more chaos before the calm. As crazy as the world is now, it will react to you by becoming even crazier. You will be blamed for much. You will be insulted, tempted, and attacked. And even when you turn away from your enemies to help this world, you will face slander and lies. Are you prepared for that?"

"Yes, yes I am."

When Prince rose from the bed, his soul had been reborn, in the same body, during those Ten "Days of Awe". His strength came back very quickly. He turned his attention to Yom Kippur and fasted with his renewed fortitude.

On Rosh Hashanah, the Jews had celebrated the birthday of the world's creation—life. On Yom Kippur, Jews had denied their physical existence through fasting and physical discomfort, a form of death, so that their Divine souls would predominate over the desires of their bodies. During those ten days, the world had swung between life and death. Divine decisions had been made, from the most monumental for human existence, to the placement of a leaf falling later that autumn. Nothing had been left to chance. But human choice had been critical to the Divine decree. Prince had chosen life over death.

11

To those who were able to follow the general existence and whereabouts of Prince throughout his early life, his late teenage years and early twenties, before he gained full blown celebrity, and while he attended Stanford University, must have seemed reminiscent of earlier times. Prince had sought anonymity in earlier life. In like manner now, he was hardly interested just yet in public exposure at the university; it was more important that he take the time to develop his character and learn more about the business and political world before facing public scrutiny. But there were those forces who sought to bring him to light. If it wasn't his great financial fortune, it was his charm, beauty, size, and great magnetism. Everyone on the campus could identify him from a great distance. And as in previous times, enough of a reputation preceded him, so that even strangers a considerable distance away had heard tale of him.

There were other factors as well that propelled Prince to the spotlight. His intellect was unmatched and this was true in any course in which he was enrolled, from English to physics. It was said that no one had gone through the university with such abilities. His teachers deferred to him in the classroom. When they would answer another student's question, they would sometimes ask him to confirm their reply. As time went on, both the students and teachers realized to their surprise that Prince was a very humble individual, who made no distinction between his own worth and those of his colleagues. He would reach out and help others in need and further, he had the uncanny ability to distinguish who was really needy and what they needed. So, while there were many on campus who resented and were jealous of his abilities, there were those who saw great merit in him and in his skills, and reached out to him in true friendship. There was a third group too, who selfishly sought to meet Prince in order to profit in any way from his future wealth and position. But Prince, with his unusual ability to assess others and their motivations, easily made the distinction. After becoming accustomed to his new environment—it was quite a change from his unstructured wanderings—Prince began the slow process of making true friends. Friendship was another area of his life in which he had so little experience.

And if all the previously mentioned characteristics were not enough to bring early publicity to him, Prince gained a reputation in the athletic arena. With relatively minimal preparation, he began to compete once again in swimming and track events, with great success. As he won all of his collegiate competitions, and his studies required only minimal time, he began to train for the Olympics in the decathlon. Surmounting those on the U.S. team who had been preparing for years, he became the favorite to win, and then won the world championships and the gold in two different Olympic years. As in the past, there was resentment against the ease with which he had won, after what other competitors considered only minimal training. Even those competitors attracted by his charisma and good nature, and amazed by his natural ability, felt robbed of their chance to succeed after they had put in years of so much effort.

In those somewhat indistinct years of Prince's youth, he also spent considerable time in learning much more about all aspects of the Jewish tradition. The Rabbi who had counseled him in Oklahoma City for several months had set up a group of several learned men to teach Prince while he studied at Stanford. Like the three men who met Prince in Oklahoma City, this group of people lived relatively concealed spiritual lives which usually differed greatly from their more public ones. And by no means were they at that time the only kind of group of this type which was involved in teaching spirituality to other Jews. While greater and greater spiritual darkness raged throughout the world, and humans continued to wage war against each other and further foul the planet, learned Jews and righteous non-Jews sensed that a time of change, a reversal, a renewal and redemption, was ironically at hand, if they would only work with G-d to make it happen. With relatively little formal organization, a network of Jewish groups or committees had arisen around the world, to hasten the Messianic Age. Unlike previous times, when such groups of Jews traditionally originated from and were approved by observant Rabbis, these groups drew from all types of Jewish souls. In fact, the very cooperation of Jews from different backgrounds and cultures in furthering Judaism and doing its mitzvot, was as much a herald of the promise of a new time as were the buds of a tree which must survive the worst, dark winter, before they can leaf out in the spring. Reflecting the diversity of Jewish souls, these groups not only counseled Jews in spiritual matters, but in secular ones as well, mixing economic and political advice with Jewish ethics, to achieve practical results and change the world by repairing it. Much discussion revolved around gathering and uniting the pieces of the world that had been shattered during creation. Other favorite topics of discussion centered around the text *Ethics of Our Fathers* which in only a few words communicated the essence of Jewish conduct.

In the case of Prince, as well as those of other noted, rising Jewish persons that would figure importantly into this time, the spiritual advisors were specially designated ones. The designated ones were nominated by a council of senior spiritual advisors—which included the Rabbi from Oklahoma City as one of its principals—and instructed to concentrate on certain individual souls who were destined in this lifetime to have the potential power to change the world. If the designated ones chose to fulfill the mission for which they were nominated, they were instructed to physically and spiritually follow these individual souls, counsel them, and protect them from harm—spiritual as well as physical.

How these Rabbis and other senior learned individuals on this council knew the depth of the spirituality of the souls they attempted to aid was as mysterious as the reasons for the three men being called to an abandoned building in Oklahoma City to meet Prince. The most that could be explained here is that these learned men employed their spiritual senses to perform their functions. Based on esoteric and secret Kabbalistic tradition passed down from each generation to the next—starting from Abraham himself, and never lost or broken after thousands of years, despite frequent persecution and exile from their homeland—they could "see" certain souls that were presented to their consciousness by G-d. Like finding a diamond in a heap of sawdust, they could perceive through time and geography, as well as literally through clouds of masses of people toiling away on earth, each soul needing their personal attention. They might not always know G-d's specific plans for that individual. But G-d always gave them as much information as was required to perform their earthly task. The task of assigning souls to individual destinies on earth was G-d's province. But only human choice, and specifically human assistance to G-d's plan, could bring the Messianic Age to earth. G-d had set up the spiritual province in which mankind existed, but humans were specifically on earth to do the physical mitzvot that would properly unite the spirit with the earthly. G-d could not do this for them.

And regarding the tasks of these spiritual committees, it wasn't just recognized mitzvot that received the consideration of these learned individuals. Their spiritual work could carry them from one country to the next in an attempt to locate a soul. An even more difficult assignment could be the bringing together of two souls who were soul mates or who would otherwise influence each other in a way that would fulfill each one's destiny on earth. When it came down to it all, some of the spiritual advisors' work could look absolutely illogical or silly to those around them who were not familiar with their intentions. So it was important for them to have some cover, so that they could continue to maintain their anonymity, and thereby use their spiritual powers without raising the opposition of the yetzer hara, which would disrupt their delicate spiritual work. Many of them were wealthy individuals, who having satisfied their physical needs through G-d's assistance long ago, had searched for a true spiritual mission on earth. They would often travel under the pretext of business in some far off place. Others were excellent actors and actually enjoyed arriving incognito in various social situations. This was often the source of much private humor in the committees, as sometimes an individual would play several people in a developing drama, even in proximity of his or her spouse.

Still other spiritual advisors had long ago already been discounted by the society around them as slightly crazy, eccentric, perhaps even demented. These honored individuals in heaven, who had been able to overcome their egos and pride even to the point of being the object of scorn or derision from family, friends, and acquaintances, in order to do G-d's work on earth, were especially valuable in carrying out their tasks. Virtually no one suspected them of their motivations and intentions. With only the minimal ego required to establish a physical presence on earth, and with their intentions not revealed, it was almost impossible for the yetzer hara to oppose them, while they resided on earth. And how could the yetzer hara argue as prosecutor against these souls in heaven after their earthly death and their spiritual return to G-d, when they had done exactly what G-d had set out for them and their egos had grasped at nothing that was not theirs? Moreover, the yetzer hara could only function in the sphere of people's spirituality that vainly attempted to separate itself from G-d, whether this was ego, arrogance, or other forms of kelipah. It was impossible for the yetzer hara to step into a province between these individuals and G-d, when these individuals remained chariots of G-d, fully united with G-d during their earthly existence.

So, the spiritual advisor group which met with Prince on a regular basis was more than a temporary ad hoc assemblage. It knew well not only its mission regarding Prince's Jewish and moral development, but how this assignment would fit into the world's future spiritual development. The people advising Prince were prepared for long-term roles over years or even decades and concerned with providing and training successors for their positions, should this be necessary. Many of the angels had previously accused G-d, in almost a disrespectful and disbelieving way, of sending Prince down to fight the world all on his own. It is true that Prince had grown up without the usual traditional Jewish background—the reasons have been explained for that—but G-d had not abandoned Prince, nor would He abandon any individual who had agreed to fulfill his oath on earth. Prince's oath in heaven before his birth, had been much more difficult to fulfill than that of others, but he was not alone on earth in his efforts. He perceived extreme loneliness early in his life because he had tried to separate himself from G-d; since this meant of course that he would separate himself from all of G-d's creation, because G-d is present in everything, how else could he feel but alone? But once he had put his faith in G-d, and had allowed G-d's goodness and light to suffuse him, to permeate and encompass him, his soul at last felt nourished and comfortable at home united with his body. But much more than just a feeling had occurred. Now that Prince was no longer in exile, had no longer erected a wall against G-d, a physical reaction took place in the universe. The resources of G-d naturally flowed toward him, like matter being sucked into a vacuum or water running downhill. From this point in his life, he would hardly need to ask G-d for anything that he would need; chances were that that someone or something would be available to him before he was even conscious of its need. But in order for this to continue to occur, Prince would have to continue to maintain his total faith in G-d.

To most observers, maintaining faith in G-d when all of one's needs are answered would seem to be trivially easy, like falling off a slick log into water. But ironically, the reality is quite different. When life seems to treat us consistently well, we may hardly acknowledge G-d's existence; our egos may foolishly attribute our success and well-being to our own efforts, which though necessary to achieve our ends, are feeble when compared to the forces of G-d throughout our lives. Moreover, after a while, we take what we receive from our lives for granted, forgetting the feeling of pain and discomfort. But when we are down and out, and then G-d miraculously lifts us up, it is much easier to feel the trust and faith in a higher being. As human beings living in a physical world, not understanding the absolute of G-d, but only the subjectivity that we experience around us, we generally only see the relativity of our condition; we must experience the contrast of change from one position to another to understand who we are, distinguish ourselves from others, and appreciate what we are given. In our physical realm, to see the total absolute of G-d in the world, though we generally can't, would tend to extinguish our individual identities. So though G-d gave Prince everything he would need, it was deceptively easy for him to remain humble and completely trust in G-d. G-d had certainly given Prince much, but the level of His expectation was all the higher. As a general principle, whenever G-d endows us with something, it is not only a sign of abundance, but a test of our spirituality. A person who is wealthy is certainly permitted to enjoy, even celebrate that wealth, but the humble one will also ask G-d why G-d has enriched him and how he should properly use that richness to better the world.

But we have digressed in our story somewhat. The fact of the matter was that the designated spiritual advisory group that counseled Prince was an experienced and diverse group whose individuals G-d had tested in other circumstances. Before presenting advice to Prince, they were to be sure often argumentative about the direction that needed to be taken, but this was merely a means to get to the truth, which was each member's goal. In fact, all had studied Talmud for years. And if one took a side of an issue, another was sure to argue the other side, even if this sometimes meant role reversal and arguing against his or her own innate beliefs. It was all a matter of getting enough facts on the table so that a consensus—almost always unanimous—could be reached. And if that consensus took a few minutes, fine, or if G-d's work took hours or days, that was okay too. The same applied to the Jewish concepts they imparted to Prince. And as time went on, and Prince grasped what they had advised and taught him concerning his life and Judaism, they were not as concerned with those areas of instruction as they were with preparing him to face the rigors of his destiny in the world. This focused on how he should achieve his goal of changing the world and how he should react to the specific pitfalls that the yetzer hara would throw at him. At this point in time, the arguments among the counselors really grew to a feverish pitch and would last through the nights. As time went on and Prince grew in wisdom and stature, these disputations would not just occur before talking to Prince, but while he sat there, so that he too could weigh the pros and cons of the issues. Finally, as a further period of training of Prince elapsed, Prince began to participate in the argumentation. In the end, after further time went by, it was Prince himself who after listening to opposing viewpoints, made the decision about future conduct. His advisors, now in reality also his colleagues, watched this, beaming with approval, and knowing that they had succeeded well in their endeavors. This then would be the structure of the inside committee which would advise Prince throughout his public life. With this inside committee, Prince never had to question their loyalty, nor explain his own motives. There was complete understanding. Argue amongst themselves they did, but in the end they were united in their actions and their face to the world—without a question.

One of the specialties of the designated spiritual advisory group was role playing. Utilizing the diversity of the group, various members would play the major personalities and major types of personalities that they expected Prince to encounter in future years. Prince would react to the role players in the manner he reasoned would best accomplish his goals in society; afterward a discussion among the group members would ensue as to what behavioral changes Prince might consider making to improve his tactics. Many times Prince would use those suggestions to replay the role. In the replay, the various role players might realistically then alter their behavior in response to Prince's changes. The role playing was meant to simulate reality as much as possible, and in particular, arouse the strong emotions that the members of the spiritual advisory group believed that Prince would possibly feel when his integrity and self were questioned and slandered. It was important that Prince's brain rule his heart in all such instances. However, now that the evil from the left ventricle of Prince's heart had been expelled, in fact now that all of the evil in Prince's body had been chemically expelled, their concerns proved to be unfounded. After Prince had been challenged heatedly on several occasions in these confrontations, and still calmly responded, one of the older observing members would rise up out of his chair and put his hand on Prince's chest to feel his heart beat. When he felt the steady, calm beat, he would smile and say, "All tzaddiks, and all true messengers of G-d, who know that they are protected by Ein Sof, remain calm, even in the face of total adversity, like my good friend here. I now believe that you could even remain calm like the spy from our brethren did when he was challenged by Napoleon."

Some of the interaction in these sessions was less role playing than actual rehearsal of probable, specific future events. Some of the important, well known people who Prince would meet publicly in future life were actually part of the committee and participated at these sessions. Once again, their public lives—in this case very noted and newsworthy ones—masked their hidden spiritual role within the committee. So these individuals were able to perform dual roles in service to G-d's Messianic Age, both in the private spiritual sphere in committee and in public. One might expect that those with dual roles would plan to take public positions which were always sympathetic and supportive of Prince. But this was often not true. Many of them planned to take adversarial roles, even though they privately hoped and worked so hard for Prince's success. This planning occurred for several reasons. First of all, it was necessary to confuse the yetzer hara, keep it off guard, and be able to respond to it immediately.

One of the ways of doing this was by having members of the committee infiltrate the opposition and know exactly what its current thinking was at all times. And what better way to do this than by becoming one of them? Moreover, just the mere presence spiritually of one of the advanced committee members in the opposition, would have a strong impact on the group. Spiritually, the presence would dilute and tend to nullify the anger of the opposition, by providing a spiritual receptacle which would absorb and enclose their evil ideas and plans. Since all humans were spiritually and physically connected—the source of all of our Divine souls is G-d—the spiritual movement of one of the committee members in sympathy toward Prince, if only in thought and not deed, would heavily influence the others opposing him; this had a great deal to do with the strength of the committee members' brain waves, which supported not only Prince, but the harmony and peace in the universe, which was to become the basis of the Messianic Age. Not only that, but since all humans were entities suspended in the fluid of the cosmos, the pull of one human soul, particularly an extraordinary one, could literally move the others in the same direction. Though most humans could not observe this causation, its effects were nevertheless real. Finally, at some point, as Prince rose higher and the yetzer hara against Prince drew strength to oppose him with all its might, it would prove very useful, from a public relations point of view, for some of the dual role committee members, to suddenly renounce their opposition to Prince and "convert" to his side. If these tactics seemed somewhat devious for otherwise pious men to use, it was because they knew that they would have to fight the yetzer hara with everything they had. The yetzer hara would stop at nothing to defeat Prince and the Messianic Age. This was the ultimate prize and the ultimate battle. In fact, the very willingness of truly pious, G-d fearing people to leave their relatively cloistered lives and fight for their convictions in the public arena was the harbinger of the future Messianic Age.

Finally, and very importantly, the spiritual advisory group concerned itself with training Prince to use his spiritual senses. Many mystical qualities have been ascribed to the tzaddik. These mystical qualities are reflected to us through the presence of the infinite qualities of G-d, which the tzaddik brings from heaven closer to us on earth. The tzaddik actually becomes a physical receptacle for G-d's Light. By learning to use the energy from this light, the tzaddik is able to perceive Divine souls and see what remains hidden to most of the rest of us. But as with the physical senses, the tzaddik must learn to use these tools through practice. Just like a baby judging hot and cold through touch, or what morning light means to the sight, the tzaddik must have feedback, and be able to adjust the sensory input, so that it is useful to him. Despite all of his admitted perceptive powers early in life, Prince was unable to fully use his gifts without proper training. In fact, with no one to assist him in interpreting his "messages" earlier in life, he experienced a form of sensory overload and tried to shut it out. The spiritual advisory group's work with Prince's sensory perception, took at least as much time to develop as the other aspects of Prince's knowledge. But it was the final, subtle touch and the polish that enabled him to function so incredibly in the challenging years ahead.

12

Prince left Stanford with his undergraduate degree and MBA. He unceremoniously joined his family's business. At first, he was relatively quiet about his plans, so as to not arouse the yetzer hara, but the world wished to speculate.

The following is part of a larger piece that appeared in the *Los Angeles Times* at about that time:

Joseph Reed, known to the world as "Prince", sole scion of the world's greatest fortune, and multiple Olympics gold medals winner, recently joined his family's empire of businesses, World Technologies, based in San Francisco. WT, as it is known throughout the world, is the world's largest corporation in sales and profits and the leading one in the expanding computing, imaging, and publishing technologies. It is approaching a trillion dollars in sales...

Although Prince has tended to shy away from publicity, he has in recent years become the focus of a celebrity driven public. Very few photographs have been released of him, and virtually no candid one at close range is available. But he has been reported to not only be athletically built, but extraordinarily striking in appearance, with an unusual magnetism and charm. Even though he has hardly been in the public eye, several female fan clubs are reported to be following his whereabouts. His intellect is also reputed to be unmatched...

Much of the world will be watching this powerful heir and how he develops the constantly changing technologies in his industries. There is some question of how he will operate WT, since he is reported to be a very ethically concerned and religiously observant Jew. But in an unusual twist for a religious person, some sources say that he is also a very worldly individual, with past living experiences in various countries and contacts with people, cultures, and socioeconomic backgrounds which differ greatly from his wealthy origins...

The speculation about this mysterious individual has been so great that some are claiming that he will fundamentally seek to change the living conditions on the planet. Some have said that he is not only wealthy and intelligent, but has powers of perception and knowledge, that could only be specially G-d given...

As is the case with his present life, many rumors swirl around his past one. There are even those coming forward to report to local news sources throughout the world who swear that they have had contact with him on migrant farms and merchant ships. It is reported that he is the 'stranger' who about a decade ago was seen drawing crowds of onlookers in rural counties of the southeast...

While unconfirmed reports such as these are normally discounted and not normally reported by this newspaper, the sheer number of them, and the availability of some of them from what would appear to be reliable sources, would tend to indicate that they might have some validity, and should at least be investigated further by the press...

This reporter has repeatedly tried to obtain confirmed reports about Prince's upbringing, but has been unable to even confirm that he attended elementary school or had any other formal associations in his youth. His birth certificate does indicate that he was born in San Francisco, but the reporter trail becomes cold shortly after that. In fact, not much else can yet be confirmed until his appearance at Stanford several years ago, where Mr. Reed received his undergraduate degree and MBA, both with the highest level of honors...

Mr. Reed's obscure past has led some individuals to claim that he is an impostor, who has somehow assumed this post of power through unnatural means. In regard to this line of thought, some have remarked that he bears little resemblance to the attributes of his late parents. However, his uncle, who has operated WT since the death of his father, laughs in response to such a question and states that there is absolutely no question about his identity. Nevertheless, when questioned further on his nephew's earlier background or current status, the elder Mr. Reed refused to supply any additional information...

Sources in the medical field, who speak on condition of anonymity, say that his DNA and his cell typing are a clear match for his parents, though this information would have to have been arrived at by deduction by knowledgeable individuals, since no hereditary tests are thought to have been run by the family...

Given Mr. Reed's indistinct and almost shadowy past, and the limited information that is available on him currently, Mr. Reed may be the most underreported celebrity in modern times, certainly in the past generation, when instant communications around the globe—many sold by WT—have allowed virtually no powerful person or significant personality to hide or escape from scrutiny.

Despite the absence of public facts on Mr. Reed, this reporter, after much investigation, believes that there is a high probability that some of the many current unconfirmed reports surrounding Mr. Reed will eventually bear some amount of truth. If this is the case, then the congruence of Mr. Reed's current and past lives, will make for some very interesting news and analysis indeed. But whatever the true nature and origins of Prince Reed, it is clear that this mysterious individual, or the "stranger", as some refer to him, will continue to intrigue the public for some time.

Daniel Kahn, the experienced, highly esteemed, and Pulitzer Prize winning reporter at the *L. A. Times*, who had written the above article and was based in San Francisco, continued to keep a very watchful eye on Prince. The reporter was normally a very dry, factual type of guy, but he had early on become emotionally attached to the Prince story and determined subconsciously to follow its every nuance. At first, he didn't realize the real reason for this. He thought that it was simply because Prince was the first person about whom he had reported that he had been unable to fully understand, the first individual on whom he had so little detail after so much effort. Later, he would realize that those factors paled in significance to something else. Like so many others, it was the personal odyssey that he had started when he came in "contact" with Prince.

After less than a year, Prince became the chief operating officer of WT. Then, it became impossible for him to keep all of his intentions and motivations hidden. The reporter at the *L. A. Times*, Mr. Kahn, the tenacious person that he was, as well as many others, attempted to interview every individual with whom Prince came into contact. Nevertheless, strangely most people who regularly had contact with Prince would not speak. It wasn't that Prince had asked them not to say anything, even though he might have preferred less publicity at this time; believing strongly in free choice, he would never attempt to muzzle or censor anyone. It was just that everyone who developed a relationship with Prince seemed to evolve a strong loyalty to him. They felt that he gave them something immeasurable of himself for which they were immensely grateful. No one could quantify or put into words what that quality was, but virtually everyone in touch with him felt that benevolence and kindness. As a result, they treated his self-interest as their very own. So what the reporters were able to report was mostly what they overheard in conversations, possibly through snooping, and hearsay that was passed on to them by casual observers of Prince's behavior. This only added to the perception that Prince was mysterious. It had been one thing when they had heard past second and third hand reports of his enigmaticalness. It had been another when they had been able to obtain so little personal and insider professional news on someone whom they could now verify did exist so close to them. The lack of information only served to drive them harder.

If the reporters were mostly unsuccessful at obtaining private items on Prince, they were eventually to become saturated over the years with news to report on his public roles. At first however, they had to obtain even that information indirectly from the policy actions taken within WT, and that initial data was scanty. When

Prince took over the operation of WT, he had evaluated that he already had a well run company, as a result of the competent efforts of his uncle. With his unusual ability to size up people, he made a decision to meet all the managers. He would make no major policy changes for a while until he could observe the people and discuss their professional and personal goals with them. When he had finished that process over several months, he decided to meet with the top and middle management whom he had decided to retain. Later he would review with them the managers and employees working under them.

"Ladies and gentlemen, thank you for coming here," Prince said from the podium. "Since I took over at WT several months ago, I have talked with all of you in this room. If that's not the case with everyone here, then there's been an oversight on my part, and please let me know. Everyone in this room, I have decided to retain as part of WT, but there are others, for whom that is not the case. We are not in the midst of any kind of downturn in business—in fact we are still growing rapidly—so I know that it is highly unusual that I would choose at this time to lay certain people off. I will be running this corporation somewhat differently, and I am glad to discuss this with you today."

A loud buzz went up throughout the room. Prince let it continue for a short time. Then he smiled and said, "My colleagues, you are not going to learn much by gabbing to your neighbor about the surprise you may have just received. Though you may not realize it yet, I value questions, because that is the only way you can learn what's going on. I am not going to spoon feed you what you need to know. You will have to find it out for yourself. Anything is on the table today. Which one of you will have the courage to begin the process?"

There was suddenly as much silence present in the large room as there had been noise the previous minute. It seemed to go on for the longest time, until some of the participants are said to have concluded that unless someone asked a question, they would be required to stay indefinitely; certainly, Prince seemed not the least bit concerned with the wait. Finally, a small, bald headed man with glasses, holding a pen and pad in his hand, stood up from his seat and tentatively raised his hand. When immediately recognized, he said, "With all due respect, sir, could you tell me, why you have chosen to do these layoffs now in the midst of prosperity?"

"Very good question, Mr. Jardin," Prince said. Before responding, he smiled broadly and slowly looked around the room until he seemed to personally catch the eyes of each person. As the reporters heard it told later, each individual there then seemed to become almost entranced with his presence, calm down, and place their trust in him.

"Colleagues, this company is great. It was built by my family and I have the awesome responsibility of continuing this management. I pledge to you that the changes I make here today and in the future will hopefully not be frivolous or trivial. I am truly sorry for the disruption in your lives and in others that will be required by the changes.

"What makes a company great, however, is nothing more than the people who operate it. In reviewing our people, I can see that some of them are operating at cross purposes to others and against the best interests of the company. In this regard, I am not trying to change the company's course as much as I am trying to make sure that all of us are capable of working together to achieve company goals. Though I am requiring that some people leave in your departments—and I will meet with you individually to discuss those people—the actual amount of staffing in each of your departments will be determined separately based on business conditions. So even though you may be laying off people in your department, we may be still hiring."

Again, there was a long silence. Then a woman rose and said, "But Mr. Reed, how can we do this? I have reviews in my department that I do every year. Some of the people whose employment you may be terminating may have recently received an excellent review; there are others whom you may have chosen to keep that I would frankly not mind losing, if you understand what I mean."

Prince again smiled. "Another excellent question, Mrs. Rose." She jumped in surprise when she heard her name, not imagining that he could have remembered his five minute interview with her, nor still be aware of her position in the company.

"Okay," Prince said, "I know that you think that this has all the possibilities of conflict. You are worried about the worst. But I don't think in most instances that my independent assessment will disagree with yours as a manager. After all, I have also evaluated all of you personally, and think highly of you. So I believe we are likely to think alike.

"I think that for the most part, I will merely be speeding up something that you want to happen anyway. And in cases in which we disagree on a person, I think that if you will reflect on that person and situation, you will likely realize that you should now pay attention to that doubt or hunch that you may have previously tried to shut out of your mind. Sometimes we'd rather not deal with a bad situation or resolve a conflict, so we convince ourselves that it is really okay, when it isn't."

That brought on the next question immediately. "But with all due respect, Mr. Reed, how can you come into our departments and spend only five or ten minutes with a person and tell us something, when we've been evaluating someone for years? And you haven't even seen them in the work context. You've only interviewed them. Is that really fair? Please explain that to me. I don't want to kick out the wrong person."

"Good question, Mr. Goodman! That's the spirit," Prince said. "I don't want you doing something that you feel is wrong. Once we talk through my choices, then you will have a chance to disagree with me and we will discuss it. I will definitely hear you, and we will most likely reach a consensus. It will be the rare case in which we don't agree when the process is finished. You will see."

"Mr. Reed, I think what the last person was also asking is how you can make a decision in such a short time. That's also bothering me," a short lady with gray hair said.

"Yes, Mrs. Johnson, I should have answered that," Prince said. "It does seem presumptuous to almost all of you, doesn't it?" He again caught every eye in the room. His face was no longer smiling and he seemed to be in a distant place. Suddenly, like a tidal wave sweeping through their consciousness, they realized that their leader standing before them that day was a substantial person and that they were in the process of witnessing something important. They waited impatiently for him to continue.

"I'll try to explain this to you," Prince said. "If you do not understand all that I say, please know that my intentions are good and that it will work out.

"We all have our roles in life. G-d places us on this earth to play those roles and in doing them, we interact with each other. We can't do them in isolation. All of us depend upon each other.

"Now, in order to perform these roles, we are all given certain strengths and weaknesses. One of the functions that I perform in my life is that I am CEO of WT. Everyone knows that the CEO formulates strategy. What most CEO's should do, but do relatively little, is choose the people that should be working at their firm. In other words, they should be matching the people with their strategy.

"That still leaves the question of how I can choose people so quickly. Obviously, if I didn't choose people quickly, I would never finish the process, because there are so many of you. But, still you wonder how I can fairly do, what so many of you can't.

"The answer to that is simply that I have special talents in that area. Some of you are good at tennis or billiards, or debating. For me it's people. I can see people and I can see them quickly. I know what their motivations are and whether they intend to support the company or whether they are just out for themselves."

"But how can you see those things?" Mrs. Johnson said.

"Sometimes I see halos. Other times I feel their brain waves, or perceive their thoughts. In those particular instances I can tell you why I feel a certain way.

"But there are other times when I know something about a person, but can't necessarily tell you why it's true. You know that some of you are especially sensitive to certain foods. You may be unable to eat dairy products—say cheese as an example of a specific product. Your brain doesn't have to be able to identify the process by which your body has an allergic reaction. But once that reaction happens over and over again, you learn that cheese is a problem. So it is with my perception of humans. I see certain characteristics repeated in people, and after a while, I know how that person with those characteristics will react to a future event."

Then Prince left the podium and began pacing gently in front of the group. Finally, he turned to them and spoke. "I will rarely demonstrate this power to people, just for the sake of proving a point. This power is G-d given and I take no credit for it. I was born with it, just as someone is born with red hair. Still, at this moment, I must gain the confidence of all of you. Our time on this earth is limited, particularly at this juncture of the world. I cannot wait for you to trust me through a couple of years of trial and error, even though I know that would otherwise demonstrate my point."

Then he turned again to the woman with gray hair and specifically addressed her. "Mrs. Johnson, in order to demonstrate what I'm talking about, I would like to answer your next concern—it's not really a question at this time—even though you have not yet verbalized it. Would it be okay if I verbalize it and respond?"

Mrs. Johnson blushed. At first she seemed tongue tied. Then she pushed out her response. "Well...if you already know it, I can't...can't really hide it from you, can I? Normally, I wouldn't bring it up, because it's rather..."

"Rather embarrassing?" Prince said. He nodded to see if she agreed.

"Yes, very embarrassing," Mrs. Johnson said. "At least to me."

"That's why I'm asking your permission to say it," Prince said. Then focusing again on the group, he said, "But it needs to be said today, because we need to get these things out on the table. The issues that you are hiding in your heads, your worries, your constraints, need to be out in the open. We need to address them to move forward."

Catching Mrs. Johnson's gaze again, he said, "It's really not all that bad Mrs. Johnson, what you're thinking. In fact, it's very natural for you to feel that way. Do I have your permission to say it?"

"Yes," she said. Another loud buzz—this time of anticipation—went up in the room and then just as suddenly fell off, waiting eagerly for the demonstration. Prince's audience was now spellbound.

"Mrs. Johnson, what you are thinking is that this is all a lot of huey. You came to WT over a decade ago, thinking that this would be your last job, that you would retire here, at the premiere firm in the industry. You've worked hard and loyally all these years. Everything has been going well and according to plan. You received promotion after promotion and the company couldn't be doing better. And then you come here today. And I look as if I am going to disrupt everything."

Prince paused for a moment. "I'm not finished Mrs. Johnson, but I would like you to agree that so far I'm on track, and that you'll invite me to finish."

Mrs. Johnson was smiling the way someone does when they are caught in a light prank. She was almost relieved. She nodded yes.

"Thank you. There's more to it than that. Mrs. Johnson, you are seriously questioning this 'stuff' on G-d that I mentioned. You don't want any part of it. Oh, it's not that you don't believe in G-d or attend your church. It's just that you are amazed that I would choose to mix G-d with work in such a bold manner. And quite frankly, you're also really worried that I'm a little bit off my rocker, that I will not have the hard headed focus of previous family members at this company, in order to continue to dominate our markets and stay highly profitable. At this moment, you don't like the uncertainty of your future here.

"Now lest some of you think that I was smart enough to know Mrs. Johnson's background and guess well on this subject, let me say something more specific about Mrs. Johnson. At this hour, she is also worried about her daughter's performance in college and her husband's recent health; she talked to him just before the meeting. These are two things that she would have made public anyway, so I haven't violated her confidence here. Have I said that all correctly, Mrs. Johnson?"

Up to that point in time, Mrs. Johnson had been relatively composed. But with Prince's last remarks, her mouth fell open in amazement. The best she could do now was slowly nod her head. Another loud buzz went up in the room.

"Now, it is my turn to respond," Prince said. "I know that this is on the minds of a lot of you today. That's why I wanted to address these issues. I cannot allay all of your concerns overnight. Only some additional time will do that.

"When I began this meeting, I told you that I would be running this corporation somewhat differently. It doesn't mean that we will not be just as conscious of profits. But what we will realize is that profits go hand in hand with our ethical behavior and our serving G-d.

"Day to day, this might not have much impact on your world. Mr. Barnes," Prince said pointing to a man on the first row. "You're still going back to your office after the meeting to order that paper for the plant in Kansas. But on the macro scale, how we use those profits, how we use our influence, will make a difference. For example, Mrs. Johnson, one of the changes I will be instigating is that we will give ten percent of all of our corporate profits to charities. And because I am interested in charity, I am very interested in our profit being as high as it can possibly be."

A gasp went up in the audience. The chief financial officer, Mrs. Larson, was recognized. "Mr. Reed, I wish that we had discussed this before the meeting. Our stock price will surely immediately fall severely, hurting all of us with stock or options, though sir, the stock is overwhelmingly yours to do with what you'd like."

Prince smiled. "Yes, the market is irrational and the stock price will initially fall."

"With all due respect, sir, there is nothing irrational from my point of view about the stock price falling, if the investors have that much less profit to either reinvest or pay out in dividends," Mrs. Larson said.

"Yes, Mrs. Larson, that would be correct," Prince said, "if our profit was static. But a key principle of the world is that it is not static. Life is always in movement, always changing. If we are no longer changing, we are dead. We must literally exchange the air we breathe and almost all of the molecules of our body with our environment in order to stay alive.

"How do I relate that to what you're pointing out here? Well, as well as we've done in the past, it's for specific reasons up to this point. If we don't follow through on those reasons, if we instead hog our profit and keep it only for ourselves, then we will cease to become what we have been, which is the most successful firm on the planet.

"How many of the successful firms, profit wise, of the last century, remain that way today? Okay, many of you think that it's because the management wasn't smart, or the firm was unlucky. But that's superstitious; it's making up a reason that's untrue to try to explain a phenomenon. The real reason is G-d and G-d's natural order. I know that many of you think that I am superstitious with this emphasis on G-d. But it's really the other way around."

"How do you see it?" Mrs. Larson said.

"I see it very differently than you," Prince said. "It's a different model of the way life works. And I know that almost everyone in this room is going to have some trouble with it until they see not only the success that it will bring to this company, but the joy it will bring to our lives.

"You see what I perceive about those large companies that weren't successful, is that they lost their grounding, their identity, their reason to participate in G-d's world. When the egos at the top and throughout the management became too large, they failed to serve G-d's purposes. People in these companies were merely out for themselves. As Hillel of the Jewish tradition says, it's okay—even commendable—to be for yourself, but certainly not only for yourself. And when these companies were only out for themselves, when they weren't serving their customers, their suppliers, the planet, well, then they hit troubles. Of course, at first, no one noticed, like a large tree's trunk that begins to rot on the inside, but then years of abusing others caught up with them. One can not refuse to serve G-d's purposes and continue to live like a king on this planet."

Then a wiry middle aged gentleman stood up. "Mr. Reed, I've considered myself a religious man all my life. And I truly want to believe what you say. If what you say is true, then how will we know? Will it just be that our profits will stay the same, instead of our firm going into decline? If we continue to work hard at our jobs, and you decide to give all of this money to charity, then I want a sign from G-d that He appreciates it and that it has been worthwhile. What will be our sign?"

"Mr. Torres, surely you shall have a sign," Prince said. "You may rest on that.

"Mr. Torres, one of the unwritten laws of the universe about money is that in the long run no one may have wealth to which he or she is not entitled. Surely, we see that evil people have wealth. But wealth is a test and those who fail that test, that do not share it with the unfortunate, do not have the happy, fulfilled lives of which they are capable.

"G-d decides how much wealth a person will have. So when a person takes more than his share, then he must lose it. You see, each one of us is a receptacle, a spiritual container, as well as a physical body. We are capable of only holding so much. If you fill a cup too full of grape juice, it will overflow and go to waste. No one will enjoy it.

"But now, if we give some of that wealth away, so others can drink freely as well, there's room in the cup for more juice. And then we are free to, not restricted and constrained from, picking up the juice that is sweetly offered to us from the universe. You see, the first way, there's a wall built around a person spiritually and physically; they cannot partake of the pleasant beauty around them, simply because there's no room in their cup. But in the second example, the more the individual gives away, the more room there is to receive. And we are on this earth to receive, to receive G-d's abundance, His magnificence. Through the exchange with people and with our environment, we can enjoy the diversity of life here. The first example is a form of death. The second is truly holy and life itself.

"But Mrs. Larson and Mr. Torres, I have not answered your concerns yet. Mrs. Larson, you were upset about what you accurately predict will be the immediate fall in our share price. And Mr. Torres, you wanted a sign from G-d that our charity has worked its magic. The answer is one and the same. Yes, the stock price will initially decline precipitously, but the action of giving ten percent of our profits to charity, will be like an investment on which we earn a return. Our profit will be ten percent higher next year than it is now projected as a result of our charitable giving this year. Our stock price will be higher next year than the analysts now project it to be."

Then a gentleman stood up and carefully said, "It seems to me Mr. Chairman that if you can read our thoughts today, or any time, then we have no privacy in front of you. I'm trying to figure out what that means when we communicate with you."

"Mr. Richter, let me say that I cannot always read every thought that is flowing through your head. I am just a person. Just like you, I must filter most of my information; otherwise all of your thoughts bouncing around here today would prevent me from thinking my own thoughts. What I see is merely what I choose to focus on. We all have that limitation, no matter what perceptive abilities we possess.

"Having said that, it is true that I do have some abilities. But I have a sacrosanct responsibility not to misuse the information that I receive, whether it through my extraordinary abilities, or a conversation I have with someone like yourself. My responsibility is all the greater because of my perceptions. We all have that responsibility to each other regarding information we receive, for example to avoid idle gossip about people, whether it is true or not.

"Now, I want you and everyone else here to know that whether I am reading your thoughts or not, the most important factor in my relationship with you, or the company, or with anyone out on the street for that matter, is your honesty. When we are truly honest with each other, then our Divine souls shine through. When we are honest with each other, and do not let our egos get in our ways, then we give each other the essence of ourselves. We can then share each other, just like the juice in the cup."

There were many additional questions relating to the previous discussion. Then a young woman stood up and said, "Mr. Reed, what other changes can we expect at this company now that you are at its head?"

"Broadly, just like our charitable contributions, we are trying to be better citizens of this world," Prince said. "Yes, we are still concerned about operating efficiencies and costs. But we will focus on these over the long term. We will not be focused on short term results every three months. We may judge a customer or supplier to be worth a long term investment, even though that supplier or customer is not optimal for us in the short run. We will focus on doing the right thing in a situation and the profits will continue to follow.

"What does this mean regarding some of our specific policies? Well let's take environmental policy. This is the area in which we will have the greatest influence. From this point, we are setting up an environmental department in this company that will report directly to me. We will use every influence we have in Congress and around the world to preserve the wilderness, the wildness, left on this planet. We will focus on what is left of the U.S. as well as helping poor countries have an incentive to preserve their rain forests.

"If some of you do not think that this will return to our profits, then think again. This will be part of our charitable work for one thing. And part of the return on our investment will be from the technologies that we will develop which will allow more efficient transport and use of resources in the production process and from conservation measures. Another return on our investment will be from industries we develop in poorer countries in order to relieve their reliance on extractive resources. Some of our return will be from investments we make to improve the lives of people around the globe. But finally and most importantly, if we don't do this, then our existence will become unbearable, and we will simply be unable to continue to live on this planet.

"This will be our boldest effort. There is no other company or person that will take on this role at this time. We must perform it."

Because of the large size of the meeting that day, Daniel Kahn was able to finally interview several people concerning their perceptions of Prince. The following is part of that article, which appeared in the *L. A. Times* a few days later:

Unusual Corporate Meeting Recently Held at WT

On Tuesday of last week, a highly unusual corporate meeting was held at World Technology headquarters in San Francisco, according to several employees who were in attendance. Joseph "Prince" Reed, who has recently assumed the helm of his family's corporate empire, as CEO, led the meeting.

According to these sources, Mr. Reed, or Prince as he is often known to those closest to him, announced that he has decided to lay off some of the managers in the company, apparently not for profitability or efficiency concerns, but because they do not fit into the company and its goals. He reportedly decided to do this after short interviews averaging five to ten minutes with each person over the last few months. Though he pledged to discuss his decisions with his managers before taking final action, this style of management has been termed by financial analysts watching the company, as too hands on, peremptory, and abrupt.

Mr. Reed also pledged that ten percent of the profits of the company would henceforth go toward charity and that the company would enforce a new environmental policy around the world.

In after hours trading, the stock fell 40% in extremely heavy turnover. Analysts watching its steep descent pointed to several factors: concerns about Mr. Reed's management abilities because of the uncertainty surrounding his layoff of employees, profitability questions resulting from the large charitable contributions pledged, and political difficulties that WT will face around the world based on its new environmental stance.

Regarding the stock price, one analyst, Elise Sand, was quoted as saying, "It is probably unprecedented that such a heavily capitalized stock—in this case the world's largest—would plummet 40% overnight, but Mr. Reed's management style appears to be that unorthodox. And then he put the icing on the cake, by announcing that he would no longer be interested in short term profits. Analysts just don't like being told that the company is not interested in next quarter's profits. What we want is predictable earnings."

Nevertheless, several key employees interviewed after the meeting and the stock price decline expressed confidence in the new CEO's ability to run the company. This appeared very surprising to analysts following WT's strategy. WT has been known in the past as a very smart, profit oriented company, which was able to attract management through the use of stock options, as well as favorably purchase other companies with its high stock price. After the stock fall, many of the employees' options are now seen as having little value.

There were also unconfirmed reports that in discussing the firm's strategy Mr. Reed cited G-d on a number of occasions as not only his, but the firm's source of strength and authority in this world. However, employees interviewed after the meeting generally refused to specifically comment on, or confirm or deny, the nature of the discussion. This reaction is considered highly unusual, since if Mr. Reed had even touched upon religion in the practice of business, that discussion would have been expected to generate considerable public controversy, because of WT's dominant position in the business world. Independent sources outside WT describe Mr. Reed as an observant Jew, though very little is known about his specific personal beliefs.

Mr. Reed's behavior at the meeting this week is seen as being all the more mysterious because of speculation about his obscure past. Comments have continued to swirl around Mr. Reed's origins, and around whether he was the mysterious stranger seen around a decade ago in unusual ports and agricultural locations around the world.

13

The reticence of WT employees to discuss their meeting that day had nothing to do with any directive on Prince's or anyone else's part to refrain from talking to the public. As previously pointed out, this would have been contrary to Prince's wishes. Rather, it had a lot to do with the unusual loyalty which Prince developed with those with whom he came in direct contact.

And there was another factor. This resulted from Prince's higher state of consciousness, which created brain waves of harmony and peace throughout Prince's wider environment. That consciousness was strong enough to tangibly influence the brain waves of others around him, even strangers physically near him, who had no other apparent relationship with him. People in regular contact with Prince began to think as he did; they in turn began to influence those around them, to think similarly. Of course, very few consciously understood this process. But the lack of understanding didn't make the process any less real or significant. To the contrary, most of what we cannot comprehend and must take on faith—for instance G-d's creative process—is what actually sustains our well-being and life on earth.

It was like a field in nature, in the process of primary succession, being colonized. At first there had been only the glacier; virtually no life could live in those conditions. After the glacier had retreated, melting and leaving the raw, uninhabited land, conditions for the growth of any species were still highly inhospitable. But there would be lichens and then that one pioneer plant which would move in and brave the new, difficult world—with its lack of shelter against the strong wind and sunlight—and thereby prepare the area for other similar plants; eventually smaller trees would follow, then bigger ones, and the changed world would become very inviting for the diversity of life. So too Prince was the pioneer who entered an environment essentially antithetical to life and also began the slow process of changing the culture, so that other people could follow him. Like the plants seeking to follow in the pioneer's footsteps, there were those who were initially attracted to Prince's vision of a world. And after those initial settlers in the relatively new environment, there would be the larger trees, the people with power and fame who would eventually follow. Those last people, the political, cultural, and business leaders, and the celebrities, would be ones who would lend their reputation to a movement that would finally attract the diversity of peoples around the globe.

Prince's choice to terminate the employment of certain individuals at WT was based on his recognition that those people would never, or at least would not in the near short-term period, be able to adapt to the new culture that he was creating at the company. No matter if Prince, or the people who followed him, colonized the land as pioneers, their soul types were not going to be able to adapt and grow in the new environment. For their sake, as well as the company's, it was better to break that tie immediately.

The practical result of the remaining employees refusing to talk, though perhaps seemingly incidental, was in fact not that way at all, and was quite significant indeed. The new culture in the firm that was developing needed time to mature; pioneer species that colonized new land almost always would initially face little competition from other plants. Their conditions were harsh enough, and they would surely expire if they also had to deal with the additional adversity of other species vying for their space and light. The lack of publicity into the interior workings of WT meant that positions on issues and relationships within the firm would not arbitrarily freeze and that the culture could evolve and continue to grow, expand, and strengthen, until its participants could face the harshness of the outside world of kelipah. Had there instead been dissension and disagreement with Prince, and not a united front presented to the world, then this would surely have cracked the protective surface around the firm, enough to invite the yetzer hara in. Then the sensitive, new life being created within WT would have likely been snuffed out; and if not suffocated, many of the resources of that new life would have been diverted to fight the enemy, severely retarding its future growth for years to come.

But the new culture taking root in the company, which would eventually spread from there, had that critical space, that necessary spiritual dimension, to grow stronger, and extend its range. Nevertheless, its first hold, though slightly protected at the initial stages, was extremely tenuous. Even though the hearts of the remaining employees prevented them from voicing their concerns to the outside world, many of their minds remained extremely critical, fighting with their hearts, and creating great conflict—the kind that had so afflicted Prince in his own coming of age. Their minds were highly rational instruments that told them that either Prince's predictions and model of the universe were the wonderful beginning of a new world order—one which they were incredibly privileged to personally watch and to participate in—or the craziest con job performed by a person of note. In fact, the level of discernment in the mind of a WT employee was one of the criteria which Prince had used to decide whether to retain that person. Those with a lower level of reasoning and emotional powers, whom he had decided not to retain at WT, would surely be the easiest to convert to his cause. Yet, with little substantive cognitive ownership, they would also be the easiest to be persuaded to abandon his spiritual concepts, especially in the case of the adverse reaction they would later face by opponents. Not only would they be poor representatives and advocates of his movement to thinking and influential people, because of their lesser mental and emotional abilities, but their significant rate of defection to Prince's opponents would give them great comfort and propaganda value. To the very contrary with the employees remaining at WT; though they tended to be the most skeptical, they would make the best converts. It would take them much longer to eliminate their doubts, but their doubts were only rational, and not so highly influenced by their immediate environment. Once their doubts were gone, they would support Prince with the intelligence, stability, knowledge, and steadfast advocacy, which he needed in a world full of the grave skepticism and suspicion that they had overcome.

The most important means for Prince to retain his delicate support among his remaining employees was for his predictions to prove to be true. The stock price hovered at a forty percent discount to its previous high for several weeks and then tried to rally several times, each instance chronically falling back to the lower resistance level on heavy volume. It was rumored that the stock price would have fallen even further except for the existence of a large purchaser at that price. The inability of such a major stock to recover, along with the general lack of news available about such a major company with an unknown new leader, did not inspire confidence among analysts. In the absence of news, analysts trafficked in rumors, and even when harder news emerged, refused to believe its authenticity. Thus, when profit of the company continued to rise, as had been originally projected, the stock price continued to hover close to its lowest levels of the year. The employees of WT were encouraged by the company's continued high level of profitability, but questioned whether the stock price would ever recover. This pessimism about the stock price was particularly prevalent during the first six to nine months, as stories circulated about management's decision to use a large portion of cash flow to invest in developing countries, not to mention the charitable donations that had already been fully factored into the stock price. The international investment was correctly perceived as having a long period of pay back, if it could even be said to have any return on investment at all.

But G-d was watching over Prince, just as he watches over us all, though we so often fail to recognize this reality. And though it was true that WT's investments in poorer, developing countries would not be immediately profitable, the cash flow from the other parts of the business began to increase immensely. No analyst could explain the exact reason for this, but once buying resumed in the oversold stock, there were many on the sidelines who were afraid of missing the rally. In a few months the stock price more than doubled from its previous low. It was suddenly—

and ironically, because of its much higher value—back on the buy list of virtually every analyst. The stories about the company, though perhaps as absent in details as the previous, cynical ones, touted the apparent amazing abilities of WT's new leader and his newfound vision in diversification around the world.

Though the stock price was important, a much more critical element was the progression of Prince's interpersonal relationships at WT. Perhaps the central question totally left unanswered by the meeting with management that day at WT was not as much whether Prince had the possibility of vision and good judgment—though the resolution of those issues still very much remained on the table—but that of his daily management style. In order to effect the changes he had discussed, he would have to be initially intimately involved in much of the company's individual decision making. He could not delegate the transmission of a culture that no one had fully learned. More critically still, the employees were concerned whether he could take his different vision and translate it into specific actions, when the demands of daily business might create an insurmountable inertia to doing so. Would he take the normal CEO route by distancing himself from the daily action; in fact, the question was more how he could not take the traditional CEO route, because it seemed impossible to be involved in specific decisions on issues while also necessarily setting the overall direction of such a large company?

With Prince's seemingly boundless energy, and singular commitment at this time to his business, he was able to resolve the above concerns by dividing his day into three parts. In the first part of the day, Prince chose to demonstrate foremost to his employees that he was a field commander among his own troops. Each morning he would be seen in a different department of the company reviewing the business at hand. With his superior intellect and judgment of people, he was quickly able to grasp the specific business concepts and contribute, no matter at what level, to the actual business taking place. To have a charming leader of such a firm call upon you, and discuss your individual concerns, was not only gratifying but engendered unusual loyalty. And to watch his reasoning abilities, inspired great confidence in his leadership; his suggestions were specific, knowledgeable, and helpful. Moreover, Prince would not just exchange ideas, but would often be found helping a person complete their tasks, particularly if they were behind schedule; employees were delighted, not scared or concerned, with his visits, because they actually found them helpful and time saving. Prince's departmental work did not exclude anything occurring around him at the time, including filing or running computer reports, leaving messages or getting specific questions answered. More than one person was surprised to receive a voice or e-mail from Prince asking him when a shipment of parts was likely to arrive at a factory in a part of the world. Such activity on Prince's part really did seal his reputation that he was omnipresent and took responsibility for everything that was happening at the company. Far more importantly, however, his employees saw a humble individual, one who despite his great wealth, intelligence, role, good looks, athletic prowess, and charm, never found a person with whom he didn't want to associate or value. Once an employee had contact with Prince, he no longer questioned why Prince was his leader. In fact, the opposite was true; that employee was determined to serve Prince in any way he could. Prince was the employee's guide, his mentor, the person seen taking his limited time to teach that person about himself and his role in the world. Through Prince, each person felt G-d's special touch and concern just for him.

In the afternoons, Prince would meet with his staff, those he directly supervised, and set the firm's goals and agendas. With these major company department heads, including the newly created environmental department, he would set company policy, and learn what was occurring in those areas of the company he had not recently visited. These employees were the ones in whom he had greatest confidence, whom he expected to intimately learn the company's new culture. They were the group that would operate the company and teach others when Prince was absent, because Prince knew that he could not continue to work in such a detailed capacity in the company in the future. Finally, after work hours Prince spent his time reading company reports, analyzing financial statements, and thinking about company and personal strategy. Nights were also usually the time when he met with the spiritual advisory group and discussed a mixture of business and spiritual concepts.

In various articles, Daniel Kahn continued to report on Prince. He had now become the leading news authority on him and this is what he said in part at various times during this period:

Joseph "Prince" Reed continues to surprise analysts with sterling sales and profits. Shortly after Mr. Reed took over his family's business, WT, the stock sank in reaction to uncertainty about his abilities and his unprecedented decision to give ten percent of the company future profits to charity. Analysts also questioned his "green" stance throughout the world...

It appears as if Mr. Reed is having the last laugh on these matters. Mr. Van James, who follows the stock closely, commented that he apparently has the golden touch. "I don't know how he does it. No one thought he could do better with the company. Yet, quarter after quarter, he exceeds our expectations for sales and profits. I don't know where he pulls these numbers out of the air..."

Today, WT announced that it was signing a major environmental agreement with Brazil. This type of agreement is unprecedented between countries, so it is even more surprising between a company and a country. Because of its size, recent success, and international presence, WT has been compared to a country and this agreement is sure to add to that characterization...

All the details of that agreement will not be made public for some time. Apparently, WT officials, led closely by Mr. Reed himself, have been meeting with Brazilian officials for some time. Brazil's finance minister, Mr. Cardozo, commented that Brazil was very pleased with the outcome. He said, "Mr. Reed is a very special person who listens to our concerns. He himself approached my government and the

Brazilian people and asked us what he could do for us. He didn't just walk in and tell us what he wanted. We feel that this agreement will be good for both parties..."

As analysts study some of the details made public from the agreement signed last week between WT and Brazil, they are amazed by its ground setting principles. Several remarked that the U.S. government could have done the same years ago, before such environmental devastation occurred. Other agreements are thought to be currently being negotiated by WT with other countries, including one with Indonesia...

Apparently, in exchange for major investment in Brazil and a guarantee of employment of a certain number of Brazilian citizens, the Brazil government has agreed on a joint pact to stop the destruction of the remnants of one of the greatest rain forests on earth...

The WT agreement with Brazil prompted some surprise among U.S. governmental officials. A U.S. State Department spokesperson refused comment. But several Congressmen commented yesterday. Typical of some of the remarks was that of Republican Senator James Orton of Texas who said, "I honestly don't know what Mr. Reed is trying to do here. Perhaps he doesn't trust our government to go out there and make its own good decisions, so he has to do it all by himself. The American people elect representatives to lead them in this good democracy and I question why anyone should go around this process, no matter what their reputation might be..."

Prince remained focused on WT and its strategy and culture for about two years. During that period he cemented his reputation as a true business visionary. According to one of Daniel Kahn's columns,

...his style [was] a unique mixture of intelligence and humility...Here is a business leader who actually gets out into the field in order to get things done, and yet does it without threatening those around him. He seems to have no ego. People who work for him surprisingly want to do the right thing. They want to follow his suggestions and don't at all feel coerced into the changes he has been making at WT...In fact, there has been so much harmony and so little of the predicted conflict within WT, that some competitors and other detractors have intimated that he has cult like qualities of leadership, that he can convince those around him into doing whatever he wishes... Still, no one can argue with Mr. Reed's results. He has taken a company that was doing extremely well to new heights in a very short period of time. Now, "Prince watchers", as they call themselves, are wondering what the twenty something year old will do next.

Daniel Kahn's commentary was by far the best on Prince found in the media. From his base in San Francisco, Kahn had maintained the most contacts in WT and his pieces had been widely syndicated throughout the country and the world. The media would call on him to remark on the latest specifics on Prince. But while successful as a reporter on the subject, he was extremely frustrated personally. He knew, particularly as an award winning journalist, that all he essentially had reported about Prince was hearsay. Prince had refused to grant him or any other reporter an interview, unlike virtually all other well known personalities he had ever encountered. What was even stranger to him was what he saw as Prince's avoidance, almost eschewal, of any outside publicity. Why wasn't Prince willing to try to use the media to his advantage as all other business or political leaders, he wondered? And what really motivated this guy? Essentially, he knew little more about what made him tick than when Prince had suddenly moved into the spotlight at WT a couple of years earlier.

Kahn's natural reaction was to scrutinize Prince even harder, to stay up later at night in order to dig deeper. He had always found the answer before. Usually the explanation involved some kind of "dirt", perhaps relationships, from the past that would elucidate everything. But the harder he tried, the less real news stuff he could find. And what little he could see only continued to support the validity of the reputation Prince was building. Still, Kahn waited and kept looking. Before, he had been almost fooled by other prominent individuals; just when he had almost thought that they were straight arrows, almost nobility in a corrupt world, they had let him down. Now he didn't believe that anyone could be that good, particularly at twenty something. Prince would prove him right, he thought. It was just a matter of time.

14

When Prince had grown the WT culture to a point of self sustentation, when his staff had gained the wisdom and knowledge to lead the company in his absence, and when he had solidified his reputation as a business leader, then Prince substantially reduced his hours at WT, and looked outward. Puzzling all like Daniel Kahn who tried to follow his activities, he continued to walk two roads, a more public civic one, and a personal, religious one. The two would eventually merge and lead to the same place.

In what seemed be a rapid succession of events on the public side, Prince surprised the local political community by beginning to comment on community activities and then announcing that he would be an independent candidate for mayor of San Francisco. Despite his rising reputation, because of his extreme youth and lack of political experience, he was immediately discounted among a large field of prominent candidates. The power sharers at city hall and their retinue, with whom Prince had no previous alliances, looked up from activities upon the announcement, merely smiled knowingly, and then quickly went back to whatever their preoccupation was at the time, whether city hall or some extra curricular activity. He never even figured into their political calculations, nor much in the limited polls taken before the vote.

Prince ignored those established in power. He went directly to the public with his agenda and managed to publicize it. While the other candidates took shots at each others' turf, Prince focused strictly on the issues. Prince first engaged in a rational discussion of what the local government could and couldn't do, based on its abilities and resources, and then detailed how he could improve each area. The media viewed his approach as much too intellectual for the public at large; moreover, Prince offered little in the way of "goodies" to any established constituency. His policies, or agendas, if they could be called that, couldn't be pinned down as either liberal or conservative. They satisfied no particular faction, persuasion, or particular community. The environmentalists were very pleased with his recent actions in developing countries and endorsed his campaign ideas concerning local recycling and urban development. Yet many of them remained deeply suspicious of Prince because of his position at WT; and to add to that, Prince's campaign positions also still seemed to be pro-business. He had a detailed plan for regional business development that the chamber of commerce had approved, yet business leaders remained wary of this newly minted "green" leader. Consequently, no political analyst could observe Prince and see any comparable historical instance or model which would allow him to be taken seriously as a potential winning candidate.

Daniel Kahn commented in a column on the local mayor's race that,

...political analysts are puzzled, almost amused, by Mr. Reed's program. He seems to resonate most with intellectuals at the Stanford philosophy department, who have commented on his dialectical approach to reasoning, wherein he can seemingly resolve the conflict of two opposite issues. Mr. Reed sees no contradiction between what the environmentalists want and the business community needs...

Some have ascribed Mr. Reed's approach to the Talmudic learning he is reported to participate in through his Orthodox observance of Judaism. In those discourses, Mr. Reed is said to be able to resolve conflict between major Talmudic schools of thought. But one knowledgeable anonymous source states that his approach is much deeper than that. "Prince has the finest rational mind of this generation, but lest anyone underestimate him and think that he only operates on a rational plane, it should be said that he also thinks mystically, which is at a much more fundamental level. He believes that all oppositions in this life are illusions from a human viewpoint and are nothing but different physical characteristics of the absolute qualities given by G-d that underlie all life"...

Hmm! Sounds pretty deep to me. Has Mr. Moonbeam arrived in town to save us? Maybe his ideas are pretty good on the major issues, but I don't see how he can be all things to all people. Don't think the natives are going to bite on this one, even if they could understand it all. In fact, except for his business position, it's fair to say that he'd most likely be sized up as a crank, the category that so many current and previous independent candidates fall into...

And I certainly don't see any—I mean any—major organizations endorsing him, or privately encouraging their members to vote for him. Still, he has been totally underestimated before and come through. I must say that Mr. Reed certainly adds spice and drama to the election.

But the politicos were too involved in slinging mud in paid advertisements to notice Prince's very late movement in the polls. Munching grass contentedly in the sunset, they were unaware of the powerful force sweeping through the fields. By the end of the campaign, Prince had reached almost every household through mail and email in order to describe his philosophy of governing.

More importantly, unnoticed by his opponents, a small, but rapidly growing movement of people had gathered around his campaign office in support of him, and then fanned out through the streets to make personal contact with neighbors and friends. The first of these were WT workers on their own time, but then some of their acquaintances followed, and so on. Strange as it seemed, these supporters were not primarily concerned with the issues, though they were certainly in general agreement with Prince's positions. They advocated for him foremost because of his personal qualities. Unlike so many other politicians, Prince spent much of his day, just meeting and talking to the public. His idea was that five minutes with an individual, or a small group, was worth considerably more than all the high profile speeches he could make. As a result of that personal contact, his supporters spoke strongly of his spirituality and how they felt a connection to the process when they met him. They spoke of the fact that he seemed so real, so genuine, and as one person put it, so "nice, given that he's a politician". They said that even though he was running a campaign, he didn't seem to want anything from them, that he seemed to simply value his relationship with each one of them for who they were, not for what each could offer to him. One person said his presence created "a calm" within her, because he seemed to have no fear of the future. Another spoke of his blue eyes piercing her soul.

The rumors which circulated about Prince's supporters fit with the "Mr. Moonbeam" characterization by Daniel Kahn. It only made sense that if Prince were a little eccentric, his supporters might be a little unconventional, if not unbalanced, as well. And in general, it was thought that only impractical, whimsical people supported independent candidates, who had so little chance of winning. Why throw away your vote or support on such a person, the commentators wondered? Consequently, as the campaign wound down to the wire, virtually no one was publicly admitting to voting for Prince. To be sure, the pollsters were having trouble finding movement in the polls; there was a very large percentage of undecided and the numbers were not coalescing around any one person. As one pollster privately remarked, "I wouldn't want to admit it to the public, but we know less about this election than when we started the campaign." Still, no seasoned observer gave Prince any chance. They were quite wrong.

The Sunday *Los Angeles Times* following the election had the following column in part by Daniel Kahn. His editor, Ken Graves, worried that his column was quite a bit more speculative than most of his hard hitting work, but given Kahn's reputation, and the unusual political circumstances, he allowed it to print as originally written:

The United States has a new political phenomenon, Joseph "Prince" Reed! California has always led the nation in new political movements and now apparently a powerful, new one has been born this week...

Prince Reed took the political establishment by total surprise this past Tuesday when he achieved a 50% majority at the polls and became the new mayor elect of

San Francisco. No poll had even indicated that he had climbed out of the single digits in support, and now he has won without a runoff!

No established constituency had even endorsed him. One observer at city hall even remarked that he had wondered if the voting machines had erred and chosen the wrong candidate. Other politicians and political watchers expressed complete shock at his election. His election was such a surprise that virtually no one has considered what it might mean. In fact, no one I spoke with has any knowledge of people that Prince will bring into his administration...

The election of Prince sent political analysts of all persuasions scurrying to figure out what the public was thinking when they entered the polling booth. Prince's election breaks the rule book in more than one area. As one seasoned analyst, who's seen it all, put it, "We'd be scratching our heads if he did it as an independent, but look, the guy's also got no political experience, no political machine, ran a highly unconventional campaign, and isn't close to cracking 30. And that doesn't even get to the campaign issues, which were confusing. All he had was money—plenty of that—but there's no evidence that he even used much of his fortune. Based on those realities, it was no surprise when he didn't even register in the polls. And now these results! It's unreal. It turns all political wisdom upside down. Does he have some kind of magic, or some kind of connection with G-d?"...

Maybe that's not so far fetched as it sounds. Seriously, folks, that's the word on the street. It's not my job to report hearsay, but in this case, I'm hearing from those who know him well, or not so well, that this guy seems to have some kind of supernatural connection.

Oh, some of you will say it's just a streak of good luck. A lot of people have their time, but it passes and they float down to earth. It all balances out. But something's different about this guy. And now, now that he will be the mayor of a major city, we'll have to figure it out.

Different, I say, because look at his accomplishments by his mid-twenties: rare intellectual ability and Hollywood looks, CEO and majority owner of the largest firm in the world, multiple Olympic gold winner, and now mayor.

Is this luck? Luck is something that seems to happen at random, like you win the lottery. Can it also be consistent winning behavior over odds that seemingly defy you? I don't know. How do we explain this past election win? No logic will explain it; yet, we cannot call it some kind of random event either. Hundreds of thousands of people went to the polls and voted for him.

It must be that Prince has a unique ability to convince people. What is it that they see in him? Other people have certainly had good looks, and though his intellectual ability is rare, it is not unequaled in history. Certainly many previous great minds had no particular ability to influence others.

I must tell you I'd like to explore this with him personally. But he has granted no interviews. So I've had to rely on those who've met him individually.

Admittedly, my sample is not big enough to be scientific. And each has a different story to tell. But what I sense is that they all have the look of someone who has been converted. I mean that when I mention his name each one of their faces lights up with a glow, almost as if each one is referring to a religious experience. I don't think that I heard a negative word about him. Each seemed to have a loyalty to him. It was like he was a member of the family, and only a revered one at that.

I heard comments such as, "It's amazing. He doesn't care one bit about himself." Or, "His motivations are totally pure." Or "He's only interested in others." Or finally, "He's focused on building a better world."

Now guys, I try to take things at face value. But in all sincerity, I can't fathom all of this. I mean this world is just not generally made up of angels or saints. If they really do exist—beat on me for saying that even that's debatable—they seem to concentrate in some religious cloister. I mean how many do we know outside running the business world? If you even answered one, I'd like to know who you think qualifies. Maybe we should have a contest. Wait, I think that Prince would surely win.

Some have said that Prince must be a leader of a cult. The way people light up when I talk about him makes you think so. But how does a cult leader run a modern corporation?

Some have said he could be a prophet or a leader sent from G-d. Of course, history is full of false leaders and crowds following them, only to be let down. But those false leaders occurred before modern times, before the vast public read, before scientific reasoning and a free press ruled the land. We have no model for those who would delude us for long in our democracy.

We still have our false idols of course. They're the products we buy, the images we chase, but our idols are not generally people who we wish to worship. A healthy skepticism prevails, the very opposite of the expressions on the faces of the true believers around Prince that I talked with.

It almost reminds me of androids from another solar system in a sci-fi flick. These people talk logically, and perfectly organize their lives with intelligence, yet apparently blindly follow some person they hardly know.

Okay, I admit that I am outside the limits. It's not fair to criticize someone, or their followers, because they're different. But is my analogy so wrong?

Mr. Reed comes at us like a tidal wave. The world knows very little about him, or his motivation. Like a visitor from another planet, he descends upon us. Like a sci-fi story, he totally turns our world upside down, over night, without our so much as noticing that it is happening. We suddenly wake up with new leadership—with no loyalties to anyone and a youngster at that. This is scary, only we can't shield our eyes in the dark theater, because it's real life.

It was all right for him to do whatever he wanted before. But now he's in the public domain. He's running a major city. He should speak to the press and be interviewed. He should be understood by all of us.

Who is this person who can motivate so many of those around him to serve him? What are his goals and what are his intentions towards us?

But that Sunday when many were munching brunches over Daniel Kahn's column, Prince had temporarily turned his head away from politics. Politics was a bit of an unsavory necessity for his purposes. For the first time in months, he was free of the campaign and able to fully pursue his real love in life, his eternal relationship with G-d.

In a stand of sequoias on property which he had recently purchased, Prince stood with several dozen other Jews, his spiritual advisory group and others whom he knew that he could trust, and dedicated a new congregation. His "followers" watched as he chose the largest and most ancient tree and hugged it with all of his strength. Then, from that highest point in the forest, he turned to face them all.

The Hasidic Rabbi who had counseled him in Oklahoma City brought over a tub of water which he had gathered from the permanent stream some distance away. As he gently removed Prince's shoes and socks and then lovingly washed his hands and feet, the Rabbi's companion, the businessman from the Oklahoma City experience, spoke to those gathered. "When our honored Rabbi finishes his duties as a Levite in service to the Cohen, our leader will bless us with the priestly blessing. You know, in the Messianic world we will have, the Levite will be justly rewarded for his service in the Temple, and thereafter, to the Cohen; the Cohen will then serve the Levite in the World to Come."

After he had blessed his fellow Jews, channeling the Divine spirit to their souls, and they had raised their bowed heads and no longer diverted their gaze from him, Prince fell onto his knees and began a silent prayer. The fingers of both hands dug into the ground in front of him and raised clumps of soil. Then—all the witnesses later swore that it happened—Prince dropped the earth and reached into a container and brought out a piece of meat with each hand. He became perfectly still and waited. Soon two song birds crisscrossed in flight just before his face, coming so close as to seem to "kiss" him. Then an eagle landed on his shoulder and took the meat from one hand, but seemed to studiously avoid touching the meat in the other.

As the group gasped in awe—with a mixture of disbelief, fear, respect, and sense of the Divine—they became overwhelmed by yet another presence. A bobcat stood at the edge of their small gathering. Many of them instinctively drew back.

"Do not be afraid," Prince said. "The spirit of the L-rd is with this creature. Otherwise, it too would be afraid to approach us." Then he offered the palm still holding the meat and the cat approached and ate it carefully from his hand.

"You see the cat and the bird, usual enemies, sometimes competitors, stand here together in perfect accord, still and confident in the other's motivation. They stand with us humans and neither we, nor they, have fear. This—what you see here today in this moment—is the natural course of our existence. Our usual, or daily common experience, out there in our physical world, where we fight, and carve up, and possess, is anything but natural." With the last sentence he gestured toward the light filtering in from the outside of the grove.

"G-d has given to all categories of existence corresponding to the four letters of the Divine Name—the inanimate, the vegetative, the animal, and the human—a bounty to enjoy in this world. What we humans need, we have. To satisfy our needs and wants, G-d grants us—humans—dominion—free choice—over the earth, plants, and creatures, as well as ourselves. As *Genesis* says, we are the stewards of the earth. We are given great and good power, considerable resources, but with that comes great responsibility. We are responsible not just to ourselves, but to our families, our countries, and all mankind. Most of all, we are responsible to this earth, these trees, this stream, these rocks, these animals who sit in peace among us today, because they are defenseless and powerless in the midst of our fury. How dare us tear up this place, this world, which nurtures us!" Prince's face suddenly took on a mixture of passion and rage.

"We complain to G-d about our circumstances, our plight, and yes, it is harder in this world than in Gan Eden. But it is our error, our ego, our stupidity, that leads to our plight. It is our behavior, and the consequences of that behavior, that lead to our fear and pain, to the pain and fear of animals, and it is that fear which leads to our and their fighting. That fear constricts the life flow, the Divine Light, which would flow freely throughout our systems, if only we would allow it. You see we must receive back what we give, and we must give back what we unjustifiably take from our environment, from our neighbors, our pets, and everything else in this world.

"It is within our power to bring the peace you see here today. G-d has granted us goodness and life. It is our choice. But unfortunately we often cannot see this. If we could, our choices would be obvious in this life. That is our challenge in this world—to make the right choices when they are not so obvious, when it is a matter of faith in G-d, and not a matter of reward to ourselves."

When he had finished speaking, the doctor who had aided him in Oklahoma City approached him with a container of olive oil. He poured all of its contents over Prince's head.

Prince returned to San Francisco with the three advisors from Oklahoma City, whom he had not seen for several years. The lively and enjoyable conversation ranged from suggestions for Prince, to Talmudic arguments, to jokes, but Prince knew that they wished to accompany him for a more important, if yet unknown, reason. When they reached the driveway of his home, they could make out a large crowd which stood in a line outside the entrance of his house.

"Please pull over to the side of the road and do not go into the driveway," the Hasidic Rabbi said to the driver.

"What's this?" Prince said. "I expect publicity now, but why would they be lined up outside my house?"

"You serve two roles now," the Rabbi said. "You're going to be a mayor, and from there, who knows? But you have a more important role. You're also now a Rebbe. You are a leader of the Jewish people. You will feel the pain and joy of those Jews you do not personally know. This combination is a first for this world."

"But..."

"But nothing. You have made your teachers proud and you will serve G-d well in your task," the Rabbi said.

"But I am not only humbled," Prince said, "but puzzled. Why are they suddenly lined up? They weren't here before."

The Rabbi's eyes twinkled, just as they had done in Oklahoma City. "I am still glad to be of assistance to my former student, whom the world knows as brilliant. The wind blows them in." Watching Prince shake his head in some disbelief, he added, "I give you my word that not one of us, nor anyone else I'm aware of, relayed, or said anything, that would lead to this."

"Then why have you ridden with me all this distance? It's because you knew that I would face this," Prince said.

"That is true," the Rabbi said. His eyes were twinkling more intensely than ever just then. "We did. And even though generally your powers of perception are greater now than ours, still it is possible, even likely, that we might see some things, which relate specifically to you, which you may not be able to see yourself. That's because you must still carry around a little bit of an ego, to physically exist in this world and do G-d's Will. For that reason, we and the spiritual advisory committee will always be available to protect you. We will be your extra senses, when you cannot physically be present, or when the act of physically viewing something keeps you from spiritually viewing it in the proper light."

"So, how did they all decide to come now?" Prince said.

"It's Sunday night. They've been waiting since the afternoon. Every Sunday, they will come now and ask for your advice. You must give it. This is what G-d wants," the Rabbi said.

"And they just knew it would start today?"

"As I said, when the wind blows," the Rabbi said. "When there's a spiritual need, and there is a source which can satisfy that need, then the two of them are drawn together. These people didn't all know to consciously come here; many of them were simply drawn here and others followed. It's a big vacuum. There's a huge force out there. The universe is propelling this."

"But I've not even taken the oath of office yet. I'm supposed to represent all groups in the City. It will look unseemly for a mayor to also be a 'preacher man' already. Especially when I'm not even an ordained Rabbi, and did not run on that premise," Prince said.

"Yes," the Rabbi said, "that's the challenge you face. It will not be easy. But there's no turning back. You accepted the challenge. These people need you now. The time is short to establish a Messianic Age. And if we are to get there from here, we've got a tremendous amount of work to do." He looked at Prince with the same ferocity that had caused Prince to jump in his bed in Oklahoma City. Then he added, "The heart of this whole thing is marrying the Divine presence with the political. You must be both the administrator and leader in the physical world and G-d's representative on earth. You must carry the Divine Light into the darkness of the physical world, and your acts of good must sweeten the bitterness of this world. You must transform the evil into goodness."

Prince sat back stunned. As great as his powers were, he was tired. So much had happened that day and that week. Only some private time with G-d, and the Divine Light, would rejuvenate him. Yet that was unavailable to him at that time. Only his faith in G-d could carry him at that moment.

Suddenly the tone of the Rabbi changed. His eyes misted over and he grabbed Prince's hand. "I can't exactly know how you feel," the Rabbi said," but I'm fairly sure I know. What a time to leave you! I know how I personally feel.

"From this point, the anonymity, whatever is left of it, and the concealment of your purpose and your powers on this earth, will dissipate—quickly vanish. Your enemies—the yetzer hara—will be out in full force. No longer will we have the advantage of plotting slowly to try to avoid mistakes. Our opposition will force our hand, and only our advance preparation and determination will help us. It will also be harder for the spiritual advisory committee and all of us to communicate with each other, without losing the cover that we need later. We must rely on our bonds of trust, our intimate knowledge of each other, and our ability to signal one another. Even now, to maintain that cover, it will be necessary for you to depart at this moment from the car. We can't stay here longer, and we absolutely cannot drive you to the house. You must walk."

"How do you feel, right now, Joseph?" the doctor said.

"Alone," Prince said. Then he smiled. "But I am not alone at all. G-d is with me. Thank you all, for everything, and if I don't talk to you again before Gan Eden, then it's been a pleasure. One could not ask for better teachers." As he grabbed the door handle, he said, "I'm truly blessed. G-d has blessed me. Praise the L-rd."

"Don't go quite yet," the businessman said. "Joseph, I want to tell you that you've exceeded all of our expectations. We are the ones who are blessed." The other two of them nodded. "Remember that despite the divide, the deafening noise and kelipah which will separate us, you can reach out. We may not be able to respond in a traditional fashion, but we will hear you and we will help you bear your pain, through our thought, speech, and action. Just as G-d will support you when you ask for assistance, so we too, as G-d's agents, will do the same. Our response may not be directly apparent to you, but there is no doubt that you will feel it. The universe will support you."

"Go with our love and may we see you soon in the Messianic Age," the Rabbi said.

15

When Prince left the vehicle, he once again had the sinking feeling of aloneness. He had not felt such abandonment since before his entrance into the building in Oklahoma City. Even with his acute powers, which he had polished, and even with his intense training, he felt personally unprepared to face those who patiently waited for him. For a moment he paused, praying to G-d, "Oh Ein Sof, why me now? I am willing, but I cannot possibly do the kind of service which is needed here. I will let you down."

He did not expect an answer, at least at that time. Though G-d listens to our prayers and is concerned, Prince knew that G-d doesn't always answer us at the time and place, and in the manner, we might choose. Like a parent watching over His children, G-d is always looking out for our best welfare. Like children making a request of a parent, our views of our needs are subjective and narrow, and our solicitations, if granted, might actually adversely affect our welfare. So, it is not surprising that we often do not receive the response for which we ask. More often than not, we are answered, but cannot, or perhaps are not willing, to hear the answer. Good communication takes both a good receiver, as well as a giver, and very often we are poor receivers. We might expect something like a lightning bolt as an answer, but often our response is in the subtle form of a gentle touch, or a small comfort. Then there are the times when some dramatic event indeed occurs in direct response to our prayers, but our restricted consciousness cannot make the connection.

So Prince was somewhat surprised when he did receive an immediate answer to his prayer. Mind you, it wasn't specific spoken words, but rather a sudden understanding which calmed him. It was chochmah, the flash of wisdom, which can only originate with G-d, though humans, with their egos, will often take credit for it.

As Prince demurred on the edge of his lawn, he felt this intense feeling of pleasant warmth surround him and if the instant comprehension from G-d could be spoken, it might be put something as this: "Do not fear. I am with you My son. I will be with you always. I do not ever expect more than you can do. I only expect your best. Everyone who enters this world, no matter the status of his soul, whether tzaddik, or common person, has a specific purpose, a specific set of tasks that only he can perform, and those who honestly, faithfully, and humbly try to serve Me, by fulfilling their destinies, will inevitably question their own abilities. That is because every one of My children, no matter their ability or station in life, is nullified in My presence. Therefore, to go forward, you must have faith in Me. Now imagine My son, with all your powers, the humility, the insecurity, the smallness you feel now in My universe. Magnify this many times, and you will feel the pain of some of those who are now approaching you for help. I have given you the power to help them."

"You, oh L-rd, have indeed aided me. You have greatly empowered me," Prince said, "but I do not know how I can specifically help these people."

"I have given you the gift. Now you must start. If you will merely believe, it will happen."

Prince walked toward the group of people. They had stopped their conversations or their thoughts and had turned toward him. Some of the faces broke in smiles expressing joy at his presence; others seemed motionless, their dull eyes merely starring at each of his strides.

When he was in their midst, he paused and spoke softly. "I am sorry that each of you had to wait. In the future, I will have regular hours on Sunday."

They crowded around him before he could consider where and how he would greet and meet and talk to each person. Several of the men grabbed his hand in appreciation. Then as he examined all of them further, it seemed that a great veil had been lifted from around each one. Suddenly, he could see inside them, feel their thoughts, and sense their pain. They were connected to him as much as his limbs. Their concerns, their prayers, were now his. He could feel their passion as if he were inside them, yet he still retained the viewpoint, and objectivity—without ego—of an outsider. Their emotions were so overwhelming for him, on this first encounter, that he was forced to bend his large frame over in pain, gasping for breath. Then tears streamed down his face.

He sat for several hours listening to each story, assisting where he could. The words spoken covered the gamut of human experience and it is not possible to characterize all of the situations discussed then or in each future week. But in each situation, Prince was able to "read" the soul of the person and that person's connection to other souls. After several hours he even began to see a pattern, a general purpose among souls that had been established. For example, the answer to Susan's dilemma resided with Aaron to whom Prince spoke two hours later. Even though they might not even know each other, their destinies collided in some fundamental way, so the decision one made was crucial to the decisions available to the other. With his legendary memory, Prince put together this web of information about his followers, and continued to add to it in his mind from week to week, as additional Jews visited.

And it wasn't just his visitors whom he came to "know", but many of the people with whom they interacted. Within a year, he knew personal data, which he could recall at will, about several hundred thousand of his constituents in the City. While he was otherwise generally careful how he used private information, he did not hesitate to walk up to those whom he had not even been introduced and greet them, and ask them about the loss of a parent, or congratulate them on their son's acceptance at a university. People would be both stupefied and honored when something like that happened. It only served to cement his political and personal popularity and added to the supernatural, if not infallible, aura surrounding Prince, which had been created through rumor and media. Many a story told at cocktail parties about his street conversations with apparent strangers ended with "I don't know how he does it!"

But Prince more often used such information for more critical purposes. For instance, from the beginning of the Sunday visits, he would know when a particular person would be in danger, because of his ability to see his soul. As inscrutable as such an instruction might be, he would tell that person not to leave their home, or avoid a certain country in their travels. But as time progressed and he could see more—both because his powers of perception increased with practice, and because he knew about more individuals—he could even identify the specific danger facing a person. Sometimes he would advise his police staff to follow a certain person and stop him as a crime was about to take place, or search a place for evidence. The repeated apprehension of criminals with the mayor's help only added to the impression that the new mayor was psychic or had eyes in the back of his head.

The majority of Prince's discussions centered around general advice and consumed much of his time. In the first part of the twenty-first century, there had arisen many new ways to obtain advice, in addition to the traditional sources, such as a friend, clergyman, or therapist. It was available in books and newspapers (the kinds they had at the time), on TV and radio, and over the internet. Many claimed to be qualified to give it. Lists of recommended actions were produced in great quantity that their proponents claimed would lead to happiness, if only diligently followed. As with any item in great supply, the considered worth of "advice" became cheapened. Consequently, those clergy and friends, who had traditionally given assistance and advice, tended to see their role as less necessary, and tended to remove themselves. Moreover, most individuals claimed to be so busy with their work, family, and leisure activities that they could not possibly fit another activity into their schedules. As a corollary to this viewpoint, there was the strange presumption in America at the time that each person was entitled to his own personal happiness, almost regardless of its effect on others, and in order to "have it all", each person should make sure that he selfishly took the time to obtain everything to which he was entitled. As a result, friendships fell apart, and it often seemed that very few people would take the time to actually talk to a person, unless they were paid to do so. It also seemed that people had lost the ability to sit and reflect on their reason for being.

Another casualty of the first half of the twenty-first century was the idea of truth. In previous times, there had always been the problem of subjective interpretation of events. One person's viewpoint of what happened could be quite different from another's, simply because what each saw was filtered through his own level of consciousness and understanding of the universe. But a much more insidious course took hold of America in those years. Probably because of the growth of media, truth became something that a person could manipulate considerably more than in the past, and the temptation became too strong for many. Even if a person had committed an immoral action, or worse—a heinous crime—he could nevertheless hire a "spin" master to handle the media in the former case, or a lawyer in the latter case, to simply maintain that such an event never happened, or that the circumstances had been completely different. Barring that avenue as an acceptable excuse to the public, the advocate of the person who had committed the grievous action could simply argue that his client had been forced to do it because of certain circumstances beyond his control; individual responsibility among public officials and private individuals for their actions waned greatly.

Moreover, truth became something that the entire society was willing to conveniently ignore. On civic issues which were generally debated through the media, those advocating a specific position maintained that certain facts were off limits to the discussion. Social commentators at the time called such restriction of dialogue and communication by the name of "political correctness." By its critics it was considered censorship; in their view, society could never deal with the underlying issues of disagreement between certain groups. By its advocates, it was almost considered a sign of courtesy; in their eyes, it would be considered offensive, and of course bad taste, to bring up subjects which made certain groups, particularly minority groups, feel uncomfortable. Regardless our current viewpoint on "political correctness", it seems clear from a historical perspective that it limited the debate to a narrower field of facts. Discerning political observers, who read widely and thought deeply about a subject, knew that the "truth" was considerably more complex than usually presented. But these observers constituted an extremely small minority of the population. As mentioned earlier, most of the public was much too busy to read, and in reality much too self-absorbed to care about subtle, or not so subtle distinctions, in the facts. In fact, those who would distort or deny a reality could count on a certain weariness to set in amongst the public after a prescribed period; most of the public's attention span for news was extremely limited and they would simply tune out after they had heard enough spoken through the media on a subject. Chasing ratings, which was their main avenue to earn profits, the media would usually eventually oblige the public and limit the news coverage of an old item, moving on to newer subjects. In fact, one of the effective ways a "spin" master could cut off discussion was to refer to something as "old news". The implication was not only that a subject had already been heard and discounted among the public, but that the news media was too lazy to move on and find new, more critical items for public debate.

The result of this obscurantism was a confusion about truth. In previous periods, truth had been seen as having a certain objectivity, a part of the orderly and rational world, which was our heritage from G-d. But during Prince's time, truth became relative. It became anything that anyone wanted to make it. Instead of truth being a quality inherent and fixed in a person, idea, or object, it became whatever "face" or position a person chose to present to the public. If you didn't like the looks that G-d bequeathed you, then you changed them. It might start with something smaller such as dyed hair, and then move on to something on the order of a tummy tuck. But there being no boundaries to this thought process, it had proceeded to even the essence of people's souls. People thought little about falsifying resumes, even teaching about subjects from a first person point of view which they had never experienced. There seemed to be little cost to this, as few were caught, and if they were, there were again ways to deny it—and failing everything else—there would always be a certain sympathy for the accused person, if for nothing more than his underdog status, or the observation that he had "helped" so many people. In some people's minds, history became merely an imagined narrative from a certain viewpoint. Many marriages—not to again mention friendships—became shambles as it became common to lie to a spouse. Because many no longer acknowledged the existence of G-d, there seemed no higher authority. Each person became his own guide, validity, and sufficiency. Caught in this milieu, and concerned about their changing positions within their congregations, even many clergymen had subscribed to this point of view.

But there were those souls whom G-d had placed in this world who refused to agree to this view of life. When the Jews among these souls heard of Prince, they came running to him. Here was someone whom they had heard would not only "see" their souls, but would give them advice which was both disinterested and truly designed to help them. Better yet, he seemed to have a direct link to G-d and His truth. Prince's intelligence and success in the outside world, and his reputed faith and calm in the midst of adversity, assured them of that. The non-Jews were known to gripe to their Jewish friends that they only wished that they had a similar figure to counsel them. One of the conversations occurred with a 45 year-old woman.

"Have a seat, Mrs. Shapiro," Prince said.

"Thank you so much for seeing me, Rebbe," she said. She was suddenly aware of being in the presence of a great person and could not speak. All she could do was stare at the stacks of books piled on the shelves leading up to the high ceiling.

Prince smiled broadly at her. "Don't be afraid of me, Mrs. Shapiro. I'm just like you. My soul descends from G-d, just as yours does."

She relaxed in her chair. "Thank you. I, ah, came to talk about several things bothering me. But first, I'd like to ask about my family. Is everything okay with them? Do I need to worry about anything?"

"Yes, your family is well," he said, smiling. "But, there will be challenges for you and your family. There are always challenges. I cannot get into all the details of the future here, because it is important that you and your family make your own choices. This is the reason we enter this world. But your life will have meaning, good meaning."

"Rebbe, I am here, I suppose, because I feel—I hope—that talking to you will give me a greater connection to G-d. I know that there is a lot of purpose in this world, and I am connected to it. But, I am struggling at this time, with that connection. I was hoping that talking to you would help me."

Prince sat motionless for a moment before he spoke. "I see a fine, old soul in my midst. You are waging good battles against evil in this world."

"I know that I have been trying to do the right thing. I know that. But I am so tired, and sad, right now. Is there anything wrong with me?" she said.

Prince shook his head. "There is nothing wrong with you Mrs. Shapiro."

"Then why do I feel the way I do?" she said.

"You are not clinically depressed—that much you know from your own profession, psychotherapy," he said. "Instead, what you feel is completely normal. I'm seeing that you feel a kind of malaise, but that happens to most of us at times. It is nothing to be overly concerned about. You will come out of it. The important thing is that you accept your condition for what it is, and do not become overly concerned, or more depressed, about your feelings."

"But why do I feel it?" she said.

"Ah, that's a good question. The sages say, 'In every sadness there will be profit.'"

"But what profit will this sadness possibly bring?" she said.

"Mrs. Shapiro, the fact that you feel sad doesn't mean that there is anything wrong with you. To the contrary, it means in your case just the opposite. The fact that you feel sadness indicates that you are both intelligent and sensitive, and that you wish to do right in this world. It is often not easy to do right in this evil world."

"You're saying that my feelings make sense?"

"Yes," he said. Let's examine the way life works. Life is composed of activity and rest. We work six days and then we have Shabbat for rest. When we walk, one leg works some muscles, while the other rests those muscles. Our hearts beat and then they rest. Even the general universe reflects this condition, with the contraction leading to the big bang and then its expansion again. The Kabbalists talk about Chesed, or kindness or generosity which flows, and Gevurah, which is contraction or restriction. But though Chesed and Gevurah appear to be opposites at one level, one cannot operate without the other, so that the quality of Gevurah must in fact be included in the quality of Chesed, in order for Chesed to be fully expressed in our world. This is true for the very creation of our world, which occurred through many contractions. And so this is true for the birth of a baby, which enters this world through the multiple contractions of her mother. But a mother cannot deliver a baby with just contractions; there must be rest in between for those contractions to do their work.

"Through this activity and rest, the world turns. Life is a turning, from birth to death, to birth again. When we are born, we leave a totally spiritual realm to enter a physical one. As our bodies age during this life, we become more spiritual. Some would say it's because of the wisdom we've gained, and there is some truth to this, but how much wisdom of the soul is gained in a few decades of a life, when compared to the experience of many past lifetimes? Rather, as our bodies age, as our physical desires wane, our Divine souls wage a more successful fight with our animal, or vital, souls. As our physical desires decline, we prepare again to enter the spiritual realm after our physical death. Everything returns."

"But how does this apply to my feelings?" she said.

"For there to be progress in this world, for us to do G-d's work, and move toward the Messianic Age, there must be activity and then rest. Your slight depression is a resting phase, before you move on."

"But why the need for sadness? Why the need for rest?" she said.

"We are relative beings in this physical world. Without sadness, would it be possible to appreciate the joy? Would we value summer without winter? Would we appreciate the day so much, if there were no night? What would our days be without the nights to give us our dreams, and to reorganize our psyches?"

"But, sometimes I feel mad, angered at this world. This cannot be right," she said.

Prince smiled. "By Divine Providence, Mrs. Shapiro, everything that occurs by design is right. The leaf in the forest falls in just the right spot for the caterpillar. Only we may not be able to see it. What may not be right are our reactions to the situation presented to us. If your depression and anger lead you to greater depression, so that you become apathetic and do not care about this world, and refuse to continue to act, which is your purpose for being here, then this is not right. But if your anger leads you to a kind of genuine bitterness, which eventually forces you to properly act in the future with renewed vigor, then this is natural. In the latter case, and in your specific case, the spirit of the sitra achra, or literally the 'other side' is broken within you; its molecules then become available to be reconstituted for use in the mitzvot, or good deeds, you do in this world. With the good deeds, a part of the profane of the common world becomes holy. It becomes separated and becomes consigned to the service of G-d. The good deeds become the oil for the wick of a candle that lights the world. The first example of greater depression leads to death; the second example leads to life."

"Okay," she said, and then sighed. "Rebbe, I will do what's right for G-d. Yes, I'll do the good deeds, charity, and as many of the 613 commandments as I can. But, I am ashamed to say that I do not like my choices in life. Sometimes, I just get up in the morning and feel like screaming at G-d because of what I am faced with during the day. I mean the stupidity of this world is just baffling. I'm sorry, but I don't get up cheery eyed and face the crazy demons on the road, or the environmental carnage, or the politicians lying up there in Washington. Now really, am I supposed to think that this is fun? Do I always thank G-d for this?" She had suddenly realized how agitated she had become and had quickly cut her words off.

Prince smiled at her. "You should serve G-d as joyously as possible. A true servant will want to serve her master. This particularly applies to prayer, such as the Amidah, when we make specific requests of G-d, but in all other instances as well. But Mrs. Shapiro, you are not required or obligated in any sense to like your choices in your life. Many of us do not like our choices. We'd rather be doing something else."

"So, how do I deal with that feeling?" she said.

"Well, you certainly don't deny it. But through prayer and time, the suffering dissipates."

"Why?"

"Mrs. Shapiro, there's a certain point in life when we stop fighting. I'm not telling you to ignore the pain. But at some level there is an acceptance of the human condition, the fact that we are caught in this web. You see, maybe you or I would wish not to pollute the environment with our cars. We'd wish to stop plowing marginal fields that erode and muddy our rivers. And maybe we hate the latest technological gadgets out there which we are required to use to be a part of this society, because they destroy a part of our humanity. But we are boxed in. Not only that, but we are not able to do what we'd like for someone in need, because we are so tired from the coarse demands of life, or from defending ourselves from a neighbor who picks a fight. We simply do not have the specific choices we want.

"But that doesn't mean that we do not have choices. For example, we could just lay down on the railroad tracks and commit suicide, G-d forbid. Some do. Others take a middle course. They just get by. They don't do much that they don't have to. They let others fend for themselves. Then there are those, the rashas, the wicked of this world, who take pleasure, physical mostly, in serving only themselves, even at the expense of others. Many of the rashas seem to profit—only though they don't often realize that such profit is temporary—at what they do. They seem perfectly content with this world, because they have found ways for it to serve them, instead of them serving it.

"And then, there are those like yourself, who perceive that the human world is highly imperfect and often disgusting, but continue to do the small things that they can, to make it better. Maybe it is spontaneously helping a stranger at the store, or just smiling at someone who needs a friend. Some souls return to this earthly existence to do nothing but a small act of kindness—that is their sole reason for being here. All those small acts of kindness add up. The point is that we don't just stop driving a car or become hermits because we can't stomach the consequences. We deal with the hand we have, and do the best we can. When you think about it, there is great beauty in this. We are like craftsman perfecting the small space around us, which we really can influence. Knowing that we are doing the right thing, that we are warriors for G-d, gives us great peace. When you accept your limitations, when you accept your destiny, and the reasons that you are put on this earth, then you can find spontaneous joy in your existence."

"Some say that this acceptance of following G-d is blind, that we are just a bunch of sheep that do that not know better," she said.

"I say that the blind are those who deny the existence of G-d. In every generation, G-d shows His might."

She sat quietly for a minute. "I'm just curious, if I may ask, but do you talk to everyone this way?"

"With these concepts, this kind of vocabulary? No. I try to speak to the specific level of the listener, or slightly above. I perceived when you walked in, that while you had relatively little formal training in Judaism, your soul, with its experience in previous lives, would understand this communication."

"And you can see my soul? —I can't believe that I'm asking this," she said.

"You should ask whatever is on your mind, Mrs. Shapiro. There are no stupid questions. We've all been and continue to be students. And my role is no more important in G-d's plan than yours. We all have our part. To come back to your question, yes I perceive your soul. You have a halo, past lives, and other very nice characteristics."

"I always thought of myself as having this body and mind," she said. "But my mind was a function of my genetics, or my body, and the environment around me. I never thought much about souls. How come you don't hear more Rabbis talking much about them?"

"I am no Rabbi, and do not deserve such recognition," he said. "As for souls, this is your essence, the part of your heritage from G-d. You have had a special Jewish soul for many generations, since the revelation at Sinai. This knowledge of souls has been relatively hidden, and often distorted by those who did not understand it, but has been available to the learned and to the Kabbalists for use since before recorded time. The fact that it is starting to reach the greater consciousness of the world is a harbinger of the Messianic Age."

"Rebbe, I think I understand about sadness, and yes there are cycles to my life, between joy and sadness. But I must say that I am not totally comfortable at any time in this world. Even when I am at my most joyous, I still feel this loss. It is this very heavy burden of heavy-heartedness. Why is that?"

"First of all, we Jews are a people who feel loss. We have had great things given to us by G-d which we have lost, such as the two Temples, and the first tablets with the Ten Commandments. For two-thousand years, we had even lost our land. Those losses never go away. We pass that feeling, unconsciously as well as consciously, from one generation to another. Of course, we could choose to forget those losses by losing our identity, as other peoples have done throughout history. Ask yourself, why we don't choose to do that.

"We are also a people, who more than any other, understand and record time, most importantly through the Torah and Shabbat. Our religion doesn't just commit us to beliefs. More importantly, it involves a covenant with G-d and commits us to actions based on expectations. G-d has expectations of us, and we have expectations of G-d, and ourselves. Expectations operate through the element of time. We work toward a better world over time, and when it doesn't happen as we wish, we feel this great loss. Without expectations, without a Divine standard, we would feel no loss.

"And then there is something else in your case. Your soul is elevated. Often your Divine soul dominates your animal one, and your Divine soul truly wishes to return to its source, which is G-d. It is not usually charmed by the affairs of this world. Your sadness is a genuine one, which is derived from your Divine soul's natural love and fear of G-d."

"What must I do?" she said.

"You must meditate on the greatness of G-d. You must realize that the greatness of G-d is all around you, and in you, and that you are never separated from G-d. You must stay focused on the purpose of your life, and the actions which will bring G-d's presence into this world. You must help make a dira, an apartment, for G-d, on this earth. These actions will bring your Divine soul closer to its source. You must avoid the sitra achra, and fight the yetzer hara, which seek to separate your Divine soul from its source, and inevitably lead to your unhappiness."

"But if what you say is true, and my, ah, Divine soul is, ah, repulsed by operating in this world, then it will be very hard for me to help bring G-d's presence here," she said.

"Very true, Mrs. Shapiro. You will receive a lot of credit in heaven for such efforts, because they do not come easily for you. Some of the sages might wish that they could be in your shoes, so that they too could face the same challenges you do, and could prove their devotion to G-d under such difficult circumstances. Remember, G-d determines the type of soul that each of us will possess. Some are more elevated than others. The key is not where you start, as much as where you go with what you have. The greatest tzaddik and prophet of all time, Moses, the one with the greatest communication with G-d, was not allowed to enter the Promised Land. Why? Just because he struck a rock in error. You see, because of the elevated status of his soul, G-d had a much greater expectation of him than of others.

"What you should also understand is that G-d will support you. G-d never asks more of us than we are capable. And though your challenges will be difficult, G-d has brought you to this place and time for a specific purpose. Many, many other worthy souls, such as yourself, have been placed here now. With all of your efforts, we can build the better world. It is no accident that you have sought spiritual guidance here today."

16

When Prince finally returned to his desk after the mayoral election—the day after dedicating the congregation among the sequoias and counseling those at his residence the same evening—he faced a huge pile of mail from the media and well-wishers, which his secretary had organized. "Of all these barrels of mail, which I have gone through," the secretary said, "this one letter marked personal and confidential seemed to become separated from the rest. In fact, I'm at a loss to tell you how it exactly got here, since it has neither a stamp nor a postmark. You'd think that someone dropped it off, but I would have known if anyone had." He handed Prince the letter early that morning before they had even discussed any other matters.

Even before he took the envelope, Prince knew that he shouldn't look at it just yet. "Jacob, leave me for a few minutes. I want to get organized and then I will call you."

Only after Jacob left the room did he permit himself to consider it. The faint odor was unmistakable and he would know that beautiful scrawl for eternity. His hands trembled and his body fell limp. He doubled over and began weeping before he could even open it. Finally, he ripped the envelope with such force that the card popped out across the room.

"Joseph, do not shed any more tears, my dearest one. I am with you now, in this moment, as I am always with you. I have followed you closely through all these years—you have never been far from me. I love you and will wait for you forever.

Congratulations my mayor and Rebbe. Keep up the good work!

Judy"

For the longest time he sat contemplating the card, reading it over and over again. As with all matters this message had both its intellectual and emotional qualities for him to consider—trained as he was in Kabbalah—and for such a short message, it had a great abundance of both.

He had reacted emotionally first. There had not been a day in which he had not thought about her. But she had been as someone from another life, one to which he could never return. He had forgotten that intensity of feeling. In the years since he had been with her, no one else had touched him to the core of his soul, except the Rabbis and the spiritual advisory group, but that had been totally different. After all this time, this note was like a great storm that had shaken the foundation of a huge tree. No one else had such a power over him—no one. He had not wanted for anything recently in this physical existence, or so he had thought. Now he again realized that a huge part of him had been missing. He now acknowledged that huge hole in his being.

Then the intellectual in him had taken over. G-d had His purpose and Judy was certainly part of it. Given her elevated soul and his relationship to her, she was surely G-d's agent, and not just speaking for herself. Further, he knew that she surely knew that she was acting with Divine purpose. Why had she suddenly chosen to contact him now, after all these years? What did she know that he didn't at this time? What was he missing, he wondered? Come to think of it, how did she know that he was now considered a Rebbe by some? That communication with the Rabbis in the vehicle had happened just last night and it seemed that it would have been impossible for her to know that information when she had written the note. Yet, he knew that she had the power. He smiled, knowing once again that he had met his match.

Was she about to reenter his life and he didn't know it? Better yet, had she already reentered his life and he wasn't even aware of it? But how could any relationship possibly work? When he focused on the situation, he could perceive that his friend John was still well. What was the point?

Then he remembered something very important about his relationship with Judy. His powers of perception had always been curbed under her influence. Yet, she had always compensated for that loss of powers; she had spoken for him when he couldn't. Was this about to happen now, as he entered a different phase of his life?

When he thought further about it, he realized that it could be something quite different. G-d was trying to strengthen him by causing him to acknowledge his own personal weakness. No, he had not acted with condescension to anyone, but perhaps he still had not been humble enough. Perhaps he had taken his recent worldly success for granted and had considered himself too busy to thank G-d properly. And perhaps he should remember that every human had some weakness. Perhaps this recognition of the pain in his soul would help him better reach people. Maybe this realization would help him serve G-d better.

Finally, he realized what he had taught to so many others. While there is a Divine purpose to everything, it is not always readily evident, or for that matter understandable by humans, no matter the status of their souls. Perhaps the importance of her communication would not be evident for several years to come.

The communication from Judy also engendered a great deal of discussion among the angels in heaven. The discussions concerning the developments in Prince's life had never stopped; with each movement and decision in his life, there arose a new debate concerning the Divine purpose. The angels had seen many events centered around many great individuals, but they had rarely watched something which they knew would have such significance for the world.

Some of the angels had never stopped chattering about G-d's decision to send such a spiritual soul into the common world. They admitted to some surprise, along Prince's journey so far, that he had been able to negotiate the world as well as he had, but they maintained that the worst was yet to come. As they saw it, he would be absolutely crushed by the yetzer hara, once he started to have a significant impact on world affairs, and that day was close at hand. Either G-d had some trick up His sleeve, which they had not seen since the days of Mt. Sinai and the parting of the Red Sea, or Prince would face a cruel end. Remember, they intoned, this time G-d had explicitly left the choice of a better (or worse) world up to the humans. And unless the humans agreed to change on their own—specifically without the vast miracles from G-d that would convince even the rashas, or wicked, to give up their ways—there would be no avenue for a Messianic world. Prince could not simply overpower the world with his intelligence, good looks, money, and charm. He would have to convince the world to change. How would he do this, they asked? It would seem that only G-d had such power. Other angels responded that G-d had His ways, that he would not abandon his servant Prince any more than he had abandoned any other of His children, Moses or David, who had faithfully followed in His ways. Another group of angels subscribed to both views. They believed that G-d would support Prince, but also saw no way for humans to fundamentally change, no matter what Prince did on earth; therein lay the conundrum for them. And so the debate went on and angels would switch sides, passionately convinced by the discussions; humans might have compared it to the earthly children's game of those years, red rover, red rover.

But the event which stirred the angels to most deliberation and agitation was Prince's relationship with Judy Jones. Despite the spirited discussions, it was a rare point of agreement among the celestial beings. They all believed that when she was involved, something of significance would happen to Prince. Like heaven and earth, like G-d and humans, when one acted, the other was affected. Part of the same soul, the two of them danced in space. Even when out of conscious contact with each other, the simple daily activity of one would move the other. Those persons who came through the space between them, who coincidentally traveled across the physical energy field that connected their souls and psyches, would find their thoughts and sensibilities disrupted in some unexplainable way. And the angels would watch as John would quietly observe Judy and say, "Thinking about Joseph, again, aren't you?" and she would silently nod.

So it was that after Prince received the note from Judy, there was a din of voices going on throughout the heavens. There was so much speculation that few could have substantive exchanges of suitably acknowledged views at that point. Rather, many of the angels could be observed talking at each other, hardly listening to what their neighbors were saying. Still there were some substantive discussions and one of the better ones was fortunately recorded for posterity.

"Wow," Seraph said. "Did you know that this was going to happen?"

"You mean with the note?" Ophan said. "Yes, as luck would have it, or Divine Providence, I was actually assigned to the delivery service and responsible for helping make sure that note was delivered to Prince's office, and not intercepted."

"Really?" Seraph said. "You always seem to get the good assignments. I don't know how you do it."

Ophan laughed. "Believe me, I don't have a special connection, or anything. Your time will come too."

Seraph sighed.

"I may have gotten a first row seat this time," Ophan said, "but that doesn't mean I understand it all. Did you see how Judy told him to stop crying in the note. How did she know that he would be crying before he even opened that note?"

"Easy," Seraph said. "I figure she's so connected with him that she knows everything he will do, if she will only think about it, painful as it may be at times for her to do so."

"Well," Ophan said, "she must be some lady. If she really is so joined, so linked, that she knows all that, how in the world does she have the self control not to go running to him? I mean the attraction between them must be supernaturally strong, practically irresistible."

"True, so true," Seraph said. "But her love for him is stronger than that. Their love for each other is so strong that even two thousand miles apart they act in symphony with each other. He is on the outside, preparing the world for the physical changes it must make. She plays the traditional female role, often even more important than the male one, preparing the hidden spiritual side, laying the hidden, but strong foundation for the manifest changes that he makes."

"Very much as the Jewish woman prepares the spiritual Jewish home for her family," Ophan said. "But I haven't followed this in as much detail as you have. What has she been doing?"

"Well, it doesn't outwardly look like much, at least yet," Seraph said. "We don't notice her much doing what she's doing, but we'd sure notice it if she weren't there. It almost reminds you of that woman knitting in *A Tale of Two Cities*. Judy'll become more active in organizing people as time goes on, I expect. But right now, what is so critical is that she balances him. You see, it's simple physics. When he steps out to do something, it's not like someone else stepping out. I mean, what he is doing, and will be doing, of course, is much more significant in the universe. Every time he does something, it's of great importance and consequently it will be opposed or resisted by a great force out there—"

"—Great forces create great winds."

"Yes, and when he creates that gale force wind around him, she anchors him, and makes sure that he doesn't fall," Seraph said. "But it's more than that. You see, he may be a tzaddik, but even a tzaddik may fall seven times and then rise again."

"A tzaddik?" Ophan said. "But…"

"Yes, especially a tzaddik. Focus on the rising again. The wicked stumble, but the tzaddik is climbing to the next level, only his climb each time is from one level to an infinitely higher one, not some tiny finite steps."

"Ah, so he is stumbling for the very reason that he is climbing," Ophan said.

"Yes, that's absolutely true. If you're just taking finite steps, for example on a ladder, you don't let go of one level before you take the next step, so that you protect yourself from falling. But a tzaddik…well he's moving unsupported in space to the next level, which is infinitely greater than the last," Seraph said. "He falls back for a while, before he moves forward. But now, that's the essence of life, whether you are a tzaddik, or not. Life is movement, and all humans are destined to advance their spiritual level, but so many ignore that spiritual journey."

"That must require great faith and trust in G-d by him," Ophan said. "I mean, believing between those great steps of growth that G-d will catch you and that you will not continue to fall."

"For that faith, he, as other souls, must rely on his love of G-d, the love of G-d that he learned in his youth, that which he had been educated in by his uncle," Seraph said.

"Before he left his home," Ophan said. "So, that's the reason for that Jewish education early in life. I wondered, because he never used it then. It seemed like such a waste for a time."

"Not a waste at all. That is his foundation, the hidden floor that supports his growth," Seraph said. It is critical that all children receive it, because as adults they need to be able to return to it, even though they hopefully have grown much beyond it. You see, he was running away from his Jewish upbringing, to be sure, but at least he had something to run away from, and thus something to return to."

"That—the stumbling—also explains why there have been major ups and downs in his life," Ophan said. "But coming back to Judy…"

"Well," Seraph said, "she provides him that foundation that supports him. There's G-d's support from the heavens, but there's the earthly love too. He's a tzaddik, and his love and awe of G-d sustain him in ways unavailable to other neshamahs, or souls, but he is also human. And under the difficult and extremely demanding conditions he faces, he very much needs her human assistance."

"Why her particularly?" Ophan said.

"Her devotion to him cannot be compared in any way to the support he receives from G-d. But in the human department, it is far superior to anyone else. You see, he is elevated to a point where few on this earth can really understand him. There is extreme loneliness. It is different with her. They have shared many lifetimes together. And sharing an elevated soul, as they do, her pleas and wishes for him double the effect in heaven."

"And how does she do that, especially so far away?"

"Prayer and love. They travel all the way to heaven, and so they certainly will also travel a few thousand miles. Being part of the same soul as he, she has as much power as he does. It was just destined that his would be manifest and hers hidden. She accomplishes in thought what he does in speech and action. Perhaps you could say that she provides so much of the thought behind his action."

"What does that mean?" Ophan said.

"I mean she is able to follow everything that he does. And every one of his actions, every one of his speeches, she contemplates, and prays to G-d that it will fall into the proper spiritual context. And not only that, she protects him. Her love provides a force around him that shields him from those who would wish to harm him."

"But she's only human. She's not out there with him," Ophan said.

"True enough, but love, true love, can do that. How do you think you got requisitioned to get that note delivered? Her thoughts, her love, set that in motion. By the way, this is sometimes in the power of a few other humans, but they hardly realize it."

"Wow, the way you talk they could practically switch bodies with each other," Ophan said.

"When we are talking about the power of souls and soul mates, bodies lose their significance."

"But she knew nothing before he came to the Jones' ranch. She even denied her Judaism," Ophan said.

"As he denied his," Seraph said. "But she was like the sleeping princess that was awoken by her prince, no pun intended. Neither one of them could be active in this life without the other. Now that both of them are lit by the Divine spark, they can sustain a chain reaction. That chain reaction is getting ready to set a bonfire on earth. Just watch."

"Since you are so smart, my fellow angel," Ophan said, "enlighten me further. "Why is it that she has suddenly, after all these long years in their lives, suddenly contacted him?"

"Good question," Seraph said. "Now we can speculate about that all day."

"Go ahead!"

"Well, I figure for at least a couple of reasons. First of all, she's letting him know that she's part of his life," Seraph said.

"Why now?"

"Simply because she's taking on a more active role in assisting him and she needs his assistance, his consciousness about her, to enable her to do that," Seraph said.

"What do you mean?"

"It's Kaballah," Seraph said. "For her to assist him, he must be a spiritual receptacle. And in order to do that, he must keep his container open, to receive. She's signaling him that she wants him to do that. You know, it's still his choice whether to accept her help or not. And it's not so easy accepting help in this world."

"But he's a little befuddled about this, or is he?" Ophan said.

"I think under the circumstances we all would be, and under her influence, his powers of perception are often clouded. But that doesn't matter too much. She's got him thinking about her, and just that, opens his soul up to hers," Seraph said.

"And why is she starting to assist him more at this time?" Ophan said.

"Well, as we approach the time of the Messiah, the hidden spiritual world and the manifest, or revealed, physical world will begin to unite. And Prince and Judy's relationship will begin to do the same. Her activity will necessarily become more manifest, so that it matches his. But in order for her role to become more open, his must become more thoughtful, to compensate for what she no longer does," Seraph said.

"Why's that?"

"It's back to balance and Kaballah. They are dancing with each other, these two beautiful souls in space. And when one leans back, the other must lean forward to compensate. She cannot give without his receiving. When one goes to the right, the other must go to the left. It's like seeing another part of yourself in the mirror."

"But what does it mean to the world for her to suddenly be communicating with him?" Ophan said. "I mean I can subscribe to your theories—they're quite good and all that—but G-d's got a plan, you know. What's G-d thinking? Does it mean the Messianic Age is any closer?"

"I don't know. The ways of G-d are mysterious. G-d may be indicating that the two of them are going to eventually get together. But what that means...well, I think it's been clear all along that that will be up to the humans to decide. Certain souls are destined to travel together, but where they travel, may depend upon human choices."

17

Prince turned his attention to governing the city of San Francisco. His detractors, and there were many, openly questioned his ability. They would, at the very least, have given another politician, even a hated one, a small honeymoon, or a little benefit of the doubt at the beginning. But Prince was not just some politician in their book. In a follow up column to the Sunday one he wrote after the election, Daniel Kahn threw the gauntlet down. He said in part,

It seems clear that Mr. Reed can order others around in his own corporation, and get things done. But that style won't work in our modern city. He'll have to convince others now. And in order to do that, you have to have paid your dues. Mr. Reed has paid no dues. Furthermore, it's not clear to us what he even wishes to do.

If Prince was afraid, he didn't show it. And this was the first reality that threw his opponents off. Fear was a sign of weakness to them, and something they understood and could control. You simply manipulated that fear to achieve what you wanted. The fact that Prince showed no fear either meant in their books that he was crazy—that is had a tenuous grip on reality—or that he was so talented that he had no need to fear. With someone else, they might have laughed, but Prince clearly had a major corporation, wealth, intelligence, and charm behind him—not to mention the unexplainable way he had been elected—which caused each one of them to question their own grip on the electorate, and thus their future political prospects.

Prince's first act was to meet with the leaders of city council and civic organizations, as a matter of political correctness. Then he sagely focused his attention on others who might assist him, as well as those who might cause him specific problems. To those who he thought would ally with him, he offered "love", that is inducements, or the carrot approach, laying out what he could achieve with their help, and how that would help them reach their own personal and political goals. To those who would oppose him, he showed a path of "fear", that is how they would be hurt if they crossed him. His first assistants, from the previous mayoral administration, who heard the meetings, remarked that this man could not be suitably characterized in words. He would show several human sides at once, being both compassionate and firm, and not only soft and inviting, but hard as nails at the same time. He was constant in his choice of goals; yet his methods in achieving those goals were as numerous—and unpredictable—as the different persons he met. A person who came to see Prince, who thought he had figured Prince out and was in control, would usually be spiritually wrestled to the floor immediately, and would suddenly realize that he was totally outclassed. He would quickly fall into line. But then, near the end of this process, several weeks into Prince's mayoral term, there was still Big Al left to deal with. Everyone said he would show Prince his place.

Before Prince "came to town", Big Al was the guy that seemed to have the power. Through thick and thin, through each mayor, or tax increase, it seemed that he was the hay maker. One had to come to him to negotiate a final deal, if for nothing else than to have it rubber stamped with his approval. It was said that he had tied up one of the previous mayor's programs so badly that nothing would pass, and that was merely because he didn't like the person. That mayor had resigned before his term was over. Big Al was the one person whom Prince's opponents were counting on to organize the mob which would lynch the new mayor.

When Big Al came calling to the receptionist outside Prince's office for his scheduled meeting, even Prince's first assistants cowered in the office wings, and the receptionist deferred ever so politely to him. "I'm so sorry, Mr. Al, to keep you waiting out here like this. It's so discourteous for him to still be tied up in that 2:30 meeting. He should have scheduled his day better than this."

"Don't you worry your pretty little head about this. It's not your fault, you sweet thing," Big Al said. His beefy, hairy hand reached around her shoulder in a suggestive way.

"Oh, Mr. Al..." she said, grinning.

Prince had then walked out of the office, and after bidding farewell to his visitors, he said, "Ms. Logan, have I told you that you would be transferring to another city office building across town?"

Her mouth dropped open. "Why...why no. You haven't," she said.

"Well, I'm, telling you now, effective immediately—that is tomorrow morning, so begin gathering your personal things together. You may discuss it with me after my meeting with Mr. Groudson," Prince said.

Before they could even reach Prince's office just a few strides away, Big Al said, "What d'ya want to pick on that gal for? What's she done to you?"

As he motioned Big Al into his office and closed the door, Prince said, "That's not really your business, now is it?"

"Well, now I disagree with that," Big Al said. "Everything in your office has always been my business."

"Well, that may have been true in the past, but I can assure you that it will not be the case in the future,"

Big Al's face had turned beet red. "No one, no one, has ever treated me this way. Who do you think you are? I got that gal that job. She's in there because of me, and as far as I'm concerned, you'll have your job as long as I want you to have it."

Prince walked up to Big Al. His large athletic frame came closer, and then closer, until he was less than a foot away and his blue eyes stared at Big Al, until they seemed to pierce him. Big Al winced as if his body had been severed. Then he backed into the corner, and Prince moved with him. His heavy weight began to sweat. "I'll tell you who I am," Prince said. "I am the new mayor of this city."

Big Al shivered. "I'll tell you what son, you just don't get it. You're new. I'm the respected elder around these parts. Nothing passes, nothing gets done, without me."

"No," Prince said. "You're the one that doesn't get it. Things are changing around here. We aren't going to run things the same way."

Big Al tried to laugh, the way he always did when he was in charge, but only a whimper came out. He continued anyway. "You ain't got no ability to change anything in this town. Look what the newspapers are saying about you. I give you a few months, if that. The vultures are already circling. It should be a pretty spectacle." His throat was so tight that he could barely get the words out.

Prince smiled at him. He backed away from him and began to circle around to his desk. "Have a seat, Mr. Groudson. You're going to need it." Big Al needed no more suggestion on that matter. He shuffled with great effort to one of the seats in front of Prince's desk. He was completely out of breath.

Prince picked up a stack of papers which he waved at Big Al. "Mr. Groudson, I seem to know everything I already want to know about you. Where would you like to start?"

"What are you talking about?"

"I'm talking about you. You sit there threatening me, telling me how to run my job. What about you and this sordid mess of a life that you apparently lead?"

"How dare you! My life is outstanding...upstanding," he said, stumbling on the words.

"Well," Prince said, "it's generally not my policy to judge others. That's usually G-d's business, since we can't always see into the hearts and motivations of others.

But there are times when it is absolutely necessary to rebuke a person, especially when he is hurting others."

"Don't you go bringing your religion into this matter. You're one of those observant Jews. But it doesn't work. G-d doesn't protect you, no matter how much you pray to him."

Prince began. "It's prostitution here, and a mix up in a drug scene—only you weren't arrested for it."

Big Al nodded. "I've got plenty of friends in high places."

"No more," Prince said. "I'm following your trail like a blood hound. I'm taking out everyone who ever protected you. I won't have any more of this filth around city hall."

"Let's see you do it. I've got too many friends, and we'll take you out first," Big Al said.

"Your police chief is gone. While we speak, he's been indicted, and arrested, without bail this afternoon," Prince said. You won't be able to call him when you leave here."

"I don't believe you," Big Al said. But his normally red face had turned almost white.

"You don't? How about your friend, Crieve? He knew something's up. He committed suicide this morning," Prince said.

"I don't believe that. I would know about it."

Prince shook his head. "No, the details have been withheld from the media for a while."

Big Al sat there gasping for air. He couldn't force any words out.

"I could arrange for your arrest right now, but then they'd say I did it because of politics. So I'm going to let the news media do their work. And although I didn't call them, I expect that they'll be out there in mass as you walk out of this office," Prince said.

"Your time will come," Big Al said, almost falling out of his seat.

"Why is that?" Prince said.

"'Cause you're no saint," Big Al said. "They say that you're a saint, but no saint can be this tough and this smart and this wealthy."

"Been doing some checking on your own," Prince said. "Only you haven't been able to find anything."

"You bet I have," Big Al said. "I just didn't have enough time. I should have started earlier. Big mistake on my part. But they'll find something on you. And if they don't, they'll invent something. You'll be forced to accommodate people like me. You can't survive being ethical and so perfect. You're going to get real dirty, doing what you're doing." But he hardly seemed to convince himself of what he was saying, so he then stopped abruptly.

Prince said nothing. So Big Al continued. "Tell me something, mayor, before I go out there and face that crowd. Why did you even have me here today? You could have just disposed of me without this meeting."

Prince's gaze hit him directly once again, and he shrank in his seat. "Because," Prince said, "it is not fair to condemn another person until you have stood in his place. I wanted to meet your personage first and see your soul for myself. I wanted to give you the chance to be different from the person I thought you were. I wanted to give you that choice. It's never too late to repent. Perhaps you would have come into this room and told me that you wanted to do things differently now, and that while you hadn't been proud of your past, and the way that you had treated others—especially your treatment of others—you wanted to change. You know, there still would have been some consequences for your past behavior, but I would have helped you. But your soul is very sick."

It was very shortly after his meeting with Big Al that Prince had replaced his two assistants from the earlier administration. While others just beginning their administrations would have likely asked for all resignations of previous political appointees, particularly ones of a different political party, Prince had thought it only fair to observe all his assistants and department heads before making a final decision on their status. Moreover, he valued the continuity and knowledge that some could bring, but only if their motivation and heart was in the right place. He was also keenly aware that his future success, and that of the new independent party which was developing around him, would be predicated in part on the ties which he could develop with those from other political persuasions. The two new assistants Prince had appointed to report directly to him were Jeff, a brilliant young Talmudic student of his who just had turned down a partnership in a prestigious law firm in order to work with him, and Richard, a sixty-year-old retired successful businessman, very active for years in the leadership of Reform Judaism, and now attracted to Prince's causes. He trusted them implicitly. "I want you to be my eyes and ears," he said to both of them.

After just a few months, Prince had sifted through the employees of his administration and had established what seemed to be excellent relations with the city council and other organizations. Now that Big Al was gone from the scene, Prince had acquired an air of invincibility, once again in his life. And that wasn't even mentioning all the honest folks who were seemingly eternally grateful to Prince for Big Al's demise; as one influential councilwoman put it, "we are all so relieved that this reign of terror is over. I'll do anything political for that man [Prince] now."

Everyone seemed happy but the media, led principally by Daniel Kahn. When the council easily passed the first of Prince's programs, as expected, Daniel Kahn, quickly called the council a bunch of "spineless pussy cats". Richard had approached Prince with the morning paper.

"You've taken care of everything else political in town so far," Richard said. "Now, it's time to focus on the media. I'll be glad to place a call to him today and schedule a meeting."

Prince sat with his eyes focused into space, his elbows supported by his desk, and huge hands folded in front of his mouth. He slowly shook his head.

"Why not?" Richard said. "You've got to affect the media. All this guy wants is his due. Why not give it to him?"

"What he wants," Prince said, "is very simply an interview, and I'm not going to be blackmailed by his insistent comments and slander to appease him."

"You are a tough nut—a nice one too—but that's what I value about you. You don't give in to anybody unless it's right. I have to say I admire that about you," Richard said. "But now, shouldn't we talk about what's practical in accomplishing our goals here."

"True," Prince said. "Now, Richard, I've evaluated this character. He's not going to give us good press at this point."

"Why not?"

"Because his ego is in the way. He's set on proving a point at this time, and he is simply incapable of even hearing us. And I have other reasons for waiting too," Prince said.

"But he'll never come around," Richard said.

"Oh, yes he will," Prince said. "When the sitra achra and kelipah in his heart break down, he will be humble enough to hear us."

"That doesn't happen with Pulitzer Prize winners," Richard said.

"Richard, we should take this to heart. Everyone, no matter his status in life, or his soul, can fall, when they have too much ego. Ego is having too much of the element of air in a personality, and too little of the element earth. But that always corrects itself, as everything else does in nature. Gravity will then rule. Ego is a big balloon of hot air that someone can burst overnight, so that you come crashing down to earth. If we don't answer him, Kahn will keep going, will keep rising, will put something completely embarrassing in print, probably even have a fight with his editor, if that isn't happening already. Let's don't give him the chance to twist what we are doing right now. Let's just keep doing what we're doing so well. That is the best defense. The more that we do well, the more ridiculous his criticism must become, until the world will force him to cease."

"And you see this?" Richard said. "But what about the damage now?"

"Nothing compared to the benefits we receive later, when we do finally allow him to interview me," Prince said. "At that point, he becomes our best convert. His conversion to our side has an incredible drama and the element of surprise. He will admit that he is wrong. Our remaining foes will be shaken to their core."

"I'm just afraid," Richard said, "that it will be the other way around. He will remember what he considers our sleight and will never join with us. He will continue to comfort our enemies, who will grow stronger, and then he will grow in credibility. And if we then reach out to him, he will do more damage than ever."

Prince sat very still for a moment before speaking, deep in contemplation, as he always did before a final major decision. Finally he spoke slowly. "That is possible. "But I don't see it happening that way. His soul has great needs, which simply cannot be satisfied without eventually coming to us. G-d will bring him to us, for his sake as well as ours. At that time, our interests will be mutual. Yes, our association, strange as it seems, is for a reason. And, in any case, the decision fork we must face now is whether to give him the interview. And I believe that there is no way that he will be fair to us now."

"So we continue to take this unfair drubbing from the press?" Richard said.

"So we do," Prince said. "We get up in the morning and with discipline and self control we smile at them. But Richard, look at it this way. If the press were not on our case, then there would be someone else. That's because, with the press on our side, we would look successful, and that would draw in other enemies—more dangerous ones I fear. The negative press coverage actually lulls our enemies into thinking that we will never make it. We are thus able to continue to grow."

Despite the carping in the press, the Prince administration was recognized as a time of exceptional peace and progress in San Francisco. It was rare to hear a citizen complain. Using the political capital which he had built up early in his administration, Prince struck quickly. Within one year, he had cut the city budget by more than ten percent, and had still improved the effectiveness of the existing programs. Much of this had to do with the cutting of programs which had been put into place merely to feather a councilman's district. Those few councilmen who tried to retain programs of that nature were warned, and then eventually punished through funding decisions, so that after a short time, the council learned to police itself.

With the money saved from the budget, Prince funded a few new programs which he considered critical. Then he proposed to take the remaining money and give tax relief with one stipulation. For those in the higher tax brackets, he required that they give a minimum of ten percent of their tax relief to charity. The money was administratively deducted from the refund and sent to the charity of choice, after the taxpayer submitted a form for tax relief.

"What we're doing is all fine and good," Jeff said, "but you know that money is fungible and most of those folks are probably not going to increase their charity this year."

"Oh," Prince said, "I've certainly considered that and I hate the paperwork of this thing as much as anyone. Government simply has too much paperwork and we've created more. But then I began to think about it. Charity is so critical for our society, both in our attitude toward our fellow man, and our attitude toward G-d. And a lot of that money will be increases to charity. You see, most of those people simply do not give anything outside simple donations to their churches and synagogues, and this will be a way for them to give something else. And more importantly, it'll make them think about charity in general and what they actually want to donate. I think it will have benefits well into the future, as some begin to build associations with new charities and raise the level of their awareness. And look at the local charities going after that money. We've caused them to do a better job of charitable work, and to market their programs better."

The charitable refund program, as it was called nationally, was only the latest event to propel Prince onto the national news programs, where it was debated. Some traditional liberals argued that it was a great idea to emulate, while others—mainly conservatives—chaffed at the idea that big government was forcing its citizens to do anything to receive tax relief.

But surprising to the media, quite a number of other conservatives argued that the city of San Francisco should instead be grateful to a man who had been wise enough to save the money to donate to charity. They said that it was not too much for good government—emphasizing good—to give back ninety percent of its savings to its citizens, and only require that ten percent be paid, and then only to the charity of the taxpayer's choice. As with all other issues which Prince had brought to the public attention, the distinction between liberal and conservative was becoming blurred. It had been replaced instead in the public's mind by the question of whether the program was right or not. Consequently, it had now become hard to predict how a person with a certain economic, social, or ethnic profile would view Prince's programs. As one conservative, who had previously been so rabid anti-government said, "I can't believe I'm saying this, but I don't mind this guy having control of some of my money. Anyone who would run the government as efficiently as he has and save money, I trust. It was never whether there was a need for government, but whether government could ever be effective and not a total waste."

As a result of this national debate, as well as the several major other ones that reached the national consciousness at the time, a slew of contributions began coming to Prince's nascent political party, which still had no name. Prince developed a national reputation and every list of rising young national political stars mentioned his name. But in his case, his name was asterisked, because he was then so young that he could not yet qualify for some of the elected national offices.

Sixteen months after Prince became mayor, he announced his intention to run for Congressman in his native district. With his popularity and his independence from other politicians, he ran far ahead in the early polls at the time, even though his main opponent was a relatively popular incumbent. Political commentators said that his name was golden, and that barring any foolish mistakes, he should take the election in a landslide. And there was nowhere to go from there but up. Then he made a fateful speech, live on national television.

18

Be careful not to be lured away to serve other gods and bow down to them. For G-d's anger will flare up against you, and He will close the heavens so that there will be no rain, and the earth will not yield its produce, and you will soon perish from the good land that G-d is assigning to you.

Deuteronomy Chapter 11, vs. 16-17

Asked to make a keynote speech at one of the national political organization meetings, Prince spoke first on several points and then veered into a discussion of environmental issues. This surprised no one at first, because Prince almost always spoke about the environment, about which he felt passionately; it was his signature imprint. But what followed, shocked almost everyone in attendance.

"We are getting to a point, a point of no return, on this sacred earth, which G-d grants us. Soon, if we continue to despoil her, if we continue to add to our carbon dioxide emissions, if we continue to cut the pitiful rain forests still left on this planet, and pollute our streams, and erode our farmland, while we continue to add to the world's population of nine billion people, it will be irreversible. We shall suffer famine and war. We shall be destitute, and our civilization shall slide off a cliff. Every individual civilization in history that has destroyed its immediate environment has declined and then died. But now, it is this green planet which will die. And we will die with it.

"The politicians in Washington sit there and fiddle while Rome burns. To them it is a marginal game. Do I satisfy this constituency or that one, the car industry, the coal miners, or the environmentalists? But this is a game of stupidity. We are now burning the furniture in our house and have no recourse. Soon we will burn the house itself merely to stay warm."

Prince had caught the audience's attention now. The first paragraph had been more than the usual stock from him advocating environmental action. And the second perhaps clued them in, that where Prince was headed, wasn't going to be so pleasant. He was still fixed on the subject. Prince wasn't going to throw out some strong political statement and then get back to a nicer subject, as he might have done in the past.

"How can we honestly bring any children into this world?" Prince continued. "It is not my imagination any longer, but a scientific fact, that this planet will not be able to support these children throughout their adult life expectancies, which are now more than eighty-five in this country. Even if we could find the energy resources, we are running out of water. Even this grand country is running out of water. And within the next century, major ports on the Atlantic will be flooded because the polar ice is melting. When will we believe this sad reality?"

Then what Prince said sent the convention into such an uproar that order could not be reestablished that evening:

"Some have said G-d will provide. Yes, G-d provides, but only if we try to do the right thing. But G-d does care. He is sending a signal, in the strongest terms, so that we will change our ways now, before it is irreversible. We are now in the midst of seven years of very plentiful harvests here in the U.S. and around the world. We are enjoying the fifth year of that cycle. In two short years, we are going to experience major drought in much of our heartland, which will last for approximately seven years. We know this now, so that we may prepare for the drought, by storing as many grains as possible, and by protecting the land from the dust bowl conditions suffered in the Great Depression. And we will also know when the drought occurs, that it is an unmistakable sign from G-d that we must immediately change our ways. A Canadian high will plant itself over the Midwest and eastern U.S., preventing the usual rains from developing out of the Gulf of Mexico..."

By this point there was so much confusion and noise on the floor of the convention that Prince's voice could no longer be heard over the speaker system. It was hard to discern what was really happening. Some delegates were pushing to get to the stage or the door, while others were seemingly locked in their place and unable to move because of the shock. Some delegates had fallen onto the floor; whether this was from fainting, or because they had been stampeded and trampled, was unclear. Other delegates were screaming at the top of their lungs at whomever. Many were hugging each other in despair. The police had to be called to evacuate the hall, which took more than three hours.

When Prince reached the back door, he slipped out with Richard, and they made their way as quickly as possible to the hotel. Richard said nothing, merely glaring at Prince. When they reached the room, he quickly shut the door, and began speaking.

"Jefferson, have you completely checked this place for bugs, because this is definitely a conversation I don't want to get out?"

"Yes sir. Every time someone enters the room, sir."

"Thank you. You may leave now." Then Richard turned toward Prince and said, "What the …? What was that all about?"

"I know it wasn't in the speech…" Prince said.

"Yep, it sure wasn't in that speech. I've never seen you do that before. I've always trusted…we've always agreed on major things like this, and I can't even believe what you said."

"I'm sorry Richard. It probably will never happen again. This was a very unusual circumstance."

"It must have been," Richard said. He shook his head in disbelief and slumped on the edge of the couch. "Prince, you may never have the opportunity to do this again. It seems to me that you have destroyed your political career." But then he paused. "And yet, each time you surprise me, it's for a good reason, and you say something which changes my mind. But this…well…I don't know. It's beyond my comprehension." He had been gesturing furiously with both of his hands, and as he finished speaking, he threw both of his hands out from his sides to manifest his exasperation.

"Richard, there's more than winning a political campaign. That's why we're out there fighting—because we are different. Our motivation is not to merely get elected, as others wish. That's not our goal. It's our means, so that we can change mankind. What I said tonight, I know to be true. Look, I hate the thought of this prophecy. But it's absolutely going to happen. Forget my campaign. I had to do it for humanity. My soul cried this morning when I knew I would have to say this. I prayed to G-d, but ultimately I must do what G-d wants. I am His servant."

"And how could you know that?" Richard said.

"It was a dream. It was so clear in the dream, so clairvoyant. I awoke, and then I had the dream again, and lest there be any doubt, a third time," Prince said.

"But why didn't you tell me?"

"Because this would have been a great burden for you. It was enough for me to contemplate the confusion that I would cause tonight. It's much easier to react to a calamity than to anticipate that you will be creating one. You might have felt compelled to stop me," Prince said.

"Now what?" Richard said.

"Now, we move on, that is, if you will stay with me," Prince said.

Richard grinned. "You know the answer to that. I believe in you and what you are doing. What else is there in this life? I am privileged to assist you, and I'll be there till the end. But having said that, I don't know how we'll get out of this."

"We'll fall thirty points in the polls, and everyone will write me off, even more so than my election for mayor. Kahn and the media will have proved their point, at least for now. They're already celebrating with champagne. But we will recover and win in a narrow race. We have time now." Prince looked over at Richard for confirmation.

Richard thoughtfully nodded his assent. "Speaking of Kahn, I sure wish now that you had let me bring him in. We might have had a little sympathy from the press at this time, when we really needed it."

Prince smiled and shook his head. "No, it wasn't an option. It'll work out, Richard. Believe me, as hard as it seems now, as hard as the knocks are, it will work out. It's times like this, when we are down, that we have to trust in G-d. We will do all we can, and then it's in His hands." Then after a pause, he continued.

"But Richard there is much more to this than the election, as you can well imagine. There is the condition of humanity and the earth, which is what this ultimately is all about. There are also future prospects for us.

"You see, I did what I must do tonight, regardless of the consequences. But this condition, the drought, will help our friends and hurt our enemies. In setting up the drought, G-d has also provided a means of alleviating that condition by empowering those who would do His Will. Those who would do G-d's Will allow G-d to do their will."

"How's that?" Richard said.

"We have many followers already. And the spiritual advisory group has begun to organize them. I knew this morning, that after my speech of tonight, I would be carefully monitored by the media. So I prepared in advance. I spoke personally today with the Hasidic Rabbi who has tutored me."

"Is that why you insisted on stopping to make a phone call this morning?" Richard said. "I thought it strange."

"Yes, and they were apprised of what they should do. They will speak immediately to the commodity and stock traders associated with the spiritual advisory group," Prince said.

"Commodity and stock traders?" Richard said.

"Yes," Prince said. The stock market will crash tomorrow."

"Wow!" Richard said.

"Yes, but the most important situation is what will follow after that," Prince said. "You see, when the commodity markets open tomorrow, the grains, as well as many other items will hit their trading increase limits for some time to come. Greed will prevail, as it often does in human affairs. But then there will come a time when our people will want to enter the markets."

"How's that?"

"Our natural enemies, the ones who would wish to continue to tear up the planet in a vain search for profits, now have control of many of the earth's resources. They will not believe this prophecy, and will laugh at it, much as they now thumb their fingers at G-d. So they will let the commodity prices run up as much as they can, but after that, they will be eager to sell and lock in what they will regard as unbelievable profits."

"But that will mean that in their greed they will probably be selling commodities they don't even have. They will be shorting the market," Richard said.

"That's exactly right," Prince said. "They will sell their control over these resources, and more, with the thought that when the prophecy doesn't become true, that they can buy the commodities back at much cheaper prices."

"But our people will know differently," Richard said.

"That's right. When the prices back down from their sky high levels—that is when these corporations wish to sell in the next few months, to lock in their profits—our people will be the buyers. At that time, we'll look like fools for sure, but it will be the wisest decision that we have ever made."

On the Aardvark National News the following night, an interviewer began. "As Ellen just reported, the Dow Jones Industrial average fell more than fifteen percent today on very heavy trading volume in response to comments that Joseph 'Prince Reed' made to a convention of professionals last night. Here, with us, to help us analyze the reasons behind Prince Reed's speech, and its implications, is Pulitzer Prize winning writer Daniel Kahn, who has closely followed Mr. Reed during the last few years."

"Thank you," Kahn said smiling sweetly into the camera. "It's a pleasure to be here."

"Mr. Kahn, have we ever had anyone make a prediction of any kind, and had such a response from the public or business community?"

"No, Jim, we haven't, and frankly, it's quite puzzling to me why there's such an uproar about this matter."

"Well clearly, the public takes Mr. Reed's statements very seriously," Jim said.

"Yes, but that would make more sense to me, if he were speaking on a subject about which he had some authority, say business, or perhaps politics, or even religion—in his case. But I can't imagine why he would speak on the weather. One doesn't want to question his personal judgment, but this seems to be a bad mistake on his part," Kahn said.

"This is a person though, that has an unusual track record of being correct in everything he does, so as strange as it may seem, we have to consider that he may be right," Jim said.

"Well, that's what some of the public are saying. That's why the market is down so much today. But the public can sometimes be irrational. And at this point, I would say that he has really gone too far," Kahn said.

"So you would have to question his credibility here?"

"Yes, I would," Kahn said. "And I would have to add, that it seems irresponsible to make bold statements the way he has done, and to move the markets the way he did. A lot of innocent people lost large amounts of money today."

"Let's just say, that his specific prediction regarding the drought is not correct, but should we not assume that perhaps his other statements are correct? Many scientists have made similar statements," Jim said.

"Which statements are those?"

"The ones regarding the inability of the planet to continue supporting nine billion people, predicted to go to at least 12 billion in twenty five years," Jim said. "I believe he was specifically stating that we could not continue to live the way we have, that we would have to become more environmentally responsible. One of the areas he identified was water."

Kahn gave the camera his sweetest smile, the one he had saved up for what he perceived to be the climatic point of the night. "Jim, since at least Thomas Malthus, people have been saying that the earth could not sustain more population and more economic activity. Yet, mankind has always found a better technology, a better way to make things work. I feel confident that we will again and that Mr. Reed's comments are in grave error. And frankly, I am very surprised that a businessman, who owns World Technologies, and who was listed last month as the wealthiest man on earth, would be so anti-business and, if I may say so, so anti-economic activity. He has benefited from the very activity which he claims to abhor." As he spoke, Kahn covered his heart with his right hand.

"Mr. Kahn, since your syndicated column published tomorrow morning is on Mr. Reed, we asked to be shown an advance copy of it. I've received your permission to discuss this column here for our viewers because in it I believe that you are considerably stronger in your use of words than you have been so far tonight."

The camera turned from the interviewer back toward Kahn and zeroed in on his face. He nodded. "If I may quote you here, you say,

This is not just some innocent opinion put out by some minor citizen. These are comments that are irresponsibly said for personal gain. Mr. Reed already controls a huge part of the market for wealth (through investments), technology, and religion. Now he is angling for the politics and the news media. If you really think that Mr. Reed made his comments out of altruism, then have I got a deal for you!

It sure looks as if Mr. Reed wants to control everything we do. What other reasoning could there be? He surely has no knowledge about the weather. Either this prediction is done merely to manipulate us, or I must question his sanity. Does

he think that he is the Biblical Joseph predicting the years of plenty and famine? He has even said there would be seven years of both.

Either way, the public should keep its hands off of him. His motivation cannot be good. Perhaps he fancies himself ready to fill the role of the most powerful person, in the most powerful country in the world. Only now, the most powerful country in the world is the U.S., not Egypt. Perhaps he is looking for the role of dictator. Our democracy does not need him.

"These are powerful statements, Mr. Kahn, are they not? Do you not to try to match the power you claim he has, with the power of your pen?"

Listening to the quote, Kahn had wished that he had not shown an advance copy of the column to the network, just prior to his television appearance. He had been so flattered by network praise about the column that he had allowed the interviewer to quote it; of course the quote seemed slightly out of context. He thought his statements were fine for his reputedly strongly opinionated columns, but they were admittedly too forceful for the cool medium of the tube. But it was too late to stop the moderator, and now he was surprised by the strength of the follow up question. With the spin of just a few words, Prince no longer seemed to be the Goliath, and Kahn no longer had the sympathy of the underdog. After all, the public always liked the underdog. He tried to recover as quickly as he could. He smiled sweetly and said, "Yes, all's fair in love and war. I, of course, mean Mr. Reed no harm. And time will tell. One of us will be right."

19

Prince was correct once again. Despite the drubbing he received from the press for his comments regarding future drought at the convention, and the embarrassing evacuation which followed, he was able to prevail in his bid to become a Congressman from his district in California. He had indeed fallen thirty something points in the polls from the sixties to the lower thirties, before beginning a recovery.

Several factors had helped him miraculously recover enough in the late polls to even be given a small chance to win. First had been his outstanding record in his short time in both the public and private sectors. Though the press, led by Daniel Kahn, had once again resurrected the Mr. Moonbeam analogy in the wake of the drought prediction, and though his opponent had skillfully made reference to it, Prince was able to counter the perception by referring to concrete accomplishments which he had personally implemented. Moreover, Prince's mastery of material was unparalleled to the point that his opponent knew that he should avoid debating him at all costs; this was even more so since Prince's opponent was an incumbent and well ahead in the polls. But in the end, Prince made the cost of not debating him quite high, by frequently bringing it up. The reality was that Prince was quite charming on television, as well as in person, and the public really did like to view him. They liked to see this brilliant man perform, and the fact that his opponent would not debate him, meant that some voters were subconsciously mad at their Congressman when they went to the polls. Such an election strategy might seem a bit strange, but Prince was a man who more than anyone else understood human personality. He was an expert in human souls. He could see what the voter was thinking.

Regarding his comeback, there was also the fact, that after the convention, Prince ran a campaign that was virtually error free, while his opponent seemed to make the usual number of gaffes. In the end, with the passage of time, Prince's speech at the convention became old news, and seemed not much more ludicrous to the voter than some of the rather stupid remarks of his opponent. Finally, the environmental movement had taken to the streets to bring a huge group for him to the voting booths.

Still, the weekend before election day a respected pollster produced a poll which showed that Prince trailed his opponent by a margin of 55 to 45. Even Prince's supporters were resigned to his defeat. "We've fought the good fight, but it doesn't look good for us," Jeff had said. But Prince was not at all discouraged. "Our voters will get out because they care for us and what we advocate," he said. "Many of our opponent's voters are going to stay home. He just doesn't excite them anymore. That's because he has no fire, no passion, about what he is doing. He has no real issues. Just like 99% of them in Washington, he's not fighting for anything other than the right to occupy the office."

Once again Prince confounded his watchers. By the barest majority, he was elected to Congress at the age of only twenty-eight. The victory party was said to be the largest ever for a Congressman. Prince's supporters not only filled the campaign headquarters at the hotel, but fanned out throughout the surrounding streets. Once again, Prince was heralded as one of the leaders of a new political future.

Washington was at that time a place where most freshmen Congressmen went to get in line to wait for their turn, their turn to be heard, their turn for committee positions, their turn to get appropriations for their district, their turn to gather a consensus and pass serious legislation, and finally their turn at distinguishing themselves in a way which would gain them national exposure. It was a path in those days of fixed ways, one of deference to the elder Congressmen. Prince would have little of that.

Normally, anyone with bright ideas of acting differently in such a culture would have been simply ignored, if not squashed. That would have been the greatest insult. True, Prince had unusual wealth and power, but so did many other Congressmen, and though his was undeniably greater, it made little difference in that small, closed legislative, fraternal world, with its own arcane rules, sense of ethics, and view of power and reality. Still, Prince was not your typical freshman.

His feats were already well known in the capital. It had not escaped anyone how far Prince had come in just twenty-eight years of life, nor just how unique he really was. Somehow he had prevailed in political contests which he shouldn't; he had been written off and discounted repeatedly, and still succeeded. Moreover, what impressed his compatriots was that Prince was not just a political phenomenon. Amazingly, he was still head of the largest corporation in the world. And just several years earlier, many had recalled seeing him heroically win twice at the Olympics. And if that weren't enough, there was the extraordinary following which he was developing among his co-religionists. He had developed an air of invincibility, and most of his fellow Congressmen were afraid to ignore him. In their eyes, his opponents had been trampled.

But there wasn't just the fear/awe factor. Several shrewd Congressmen had quickly concluded that great opportunity lay in uniting with him on issues. They figured that he knew how to get things done, regardless of the fact that he had never served in the House before. To add to that, he brought them immediate national exposure; just being associated with him would boost their status. Prince also brought his good old fashioned charm: first the tremendous charisma that naturally emanated from him and second his uncanny ability to tack between a hard and soft response on an issue. Finally, there was a group of Congressmen, mainly those with short tenure, who welcomed someone with the ability to fundamentally change the system.

For a guy who had been in executive roles during his short career, Prince brought the crucial coalition building skills that he needed to succeed in a legislature. In a few short minutes, he could size up a person and make a proposal that would accommodate mutual interests. After a while, the early resentment at his success at such a young age and at his celebrity status faded. It was replaced by sheer admiration for his talents. As one veteran legislator put it in a private conversation with a reporter, "That kid brings order to a place that we would now have to admit is chaotic. When he gets behind something, I, as well as others, feel confident that it is usually going to go. Another thing—he doesn't stand for pettiness, or stalling out, or obscurantism in his work. He's after the truth and wants everything out on the table. In his book, it's okay to oppose him—he'll listen carefully to your position and may even change his mind. What will get you in trouble with him is saying one thing and meaning another, or not living up to your word—and I wouldn't want to get on his wrong side. Regardless, I'd have to say that this place is a lot better with him. It's hard to believe that one person could make such a difference. I even like coming to work better in the morning, and as far as I'm concerned, he's due all the regard given to him."

Not surprisingly, Prince concentrated on environmental and charitable legislation, and then turned his talents to simplifying a tax code that had become so complex, even government administrators could not understand it. After a year, he came back to the one issue that might again topple his political prospects, the issue of the drought, now according to Prince's earlier prediction, only one year away. Richard had shaken his head, and said, "I didn't figure you'd really let go of this thing. But I don't know Prince. You're doing so well now. Do you really want to tackle this again?"

But Prince was not to be deterred. This time, however, he addressed the issue of credibility. Rising on the House floor, he said, "More than a year ago, I made a prediction that our great country would suffer a long devastating drought. I still feel strongly that this will occur, starting with the harvest after the next one. I know that many have laughed at me, regarding this prediction. And I know that it may be political suicide for me to even bring it up now. But I must ultimately do the right thing, regardless of the consequences to me.

"Assume for a moment that I am wrong and that the drought will not happen next year, or even for ten years. We still know two things: that a drought like the one in the Great Depression will repeat itself at some point in time, and that we are ill-prepared to handle one, if it does occur. The first thing we must do is to drastically increase our government stocks of grains, and then we must have a contingency plan for distributing those stocks. Yes, it hasn't happened for one-hundred years, but a large part of America and the world could go hungry again, if we don't act immediately."

Prince threw all the considerable political capital that he had built in his short time in the House at the bill that he sponsored. He also used his contacts in the U.S. Senate. In addition to his persuasive talents, Prince shrewdly used several factors in his favor. The farm lobby had become increasingly upset by the incredible surplus of grains in recent years, which had caused grain prices to fall to real levels not seen in generations; many farms had failed. They welcomed Prince's bill because it supported farm prices and would immediately double the price of corn and wheat. In fact, the already oversold futures markets had reacted to Prince's bill by beginning a tremendous rally, and many Congressmen were loathe to fight the bill and send prices spiraling downward again, forcing more farmers out of business. The President and his administration knew that they could ill afford to lose the farm belt, one of their party's natural constituencies, in the next election.

Moreover, the Senators, normally a little more isolated in their small club, were looking over their shoulders at Prince. It was rumored, and not denied, that Prince would run for the open California Senate seat in the next election. Some Senators had expressed concern that when Prince came into their chamber, he would remember their votes. Finally, many Congressmen in both houses considered that Prince had yet to be proven wrong in any matter; if he was indeed correct in his prediction, however crazy it seemed then, they had best support the bill, or face the consequences.

Thus, Prince was able to get a substantial piece of farm legislation passed and signed by the President. It would give the country a basis on which to swiftly act when the drought began. A few months later he announced that he would seek California's U.S. Senate seat.

The press did not let up on him. He had been too successful in their book to be real. Daniel Kahn continued to reprove him for his position on the drought, and continued to suggest that he must be profiting economically from such an outlandish position. But the California voters had grown tired of listening to the press regarding Prince. When it came down to it, they simply liked him. They found him highly intelligent, attractive, progressive, and particularly attuned to their environmental concerns. And as Prince went from success to success, the press beating gave him a kind of desirable notoriety. At the age of thirty, the minimum age to enter that higher House of Congress, Prince was elected to the U.S. Senate.

20

Established politically, and apparently secure in his position for at least six years, Prince turned his attention to the congregation he had dedicated in the stand of sequoias four years earlier. He had continued every Sunday since that time to meet with Jews who had approached him for advice. When he had arrived in Washington, he had set up similar meetings there, alternating between the coasts, depending upon his location. The congregation, now congregations because Washington had been added, were unique. They were Jewish—very Jewish—to be sure, but they belonged to no particular denomination, and thus were affiliated with no other congregations or governing bodies at the time.

The independence of these two congregations had served two purposes. As with so many other factors in our daily existence, one purpose was practical and manifest, and the other one was spiritual and more hidden. The practical one up to that point in time had simply been that, if either congregation had affiliated with a denomination and joined that denomination's umbrella organization, this would have highlighted Prince's role as a religious leader. The public was highly sensitive to a political leader, not to mention a young untested one, mixing religion with politics. On the other hand, while there were many prejudiced voters who might not care for Prince's religious observances, most voters were unlikely to question Prince's religious activities, if they could be viewed as occurring on a more private scale. It was understood, for instance, that a wealthy businessman, in addition to his other charitable projects, might wish to sponsor and fund private religious activities. It was even viewed as admirable that Prince spent so much time advising others, otherwise known in the parlance as donating his precious time. The point was whether he performed these activities in the context of being a spiritual leader of a synagogue.

But there was a much more basic and spiritual reason that the congregations were independent. Prince and his spiritual advisory group had debated this issue many times. Finally, everyone had been in accord with Prince's viewpoint. As Prince had argued, "When we are talking about Jews, we are specifically talking about Jewish souls. Souls are our heritage, our inheritance from G-d. On that fundamental level, there is spiritually no distinction between Reform and Orthodox, or any other denomination. To concentrate on some artificial distinction, only lowers the level of our spirituality, by focusing our minds on division. Rather than looking for levels of separation, we should look for union. All peoples, all living things, have a common destiny in this world. Do we not all inhabit the same space and spiritual sphere? The diversity we see in our world does not exist in order to segregate and isolate us, but represents the components of a vast super glue that joins us and binds us together. Diversity is the closest path we possess to viewing G-d's infinite creation, because the infinite cannot adequately be expressed in our physical world. To see diversity, is to understand how small we are, and how great G-d really is. Only when the Jews of the world, with all their beautiful differences, are united, will there be a Messianic Age. Only when the peoples of the world see their common destiny, and come together, will there be a Messianic Age.

"For the Messianic Age to happen, opposites must be combined into higher truths, differences must be bridged, paths must converge. Every living and nonliving thing must be linked into a network which has balance and proportion. The absence of the smallest part of this web of existence means that there can be no wholeness, and that there will exist an infinite longing between one part of the universe and another. It is a basis for pain, rather than pleasance. The determination of people to go their separate ways, and to emphasize their differences, rather than their propinquity, prevents the Messianic Age from ripening.

"For example, let us take a peach, just an infinitesimal part of the universe. We can discuss the infinitely numerous characteristics of an individual peach. There is its smell before we eat it or anything else, or its smell after we eat another food. There is its taste when eaten by itself, and its taste when eaten with another food. There is its color, but not just its general color, but the infinite number of different shades of colors, and the way that infinite shading connects with each other. There is its texture, but there are an infinite number of textures around that small sphere, and there are so many ways that we can personally experience that texture. There is its size and the way the skin tears off in your mouth, and how juicy it is, and its seed, and how it was connected to the tree, and how it compares with other peaches. And on and on. There are all these characteristics which G-d has given us in one mere object, and yet they are beyond our ability to count; but if we remove any one of those characteristics, just one of those individualisms, traits, properties, attributes, or qualities, then that peach is not the same. It is missing something distinctive, and once one of its aspects is separated from it, it is virtually impossible to return that feature back, and make the peach whole again. So that peach can never be the same. This is why we must often live many lives, because what we separate on this earth is often irretrievable, and cannot be returned on this physical plane, so that we must die a physical death in order to be purified and made whole again. Now the Jewish people are no different than the peach. Once one of its souls becomes disconnected from the whole Jewish soul, the Jewish people lose something that is not restorable.

"As far as denominations, only rarely was there a similar distinction during the time of the Temples, and there was no distinction after the time of the Temples, until about 150 years ago, when some people believed that they did not have the choice of observance, unless they broke away. But Judaism has always been a religion of choice. Ironically, the denominations have made the Jewish people feel uncomfortable with choice. It is implied that if you are uncomfortable with the dominant observance in a particular synagogue, you are free to worship somewhere else. What happened to all types of Jews coming together to challenge each other and learn from each other? What happened to changing beliefs within Judaism? Should a person find it necessary to change synagogues, and Jewish congregational friends, merely because he now wishes to have more or less in the way of observance? The very way of human life and destiny is growth and therefore a Jew must be able to experience movement and change within the context of a single institution; the lack of that flexibility within the synagogue is why so many Jews have forsaken their religion and their synagogue. Why can't a person feel comfortable both keeping a non-kosher home and laying tefillin, until he might see the merits of keeping kosher? And what will convince a Jew to keep a kosher home and become more observant, if he cannot feel comfortable in either a Reform or Orthodox context, because he cannot fully relate to either. Clearly," Prince said, "a Jew is a Jew is a Jew. We must bring all Jews together. We must have all levels of Jews in our synagogue."

The point in Prince's mind was not to dilute the highest level of observance, which he rigorously maintained in his own life, but to provide a path whereby others, who chose different levels of observance, or who related to their Judaism in a different way, would feel included. Prince said, "Remember, G-d has set forth certain commandments, certain laws, which are very important to follow. But the fact that a Jew does not keep all those commandments, does not make that person any less of a Jew. He is a Jew by virtue of his inheritance from G-d, and by virtue of his ancestry. We all stood at Sinai, and throughout our history we have all felt the persecution of our neighbors, and yet have still chosen to maintain our identities. A Jew, who proclaims himself a Jew, who will say the Sh'ma, and will be G-d's witness on earth by doing righteous acts, and unequivocally affiliates with our community, promoting our goals and aims, clearly has just as much claim to his inheritance. Furthermore, none of us knows the mysteries of G-d and all the reasons why certain souls are sent here to this earth. Just as the qualities of the peach, one Jew is a leader in the community, while another is destined to be a businessman and add to the community's wealth. Some Jews provide the head, some the heart, and some the hands of the community. Some do multiple tasks. Can we really say that one Jew is more important than the other, when each Jew is in fact needed to perfect the health of the community and make it whole? If there is then spiritual equality between Jews—as distinguished between spiritual equality between souls, which is G-d's matter—how can we not maintain such a spiritual equality in our synagogue, which is G-d's house on earth?"

To put his philosophy into practice, Prince had designated that all Jewish holidays, and particularly Shabbat, would be strictly observed through prayer and services at the two synagogues. This would set the example for each synagogue. But other Jews with different practices, religious and lay leaders, had been brought in to offer alternative services, and to also fully participate in the organization of the synagogue. Respect between the different congregants was the key, and this is what was continually stressed. Those who chose less observance could not act within the context of the synagogue to violate the Jewish observance of commandments by others. For example, it might not be possible for the less observant Jews to plan certain functions on Shabbat or certain religious holidays, which might violate the precepts of the more observant. Similarly, it was understood and necessary, that no observant Jew should condescendingly approach another Jew's choice of worship, but rather respect and encourage what was in that Jew's heart to do; when it came to serving G-d, no one had absolute perfection, so complete humility was required. To add to that, virtually no one could be aware of the level of neshamah, or soul, that spiritually vivified a person, regardless of his level of observance. This is because certain people, with lofty levels of souls, had been born into particularly nonobservant stations of life, especially before the Messianic Age. It was these souls' very path back to observance which would herald the Messianic Age. As their every day affairs were bound with spiritual observance, opposites would unite and conflicts would dissipate. Prince knew this from his own experience of becoming observant.

Moreover, it was each Jew's kavanah, or spiritual intent and motivation that counted. If a Jew intended to join himself to G-d by fulfilling His Will, since G-d and His Will are one, and sincerely attached his thought and intellect to G-d, then this is what mattered. Of course, worshipping G-d, observing the holidays, and doing mitzvot were absolutely critical, but a Jew should also have the right intent behind his thought, speech and action. Kavanah was the soul for the body of the mitzvah. And kavanah came in two basic levels. The lowest level was related to the natural love and fear hidden in a Jew's heart. Since it originated at an emotional level, and was associated with that person's natural and instinctive fear of the injurious aspects of life, as well as love of its pleasant aspects, it was analogous to that of the soul of an animal. The higher level related to that of human intelligence and thought. At that level, a person could discern and reflect on G-d's greatness. That person, through his understanding, had a soul which wished to cleave to G-d. That higher level was far superior, because that person chose with his intelligence and freedom of choice to pursue religious observance and mitzvot. This lofty level of kavanah was then analogous to the soul of a human being. "Clearly," Prince said, "we have many nonobservant Jews in our midst that have lofty souls with kavanah. They must be brought into our fold and be just as valued as any other Jew within our synagogue."

So different groups sprang up within the two synagogues. There were several very observant minyans, several woman's minyans, elderly ones and those of young couples, and various different alternative services, some creatively written from Jewish texts. Groups of Jews met and designed their own worship and times of worship; the only rule was that it comport with the sanctity of the synagogue and Jewish law. It became so difficult to schedule all the services and meetings at times, that the first synagogue was forced to relocate to a much larger building; as fate would have it, the very one that Prince had visited with his parents, to escape the rain that Saturday morning in San Francisco, had become available when the congregation previously occupying it had moved; Prince had remembered its beauty well.

Then another interesting development occurred. The groups became quite fluid. There was the less observant moving into more observant groups, and more observant Jews appearing in the less observant ones, because of friendships, or because a more observant worshipper would lend his voice or her talent with prayers and Hebrew to another group. And there were those Jews who constantly moved between groups, sampling different types of worship, taking advantage of special events and services, and following their spiritual inclination of the moment. There were multiple newsletters with activities put out by the groups. And then a general counsel was formed with representatives of the groups to report to the board of the synagogue. The same phenomenon occurred in its own way with adult education and the synagogues' religious schools. Three different religious schools, which shared teachers and information, had already been formed in the San Francisco congregation.

With all this religious diversity, the members of the congregations nevertheless united on social occasions—sometimes joking with each other in a friendly way about each person's religious practices—and on its profile in the general community. And its funding came from the same source, which was its rapidly growing membership; in that funding, no one group was given priority over another. Most importantly, what had been created, was a community of caring. It did not matter if someone who had experienced joy or misfortune was in your group(s); you probably knew them, and if you didn't, it was almost certain that you knew someone who knew that person very well. Life cycle events of members often became yours. Consequently, Bar Mitzvahs, namings, and funerals were always attended by very large percentages of the congregation.

What also emerged after a time was an incredible outpouring of writing and intellectual thought from the congregation. Several members were on the verge of publishing Jewish oriented books. Just as the best and brightest had had the drive and intelligence to take the hard course and immigrate to America, so the Jews who came to Prince's synagogues were of the highest caliber. They had been the ones who had questioned their previous synagogues, and had chosen to be different. They had initially taken the risk of moving their families away from familiar worship surroundings for something that originally seemed only a promise. Now the seeds of their thoughts and aspirations had fallen on fertile spiritual ground and blossomed.

This is the situation Prince faced when he came to the San Francisco congregation to meet his spiritual advisory committee. In four years time, the original startup congregation, with only several dozen Jews, had grown to the largest synagogue in America. The two synagogues had quickly become known among all kinds of American clergymen to be the most progressive, cutting edge religious institutions in America. And it seemed to be the perfect choice for an American Jew who wanted something both new and old, something that would allow discovery of Jewish self, but also would be steeped in tradition. In fact, both congregations had been so successful that they were now faced with a deluge of membership applications, more than either could possibly handle in their current setup.

But the growth had to this point occurred under the radar of the media. First, as mentioned previously, Prince had been very discreet about his association with the synagogues. He had originally started them with religious scholars, gifted educators, and souls with commitment and social grace, whom he had personally interviewed and greatly trusted. But once the synagogues had started, he had been careful to refrain from the day to day administration of the institutions, only advising them occasionally, and yet always attending his Sunday meetings with the congregants. This distance was not just for reasons of public perception. No human could handle more details than Prince was already doing; his days extended into nights, which extended into days again, with only short interludes for sleep.

More importantly, for the spiritual transformation to occur in the Messianic Age, each individual would have to rise from his present level to a higher one. Prince would have to rely on those beneath him, and they in turn would have to find those beneath them, whom they could rely upon, and could pull up. And so the entire world, through this process, would be raised a notch in spiritual consciousness and responsibility. And once enough people in the world had raised themselves by that additional madreigah, or degree, then this would be the spiritual and physical support for Prince's present rung or plane, which would then allow him to take that next higher step on the ladder to G-d. So, Prince was the lead person up the mountain of G-d, taking that leap into space to the next grade, relying on his faith in G-d to propel him there. In turn, those who followed him, relied on their faith in G-d, as they grew spiritually, and if their faith in G-d were not great enough, they could see with their own eyes the physical example of G-d's prophet on our earth. And for those whose smaller spiritual capacity could not relate to Prince's elevated soul, or for those who could not speak or personally observe him because of distance, there was also faith in G-d—though often to their more limited extent—or failing that—as might indeed be the case with souls of more limited spiritual volume—there were those corporeal teachers and leaders at each capacity who were in turn getting their spiritual sustenance from the higher levels. And so it went down from one level to another. Just as G-d created our present world through tzimtzumim, or contractions, and caused His energy, His Divine Light, to descend from one world to another, from Atzilut, to Beriah, to Yetzirah, and Asiyah, until His energy, was so minute, so infinitesimal, as to be grasped by even the human with the tiniest capacity, or even the rocks on the hills, so Prince began to construct the Messianic world, sending spiritual energy, the Divine Light emanating from his soul, through the chains of humanity. Human creation, human construction, is nothing but an imitation of, or an unfolding of G-d's Plan, and this was no different. In fact, Prince had attained great Kabbalistic knowledge of G-d's creative process and had tried consciously to construct the human world to fit the natural world; to do otherwise, he knew would have been fighting the energy of the universe and would have been a prescription for failure.

Another reason why the media had not picked up on the growth of the two synagogues is that it had happened so quickly. And then again, unlike other religious institutions, the synagogues had remained in the background, not affiliating with anyone else, and up to this point, not really marketing themselves. All this growth had happened through sheer word of mouth. The media still had in their minds that small original band of people in the woods which had dedicated the first congregation, as well as the crowds that gathered every Sunday to meet with Prince personally; this did not signify to them a sizable, established institution. The fact that the San Francisco congregation had located to a large, former synagogue was attributed more to Prince's largess than growth. It was assumed that no synagogue or church ever grew quite that fast.

When Prince arrived in front of his spiritual advisory committee, its operating head for day to day affairs framed the issue. "Now that we have been through some of the details of what our two congregations are doing and reviewed some of their boards' actions, we come to the major issue of today," he said. "As I've discussed with many of you in the last few weeks, we are experiencing such explosive membership demands, that we cannot stay in this building, nor could we even find an existing one that is big enough any more. We would have to build, but that would take quite some time, and even if we built, I can't see, at our present growth rate, that we could hold everyone. We are simply growing too fast. And that won't even address our organizational needs. I don't foresee how we could organize the more than twenty thousand member families that we might have at the end of this year, if trends continue."

"I expect that you may indeed have more than that number," the businessman from Oklahoma City said. "We must immediately consider creating new synagogues that follow our model."

"But now here's the problem," the operating head said. "We certainly can no longer operate the way we have been. But if we go out in the community, and start building synagogues, then everyone will notice."

"Yes," the doctor from Oklahoma City said, "and if we go building several synagogues, then it will become obvious that we are a new Jewish movement. And suddenly it will look as if our Rebbe here is not merely following his private beliefs, but is associated with a major new religious movement and philosophy. Before we could say that our Rebbe was an intensely spiritual and religious man, and had the individual means to create synagogues for his minyans on both coasts, depending upon where he might be. Now we cannot say that..."

"...Unless of course our Rebbe was not publicly associated with our movement," another advisor said.

The eyes of the Hasidic Rabbi from Oklahoma City were twinkling. "This, my friends, is a good problem to have. G-d has given us success. Success is outgrowing your clothes. Success always brings new decisions."

"Let us assume that we build new satellite synagogues and consider what will happen if our Rebbe continues to publicly be associated with us," a sixth advisor said. "I believe that it will be disastrous for us. The American public will not stand at this point for a U.S. Senator to be associated with a religious movement."

"And not just any movement," a seventh advisor said. "Remember this is a Jewish movement. And not just any Jewish movement—not an assimilated one that others might understand. It's associated with observant Judaism. And to make matters more delicate, it's also new. We have no allies in other congregations in other political constituencies that would aid us politically in Congress. To the contrary, Jews in other congregations will view us as competition, and at best, will let us flail in the political wind, and at worst, will try to destroy us."

"And we have no history as an institution, as part of a movement, which people might view and assure themselves of our stability and veracity," an eighth advisor said. "And with all due respect to our Rebbe, remember that from the public's perceptions, not G-d forbid our own, that he is only thirty, and people still harbor suspicions about his background and track record."

Then suddenly a silence enveloped the room. Everyone turned to Prince, to see what he might say. Prince smiled. His face was relaxed and his hands and posture showed no signs of strain or conflict. As his committee watched him, they felt their tensions drain away. "Fear, my friends, has no place in this room. G-d has brought us to this point, and G-d will look after us. Who would have thought that we would be at this point at this time? We must have faith in G-d. Do our part to be sure, but have faith. Now let us consider, without fear, what we might do."

"But Rebbe, how might we counter the perception of you as a religious leader of a major religious movement?" a ninth advisor said.

"Is this a problem? Or is it success?" Prince said. "I have to defer to my esteemed teacher and Rabbi, who I must add, always is more knowledgeable in these matters than I am." As he spoke, he looked over at the Hasidic Rabbi from Oklahoma City, gestured, and smiled. He always liked bantering with him.

"But Rebbe, if we become a full movement, with you at our head, will this not bring out the yetzer hara, and trounce us?" the seventh advisor said.

"The yetzer hara will now be out in full force, regardless of what we do," Prince said. "This is because we are successful, and now our enemies will rise up. The question is how to handle it."

"Do we gain more ground if our Rebbe is clearly the head of our movement now, or should we wait for greater advantage later?" a tenth advisor said.

"Yes," the doctor from Oklahoma City said, "that is the question."

"We are relatively weak now," the seventh advisor said. "Would it not be better if we do not wait until our Rebbe establishes himself better politically? Until he has the experience of a term or so? Then he can proclaim to lead our movement."

"Yes, it seems so," the sixth advisor said. Several other heads nodded.

"And if we do that, it may give our religious movement more time to grow and be even more powerful, with even more people," an eleventh voice said.

Suddenly, there was silence again. Almost everyone looked over to Prince. The Hasidic Rabbi was focused on the wall in front of him, as he dangled a pencil in his hand. After what seemed a long moment, Prince spoke. "Now, friends, if I waited to proclaim my leadership of our synagogue movement for several years, what kind of credibility do you think that I would have with the American public?"

No one answered and there was again an uncomfortable silence. Prince's face then took on a look of determination. "We best get to doing the L-rd's work right now," he said. Now that everyone knew Prince's decision, they quickly straightened their bodies to hear the reasons and the details.

"G-d often gives us only a few opportunities in life to do the right thing. We have a spiritual choice, which is a uniquely human condition. Our choice is really quite simple. We must choose to grow or not to grow spiritually as a movement, and as individual souls in a movement. Growth is the way of human destiny and is life. If we choose not to grow, we shall die. We may not choose to stand still where we are. Nothing stands still in life. Everything is in movement. And all things that are not growing are in the process of decay.

"If we choose to grow, and to do otherwise is to defeat our purposes on this earth, then it is certain that the yetzer hara will be out in full force. Our opponents will try to hurt us, no matter whether I am identified as the spiritual leader of our movement. And if I am not the public leader, the press will certainly try to link me. We will spend so much of our precious spiritual energy maintaining that I have no connection. The truth is that everyone will know that I have a natural bond with this movement, so that they will hardly believe what we say. By the time that I do assume the public leadership of our movement, we will be weakened. Our enemies will be trying to reopen the wound of credibility that we have afflicted on ourselves.

"We must strike now while no one suspects what we are. G-d has opened up the Red Sea and laid out a path for our redemption back to Mt. Sinai. G-d has performed a miracle for us and mankind. Shall we then complain about this miracle, which is the cause of our success, and wish that we had failed prior to this point?

Shall we be so ungrateful, foolish, and faithless in front of G-d, as to wait for the Egyptians to arrive? Shall we stay at the lowest level of kelipah—the one which our ancestors experienced in Egypt before their deliverance—or break out of our pit, and topple the constraints which we have imposed upon ourselves? I admit that what we will do now will take bold and creative imagination, but that is what G-d wants from us now. We are all here in our individual roles to serve the Master of the Universe now." He said "now" with such an emphasis and insistence as to make several jump from their seats.

Prince paused for a moment to give everyone time to absorb his words. Most sat on their chairs riveted by that decisive moment in time. The Hasidic Rabbi was more relaxed. He sat smiling, very proud of his former student.

"From this point in time," Prince began again, "we shall show our heads proudly. We shall not wait for anyone to come to us to join our movement. This week we shall figure out the number of synagogues which we project that we should logically need in the next two years, and triple that number as a starting point. We shall now publish marketing literature that explains our philosophy and goals and invites all Jews to join us. We shall use our contacts in the local media, which we have cultivated, to explain our positions. And we shall use the many talents of our present congregants; they will provide examples for prospective members, and further our public relations."

"And how shall we reply to those who say that we mix religion and politics?" the seventh advisor said.

"I shall be largely responsible for handling that with the press," Prince said. "I shall say something along the order of, 'Who has been fooling who here? As the individuals that we are, we've always mixed religion and politics in America in our personal lives, just as the rest of the world has. Both of these disciplines specifically deal with our relationships with our fellow man. The difference is that in America, we've correctly tried to preserve a fine line, according to our Constitution. No political leader in his public life should favor the interests of his own religion over the general public.

"The presumption here is that I favor my Jewish movement over the public good, because I am a leader of a Jewish movement. This is simply not true, any more than my esteemed colleagues in the Senate, favor the adherents of their individual religions, which they observe. Instead of making me more partisan toward my religionists, this leadership role and my relationship with G-d has made me more sensitive, caring, and respondent to the needs of all Americans.'"

"And you think that they will believe that, even though it might be true?" the doctor from Oklahoma City said.

Prince smiled. "I don't expect anyone to believe me, or any of us, immediately. But this is why we are around. We must change perceptions. Come on, if this were easy, we wouldn't be here. We've just got a lot of work to do.

"You see the truth always wins out. It may not win promptly. But it always prevails. As truth originates with G-d, it is eternal. On the other hand, the oppositions told by some, are ephemeral. Eventually, the dye used by some, to color the people's perception of the world, fades, and leaves the ultimate bare reality. And the truth here is that the general public and all religions will benefit by what our movement brings to the table, especially other Jews, many of whom will oppose us. All religions will flourish in the perfect world, and all their truths will be established in the heavens. Over time, our message will get through. This is why we must start immediately."

"But I know," the twelfth adviser—one voice who had not previously spoken—said, "from my own experience, that it will not just be whether you lead a religious movement, Rebbe. I expect that it will be that many Christians will be attracted to what we say and are. We will actually be competition to the Christians."

"Why do you see that?" the operating head said.

"For one thing, we are going to be doing now what the Christians did so well after the fall of our Temple. They mixed religion and politics very successfully, to the point that the Roman emperor actually converted the entire empire to Christianity. The Jews were forced out of their land and could not both honor their religion and serve their country, or any country for very long...until there was America, where the two were separated as a matter of course, and now Israel," the twelfth advisor said.

"Yes, this is true," Prince said. "And for the first time since the Roman empire, we will be a welcoming religion, even if we are not a fully proselytizing one. And ironically, it will be like old times, with Judaism and Christianity more in a kind of competition with each other, except that everything will be in a historical kind of reverse. Instead of pulling away from each other, and then separating, as we did two thousand years ago, we will be approaching each other in attitude, and as a result, starting to come together again.

"We can think about all the events that happened at the time of the destruction of the second Temple and see that, one at a time, they are happening in reverse, so as to make the spiritual world whole again. First, in the late nineteenth century, there was some settlement in the land of Israel, which was the counterpart or reverse of the groups of Jews that settled outside the land of Israel, for example in Alexandria, Greece, and Syria, just before the destruction of the second Temple. Jews settling early in Israel one-hundred fifty years ago heralded our return to our homeland, just as Jews leaving their homeland heralded the exile from our land. The Holocaust, the great destruction that happened in Galut, the Diaspora, was commensurate in that realm to the destruction of the Temple, which occurred during our residence in Israel. Then, as a response to the Holocaust, which was great death, we have settled the land of Israel, and ended our exile. This is of course a fitting antithesis to our former exile.

"And further, you will note that just as many Jewish institutions were changing, being both destroyed and created, at the time of the second Temple, so they too are in great flux now. And our model of the synagogue reverts back in some ways to the organization in the Temples. If we look back to the time between the first and second Temples, we might find similar patterns. What we have here are historical bookends. What comes around, must go around. But now that we approach the Messianic Age, we should not expect to have another cycle. The Messianic Age will occur before the building of the third Temple."

"So what should we tell Christians who wish to visit us and may wish to associate with us?" the seventh advisor said.

"We shall be welcoming," Prince said. "We shall recognize that all religions lead to redemption and to unity with G-d. Their path is just as valid for them as ours is for us."

"But what if they wish to join us? Shall we convert them, or should we attempt to discourage them, as we have usually done in the past?" the seventh advisor said.

"Honesty is the only path," Prince said. "We must determine what each one's goals are, and whether joining us would assist him spiritually. The answer is not obvious, as many of our Christian brethren would have the world believe, when trying to attract Jews to their cause. It depends on the individual's soul."

Then Prince paused. "It is true that we will have many Judaizing Christians. Many will not formally convert, but will choose to associate with us, practice holidays with us, and allow us to raise their children from mixed marriages, or even Christian marriages, to be Jewish. This is a sign of convergence, and a sign that the Messianic Age is drawing closer. But we will also work to strengthen the practice of other religions in America. This will be part of my mission, because without the strength of the other religions, it will be impossible to have that meeting. Diversity is necessary for unity."

"And what else must we do?" the Hassidic Rabbi said.

"We must strengthen Israel," Prince said. "Israel must continue to gather in our people, so that the exile will fully end. And just as Israel will gather Jewish souls, so many groups will discover, or admit to their Jewish identities, and be gathered into our collective Jewish soul. And here, I'm not talking about Christians that wish to associate with us. I am specifically talking about lost Jewish souls, who return to our fold."

Then the group prayed. Before beginning their specific planning, Prince spoke one more time to them. "It may be that we will not come together again for some time. You should know that the advent of the Messianic Age and the Divine Light is finally upon us. What we do now will be critical. Every action, even something as light as the weight of a feather, will determine the results.

"The rush of events is so fast that the question of our success will become apparent to us all in the next three years. We and others will do what we can do. G-d will do all He can do. Now, it will be up to the rest of mankind to hear our message and accept or reject us."

21

Now there was no bread in all of the world, for the famine was very severe...

Genesis Chapter 47, vs. 13

And G-d will strike you with...scorching heat and drought—and they will pursue you until you perish. The skies above your head shall be copper, and the earth beneath you iron. And G-d will make the rain of your land dust, and sand shall drop on you from the sky, until you are wiped out.

Deuteronomy Chapter 28, vs. 22-24

Daniel Kahn bellowed in the press about what he saw happening in the Jewish movement created by Prince. "I hate to tell you that I told you so," he wrote in a column shortly after the meeting of the spiritual advisory committee, "but the newly elected junior Senator from California, is using his political connections to further his religious ambitions. He has always wanted to establish a Kingdom of G-d on earth. And here right before our eyes, he is boldly asserting himself.

"Wake up Americans. Our ancestors came to this country for religious freedom. We established it in the First Amendment, the most precious part of our Constitution. And now we have this figure, who would be king, attempting to establish a state religion. We must take to the streets and demonstrate before our most fundamental liberties are taken away."

But most of the rest of the country was preoccupied with its prosperity at that point, and hardly paid much attention. Few serious religious figures or social scientists believed that a large religious movement could spring up overnight. And one columnist actually rebutted Kahn's column, remarking at the time, "Here we are, back to the old canard, that this tiny minority of Jews in this country, or in any country, controls everything. It's really kind of hard to believe that less than two percent of America's population, no matter how educated or influential, is really going to take over the country with its state religion. Daniel Kahn, I think that you ought to get off of this subject."

But Kahn kept attacking. He listed everything he could find about the spiritual advisory committee's decisions, detailing the sites upon which it would build, as well as hearsay on the numbers attending services. But initially, many of his syndicated column's readership throughout the country had grown tired of Daniel Kahn's attacks. In many ways his criticisms had become counterproductive, as a result of previous lack of credibility; as more than one person remarked at the time, "...if Daniel Kahn still doesn't like him, he must still be okay." What did happen though, is that Kahn had begun to receive a lot of inquiries regarding Prince from shadowy hate organizations.

After a few months, however, Kahn had begun to do damage on a rather fundamental level. This time he was on to something. First of all, some of the local newspapers in various areas had noticed that Prince's religious movement was buying land, discussing zoning, and arranging building permits in their communities. And a reporter for the *New York Times*, who had begun to closely follow Prince after his election to Congress, had put the reports from the various areas together. He had been able to confirm much of what Kahn had been saying. That reporter had also found that membership in the two original congregations was increasing at what seemed to be an exponential rate. He prepared a long article about Prince and his organization, in which he questioned Prince's motivation. His editors considered it so thoughtful, incisive, lengthy, and timely, that they decided not publish it right away in the daily paper, but to wait for a number of weeks, until they could place it in the Sunday magazine section, wherein they hoped to give it maximum exposure. Thus, it appeared that a major turning point might occur in the press. Prince's people had of course been approached about the article; they had put the best face they could onto the movement, but they were resigned to a major public relations setback. This much they had expected as they changed their religious profile.

But the article was never published in that form. Like a downgraded hurricane, some of its contents eventually made their way into a shorter article. But the tone was changed, and the subtle, or not so subtle, fill in the blanks answers for the reader, were no longer suggested.

What intervened was the drought. Like a plague out of Egypt, it disrupted the course of the most powerful country on the earth, and set forth a supernatural result.

At first almost no one had noticed. During the previous season there had been more than ample rains in the U.S. heartland. Most had forgotten Prince's specific prediction, even though he had passed the farm act in the previous Congress for that purpose. Many of those who remembered it had considered his speech and his forecast to be the kind of grandstanding which politicians did to get attention for their pet causes, in this case environmentalism. From that point of view, it was better in the politician's handbook to take the risk of negative publicity, than to chance receiving too little visibility and being forgotten.

It had started after downpours and flooding in much of the Midwest. The Mississippi had been more swollen and unrestrained by the flood barriers along its shores than any living person could remember. Fields had been planted late because of the water. When the sun reemerged, the farmers as well as the rest of the public welcomed the cloudless and very blue skies that followed.

Then for weeks there was no rain. That was not so unusual. But the weeks stretched into months. Then the people looked toward their weather forecasters for answers. But the forecasters could see no relief.

It became the major topic of national news. Many a forecast was begun with the tenor of words, "There is still no rain throughout most of the Midwest and eastern United States. As the drought worsens, many farmers have decided to plow their fields under and wait for the next season. The President promised relief..."

Commentators were heard to expound on the subject on talk shows. They would say such things as "I just can't believe that this would continue to happen in the U.S...." or "...my consulting firm feels that this will come to an end soon. In all the historical data we have since the weather service began keeping figures more than one-hundred fifty years ago, we've never had a drought of this intensity. Based on this data, we feel that there is virtually no chance that a drought of this nature can continue indefinitely like this. We are optimistic that..."

The wind came down from Canada, snuffing out any moisture that tried to enter from the Gulf of Mexico. Depending on the season, the wind was either very hot, or very cold, but always very dry and very uncomfortable. It was relentless, always blowing, blowing tons of topsoil off of fields which farmers thought they had adequately protected after the Great Depression, rattling and permanently bending trees that tried to stand up to its force, and requiring everyone who found it necessary to walk outdoors to lean into its fury in order to move forward. It could be heard flattening structures and whistling through almost every door in the stricken areas. It was always there as a reminder, as a hated companion. It clogged equipment, flipped children, and fanned interminable fires. People could be seen wearing earmuffs to stop the sound, but even that was ineffective.

There was no peace. There was a living hell on earth. Many died accidental or intentional deaths. But the survivors did not mourn the departed. They only felt sorry for themselves.

Prince said nothing yet. He sat grimly watching the devastation on the television and quietly preparing bills in Congress to deal with the drought.

Prince came in as a freshmen Senator. He watched as Congress first conducted business as usual—with the mindset that the drought was far away and didn't affect them—then became worried, and then fiddled in discomfort as they faced major starvation in the land. Surprisingly, few Congressmen had yet considered that the farm act passed in the previous Congress might assist the public. In their heads, farm acts were always passed for political reasons, to distribute part of the goodies, not for rational ones.

With just the passage of a little time there was desperation in Congress. The desolation and the ruin of the land had been so widespread that within a few months the consumer, the driving engine of the economy, had stopped purchasing all but basic necessities. Many of the few factories left in the country closed, hotels and restaurants shuttered, firms failed, and huge unemployment lines followed. At first, the comment in Congress was one of disbelief. As one remarked, "...just because the farm sector is wasted does not mean that the rest of the economy should tank. The farming sector represents such a small percentage of our GDP, not like it was during the Great Depression. And we don't understand, with our econometric models, how it could happen so fast, and so steeply, without our foreseeing it." The President and Federal Reserve Chairman were heard each day exhorting the consumer to remain confident and to continue purchasing. They pointed out that unlike the time of the Great Depression, government was now a safety net for the unfortunate. The Federal Reserve pushed nominal interest rates to near zero levels. But the drop in economic output not only did not end, but it intensified. Prince said nothing.

At that time of dissolution, visible and normally cocky people—you know, the ones who are always on the airwaves giving advice about politics, cooking, money, and love and marriage, as if they really know what they're talking about—were having second, and then third thoughts. For once, they were thinking before they spoke, and had begun to make some highly unusual statements, as a result of the times. One of the commentators actually went on the most popular evening talk show and said, "If any of us says that we know what is going on here, then I think that that person should be called down on the carpet. I have heard nothing but ridiculous suggestions as to the cause and cure for the present condition of this nation. I am sick of it. We should all be silenced, until we have something constructive to say."

"So you're saying that no one has a solution to the national catastrophe engulfing this country," the talk show host said.

"Yes, I would say that's...true," the commentator said. He half nodded.

"You seem to be hesitating," the talk show host said. "Could there be someone? It's important to know for the nation's sake. Perhaps someone knows what is wrong here. This seems to be even out of the realm of science."

"Well..."

"Yes?... The talk show host raised his eyebrows and leaned over toward the commentator as if he were suddenly to be privy to a secret.

"I've been thinking," the commentator said, "and you know there was this sensational prediction, and it's all become true." He spoke very tentatively, as if he were scared he would seem silly.

"Are you speaking of a prediction of the drought?" the talk show host said.

"Well yes I am," the commentator said. "Senator Prince Reed two years ago made a prediction that we would have seven years of drought, following seven years of plenty. He pinpointed the time exactly, and even managed to pass a farm bill for that purpose just last year. We all laughed at him at the time, but he's been exactly on the mark. We did have seven documented years of plenty. And the fact is that we've never had a drought that affected such a large part of the country. Ever!"

"And do you think that he might be able to help us now?" the talk show host said.

The commentator nodded. "It's certainly worth a try. You know, I've never been a fan of Prince Reed, but one thing you've got to admit about the guy, is that he's not taken advantage of this crisis. Hasn't said a word. Not a 'I told you so.' And I wonder why. Maybe what he said was true, and he's in earnest. Strange and desperate times call for unusual answers."

The second morning after the talk show the *Washington Post* carried an article on its front page entitled, *Does Answer to Drought Lie With Prince Reed?*

The Congressmen all awoke that morning in Georgetown and Alexandria to face that headline as they munched a bagel and drank coffee, and traveled to their Capital Hill offices. Before the session of Congress began, members of each party gathered as usual to discuss the day's business—again on the economy and the drought. They had been stymied for months as they attempted to form coalitions to do something, anything, to stem the down draft. The sum of their efforts had been reduced for months to making speeches on the floor of each house to represent their concerns and to appear that they were taking action. But no major legislation had passed. And it had appeared that no one in the leadership had the means or the skills to guide the group of legislators forward. It seemed that no one even fully understood the extent of the predicament.

After months of seemingly pointless discussion, this morning the Senators felt tired and helpless. Rather than discuss any new ideas, they focused their attention on the *Post* article. Huddling in their groups, they watched Prince as he arrived and stood alone on the floor, greeting and smiling at the other Senators who occasionally walked past him. Being an independent, and not associated with any major party, he had not yet integrated into the small Senate club(s). Yet, he had never been far from their attention. This morning the blond, very tall, athletic guy, with great charm, looked like a lone, magnificent buck out there in a clearing. "What do you think he knows, they wondered?" Having the read the *Post* article, and being the political animals that they were, they knew that they must now decide whether and how to embrace him.

The Senate did not convene on time that morning. Instead, the Senators huddled and then went to lunch. Prince went back to his office to work and returned later. After a while, he saw the Majority Leader break away from his pack, pick up his gavel, nod at him, and approach him on the floor.

"Good afternoon, Prince."

Prince said nothing. He merely smiled and nodded his head. He towered about one foot over the Majority Leader's head.

"Prince, I wanted to talk to you about this article in the *Post* this morning. I assume that you've seen it."

"Yes, my office staff made sure that I read it when I arrived. They're always doing the political analysis for me, you know."

"Is there anything untrue in it?"

"No."

"Then you meant what you said two years ago. And it wasn't for some effect, but then you accidentally overdid it? That's what we all assumed at the time."

"No, George, I never say things I don't mean."

The Majority Leader shook his head in disbelief. "Look, Prince, this is beyond my comprehension. We all just assumed that you couldn't know such a thing, so that you must have made it up. Should I even ask where you got this from?"

"George, I'm not trying to be opaque, but there are times when you just know something is going to happen.

"Is it G-d Prince? Does He tell you? I know how important your religion is to you. And I want to tell you something. I'm not trying to put it down right now. I just have to know, because it's critical for my understanding. I have a very important decision to make at this moment."

Prince looked squarely at the Senate leader, who quivered in his spot. "George, I know your motivation at this time. Your questions are good, and they are fair."

"You can see what I'm thinking, can't you?"

"Yes, I can."

"So what ever powers permit you to do that, permit you to see the future?" the Majority Leader said.

"I am not able to fully see the future, George. G-d allows me sometimes to foretell certain events. It was for the country's and world's benefit, not mine, that He allowed me to see the drought."

"So you believe all that about G-d warning us?"

"Yes, I certainly do," Prince said.

"And they say you can see souls. Can you?"

"Many times, yes. We're all given certain powers as individuals."

"By G-d?" the Majority Leader said, nodding his head affirmatively.

"Yes, by G-d." Prince said.

"Prince, I've been following you for a quite a while, even though we've only had a few conversations here in the Senate. All the way back to your stint at WT. Your course is remarkable. You are either the best contemporary gift this country's ever had, or you're the biggest con job going. But I figure if you were a con job, you would have messed up by now."

"Your assumption is correct, George—at least about the con job part." He smiled at the Majority Leader.

"Tell me something, Prince. Do you feel that you can do something to help this Senate, this Congress, and this country, and alleviate the drought and turn this depression around?"

Prince again looked squarely at the Majority Leader, who quivered once again. "Yes, I can help."

"Then why the dickens haven't you been doing that? Did you not care?"

"Would you have listened to me, a freshmen Senator, if I had brought the drought up before this point, or would you have laughed at me, as you did two years ago? The fact is George that as much as I cared for the situation, there has been nothing I could do about it before now. Believe me, I've shed many a private tear. I grieve for our country."

"And you knew at some time that you would be given the opportunity to do something?" the Majority Leader said.

"The purposes of G-d are never defeated. I will fill the role for which I am destined," Prince said.

The Majority Leader thought for a moment and then his tone became more somber. "Prince, I've been at this job off and on for more than ten years and have served in the Senate for more than thirty. I'm seventy-one years old now, and frankly, I'm tired. Heck, we're all tired up here now. You come at this thing fresh. Youth is on your side, and apparently G-d as well. For several weeks, I've been talking to my colleagues about what to do. I've been ready to step aside, but frankly there was no one in my own party who I thought ought to take my place, considering this catastrophe we're in, and I would say that there's no one on the other side of the aisle either—not that that could even work politically. We will have to have a new face with a totally different perspective and approach.

"I care about this country and I don't want to leave this position to someone who doesn't have a prayer to help us turn this thing around. The Majority Leader would be the second most powerful position in the land behind only the President." He looked carefully at Prince, and raised up his gavel in his open hands.

Prince waited and then answered him. "If you're asking me if I can do this job, Senator—and I think you are—I can. I can turn this around. It won't be overnight, but I can do it. But I'm going to need your help and all of your party. And if I do it, as far as I'm concerned, you'll not be retiring. I need you to keep your troops in line. And I want to tell you, I don't stand for any garbage—political or otherwise—either."

The Majority Leader smiled broadly at him, and brought his body to attention. "Yes sir! I'll look forward to watching a real pro in action, if you'll do me the honor.

And I'll tell you something else. After all this time of fighting party politics, I really don't mind at all that you're independent.

"Now if I give this to you," he said offering the gavel, "you know that it doesn't mean that you are the Senate Leader—yet. Power is grabbed in this Congress, it's not assumed. And you'll have to take it from all the other pretenders in this chamber. Of course, the fact that I'm publicly giving you this, while all the other members watch, won't hurt. You'll start with the throne, and they'll have to dethrone you."

So it was that he handed Prince the gavel. And all the Senators looked across the room at the two and nodded. And Prince rose to the podium, banged the gavel down, and spoke to all of them. "This session of Congress will now come to order. I am informed that our honored Majority Leader has today resigned his position. I believe that the proper order of business is to schedule a vote on the next leader of this great body as soon as possible."

So that is how Prince became the Senate Leader and became the highest government official specifically in charge of drought relief.

22

Now Joseph was the vizier (vice president) of the land, it was he who dispensed rations to all the people of the land.

Genesis Chapter 42, vs. 6

The press was startled again. They had barely gotten word after the *Post* article of the potential shift on Capital Hill of political allies to Prince's side. And then suddenly, within a few days, Prince was the new leader of the Senate.

"That man has some kind of fix over the people he comes in contact with," Daniel Kahn declared in his column. "One has to admire his skill, but he appears very dangerous to me." That back handed half compliment actually had been the best that Kahn had had to say about Prince. The worst statements were not fit to print and had been communicated privately. Prince had violated every paradigm about people that Kahn had possessed and consequently he had made it his personal goal, his personal struggle, to prove to his readership that Prince had been a fraud from the very beginning. "He will show his true colors in time," Kahn had said to friends, "and when he does, I shall be waiting."

Prince was leagued with no one, in a world where affiliation meant protection, and yet this meant that anyone could identify with him. It also meant that his potential enemies were less organized. He had skillfully put together a coalition to elect him and he continued to use certain alliances to assist him, as he needed them. Prince was so different from any other leader the Senators had ever experienced. Most notably, he always kept his word, but on the other hand, could never be "read" as to his future political moves. The legislators had previously known the very opposite, the devil they could predict, rather than the saint they could not understand.

Prince was shrewd in the Senators' book. He possessed a kind of canniness from their point of view, and they were afraid to cross him. He had a certain knowledge about life; in his midst, they often felt as dependent, helpless, unequaled, and ill-matched as pets with their master. Just like a pet, you could only take temporary advantage of the man; ultimately, he would prevail because of his clear superiority, his artfulness in struggle, his cunning in contest. What looked as if it were a tactical advantage over him was usually turned into a distinct inexpedience; if you were boiling a pot of hot water to dump on him, for example, it was almost surely going to be turned around to its source and end up on you; and the worst part was that he appeared to prevail in each encounter effortlessly, and without any malice toward his opponents. His adversaries not only lost their struggle, but appeared to have pettily waged it for an inane purpose. After a while, some Senators considered that even mean thoughts about Prince could be detected by him. On the other hand, to use the pet analogy once again, there were distinct political rewards of associating with him and maintaining loyalty. It always helped to be on the winning political side, not to mention that Prince was able to pass significant national legislation, as well as financing major projects in local districts. But if you wanted funding, you had better have a good reason; Prince was happy to help out a good local project, but not to fund pork barrel.

Prince dominated the air waves. The President spoke at his news conferences, to be sure, and traveled throughout the country, but it was Prince who was on the evening news night after night with another piece of legislation for the benefit of the people. With his giant intelligence, he could recall detail after detail of a bill, and argue each point. Americans back home didn't always understand the technicalities, but they knew when a person was in command of his material. And they also perceived when a person was in earnest, versus saying something for his own advantage. And Prince fit their image of the capable but good, intelligent but nevertheless decent, man who they could trust in this time of great uncertainty and change in the country.

From the beginning, Prince had immediately used the farm legislation passed in the previous Congress as a structure for funding and distributing food aid. There had been huge surpluses of food stocks in the system as a result of the seven previous years of plenty, and these overages would have been largely lost in the last year had not Prince passed a farm bill which bought up many of the stocks, supported prices, and ensured that many farmers planted all their fields in that last year. What Prince had largely sold as a political bill, aligning various interests to obtain passage, had actually been a well designed hunger document. Still, it would take a careful distribution of the food over the next few years, to make sure that no one starved.

Prince not only commanded the political front, but the private, economic one as well. His business and religious interests had accurately traded upon his prophecy, but only after that prophecy was made and published in the media. As he had instructed them, they had bought grain commodities futures several months after Prince's prediction—at what then deceptively appeared to be very high prices. Now, however, they held the rights to huge stocks at prices which had skyrocketed to levels totally unforeseen by the business community. Among other trades in commodities, they had additionally sold short cattle and hog futures, believing correctly that because of the drought, huge stocks of meat would come to market for slaughter, because there would be inadequate and costly stocks of grain available to support the animals; the huge supply of animals had driven down the price, so that these commodities could be repurchased at great profit. In the equity markets, they had also taken over control of several food and resource companies, and were poised to purchase additional control of companies which had now failed in this environment.

If Prince's forces stood to gain politically and economically by the drought, the losers on the contrapositive side were many major companies, some more than 150 years old. Those companies that had not only laughed at Prince's prediction—there was a huge number of those—but had also greedily and insidiously tried to profit greatly from the market place confusion, were suddenly on the verge of collapse. They had lost all that they had gained, much of which had gone out as special dividends to stockholders at the time anyway, plus inestimably more, as they were called upon to replace commodities, which they had sold, but did not have.

"This will be unsightly," Richard said, "even though we did everything legally and ethically. There was no insider trading before the prediction, and everyone else had the same playing field as we did afterward. They just had to follow the same prediction we did. And we had to judge when to buy and sell, just as everyone else. We didn't have any more of a crystal ball on our market moves than anyone else. Still..."

"I know," Prince said. "They will say that we knew something which they didn't, that at the very least I was privileged to receive the information leading to the prediction. At the worst, like Kahn, they will say that we made the prediction in order to profit by it."

"It's unfortunate," Richard said. "There's too often this assumption that the successful guys in our world have done something wrong. 'How else could they have gotten to the top', they say. Not only that, but so many people are always trying to lower a successful person down to their levels, instead of being inspired by example to raise themselves up. Others foolishly see it all as a zero sum game, in which one can only profit relative to another."

"They subscribe their motives to ours, because all of the sensory information of each individual is filtered through his own consciousness. And the soul—both the part which is intellect and the portion which is emotions—is the guardian, custodian, and caretaker—all these things—as well as the portal or gate, for our consciousness. There's this incredible world out there designed by G-d just for us, and yet we can only see the minute part which will fit through the tiny tube of our limited perception and the ego attached to our soul," Prince said. "And not only that, but that capacity of the soul to deal with the world is not necessarily linked to what the world perceives as intelligence. How many times do we see the incredibly talented person turn to support evil, or the supposedly simple person, who is presumed not to be so smart, do such wise things in life? Why does the simple child always catch the fish? Clearly, so called intelligence in this world and a profound soul are not the same. This is what allows evil an equal opportunity to exist, so that we may have a choice in this life."

"Yes, and if a person has a limited perception and consciousness, so that he can only imagine that no one is altruistic, then it goes without saying that there is no way for that person to sense that our motives are honest," Richard said.

"The truth is," Prince said, "that everyone is empowered with information. G-d speaks to us all. We are all receptors and it is that energy, that Divine Light, which sustains us. But therein lies the inequality. We all have different antenna, and different capabilities of holding and analyzing that information.

"So," Richard said, "that dream you had about the drought, was it meant just for you?"

"Excellent question," Prince said. "We know that ninety percent of our soul departs our bodies during sleep. The other ten percent stays to hold the body in this world. This is why we thank G-d for returning life to us with our blessings each morning after we awake—because in our sleep we come so near to death."

Prince paused and smiled at Richard before proceeding on. "Like a lot of other questions, there is a yes and no to your question. This dream is a reality out there. It exists as a truth in the night, through which my soul, or someone else's, travels. Just like a person who has died that you, or someone else, might visit in your sleep. So it is conceivable, if not likely, that others had the same dream. So in that sense, the dream was not specifically intended for me. But then the question arises who will remember the dream, believe it, interpret it, and communicate it, so that it might be used for human purposes? Who will grasp on to that reality and contract, refine, and percolate it?"

"Strain and filter it..."

"Yes," Prince said, "clarify it and purify it, separating the wheat kernel from the chaff, so that it will be understandable and actionable for our world. In that sense, the dream, though available to many, is designed, as all dreams are, for a certain person, or persons, by Divine Providence. Similarly, but on a different level, consider a dream from a departed loved one, who attempts to visit you, and talk specifically to you, in terms that only you might understand. What a shame for both the living one and the departed soul, when people discard those dreams as meaningless, upset because they awake to a harsher reality of separation; those dreams are indeed some of the most significant of all, when one human soul tries to speak to another."

"In other words, in your case, G-d was beaming, and is still beaming, a signal, a message. It's a matter of who will download it, and do it in a form that will be usable to the world?" Richard said.

"Yes, this is the essence of so much of what we experience in our existence. There are songs, books, ideas, plans for buildings and life, all kinds of creativity, which is G-d given, actually provided to us by the Ultimate Creator Himself. All these creations are hidden, and await human 'discovery', as we use the term, by individuals, who we then duly note in our history books. For example, there is the completed book or song, awaiting the person to write it. These individuals use their Chochmah, their wisdom—in our world of Asiyah it begins as a dot, a flash, an intuition—to bring these 'discoveries' down from one hidden world to the next. At each world, at each new level, the 'discovery' becomes more finite and more comprehensible by our physical beings. These same individuals, or perhaps an individual working with these persons, use their Binah, or understanding to develop the details of the discovery. Finally there is Daat, knowledge, which is how the discovery, with its details, will be used, and integrated into our society, in order to make a difference. The same person, or a new one, might be instrumental in Daat.

"People—heretics—our sages used to call them minim in the Holy Tongue, or the more familiar apikoris in Greek—mistakenly have believed for ages that man could create yesh, something, from ayin, nothingness, just as G-d did when He created our world with the letters of His ten utterances in *Genesis.* But only G-d may do that. So human creation is a misnomer. Transformation might be a better word. We use G-d given substances and create new substances from them. We divide and recombine. But we cannot create like G-d; we may only co-create in the sense that we may help manifest the creation that underlies this world; we may 'discover' what is already there."

"In that sense—that is with 'discovery'—the creation is ongoing," Richard said.

"Yes, the creation is ongoing in the direct sense, that without G-d's constant support and His Will, life cannot continue to exist, and would immediately revert back to nothingness. In the indirect sense, creation, or 'discovery', as so many of us know the meaning of the word in this world, is continuing because we have yet to uncover but a meaningless fraction of the G-d given hidden creations available to us."

"But coming back to the beginning of our conversation, how should we regard these profits that we are making, and they are losing?" Richard said.

"Those profits and concurrent losses are returning balance back to the universe," Prince said. "They had no right to take that money from the people under those circumstances and use it solely for themselves. And once you use that wealth improperly, there is no means to bring it back. There is a void that may lead to a kind of death. There is certainly nothing wrong with the abundance we have in turn collected, but it is imperative that we use what we receive wisely, fairly, and charitably."

"I assume that you are referring to the death of certain institutions and certain ways?" Richard said.

"Yes, in the long term G-d does not allow the wicked to live. This may not mean 'death' in the understood sense. It often means that evil and unnatural relationships are not allowed to stand. G-d gives no support for this way of life, so it is fated to collapse. Nothing exists without the Will of G-d.

"Now, it is actually a sign of the Messianic Age that the power structure is changing. Like humans that die to be purified, and make way for those who are born, so organizations and certain establishments will dissolve and break apart, so that the components of decay can be rapidly recycled into the growth of new associations and ideas. Why does a new organization grow so rapidly in times of ferment, as opposed to times of stability? It's analogous to a compost pile versus a garbage dump. One is designed to break down quickly and is excellent fertilizer for growing plants, while the other may contain materials that are essentially the same as they were fifty years ago. One is designed to support death, and thus life, while the other is antiseptic. Like a giant wheel going round and round, growth and death move in step with each rotation, with each cycle. Death is converted to life—this my ancestors the Cohens knew so well in the Temple, when they performed sacrifices with their blessings in the Temple more two thousand years ago."

So, it was that the forces surrounding Prince gained increased economic ascendancy, and many of the companies and individuals who had bet against Prince and his prediction were forced out of business. What Prince did, in distributing food, and salvaging an economy that was imploding, was seen by the public as fair and farsighted. His popularity had soared with the vast majority of Americans. But those who had lost greatly during the economic turmoil blamed Prince. And though they had quickly lost much of their economic and political power and authority during Prince's time in the Senate, they still retained for a time their old connections and associations. They knew how to strike back.

23

During the seven years of plenty, the land produced in abundance. And he gathered all the grain of the seven years...and he stored the grains in the cities, and he put in each city the grain of the fields around it.

Genesis Chapter 41, vs. 47-48

Prince set up major storage centers of grains sprinkled across each region of America, so that food for the hungry could be distributed quickly to large population areas. They were nicknamed granaries. As expected, at first there was considerable confusion about their function, as well as political infighting among those assigned to operate them.

The ones set up in Texas had been particularly problematical, possibly because much of the state had been hit so hard by the drought. Parts of rural Texas were steppe and received little rain in normal years anyway, and the drought had meant that virtually all the huge herds of cattle formerly present on land lacking irrigation had been sold. Many ranchers and their workers had abandoned their homes and livelihoods, and could be found wandering aimlessly in the constant wind along the long stretches of rural highways stretching from one horizon to another. A brown dust coating plastered to each object had generated a monotone. On the frequent days of dust storms, there was no separation of father sky and mother earth. And with the lack of separation, and the lack of distinction between objects, it seemed that indeed G-d's creation had reverted back to ayin, the nothingness from which it came.

Of all the national granaries, one in particular had continued to operate in a state of tremendous anarchy. Food was being handled inefficiently, sometimes wasted or lost to rodents, very similar to the way its counterpart might operate in a developing country. Though instructions directing modifications had arrived from Washington and the regional office in Dallas, and though the granary had received unfavorable press coverage, the instructions had been intentionally ignored and the center had continued to function in the disorderly alternative, and rather corrupt manner that its local managers preferred. They were confident, that in the chaos of the time, there was no one immediately available to take the time to visit, and force the changes that had been prescribed.

On a Tuesday morning during that period, a tall woman of about thirty years, drove up through clouds of dust in a small, red, old, battered pick up truck. Her confident large stride covered the short distance between what had been a parking lot prior to the dust storms and the entrance to the building. Seeing no one at the front desk, she walked into the warehouse. She could make out no one in the dim light, so she proceeded to inspect its inventory, walking through its extensive aisles.

After she rounded the third corner, she almost bumped into an older lady, who held a pencil and pad. The lady was taken totally aback, and when she recovered said, "And who are you?" Her voice was demanding.

"I am Judy Jones. And who are you?"

"I needn't tell you that. I don't believe that's any of your business, or that you have any business being here," the woman said. "I'm not aware that you scheduled any appointment."

"I came here because no one would return my telephone or e-mail messages. There was no one at the desk out front, so I walked in," Judy said. "Who's in charge here?"

"That's none of your business, young lady," the older woman said. By this time, a couple of other workers had gathered beside her to watch the stranger who had suddenly appeared in their midst.

"It is my business," Judy said. "And if no one claims to be in charge here, then I will take charge, which is probably what I ought to do anyway."

The older woman spoke up. "If that's what you really want to know lady, then I'll tell you. I'm in charge here. Now that you know that, you'd better get your tail out of here. You have no jurisdiction here."

Judy smiled back at her. "Thank you. That's what I need to know. Now, I'm not leaving here. Take a look at this mess. You can't even walk safely in the aisles. There's grain spilling out everywhere. And you're carrying a pad. Where's your computer? You don't even know what's here, or what you've distributed this week. Let's get it cleaned up now. There are people starving out there."

The older woman supervisor moved forward to confront Judy. She was used to physically intimidating people, but Judy didn't move. "Susan and Tammy," the supervisor said, "we need to forcibly remove her. You two escort her out of the building and make sure she drives off."

The two workers halfheartedly moved around Judy and grabbed both of her arms, but they couldn't force her to move. Feeling the muscles in her arm and sensing her confidence, they knew that she could flip both of them together. They quickly backed off.

"If you will not move, then I'll call the police," the supervisor said. "They'll take care of this."

"Why don't you do that?" Judy said. "I'd love to explain to them why they need to come here today. Perhaps you'd like to be on the evening news too. And by the way, I'll be out on bail and back tomorrow."

The woman suddenly backed off. "What is it you want with me? You must have a connection with those folks in Dallas or Washington."

"Just what I said," Judy said. "We are going to have this place totally cleaned up in two weeks and I will report our results back to Dallas."

"And what authority do you have for that?" the supervisor said.

"Frankly," Judy said, "I don't think I need any authority to change this pathetic situation, when people are starving. But if you're looking, find Regulation 57a, part 6, of the legislation of the last farm bill."

And so it was. Judy Jones took charge of the number 15 granary in Texas. She opened up communications with the Dallas regional office, and completely turned the operations around.

It seemed to those around her, as well as the press, that this impressive woman had arrived out of the latest dust storm. She was a stranger without a background. They could trace her back to the Jones' ranch and find her birthplace, just like they could trace Prince's birth back to San Francisco, but then the trail went cold. It was full of rumors and suppositions, but few hard facts. For years, she had been "away" and isolated from the world. What had suddenly propelled her to take over the Texas granary?

The lack of a known past in such an uncertain time would have alone secured her fame. But the absence of a preamble was the source for only a fraction of the gossip swirling about her. Her beauty was said to shock those around her. When she entered a room, she brought a certain immediate presence. All heads would turn and some would gasp at her form. Like a magnet, they would be irresistibly drawn to her. It was whispered that her blue eyes could pierce your consciousness, your inner being, find your thoughts, and make you quiver in your spot. Those who worked with her claimed that her intelligence far exceeded anyone's around her. They purported that she was equally talented at arguing a point, or putting a political coalition of support together. And they averred that she could often foretell the future, and that she could be found preparing for contingencies for situations that others could not even imagine. Her opponents learned quickly that they were ill-matched; she inspired great fear among them, but a love among her advocates. Impressed with her ratings' drawing power, the local evening news had become fascinated by her and featured her regularly. Because of this, she had been noted a few times on the national news.

In a barbershop on the main street of one of the Texas towns, a couple of older gentlemen spoke about her. "You know who she reminds me of—that fellow who used to travel around these parts and work on farms—seems like maybe ten or fifteen years ago. You know that tall one, who was so beautiful for a man."

"Why is that?" the second man said.

"Well she's on the evening news, just like he was. And she's tall and athletic—you know what I mean—for a woman, just like he was. And another thing, she's mysterious, just like he was. No one knows who she exactly is either, or why she's doing what she's doing."

"I remember that gentlemen now. He was magnetic, with people attracted to him all the time. Hey, hasn't that gentlemen come back?" the second man said.

"What do you mean?"

"Well, you know, they're doing all this drought relief stuff in Washington now. And the leader of the...of the... what do you call it—the Senate—got on the TV, and was talking on the news the other night. And I could have sworn it was him, all over again. Now don't laugh at me, like you are a'doing. I'm telling you Ralph, that it looked just like him," the second man said.

"John, you might get me to believe a lot of things. But now, I'm not going to believe that that kid running around here in the country side, all those years back, has become the leader of the Senate. Heck, how could he have been old enough yet? And if that's the best we can do in this great country, then we're in a lot of trouble."

Judy Jones' work had become so noted that within a very short time she had been promoted to run the Dallas office, and subsequently offered an assistant position in Washington advising the head of the entire granary program. With all this publicity that she had received, and her connection to Prince's soul, one would have thought that he would have at least noticed her rise. But Prince was buried in the many details of his job and his religious movement, not to mention that his perceptive powers concerning souls were often restricted when they pertained to Judy's. But if he had been more aware, the pain would still have been too great for him to follow her spiritual whereabouts.

On a day during that period, Prince sat in his office working as if he had attention deficit disorder. He had a television, computer, and radio running at the same time. Ten different piles of papers were stacked on both his desk and the floor, while three filing cabinets were opened. Prince was crawling around on the floor when Jeff walked into his office.

Jeff smiled. "Trying to do too many things at once, as usual, I see."

"I've got to go over this bill, and I'm waiting for that announcement over the airwaves, and someone is going to forward me that other information that we discussed by e-mail momentarily," Prince said. He didn't even look up, but continued working. His work sessions were now legendary, not only among his staff, but throughout Congress.

"Prince, I have to apologize before I tell you this."

"What is it, Jeff? It can't be all that bad," Prince said. He still had not looked up from his material, and was now printing a lengthy e-mail.

"Prince, there's this woman that I've scheduled for you to meet."

"When's that?" Prince said.

"In a few minutes. She's talking to our office staff right now. She just wants to meet you. Will not stay long, and you don't have to clean all this up," Jeff said.

Prince finally stopped what he was doing and looked up. "Jeff, what's going on here? You know better. Any time but now. I can't do it now. Midnight would be better—after the vote tonight."

"She is very kind and thoughtful, and says she knows how busy you are. She actually said without prompting, that she would wait till midnight. But she won't be turned away," Jeff said.

Prince paused. "What's she some kind of mind reader, or something?"

"Well, she sure read my mind," Jeff said. "And this is why she's going to see you. And you'll just have to excuse me this time, put me in the doghouse or something, because there's no way I would turn this person away. She's got an iron will. Actually, she reminds me a lot of you. In that respect, if you don't know her, I think that you ought to meet her."

"Why's that?"

"There's just something indefinable about her. It's her soul, her charm and beauty, and her darn intelligence and persistence. I think she would climb a brick wall, just like you would, to do something she thought was right. I think there's a connection here. Why don't you plug in, and think about it."

"Don't have time right now," Prince said. "Why is she even here?"

"Well, that's another thing. She's the hottest thing out of Texas. The granary administration has offered her the highest nonpolitical job available in the administration. And she wants to see the guy who did all the legislation. Says she really admires him."

"Oh, okay," Prince said. "Bring her in when she's ready. But don't expect a lot of conversation out of me."

When Jeff called again to bring her in, Prince was sprawled out on the floor. He was studying a piece of a proposed bill meticulously. Without even looking up, he said, "I apologize for this mess. I didn't know you were coming, and I'm in the middle of some difficult legislation."

"Senator, there is no need to apologize," she said. "Especially to me, of all people."

Prince's hands dropped his papers. His gaze froze and became blurry. "Give me a minute, Ms. —"

"—Ms. Jones. Of course, Senator." Her voice was deep and delicious, almost lush, and more beautiful than he had remembered it. He could now see only the straps of her high heeled shoes binding her graceful feet and the curve of her ankles flowing into her long legs.

"Have a seat at the table over there," Prince managed to blurt out, while motioning with his arm. "I didn't expect you, and I want to make sure that we talk as much as you would like." Jeff looked over at Prince, and drew back in disbelief, especially since Prince had still not looked at her.

He brought his long frame up off the floor with his back to her, afraid that he might not be able to rise if he first met her gaze. Then he turned to face her.

He had never seen her dressed up before. She wore a navy blue dress which accentuated her figure and her thick, curly hair still fell across most of her back. Her face was clear of any lines and showed no passage of time.

She was smiling at him. Her lips were turned in the manner of saying "surprise." Her eyes were piercing him, grasping and digesting his thoughts, and answering him back silently. "Yes," he perceived her as saying, "I know you didn't expect me—in fact you've been too caught up in running the world to know what I've been doing—but I know everything about you and what you're doing—I mean everything—and I still love you. Isn't it nice that we're together, if just for a moment!"

Prince approached the table and reached his long arm across it to shake her hand. "Ms. Jones, I can't tell you what an unexpected pleasure it is to have you here." Jeff's face was frozen in a look of incredulity, since he had never observed Prince to fake an emotion.

She grabbed his hand, and would not release it in a normal handshake. Her grip was firm and decisive, and he could feel the intensity of her emotion, and the electricity pulsing through her body to his. "Senator," she said, "I could not come to Washington, without seeing the man who put the program together for the granaries. I want to tell you how wonderful your work is. I have been following everything that you do."

"I can't tell you what that means to me," Prince said.

"Well," Jeff said, looking directly at her, "I know the Senator needs to get back to work on his bill."

"Jeff, we're just going to have to delay that vote until tomorrow," Prince said. "You'll notify the Senators by mid-afternoon.

"But...I'm not sure we'll have all the votes tomorrow," Jeff said.

"We will," Prince said. "It is not often that such an honored soul visits us." Jeff slumped in his seat in shock.

"Ms. Jones," Prince continued, "I've heard about your incredible work in Texas. Thank you for supporting me in so many ways. You have been a rancher yourself out there?"

"Yes, with my husband, until recently," she said.

"Tell me, how is your husband, and your ranch now?" he said.

"My husband is fine," she said. "As for my ranch, it is not good now, not operational at all, but we are financially fine, unlike so many of our neighbors. You see, ten to fifteen years ago, through an unusual set of circumstances, we had a stranger take over the operation of our ranch. He must have been sent by G-d. Everything he did, everything he touched with his hands, prospered. Our cattle became prize beef. So he found favor in our eyes, and we appointed him over everything in our household, and on his account, G-d blessed everything we owned, in the house, and in the field. In that respect, he reminds me so much of you, since Senator, you have the same G-d given golden touch.

"Anyway, that stranger ended up leaving. This was very upsetting for us, since we liked him very much. And I must admit, that I was particularly close to him, and will continue to be, no matter where he is, or what he is doing, whether he lives or not. He was the greatest friend a person could have." Her mouth quivered and she struggled to regain her composure. "But before he went, he left us very wealthy, taking nothing for himself, even though he had earned it all for us. And I've been searching for that person, all this time, because I will never be complete without him."

Prince's vocal cords had contracted to the point that he was struggling to respond. Finally, he said, "And why do you suppose the stranger left?"

"I did something very foolish in our relationship," she said. "But the reality was that Divine Providence was blowing him on."

"And you say that you've been searching for him every since?" he said. "Can you not find him?"

"People suppose, Senator, that finding someone is a matter of physically locating the person. But as hard as that might be, it is the easiest part. Truly finding a person is a spiritual task. In order for me to find him, we must both know who we are, and why we exist in this world. And then my destiny must intertwine with his, in a way that we can walk together," she said.

"I see," he said. "Does he know who he is now, and do you now know who you are?"

"Yes, I think I can confidently say that he knows exactly who he is now. I am so proud of him. He is fulfilling the oath that he took from G-d, concerning his purpose on this earth. And what a wonderful and courageous mission it is! And now, he has been an example for me and my life, just as you have been an example for me. And I know who I am," she said.

"Then the problem must be..."

"The problem is that we cannot walk together—at least not yet," she said. "And we were young when we met, and now, as Divine Providence would have it, we are both about to leave our youth, and many of the broken eggshells of our dreams behind." She held back her sobs.

Jeff left the room for just a moment and could now be heard answering a question about a telephone call that had just arrived. Prince thankfully had his back to the open door, because he could contain himself no longer. Huge tears ran down his cheeks, and fell on the pad in front of him, creating loud plopping sounds.

She took the short opportunity to extend her hands toward his. "It is so good to see you Joseph. Do not fret." Then she saw Jeff turn around to reenter the room, and abruptly pulled her hands away, and restarted the conversation.

"What must I do Rebbe, when I can not walk together with this person?

Prince had recomposed himself. "You must wait. Souls are our inheritance from G-d, and they are infinite and timeless. The physical barriers between two souls, who are destined to be together, are ephemeral, whereas the ties that bind those souls together are eternal.

"G-d does not wish us to suffer. If those souls are temporarily apart in this physical world, then it is for a reason. G-d must need those souls in two different places."

"And what could that reason be, Rebbe?" she said.

"Ms. Jones," he said, "you are obviously a very spiritual person, with a very elevated soul. The Messianic Age is upon us, and with your profound thoughts, and your work in the granary program, you are physically bringing this spiritual potentiality into a reality on earth. From what you say about the stranger and your attraction to him, he must also have possessed an elevated soul—though I believe that he would cringe at that characterization of himself, because he hopefully regards himself as merely a humble servant of G-d. With your Divine souls, both you and he channel considerable Divine Light into this world.

"Now, the two of you, by residing in two different geographical locations, form a bridge across this world. And the waves of love and energy that travel across this bridge, which are in reality a funneling of the Divine Light, are so forceful—both because the souls are so strong and elevated, and because their attraction to each other is so intense—that this energy harmonizes the disorder in the universe that surrounds the bridge. In turn, those consonant, balanced, proportional, and synchronized spiritual waves calm the waves around them. And so on. So even in the most distant part of our world, a distilled essence of your efforts and your love is having an impact. A similar analogy is that we see only a tiny, contracted part of G-d's Infinite Light filter through veils in our world; yet we could not exist without it. Similarly, your love and energy very much support our world and speed the coming of the Messianic Age."

Then he looked directly into her eyes. "Ms. Jones, it is not easy, is it? But you must know that the difficulty is indeed proportional to the importance and necessity of your role in this world."

"Rebbe, I knew that you would make me feel much better. Thank you," she said.

"Ms. Jones, what happened to your cattle? Hopefully, you did not lose all those prize cattle that the stranger developed, or have to sell them at distressed prices," he said.

"No," she said, "thanks to your prediction, we sold almost all of our herd at very high prices last year, when feed stocks were cheap and ranchers were building up their herds. We sent a few to Central America, so that we could build our stocks back up when the drought ends. We are quite comfortable thanks to you, now doubly so."

"Doubly so? I don't understand," Jeff said. He could no longer keep quiet in his confusion.

Prince smiled and ignored him. "Ms. Jones, I understand that you have been offered a major job in the administration operating the granary program. Will you be taking it?"

She smiled again at him. "Actually no. I've decided after our conversation that first, I've fulfilled my role in the granary world, and will be better suited in another role. And secondly, I've very much taken your advice today to heart. I think that based on the idea that I form the side of a bridge in this world, that it would be important that I be somewhere else at this time."

He nodded his agreement. "And where will that be?"

"A place that needs to not only be united with America at this time, but is crucial to the Messianic Age: Israel," she said.

He smiled. "That is wonderful, Ms. Jones."

She nodded. "I thought you would think so."

"And what will you be doing?" he said.

"I told you Rebbe, that I've been following and admiring everything that you do. WT is funding the Dead Sea project. I know that you have long been a proponent of building a canal from the Mediterranean to the Dead Sea, and utilizing some of the hydroelectric energy that would be generated from sea level to the lowest point on earth to desalinize water. Meanwhile, the Dead Sea will no longer be shrinking and drying up. WT has hired me to do the negotiations for the project. After all, Israel must be strong and green, when the Messianic Age arrives."

When they rose for her to leave, Jeff again turned his back momentarily on them, to receive his urgent messages from his secretary. Prince said, "Judy, it will not be long now. Whether the Messianic Age will come, I cannot say. But regardless, the flower of our youth will not be wasted. Less than two years. That is all that is required now."

"Joseph, I don't see how. I just don't see it. And if it is to be so, will it be in this life, or shall it be in death? Is it so much to ask G-d, that it be in this life?"

"I do not specifically know how either," he said. "That is not for us to worry about. It is in G-d's hands."

Then she was quickly gone, because she knew that if she stayed any longer, she would never have left. And he knew that he would not have allowed her to leave.

After a minute, Jeff had turned around, puzzled. "How did she leave so fast? First, I think that she's not supposed to stay for more than thirty seconds, then she stays forever, and then suddenly she's gone. Well that just fits with the day. Prince, you've had some weird conversations before, but really, I couldn't follow this one at all. You totally changed your mind when she entered the room, and then you spent all this time talking about this stranger on her ranch, and bridges across the universe, and then she's calling you both Senator and Rebbe in the same breath, not to mention what seem to be a lot of double entendres. Meanwhile, we have this crucial legislation you're in the middle of." Then he paused. "Prince, was I doing something wrong, or taking it all wrong?"

"No," Prince said smiling. "The extra name is her greatest sign of respect for me, just as we give G-d different names, because as the Infinite One, He has so many attributes. But other things are just inexplicable at this point in time. Still, it all goes to show, that the universe pushed you to do the right thing, by letting her in here. What a beautiful day it's been. Now let's get back to work."

The next day Judy Jones flew to Israel. For many months she translated WT's environmental and financial instructions into the specific details of a contract for the project. WT had predicated its support for the Dead Sea hydroelectric project upon Israel's investment in an updated irrigation system that would carry the desalinized water throughout the country. The project would take care of Israel's water needs for decades.

When she finished the nonstop work, she was very tired and took some additional time to travel the country. She saw a very beautiful, and relatively isolated, piece of land, and on what seemed like a whim at the time, purchased it. She spoke to her husband John about it upon her return.

"John, one thing that we haven't yet talked about it—it's very exciting—is that I bought some land while I was over there."

"You what?"

"I fell in love with it, John. It's very green. And it's a place that we could literally disappear and be hidden and not found. The government agency that sold it to me didn't put a high price on it either."

"But why?"

"John, it was a very long project, and I guess I really didn't think about it too much when I did it. But now consider that we have no future here on this ranch, the two of us. We came here under certain circumstances, but our world has changed. Now there is nothing but just dust, and even the view out the window seems depressing."

"I'm sorry Judy, but this is the only place for me. I can't see leaving. And if I did, I certainly wouldn't go to Israel."

"You wouldn't ever consider..."

"No. I know that you've come back to your Judaism. And that's really been okay with me. But it stops there. Israel's not a place I'd consider going. It's not my home."

Judy sat staring out into space, her lips pursed in disappointment. "I just thought that, now that I've bought it, you might...but you won't even look at it."

"Judy, you're the spiritual one. You've always told me that things are for a reason. This is no exception. Perhaps it's connected to Joseph..."

"No," she said firmly. "It wasn't. I wasn't even thinking about him when I bought it."

He nodded. "I believe you. But that doesn't mean I'm not right. One thing that I know is that I'm not the connection here. Perhaps you're right, and we have no future at this ranch, but then, that may mean that my future is limited, because I'm not looking past this place."

"But there's life out there, and thanks to Joseph, we have the means," she said.

"True, but this purchase is for a different life. The drought and Joseph are rapidly changing this world, and it will be one that I will not adapt to. As you have said, just as a generation between twenty and sixty years old was required to die out before the Jews entered the Promised Land, so many of our generation will choose not to make the journey to the Messianic Age. It will be left to a new cycle of souls. So, I believe that you are preparing for a time and place without me."

24

John Jones had been right in one respect. The world had been changing extremely rapidly. And it had begun to divide rather severely into two camps. There were the advocates of Prince, many who favored the changes which either rightfully or wrongfully were attributed to him. A second group either opposed him, or simply remained focused on the older, now vanishing, former world. Many of this latter group had simply been shocked by the accelerating transformation of what they had previously known and assumed about their lives, and now were attempting to shield themselves from the stress of acute choices and painful adaptation. Out of the decaying past and rubble of abandoned, worn out, disconnected, or obsolete hopes and desires, arose a new path, but no one, not even Prince, could be sure where that passage immediately led.

During the three years since the drought had begun, the birth rate had declined drastically, while many had chosen to leave the world, often in their sleep. Whole rural communities had picked up and left the land, usually scattering to the cities, where they joined many others in unemployment and food lines. Health care had suffered immensely. The public was not comfortable with the President's cavalier attitudes regarding its pain, so it was often Prince who was called upon to speak regularly to reassure the nation.

"Last century," he said on one address, "for the first time in all of mankind's history, 'modern' man foolishly assumed that our so called advanced technology could shield us from the vagaries and natural cycles of our mother earth. We thought that we had forever mastered the process of extracting food, we took for granted the abundance that usually is provided by G-d, and we accepted no responsibility to return to our planet what we grabbed from it. Now we learn once again, how dependent we really are on our land and our earth, for our prosperity. We learn that we will only receive from it, if in turn we will first give. Ancient peoples have always understood this wisdom, and now we must follow their same course."

It seemed that one part of the nation accepted this concept and resolved to modify its future lifestyle. These citizens involved themselves in following and occasionally contributing to the serious discussions that Prince had started in Washington, concerning everything from alternative energy sources and transportation methods, to the use of fertilizers and antibiotics in farming. These very specific public exchanges in Congress in the end revolved around proposals for a very basic reorganization of American and world society. In addition, in this time of insecurity, doubtfulness, and bewilderment, many of these citizens had actually accepted that they must make more of a place for G-d in their lives.

But the contrary side—particularly those who had formerly had power and wealth, and had lost much of it in the economic turmoil following the prediction of the drought and its subsequent realization—was incensed at what was happening. They viewed Prince as a young upstart, as a pretender to the throne, who had lucked out on his predictions. As for G-d, though some had been regular Sunday church goers, their attendance primarily had satisfied a socioeconomic need; few had really accepted G-d as the arbiter in their lives. Many of this second group, having lost their usual control of natural resources and overall decision making, had amazingly and ironically been transformed overnight, from relaxed and content conservatives, to apologists for radical change. The milder side of their viewpoint was expressed by one member as, "The reason why we have this drought and depression is that that Senator in Washington won't let us mine where we want, drill where we want, recreate where we want, just live like we used to. He's anti-jobs. We are the ones who used to create jobs in America. We're the ones who made this economy run. Things were fine before that guy came along and stopped our progress in this country. And if we will just return to the way things used to be, then our problems will disappear." Another said, "America was always based on free choice; now we have a dictator in power." But there were much harsher opinions.

The formerly well-to-do opponents of Prince had become especially radicalized after about two years of drought. At first, the accounting from the drought had not been so clear. Many of those who had fallen economically had assumed, or least hoped, for subsequent improvement. Even after it became apparent that there would be no immediate turnaround in their fortunes, they had been able to obtain credit and continue their lifestyles based on their pedigree, history, and contacts. Of much significance as well, as months of the drought turned into the first year, was the fact that property and business appraisals remained relatively high, tending temporarily to stick at former levels. But once a few had faced foreclosures, the resulting distressed sales made it very clear that asset values throughout the economy were in free fall. In some cases, land that had been bought for $250,000 per acre could not even fetch $20,000. And in commercial real estate, there was often no market at all, simply because there was no economic basis for the property. The result was that huge numbers of banks faced regulatory closure, as in some cases their assets garnered cents on the dollar. And many of the individuals of the old economy could no longer pay on their former inflated loan values, could obtain no new credit, and were forced into personal bankruptcy.

The economic whirlwind was recorded—not surprisingly—in the Presidential mid-term elections. Just as the elections surrounding the American Civil War had caused the creation of a new political party, and just as the 1932 election had produced sweeping political realignments, so this election, during a new time of severe stress for the country, was a further turning point in the American political landscape. The change in Congress was staggering. Within six months of his election to head the Senate, Prince had decided that he would field candidates in the Congressional elections more than a year away. The result of his new party's efforts was the election of 130 members in the House of Representatives and fifteen new members in the Senate. It went without saying that these newly elected members were extremely loyal to the leader of their new party, and generally voted as a bloc for his programs; consequently, after the elections, Prince was able to spend a lot less time building political coalitions, and a lot more time passing substantive legislation to deal with the drought, environment, and the economy.

Moreover, looking back at American history, the strategists of Prince's new party saw the ultimate prize of the Presidency within their grasp. At every mid-term political turning, such as 1858 and 1930, it seemed that the Presidency had been captured in the next election by the party out of power. As it happened, Prince would be 35, the minimum age for eligibility, just in time to run for President. However, when asked about his future political intentions, Prince replied that he was uncertain, even to his own staff.

"We're hot right now," Richard said. "And we're the new face on the block. That combination makes for a great public insatiability about us.

"And it's not just that. The public wants to see us run for President. It would be a great race, and it would make American history. You see, Americans have always been receptive to new ideas, always receptive to innovation. Our society, our westward expansion, was built on it. Just immigrating to America from another country, was a novel idea. So, I think that you should make a decision soon, and announce your intentions for the Presidency, while the iron is hot."

"But I don't know whether I shall run or not," Prince said.

"Why is that?" Richard said. "Isn't this what we have been striving for?" He was a bit exasperated.

"Whether I shall run for the Presidency in two years time, or whenever, is dependent upon the wishes of G-d, and that in turn is dependent upon the choices that humans make before that time," Prince said. "Humans, not just I, will choose—with G-d's help—the Messianic Age."

Richard nodded his head in resignation. "Yes, you, above everyone else, are a humble servant of G-d. You will truly be a harbinger of the Messianic Age. When you act, it shall be a sign of our times, not an intention on your part.

"But now, here's the problem," he continued. "The public will think that this is just another standard politician's reply. They will believe that you are less than truthful, that what fool wouldn't want to run for the highest and most powerful office in the land—the world—especially when he is already the presumed favorite. They will think that you are dissembling, merely to keep your options open, and in order to keep the opposition from attacking us head on at this time. They will not realize that you are indeed different, that you say what you mean—and not only that—but that you are in control of your brain and your heart—your intellect and your emotions—so that you, unlike so many others, indeed have the capacity to mean what you say. You have the capacity to conduct yourself, as you intend."

"Yes, this is possible, if not likely," Prince said. "But if we stay focused on the thoughts of others, or if we are afraid of what the opposition thinks, we shall not accomplish our goals.

"We should take heed of our ancestors' fears when they were about to enter the Promised Land. If we look at the story, we know that all but two of the spies sent to scout out the Promised Land reported back to the people that more powerful peoples, even giants, dwelled in the Land, and that these people would be too strong for the Children of Israel to overcome. The people believed them, and in their great fear, planned to return to Egypt. G-d punished our people, and caused them to wander in the desert another thirty-eight years—a total of forty years. More importantly, all twenty to sixty-year-olds were required to die in the wilderness, and not able to enter the Promised Land.

"But, as with all of the Torah, there is always much more than the literal aspect. A generation dying out was not just a punishment for its sins. It was a recognition that this generation, which was so distracted by its fear, and by its enemies, that it even planned to return to slavery, to spiritual death, in Egypt—because its faith in G-d was not strong, even after experiencing miracle after miracle—did not have the spiritual strength to enter the Land and be successful, even if G-d should help it prevail. Physical strength on this earth cannot ultimately prevail without commensurate spiritual strength to balance it, in a person, a people, a generation, or anything. Thus, knowing collectively as a people that G-d would help them prevail, was more critical than any might of their opponents. What was necessary was the unity of Jews in their faith in G-d. This faith is what we affirm when we say the Sh'ma.

"Each generation—as are individuals—is required to be tested again and relive G-d's Word in the Torah today. So, our fears here, our focus in this case on our opposition, our yetzer hara, would derail us. And so, while we must be sensitive to the public, we must not be afraid of misinterpretation. That fear, at a minimum, will cause us diversion; we will miss the bull's-eye on the target because our bow slips ever so slightly, or we will just hit a base hit, instead of a home run, because we were partially looking at the back field fence, where we wanted to send that ball, but as a result, did not hit the ball directly. But worse, our fear could be disabling for us. Either way, we may be required by G-d to wait for the next generation, because we here are not spiritually strong enough to enter the 'Promised Land'.

"Which brings us roundabout back to your question. Whether we go forward to the Presidency will ultimately depend upon the Jews' faith, as well as other people's faith, in G-d at this point in time. Before the World to Come can be realized here on earth, it may be necessary for successive generations after us—as there have been many generations before us—to each experience their repeated chance to accomplish, with faith, the Messianic Age."

"Is that not generally true with all human endeavors—that those who truly accomplish in their lives must have an inner faith in G-d to make that transition, that leap from one point to another?" Richard said.

"Yes, this is true. Everything in life is a microcosm of something else. Everything—all choices are in a certain sense repeated at each level, just as you will find the same DNA in each cell of a person, whether it is a brain or a foot cell."

"Faith," Richard said. "Faith—this is what you inspire in me."

It was not just the political, historical, and socioeconomic fronts that were revolving so swiftly. Man's religion, his faith and his spiritual beliefs, must perforce correspond, coextend, and correlate with the spatial and temporal boundaries of his other realities. So, it was not all that surprising that the metamorphosis in Prince's Jewish movement had been substantial. What was astonishing was the actual scope of the growth. In just three years, the spiritual advisory committee had established synagogues in thirty new metropolitan areas. Smaller synagogues were now planned and under construction in another twenty-five. This movement was estimated to have a million new Jewish adherents, and it was claimed that this was just the beginning.

At the time of Prince's spiritual advisory committee's meeting in San Francisco, there had been such fervency in the San Francisco and Washington congregations, that some of the members had leaped at the opportunity to carry their new movement's mission to new locations. Not unimportant at the time, was that there were so many members in the two congregations that by sheer natural movement— especially during this time of severe economic hardship, which had greatly increased migration from one locale to another—members came to live in new areas and establish new congregations. Since there were almost no Rabbis initially available, the lay leaders took over responsibility. This facet, which seemed unfortunate at first glance, was actually a factor in attracting even greater groups of Jews. After a while, some Rabbis seeing the success of these new models, and seeking their own personal spiritual renewal, had left their former synagogues and movements, and had accepted positions at the new synagogues.

If the new synagogues were attracting a number of Rabbis from other movements to lead them, the same could not generally be said of most of the new members who were joining them; and perhaps this influx of unaffiliated Jews was one of the reasons that these Rabbis were willing to break away from their established institutions. As one well known and highly placed American Jewish organizational person, who had closely observed the movement, said, "the Jews joining these institutions [of Prince's movement] are coming out of the woodwork. We never knew we had so many Jews in this country. Some of these are unaffiliated. Some are lost Jewish souls. Some of them vaguely remember their grandparents lighting candles. Some of them know they're Jewish just because of family stories, old menorahs, or names, but have almost nothing else. But they all have one game plan at work. They all want to get back to their roots, and they perceive something genuine here, without a political or Rabbinic agenda. They feel as if each one of the places they visit is welcoming, and that it is appropriate for their spiritual journey.

"And another thing, even though Prince incredibly has enough money to fund them all, he doesn't. He financially helped the movement get started. But then he wisely let it grow on its own, so that no one could accuse it of being his artificial construction. So, you wonder how this movement could come up with all this money to build and expand, particularly at this time, and especially because many of these Jews were unaffiliated and were not used to giving anything. But the model works. These Jews, who have re-embraced their Judaism, are so grateful that they want to give something back. They inspire all the new ones who are considering joining.

"And another thing, have you ever walked into one of those synagogues on a Friday night, after everyone's work week? I cannot describe the joy, the singing, and looks on everyone's faces."

When asked a further question about reported Christian or Moslem interest, she nodded and said, "Yes, it's true. I'm told there's been a whole lot of interest. Would you believe that they now have quite a number asking for their texts, joining their services, and then actually asking to convert?"

"Why is that?"

"I don't know. I think it's because they're so welcoming. But, of even more importance, it's because we're the real thing. Judaism is the real thing. We're the mother, and who wouldn't want to get back to their mother?"

For a while, the severe effects of the drought had obscured what was happening with this new movement. For one thing, there had always been religious growth at various times in American history. For another, the presence of great darkness during this period of drought, and the feeling of a loss of control—a futility to existence—had moved many toward the light present in all religious organizations. Thus, almost all genuine religious organizations were experiencing a major revival. Prince's new Jewish movement at first did not stand out. But it was impossible, even with all the other preoccupations of the time, for it to continue to be unheeded by the public at large.

Two very different major articles in two different newspapers had appeared one Sunday morning. It was not surprising that Daniel Kahn was writing once again in the *Los Angeles Times.* Of more note this time, the *New York Times* reporter, James Grissell, who had formerly written about Prince, was again featured; this time his article not only made the magazine section, but was the lead story there.

The Kahn piece, in many ways, was much of the same as before. He railed against Prince, claiming once again that he was mixing religion and politics. His tone had grown more vicious with each column, as if only exceeding the last polemic's claims would do. It was "if you didn't believe what I told you last time, then wait and see what I have here" kind of approach. But, as if he knew that upping the ante each time would no longer suffice—that is that people were growing tired of his constant carping—he finished the article in the sharpest tone that he could muster. It was as if he had been boxing with his opponent for fifteen rounds, and had been losing each round. Now at the end of his rope, he was looking for a lucky knockout blow—knowing that even as he was letting his own defenses weaken, in order to deliver the punch, it was still his only opportunity to prevail. "Prince Reed," he said, "has not only profited from his prediction of the drought, and from the drought itself, but I believe that he has caused the drought himself. Look at him smiling up there, doing politics while the country is suffering. He has succeeded on the success of others, risen up on their backs as they have fallen. I sincerely believe that not only is he not G-d's messenger, but he is in league with the devil."

The second article by Grissell was a much longer and more calmly researched piece. It attempted to analyze everything available on Prince and reach rational conclusions. Given its tone, thoroughness, and greater subtlety, its influence among the public was much more substantial.

Prince Reed, the article said, *is only one step away from the Presidency, should he choose to run in two years. In recent straw polls, he runs substantially ahead of the President in almost every area of the country. It is estimated by several political analysts that Prince Reed's Independent Party could take a majority of the seats in the House and hold thirty-five seats in the Senate after the next Presidential elections; at present trends, it is likely that his party will even gain a majority of the Senate within four years. Not only that, but Senator Reed's party is now fielding candidates in state and local elections throughout the country.*

What we have here is the first new party in American politics since Abraham Lincoln helped birth the Republican Party prior to the Civil War, and make it the dominant party for a generation. Both the Democratic and Republican parties are more than just looking over their shoulders; they are plain scared and trembling in their boots. And here's why. American politics has never tolerated more than two major permanent political parties. If this political tradition should continue, and there's no reason to believe that it won't, then will it be the Republican party, which is almost two hundred years old, which will partially fold into the Independent Party and thus die, or will the Democratic Party which dates back to Thomas Jefferson's political doings at the beginning of our Republic, more than two hundred thirty years ago, fail to head for posterity?

No one knows. But one thing is fairly obvious here: Senator Reed has already substantially transformed the landscape of American politics. For the first time in a very long time, these two parties are not taking their existence for granted. They have genuine competition, and that competition is scrupulously honest and on the level. They're not just some other new political faction that's interested in allowing business to be conducted as usual, as long as they get their votes on their issues and their piece of the pie. Rather, they're out to totally change the way business is done in America.

This whole business, this shaking up of the old order until it practically vomits from exhaustion and sickness, has had curious results in Congress and elsewhere. First of all, the rules are changing. No one exactly knows what will happen next. These days it's not boring in the Congress, as nothing, not even tradition, is taken for granted. Secondly, the cream of the Congressmen are rising rapidly to the top, as Senator Reed promotes them; the older ones, who are tired and losing their power, are retiring.

Furthermore, instead of taking polls and trying to twist or spin—otherwise known as market—their position to fit the results, the Democratic and Republican parties are listening to voters' needs now, with a sensitivity that they've never shown before, and then trying to lead by fashioning better legislation. Early on, the polls told them not to expect that Senator Reed's party could ever succeed. The pollsters were dead wrong. So, for the first time in about a century, the polls are in decline. And when you think about it, maybe the logic of polling to find a position never made a lot of sense. Did politicians think that the American public was so stupid as to believe someone who was always trying to agree with them? Instead, Americans apparently want leaders now who are truly concerned for their welfare, and will lead them through difficult times and weigh the tough decisions. Our system of governance was built by leaders of that caliber.

And it's not only pollsters who are out of favor these days on Capital Hill. Many of the lobbyists have joined the huge lines of unemployment. Senator Reed or his staff will politely meet with you to discuss your position. You can win on the good points for the people, but don't plan on doing any horse trading, or for that matter threatening to retaliate against him on another unrelated vote. And whatever you do, do not plan on sticking your agenda, or funding in at the last moment on a bill, when he's not looking. People who try to deal with Prince once by deception rarely win, but regardless, even a win is really a terrible defeat. His opponents say that he will then turn around and trounce you.

Prince Reed, Grissell said in a rather startling conclusion section, *is the most interesting political, socioeconomic, and religious phenomenon that America has experienced in generations. But the amazing thing is that he is not just one of these—for which he could adequately claim fame—but all these together. We have never had a person that could meld all of these traits collectively. And with our Constitution, our First Amendment, we have studiously guarded against mixing these areas.*

The Prince advocates see no difference between a better world, or a Messianic world, through the religious process, and one achieved through the political process. They are prepared to mix the two. Is this what we desire in America?

Then there is the overwhelming success of Prince's religious movement. In times past, we have said that any movement that can attract such devoted—some would claim blindly so—adherents to its cause overnight, is a cult. If you talk to these people, and I have talked to many of them, including synagogue leaders, they are some of the most intelligent and most professional and discriminating people that America offers. They support the web of life in America, and some are truly making a huge difference in this time of irregularity, poverty, and instability. Would these kinds of people be part of a cult? Yet, how do we explain the success of this movement, which all now admit has a frenetic wild eyed urgency to change the world? And how do we explain their steadfast devotion to not only Senator Reed's causes, but him personally?

Then Grissell went on to say something that eventually caused a sensation across America. *But if you still really don't think that this is a cult, then consider this. The devotion to this man is so strong that some who have met him say that they would do anything for him. They would travel to the ends of the earth, even give up their careers. This leads me to the next point. Some are even saying in this scientific age that he is truly the Messiah. The Jews among them say that he is the man that G-d has sent to lead the world into the Messianic Age. They point not just to his ability and success at every turn, but his humility and extraordinary devotion to G-d, which supersedes his own personal needs. They say he is like the great prophets of old, Joseph, Moses, and David, in that he is not just some mystic in a ghetto, as the Jewish people possessed for two thousand years, but unifies and leads the Jewish people through their real travails of life, while still being a servant of G-d. They say that G-d is speaking to them by choosing to bring this extraordinary soul, who can straddle both the physical and spiritual worlds on this earth (which is the only way that the Messianic Age can arrive), and that G-d is providing us with this highly unusual opportunity to establish the World to Come, now at this specific place and time. Their eyes gleam in ecstasy, as they contemplate the world that could be.*

But it doesn't stop there. There are also many Christians that see his presence, and his strengthening of Israel, as the heralding of a Messianic Age. Some of the Christians are even saying that he is really Jesus, and that he has not yet chosen to reveal himself, until we prepare the world properly for his coming. You need no more proof, they say, than to note his unusual powers—particularly his ability to read souls and tame wild animals, the fact that he is a Jew with a priestly background, and the date of his birth exactly two thousand years after Jesus' first coming.

But now, I detect that some of you are laughing at what these people say. Why have I devoted even a few paragraphs to these crazies, you wonder? Surely, we've also seen these phenomena among Jews and other peoples before throughout history. Because, other than their unusual opinions about Senator Reed, these people are the most intelligent, successful, circumspect, careful, meticulous, as well as skeptical— especially skeptical—ones that you will ever meet. It's only when they talk about Senator Reed that they apparently become irrational. I wonder what they know that I don't? And why has Mr. Reed never met with any reporter on a one to one basis? One has to wonder whether he has the ability to brainwash people, but then, if he did, why would he have to worry about reporters getting the best of him?

Grissell then ended his article with several more statements and questions, some of which included the following: *All this information about Senator Reed raises more questions than it answers. Do we care that Senator Reed is the wealthiest person in the world, with a majority stake in the most successful corporation in all human history? You bet. And do we care that this person who already calls the shots for this country in the Senate, and for its current critical food program, could be President in two years? You bet. But now can we trust him? Can we understand his motives? Unfortunately, we don't know yet.*

In reality, we still don't know who Prince Reed is. Because there has been no individual like him in modern times, we have no model to explain this extraordinary man, just as we have no model to explain this vast and extremely rapid transformation going on throughout our country. But it seems very clear that the two of them are linked, and it seems clear, as Prince Reed would say it, that there is a reason for everything. We'll just have to patiently wait to find out. And while we do, all we can say is that we should tread carefully.

When Prince turned thirty-three years old that year, this was the fate of the world.

25

The sensational reaction about the latter part of Grissell's piece had not surprisingly concerned the discussion about the Messiah. And quite expectedly, it had centered around the controversy, the insanity from the perspective of many, of anyone being, or potentially developing, into a Messiah. This was just not something that the media, or theological arbiters could accept in this modern world. G-d didn't just act in the manner in which He had performed in the Old Testament or New Testament. G-d was hidden now, so many theologians maintained, or He was leaving it up to humans to do His work now. These people thus reacted with disbelief and many of them accused the followers of Prince of having a lot of gall. This was the way that dictatorships were created they said, by letting those who claimed to hear G-d do things one way, and one way only. And if you didn't believe it, the article itself had said that Prince was the favorite to take the Presidency. So, for a while, the airwaves were clogged with people calling in and self righteously proclaiming that the Prince people were bent on taking over the world, by self righteously citing G-d as their basis for action.

But after a few days, a more amazing reaction was occurring. By this time, many people had had considerable time to digest the thoughts in the *Times*. Others were just getting a chance to read the article as it was disseminated throughout the country. And the angry reaction against Prince and his supporters had died down. One by one, in local papers, on local radio programs, and in barber shops and synagogues and churches in the land, people were starting to come forward. At first, one or two of them were saying that they were stunned by the visceral—and they often said liberal—reaction to the idea of the Messiah, and that at the very least, it shouldn't have been summarily dismissed. Then, a little later, many were saying that they liked the idea, regardless of its applicability to Prince or the current age, and thought that it merited further public discussion, and that the society should work toward that goal. Finally, as the atmosphere was warming more to their viewpoint, others gradually came out of the woodwork, saying that Prince could well be the Messiah. They pointed out that he had the right personal attributes, that the world he advocated was one which they could wholeheartedly support, and that he obviously had the ability to lead the country and world there—not to even mention that he was a Jew from G-d's chosen people, which, when they ruminated on it, had started to excite peoples of all origins.

At that point, the original critics of the whole concept of the Messiah had become stirred up again and had headed back to do battle with the increasing number of believers. The majority of Americans, who were initially on the outside of the argument and who had originally left the disputations alone, then gradually became pulled into the contention. This debate went on for days, then weeks, on into months. And though the talk show and radio hosts and news organizations became tired of it, and tried to move on, the people would have nothing of it. They were preoccupied with it, because it involved nothing less than the perfection of the world. And each additional discussion would polarize another person to one side, or another, until the whole nation was beginning to take positions. It had become the most contentious issue of that generation and had split families, taken over telephone conversations, and disrupted cocktail parties.

As the rage continued, it appeared to grass roots observers that the forces of Prince were gradually gaining. The opponents of Prince, many of whom consisted of the media, highly educated, pre-drought wealthy, and pretentious commentators, had thought that they would quickly destroy the Messianic concept by making trifle of it; that had worked before on ideas like this, which were not only not politically correct, but on their surface appeared preposterous, merely because there was no human experience from which to draw for comparison. But the more these ideas were discussed and debated, the more what had previously been perceived as mentally deficient, foolish, mad, demented, idiotic—all of these words and many more harsh ones had been used to describe the Messianic concept—came to seem if not perfectly normal, then not so unusual. What we as humans consider normal, is nothing more than what we expect to see on a regular basis. So America and the world, at least were contemplating and discussing something which had formerly been outside the general realm of the imagination. And this thought process was the first critical step to realizing the action. When repeatedly asked to comment on his view of these discussions, and his view of a Messianic World, Prince would only say that he must stay focused on his work in the Senate, and that by furthering certain objectives, one step at a time, he hoped to make the world a better place.

While these events were taking place, Daniel Kahn had been called into the office of Ken Graves, editor of the *Los Angeles Times*.

"How was your vacation?" Kahn said, as he closed the office door.

"It went quite well," Graves said, "until a certain point."

"Why? What happened?" Kahn was having trouble reading Graves' face, as he probed for a seat in front of his desk.

"Until I saw that article," Graves said.

"I assume you're speaking of the article in the *N Y Times* on Prince Reed. I have to admit that Grissell did some good work on him," Kahn said, and then reluctantly added, "and he has received some very good publicity for it."

Graves shook his head and his lips tightened as he held in his anger. "No, it's very true that you could go to school on what Grissell did. And it's also true that if you had been writing like that, we wouldn't be having this meeting. But this is not about his article, which indeed clearly has far outshone all your recent work on the Senator."

Kahn raised his shoulders up and drew his head back in disbelief. "Then what's it about?"

"It's about you," Graves said. "We've been talking about the tone and lack of professionalism of your work on Prince for years now. But you haven't listened to a thing I've said."

"I've listened Ken," Kahn said. "But look, that guy needs a drubbing. You'll see that I'm right."

"Daniel, I'm not going to see anything from you on this subject any more. In fact, we're finished. I've talked to everyone upstairs, and they've approved it."

Kahn's eyebrows went up. "What are you telling me? I'm fired?"

"Yes, that's exactly what I'm telling you," Graves said.

"But for what? Why so suddenly?" Kahn said. "Just because this guy Grissell has upstaged me?" The palms of his hands opened out as he expressed his disbelief.

"No, because you can only think about yourself. This thing with Reed has been all about you. You haven't been focused on the truth—not even concerned about the facts," Graves said.

"But all the facts have yet to be uncovered," Kahn said.

"Then why don't you cover the facts that are out there?" Graves said.

"And that's all this comes down to?" Kahn said.

"No, that's not it. You lied to me," Graves said.

"Lied to you?"

"Yes, I've tolerated this ranting and raving long enough, but I allowed you to do it, in deference to all the good years we had here, and the great work that you used to put out," Graves said. "But I've always told you, explicitly warned you, that you shouldn't cross the line—"

"Wait a minute," Kahn said. "Stop right there. What do you mean, 'cross the line'?"

"If you'll let me finish, I'll tell you." Graves' voice was now booming throughout the room and could be heard in the corridors outside. "Before I left on vacation, I saw the rough draft of your piece, which I must say that I had approved, only reluctantly—as usual. You knew I was out of town when you finished that piece. So you cleverly inserted those last few sentences. They didn't know the difference downstairs. You traded on my trust, on our friendship."

"I was just touching it up, just modifying it a little bit, to make it better, you know for public consumption," Kahn said.

"I hate to see a friend grow so pathetic," Graves said, shaking his head. "How could you say that you were just touching it up? You of all people know better. Let me quote from your addition: 'He has succeeded on the success of others, risen up on their backs as they have fallen. I sincerely believe that not only is he not G-d's messenger, but he is in league with the devil.'" Then looking at Kahn, he said, "Shall I continue, for example, with your line saying that he has caused the drought," Graves said sarcastically, "or is that enough?"

Kahn now sat silently.

"Daniel Kahn, this is an insult to your intelligence. You used to be a hard hitting reporter focused on facts. That's how you won your Pulitzer Prize, digging one piece of information out at a time. But there's nothing factual here. Most of it appears to be at best suppositions, at worst, a pack of lies. And the fact that you don't seem to even know the difference any more is what is so sad. I'm printing an apology for your work on the editorial page in tomorrow's paper." Then shaking his head in disgust and disbelief, he said, "I don't believe that we've ever had to do that before."

"After all this time," Kahn said, "I'm just gone like that? Is there anything I can do? No one's going to wave a welcoming flag to even a Pulitzer Prize winner, when he's sacked from such an esteemed place after all this time. "

"No, whether anyone hires you again has relatively little to do with getting fired from here. It has almost everything to do with the recent quality of your work, which has been amply displayed.

"Maybe you ought to take a hint from your nemesis, Prince Reed," Graves said, "and repent. I've thought about it a lot, considering our former friendship and the embarrassment which you have inflicted upon this newspaper and me. The only thing that might redeem you now is for you to actually interview this person, whom you have denigrated all this time, and bring me an article based on that interview—a balanced article, you understand, if you are capable of it."

"But that's impossible," Kahn said. "No one's ever interviewed him. And if I had a tiny chance to ever get that interview before, then I would say that it's out of the question now."

"Again, I think that you ought to take a hint from Senator Reed. Nothing's ever impossible," Graves said. "But your attitude will have to change in order to have a chance. He's not going to give an interview to a biased person." He paused for a minute before continuing.

"You know, Daniel, this man is no fool. Don't you think that he's been watching you all along? Do you think that he's really in league with the devil, and wants nothing but for you to suffer? The truth is that you are totally outclassed by him. He's apparently everything that you deny in him. So your bald faced assertions have ultimately done nothing but assist him."

Kahn left the office seemingly without anything. He had dedicated his entire life to his career, ignoring family, not making friends, and now he had nothing to show for it. For a long time, he did little but walk the streets. Often he forgot to eat, and it did not seem to matter to him anymore whether he slept. The days merged into nights. Time and even the news were meaningless. He had lost himself. Or maybe, he realized, he had never really possessed himself.

At first, he had been too numb to think. It had been too painful. Then, when he could think for only a few minutes at a time, he wondered if he had ever really done anything good for the world. "What could I have been thinking all this time?" he kept saying to himself. Then he had wished that he could start all over again. But he "knew" that was not possible.

Finally, after much soul searching and self questioning, and with considerable trepidation, he composed a note to Prince. "I apologize for the injustice, grief, and lashon hara and lies that I have inflicted upon you. And if there were any way that I could make amends for your pain or restore what I have taken away from you, I would certainly do it. I further want you to know, that while my apology and repentance are spontaneous and sincere, I did not arrive at the circumstances that brought me to my repentance, of my own free will. Those circumstances resulted from the evil that I inflicted on this world, which is now being returned to me.

"I know that it is very much to ask, but I would like to meet with you some time. I certainly do not deserve this consideration, nor upon reflection, did I ever deserve it, but nevertheless, this would be very important to me personally, and perhaps it might help me to set things straight."

"You're not going to meet with him, are you?" Jeff said when he brought Prince the note.

Prince sat thinking in his chair with his huge legs propped up on the office desk. "Yes, I think that I shall meet him."

"What? I don't get this. You've never met privately with a reporter before, and now, you've decided to do it for some odd reason. And it's not just any reporter. Noooo!! You've decided to meet with the person who has desecrated your name, who has tried to destroy everything that you ever stood for, not to mention that you wouldn't take Richard's suggestion and stop the vitriol earlier," Jeff said. He had said it so fast that he had run out of air. When he recovered, he added, "You've been expecting this to happen, at some point all along, haven't you?"

"Yes," Prince said, "that's all true."

"But why? This guy's dangerous. He's more dangerous now than ever."

"No, he's not. First of all Jeff, he's discredited. Whatever he would try to write against us now will have no validity. Secondly, anyone who edits his piece, and now it will be very heavily edited, will ensure that it is balanced, in fact will bend over backwards to call it our way, if it's in question. Thirdly, he's repented. We're not even dealing with the same person."

"Okay, assume that's all true. But why fool with him, especially because of the way he's treated you? Is it public relations—to have him possibly publicly come over to our side after all this time of fighting us?"

"This will be a direct result; I do not deny it," Prince said. "But it is only that doing the right thing spiritually usually also results in physical rewards. The real reason Jeff is that this man has had a relationship with me long before this life. More importantly, he's a Jew, and we must love and take care of all Jewish souls."

"I saw the part about the lashon hara. He must have some training, some knowledge," Jeff said.

"Yes, he does. We will see if we can correct something that has been amiss for a long time."

26

The spirit of G-d spoke to me, His word is upon my tongue.

Second Samuel Chapter 23, vs. 2

And G-d Himself will go before you. He will be with you, He will not fail you or forsake you. Fear not and be not dismayed.

Deuteronomy Chapter 31, vs. 8

"Come in Mr. Kahn, and have a seat," Prince said.

"Thank you," Kahn said. He looked around the room at the shelves of books from floor to ceiling. He was still surprised to be there.

After what seemed to be a lengthy silence, Prince said, "Well, Mr. Kahn, I believe that you asked for this meeting."

"Yes, I did. How shall I call you—I mean by what name?" Kahn said.

Prince smiled. "That is an excellent question, Mr. Kahn. A name is very important. It conveys a special energy which emanates from the soul. I have gone by several names in my lifetime and perhaps one of those will be adequate, or perhaps another one is more appropriate with which to address me. This is a question that you must decide."

"I don't how I would like to address you at this time. May I wait?" Kahn said.

"Yes, of course."

"I do not know why you have chosen to see me at this time?" Kahn said.

"Should I not be seeing you?" Prince said.

"Well, you had certainly never agreed to see me before," Kahn said.

Prince smiled again. "Mr. Kahn, you may think that you asked to see me before, but perhaps that was only from your perspective."

"What do you mean?"

"Well issuing an edict in the press for an interview is not really asking to see me. I don't believe you really asked to see me, as you did just recently with your note," Prince said.

"But I did. I wanted to see you. You knew that," Kahn said.

"From your perspective, yes, I knew that," Prince said. "Your intellect told you that you should see me. It was misguided by your ego, which would have been rewarded when you wrote exclusively about me in your column. Your ego clouded your vision. But now your heart, it had no intention of seeing me. Your heart was closed—it was hardened—and could not relate to me. There was no possibility of really having a dialogue with you."

"And why are you choosing to have a dialogue with me now?" Kahn said. "You could have this conversation with anyone. You are an extremely busy man in the Senate and outside."

"You are a Jew. And your soul is in distress," Prince said.

"What does being a Jew have to do with this? Okay, I've never denied my Jewish background, but it's really in the past. I haven't been in synagogue in years," Kahn said.

Prince smiled again. "Mr. Kahn, just because you don't go into a synagogue doesn't mean that you can put your Judaism on the back of a truck and have it hauled away to the dump. You can't dispose of something that is intimately yours. You have a Jewish soul. It's who you are. Now, whether you deal with it now, or later, or in another lifetime, you will have to engage it, grapple with it. As Jacob did, you will have to wrestle with it. This is not just part of your existence. It is the very purpose of your existence."

"And you think that this mess that I've put myself in is related to being Jewish?" Kahn said.

"Yes."

"If this is true, then please help me. Help me to understand," Kahn said.

"Is it not true, Mr. Kahn, that before I entered the picture, before I was noticed in the public arena, that life was going very well for you, at least by your past standards? You were recognized nationally and internationally for your reporting and had won a Pulitzer Prize. You were very bright, and would have undoubtedly won another, and another, if I hadn't come along."

"Yes, the first part is true. And I believe that my career would have continued on a trajectory," Kahn said.

"So what was the purpose of focusing on me? Why did you let me distract you?" Prince said.

Kahn was stunned. "You know, I really don't know. I guess that I thought that you were interesting and that I would have you analyzed in a short time and move on, like I always did. But it never worked out like that. And then I couldn't get away from it. I was stuck."

"You've just said a lot, Mr. Kahn. Let's take one piece at a time. First of all, you should not think that you can analyze a complex person in a short time. The higher in the service of G-d that a person travels, the harder it will be to describe in words her character and motives. Reporters routinely simplify events and people to the point of absurdity, so that they can sketch them in a few paragraphs. You were always good with what you perceived to be hard facts. That is why you chose to be a reporter in this life. But when it came to gray areas—and the universe is mostly gray—that is matters of judgment, which originate from the soul, and are our purpose for living, you struggled. That was the case with me, was it not?"

"How do you—how can you possibly know these things about me?" Kahn said. "There's no way you could have known this."

Prince did not answer him. Instead he continued on his point. "Mr. Kahn, why do you suppose that you were stuck on me? Do you really think that it was accidental?"

"I don't know any more," Kahn said. "What does a stranger who wanders throughout his childhood, and then on the edge of adulthood, suddenly arrives in his hometown, to claim the world's biggest fortune—and who is now within a whisper of the highest office in the land—specifically have to do with me?"

"If he didn't have anything to do with you, then why did you make him your business?" Prince said. "And why did you get stuck on it, like an ant trapped in honey?"

"I don't know," Kahn said.

"Perhaps," Prince said, "the answer lies with the reason that you had such a strong religious upbringing in your childhood."

"But I left that behind," Kahn said. "And how could you possibly know about that forty years ago?"

"But, as I said, leaving your Judaism behind is impossible. If you really think so, then what was your preoccupation with me?"

"It could have been politics or anything. How could it have been religion? I apologize to say this, but I have hated your brand of Judaism, absolutely hated it," Kahn said.

"Hated it or loved it, you have continued to grasp it in its entirety. You have not let go of it. Why Mr. Kahn, why? Why did you insist on scaling this wall? Why not go around it? It would have been a lot easier, wouldn't it? It would have been a lot more comfortable not being a Jew. You could have forgotten it. Did it not have to do with something in your background? Why do Jews remember their history and their ancestors most of all? Because of their ancestors' direct relationship with G-d. Because of that relationship, their ancestors were truly great."

Then Kahn looked directly at Prince and his face filled with a kind of determination, and his hands were clenched with emotion. "You know. You know who I am, and why I am here, and why I am in this life. I hope that I am worthy enough, humble enough, that you will tell me."

"Mr. Kahn, you know from your religious training that you are from the priestly line. Others would recognize it from your name. As you may know, so am I. Your ancestors were priests in the Temple with mine. We have known each other all this time. That's your fixation with me."

Kahn shook his head. "Why do I know that you are correct? There is no proof, like you could do with a theorem in math. Yet, I feel so strongly that you are so right." Then tears came down his face and his whole body began to shake. "You are truly a tzaddik and a rebbe. I am so sorry for what I have done to you."

"You see," Prince said, "our ancestors were contemporaries, friends in the Temple. We had no inheritance of land, as did the other tribes. We instead lived off the offerings of the people. We conducted sacrifices, administered the festivals, and preserved the memory of our tradition. Then the Temple was destroyed once and then twice, because the Jews could not get along with each other. And after that, the descendants of our ancestral priests fought with each other from one generation to another. And in each following generation, G-d put us on this earth with different purposes, but one of them, for our grandparents, was to repair our ancestors' breach and restore our continuity as a Jewish people. Without the repair and mending of this rift, and many others like it, there could be no Messianic World. And without overcoming this continuing obstacle, you personally were bound to hit a brick wall and progress no further in your life. And where there is no growth, there is spiritual decay. Now this deficiency, which has manifested itself in every generation, shall finally be corrected. And now, your life shall be much better. You will go out of here a much freer spiritual entity."

"And the purpose of my very serious and thorough religious training?" Kahn said.

"You were being given a choice," Prince said. "Without the knowledge, what choice would you have had to embrace Judaism? You see, your soul's and your ancestors' refusal to believe were manifested in different ways in each generation. Your ancestors were heretics or apikorsim after the destruction of the Temple. When my ancestors were Chassidim in Poland, more than two centuries ago, your ancestors were Misnagdim, our opponents. Several generations ago, several of your family members tried to water down your Jewish observance and opposed Zionism, because they were afraid that our Christian neighbors would think that the Jews were disloyal citizens in America. Others were socialists, who thought religion was a drug for the masses. Now, in a scientific and media age, you are a hard hitting reporter, who focuses on what he can see, disbelieving the subtle and hidden, which underlie all creation."

Kahn grinned. "Was a hard hitting reporter. Rebbe, what can I do now?

"Repent. Repentance is not just being sorry, but restoring what could have been, if you had not erred."

"But I am empty. I have made a mockery of my life," Kahn said. "I do not know how I will go forward now."

"Repentance is a turning. And when you make that about face, all alone, in that stiff wind, in your little sail boat, in the big ocean of life, it is so hard. You really do believe that the wind will force you over. In that small second of time, when your resolve to change tack is all that you have, so that you are forced to rely on your faith in G-d, you tap into the infinite.

"But do not think that you are really alone. Many people have had to face this expanse of water. I too have been there. The more critical a person's destiny, the more obstacles are likely to stand in his way. And the more likely he is to try to deny it. But eventually, he must face the consequences of that denial, because otherwise the spiritual sustenance available to him becomes increasingly constricted. In each generation, the stake is raised, until that person is able to perceive the path of truth."

"But I have spent all these years playing this role in error. I have so little time left," Kahn said.

"Physical time on this earth, as it concerns repentance and human intention, means nothing, because these do not operate on the finite plane. And your true repentance going forward wipes the previous errors away. G-d is concerned with what remains in your heart, that is how you would act if faced with the same situation once again. Moreover, time is not limited as you perceive it. As your soul is your inheritance from G-d, it is immortal. Your soul has operated in error for generations. Now, it may have the opportunity to rectify that misjudgment for many generations to come. Besides, Mr. Kahn, I believe that you have many good years—professional ones as well—left in this life. And your background, reputation, and ability in this life, will be a springboard. From these depths, you will climb to greater heights than ever, now that your soul is less restricted.

"And Mr. Kahn, each one of us has an individual path, an individual destiny, which will allow us to do repentance. If we will just make the attempt, that route will be set out in front of us. We will know how to do it. Let me tell you a story."

Nachmanides, known as the Ramban, once had a very learned student, Rav Avner, who converted to Catholicism. After his conversion, he rose to the highest levels of Spanish nobility. He wished to insult his former teacher. So on Yom Kippur, of all days, he called for him to come to his palace. When he arrived, Avner placed a pig in front of him. He then proceeded to slaughter it, divide it, cook it, roast it, and eat it with relish.

He asked the Rambam, "How many transgressions have I just committed?" When the Rambam responded with the number four, Avner corrected him, and proved to him in thorough detail that it was actually five. The Rambam then asked him why, if his knowledge was so great, he had forsaken Judaism and the Torah. Avner replied that it had been the Rambam's fault. The Rambam had once taught that the Song Haazinu in the Torah included within it everything which would ever occur. And he did not wish to be part of a religion with such preposterous teachings as that.

The Rambam replied that his teaching was absolutely true. "Prove it to me," Avner said. "Show me where my name is found in the Haazinu." After some thought, Rambam referred Avner to Deuteronomy 32:26, wherein every third letter of a portion of this verse, "I will scatter them and wipe out their memory from mankind," contained the spelling of his name, Rav Avner. Avner suddenly realized the truth of his teacher's message, and asked how he might correct his grave error. The Rambam directed him to follow the instruction of the verse. Shortly after, Avner mysteriously left Spain for an unknown destination, disappearing from the world which knew him.

"So, you see Mr. Kahn, while your struggle will be uncertain, there is a path specifically designed for you. G-d not only wishes us to return to Him, but has given instruction in the Torah, which applies not just to the Jewish people, but to us individually. Even before we know we require something—even before we are born— G-d has anticipated our needs, and set it forth throughout the generations. And while your struggle may be difficult, others have overcome worse. It is certainly within your power to do it."

Kahn sat pensively absorbing Prince's words. Then he said, "Your words are very kind and helpful, and I thank you very much, Rebbe. And now I believe that as much as I would like to continue here, that I should not take up any more of your time."

"Mr. Kahn, I believe that you would like to interview me. I think that it will be very important to assist you in your return to writing."

"You are an amazing individual," Kahn said. "You were right. Before, I always wanted to interview you to get the scoop. Now, that I'm in your presence, it's not the fame I care about, nor even the possibility of my rehabilitation, despite my personal need for this to happen. It is learning from you. Now, I only want to interview you to gain your wisdom, or if something good for you can result from it. Rebbe, am I even qualified to interview you?"

Prince smiled. "Mr. Kahn, you are the most qualified person of your generation to interview me. If you will now think back on your previous learning, on your heritage, and actually take ownership of it, for the first time in your life, you will realize how much knowledge you really do possess. G-d provides my opponents with superior knowledge and skill with a purpose, so that I will wage battle on equal footing, and so I may also appeal to them on a high intellectual and emotional level to follow the righteous path. This knowledge, combined with your superior professional skills and a sincere heart, will be the proper combination. Now that you do not solely wish to satisfy your ego, now that your goals are more altruistic, you are finally prepared to receive.

"Not only that, but as you now know, our association is not accidental. We've had this appointment for a very long time. I have been waiting for this moment. You know everyone thinks that a leader must push. But often what a leader does is patiently wait, wait until G-d provides the opportunity. But of course the leader must know what is opportunity, and how to seize it. That is the hard question."

Kahn shook his head. "I would never have believed that..."

"The point Mr. Kahn is that you can't bulldoze your way in life. Follow the path that G-d lays out for you, and don't spend all your time and energy bushwhacking in the wilderness."

With that, Daniel Kahn pulled out his tape recorder and tablet and prepared to begin the interview. "What are your rules for interviews?"

"Rules?"

"I mean you'll let me know what's off the record, and how you want certain concepts or information about you expressed, and what I can quote, and can't quote, won't you?"

"I do not have those kinds of rules," Prince said. "I will not tell you something about someone, and then in the same breath say that you may not publish it. If something is not publishable, then it should not be said at all. This is particularly true in the case of a person, who may be hurt by our secret speech. I have nothing to hide."

"But all this time, you haven't given the first private interview," Kahn said.

"Yes, this is true. But do not confuse my refusal to give an interview with my intention to be truthful and open when I actually do one. I have previously given no interviews, because I judged no one capable of understanding, grasping, and dissecting my communication. A person must have a certain spiritual capacity."

"And so you now believe that your former opponent will now do you justice?" Kahn said.

"Yes, I trust that you will. Though you approached me with hate, it was an intimacy that will turn to love. Now the vinegar that you have tasted will be turned to wine. It's nothing but a petite turning, a slightly different viewpoint, a little twist of the fingers and thumb, that makes something so sour or bitter, now so sweet. If it seems magical, it is what mankind can do on this planet, with only a slightly different intention."

"So you are not afraid of the truth," Kahn said.

"No, when a person has faith in G-d, she doesn't worry about what will be. There is no need to manipulate the message. You, Mr. Kahn, must have the choice to call this as you see it."

Kahn shook his head. "I believe this is the first time I have ever done a major interview with no rules at all. And some say out there that you are a cult. How wrong they are! They are the cult. Our responses in the press have been reflexive, and we have not thought for ourselves. We have not seen your discrimination.

"Rebbe, you have gone under several names. What is the significance of your names?"

"Sometimes Mr. Kahn we don't know what the significance of our names are. It may be the power over a certain moment, or the key to a story, perhaps our story, or someone related to us. We are all sent down here with a certain purpose, and the name is the creative sound which assists us.

"My names reflect my attributes, as others see them, and by calling those names, people return the energy to me, which they perceive that I project to them. 'Prince' is my worldly name, the one used in daily secular activity, and in commerce. It is like the old worn shoes that I wear. It is tolerant enough to fit around many of my attributes, so it is commonly used by most. It also connotes a regal function, which through malchut, the lowest of the sefirot, refers to our daily existence, and my management of it.

"There is 'Rebbe', which some call me. It is an acronym for the head of the Jewish people. This is not a role to which I aspired. I was called by G-d to do this work."

"Like Moses. G-d called Moses," Kahn said.

"There is simply no way that my soul may be compared to Moses. But to continue, even to this day, I remain afraid that I shall let my people down. It is a role of great feeling, because a Rebbe senses all the range of emotions of the Jewish people, from great sadness to immense joy."

"You are too modest," Kahn said. "As a Rebbe, you are a part of an esteemed tradition of spiritual masters, as opposed to an ordained Rabbi, or a Rav, who deals with Jewish law. You guide the inner and sacred life of your followers. Though your knowledge from books is legendary, it is the direct experience which you possess from your people that is the key for this name. You are out in the field leading your movement and all Jews. But now, your parents gave you the name of 'Joseph'."

"Yes, this is my Hebrew name, of greatest significance for my soul. For a while, I did not understand its implications."

"Joseph was a great tzaddik," Kahn said.

"Yes, but the part which I believe applied to me was Joseph's enslavement in the land of Egypt, and the mixed emotions at best, or the kind of mental block at worst, which he held regarding his origins. Even when he became second in command under Pharaoh, he refused to contact his family and let them know of his existence. Both his enslavement and ambiguity, are of course connected."

"And at one time you forgot your Jewish origins too?" Kahn said.

"Forgetting Judaism again is not a particularly well chosen word. My Judaism was in exile inside me, as was Joseph's, so that I too was enslaved in a kind of pit."

"What energy it takes to keep your identity in you exiled! You must have had to build a spiritual wall around it!" Kahn said.

Prince smiled. "That is true. And so you too will discover the great energy which will be released now that you have broken down the barriers that keep your soul imprisoned."

"I could think of many other specific ways—favorable ones I might add—that you could be compared to Joseph. But the main thing I see is a 'tzaddik'. Would you consider that to be one of your names?"

"That is for G-d to say. I should not be judging the condition of my heart and whether I have expelled the evil out of its right side. Only G-d can see into the subtlety of the heart."

"But now," Kahn said, "now that we are so close to the Messianic Age, is it not true that you are here, as a servant of G-d, supporting the world with all your might, holding it in the balance for a brief instance in our history, in order to give mankind a choice—a chance—for that World? Are you not the conduit, or channel, for the spiritual communication between G-d and man?"

"I cannot answer that, nor comment on the status of my soul."

"Are you not 'bnei aliyah', a 'man of ascent'? Do you not convert darkness on our earth to light and holiness, and thereby elevate mahn, the feminine waters on earth, which then effect a corresponding and reciprocal descent of mahd, the masculine waters from the heavens? Do you not by your complete love of G-d, 'a love of delights'—which is greater than even your love for yourself—and by your service, your mitzvot in this world, draw down G-d's presence here on earth? Do you not make a dwelling place for G-d in our human existence?"

"Mr. Kahn, you know that I am as incapable of answering this question about myself, as I am now on the other hand, capable of recognizing the incredible knowledge which you still possess after all these years. Now, do you understand why you were immersed in Judaism? Just because it didn't 'pay off' right away, didn't mean that it did not have a purpose."

Kahn grinned. "Rebbe, I thought that I was finished as a reporter, and now a few days later I am doing the greatest story that I will ever touch. I believe that I am interviewing the most important soul and leader of our generation. And you are right. It's strictly because of the privilege of being Jewish. What a fool I am?"

"If you will reflect upon it Mr. Kahn, Judaism provides so many other privileges for us as well, if we will only choose to receive them. As for foolishness, you are no fool, Mr. Kahn. No one intended for you to be a fool. We are all taught lessons in life.

"Now, at this point I need to break for the minyan. I know that you have chosen to avoid synagogues, but if you should choose to change your mind at this time, you are most certainly invited to come along."

"It would be an honor," Kahn said.

They talked about many personal aspects as they walked to the synagogue and back. A friendship had begun to develop. When they returned, Kahn started the interview once again, weaving from one subject to another, as if he had been studying them all his life. "Rebbe, you talk about our ancestors and our individual souls in one breath, as if they exist simultaneously. How are they related to each other?"

"The Kabbalists teach us that many souls tend to incarnate in the same family line, so that the virtue of one's ancestors might really be our own. This is really quite logical. Our souls have choices in the other world, just as we have choices here in this one. We take an oath before our souls come here, to be righteous and not wicked. By accepting this moral obligation, we agree to our destiny in this life, and to the responsible roles we shall play, and we accept the specific situations and relationships with people we shall encounter, in order to fulfill that capacity.

"What could be more sensible than to return to familiar family lines and circumstances which we, as well as the other family members with whom we will reside, already understand in a very fundamental sense at the soul level—not to leave out the similar shared cultural heritage and genetic disposition, which also play a part? Plus, there are relationships between family members which must be developed, expanded, or elaborated over many generations; these individuals can work together to accomplish common goals. Some call these grouping of individuals, who incarnate together in each generation, soul groups. To do otherwise and incarnate in unfamiliar circumstances, would mean that we would be required to master many new situations, while trying to fulfill our destinies at the same time. Of course, incarnation in an unfamiliar state happens; sometimes a different lifetime is what is needed for a specific soul's growth."

"I always wondered years ago when I read on this subject, who I was casually running into on the street whom I had known, possibly quite well, in a different life," Kahn said.

"Yes, sometimes we are thrown at someone for just an instant in time, just to provide a certain support, or to do a good deed. This action, even if small, can be the very reason for our existence." Prince said. "Sometimes, it is just necessary for two people, who are otherwise unrelated, to experience the same environment for their growth—like a parallel or convergent evolution. And then again, perhaps these common, but unconnected experiences will eventually bring them together in the future for a purpose."

"It helps me to know that our souls are not just out there dangling by themselves in that wind, that we are connected with others on the same journey," Kahn said.

"If we could just see what remains hidden in our world, we would feel a great comfort," Prince said.

"What is happening to various souls as we approach the Messianic Age?" Kahn said.

In general, the Messiah shall not come until all the souls which have been created are born into this world," Prince said. "This is one of the reasons for the great population increase on earth. In some sense, with everyone being born, we are recapitulating relationships that have existed in prior generations. Another phenomenon we see, after so many generations of separate peoples, is souls from different backgrounds mixing with each other. This provides a unity, which will precede this World to Come.

"There are also specific occurrences among Jewish souls. Those Jews lost to our faith through Galut, our exile, are returning. This is the major reason for the tremendous growth in our movement. But in recent decades we have also discovered lost groups, who having retained their Jewish origins, are being reabsorbed into our people. Finally, we are experiencing the conversion to Judaism of people whose souls have been born into non-Jewish families. This is one reason why we have so much conversion at this time. Again, this is a means of uniting all peoples in preparation for the Messianic Age. But it is also because when the Jewish people are united and strong, they shall lead the way to the Messianic Age."

"Rebbe, what has been the most difficult aspect of your mission in this life?" Kahn said. "Has it been the struggle against evil, or fighting opponents such as myself, or being out there alone, where almost no one else understands you? Has it been your relationship with G-d and what He wants you to do?"

Prince thought for a while. Then he said, "You know it wasn't easy for me to accept this role. And I fled from it."

Kahn nodded. "Yes, that's highly ironic, since people such as myself have claimed that you have profited by your role."

"I had to figure out why I was running from it. Perhaps I shall never know exactly. But I remember booing at that hockey game when I was a small child."

"What does a minor game have to do with such an important soul as yours?" Kahn said. He was intrigued.

"Well that hockey game was the essence of kelipah. Since I was old enough to discern my environment, I have always disliked the sitra achra, the other side, with a passion."

"So it wasn't fighting evil, for example, that gave you the biggest problem?" Kahn said.

"No, fighting evil, doing the right thing, has come so naturally. I couldn't have done anything else with something so repugnant. In fact, I suppose it's like someone getting up in the morning and thinking that they want to eat. I couldn't survive for an instance without doing it."

"Were you not concerned that evil would prevail?" Kahn said.

"No. Evil shall never prevail. That's just a human distortion of our world. It's our fallacy, our error. But we are such a small part of the universe. Human perversion and fabrication have no effect on the Divine Light, which shines through and around us. We have no power to create, as G-d does with His Ten Utterances. Our machinations mean nothing. G-d and His creations are good, and we have no power to change that."

"But the Holocaust? It's of such a magnitude that..."

"The Holocaust was a terrible event. But out of death, life will once again arise. Yes, so many of our people were killed, but their Jewish souls remain immortal. They do not go away, whether they stay in the World to Come, or they choose to return to this earth. Yes, many souls died horrible deaths, and were scarred. Some of them are confronting the residue of those memories in their new lives, though they may not realize it. But with time, there is a cleansing. With time, these souls choose to return to earth, and correct the deficiencies in mankind which led to that odious time. In time, everyone and everything, is whole."

"And your opponents have not bothered you?" Kahn said.

"No, my faith and knowledge has grounded me. My opponents are not just inconveniences, but opportunities. My struggles with them are my chance to assist the world. Just as in physics, there is no work done without resistance, so one cannot do good in this world, without overcoming evil. Good exists through its opposition to evil."

"So what was it with the sitra achra that made you so uneasy?" Kahn said.

"In order for a person to be able to tolerate a reality outside of himself, he must have at least some small affinity for that reality. And for that affinity, or relationship, to exist, there either must be at least a small portion of that reality present in that person, or the possibility, or potentiality of that person binding with that reality. Otherwise, it will be similar to oil and water; there will be no association—that is unless there is an intermediary such as soap which joins them.

"My Divine soul has no attraction to the sitra achra, and kelipah. Consequently, this coarse, very unrefined matter has the possibility of making my system extremely sick. Naturally, I have always been repulsed by it. But when I was young, I had not built up on the natural defenses to repel it, so I avoided it."

"It sounds very immunological, like a disease," Kahn said.

"Yes, there are comparisons."

"But other souls are able to handle this sitra achra better?" Kahn said.

"Yes, every soul has a different constitution, a different balance. Many can handle the filthy garments full of kelipah in this world, which surround their soul. Others have perforce shed them, or a portion of them."

"Not all of us can reside in a dirty hovel," Kahn said. "Some very holy souls require a place which is immaculately clean. But now realizing that this is your soul's state, why is this true with an elevated soul such as yours?"

"Let me refer you to a story which you have probably heard in different forms. But the message is the same."

There was once a person, who in search of diamonds, went to a far away world. When he arrived, there were diamonds everywhere. He could have hauled them away by the truck load from the beach alone. But because the diamonds were so common, the people in this far away location placed no value on them. When at first the man tried to gather them up in buckets, they laughed at him. What was scarce and valuable to them was fish.

After a number of years, this person was set to return to his home and family. He wanted to carry back all he could of value with him. But he had forgotten what was valuable in his previous home. Instead of carrying back diamonds, he returned with as many fish as he could. When he arrived back home, after greeting him, his family wanted to know what he had been able to bring back of value to them. When he pulled the stinking, rotting fish out of his luggage, they were incredulous. Why would you haul that back here, they asked?

"But how does this apply to the soul?" Kahn asked.

"It applies. But first, let me say that I wanted to tell the story again anyway, because it's one of my favorites. It's about what we value in our lives. Ultimately, we will be known for what we value. Will it be stinking fish or diamonds, and in reality what's the difference? It's all relative. One is hard and shiny, and the other is soft and dull, but not one of them has that much use in the long run for our souls. They're both apparitions, illusions of something which we perceive we want. But neither one will bring us closure and or happiness. Neither can affect our being, or our relationship with G-d. And thus, just like some people's hunt for money, if we obtain either one of them, we may find ourselves unsatisfied, and in constant pursuit of more of it.

"But you asked how it applies to the soul. Our story, the human story, is one of passage, of a journey from one world to another, and back again. We are always in transit, always in movement. Besides what we value, we will also be distinguished as individual souls by our good deeds, and by the memories embedded in our soul from our sojourn in each world. What will we carry in our deeds and memory away from one place to another, in order to make a difference in the next world? Will the movement to the next world be a progressive step, or will it be merely a return to the same conditions and reactions as before? Will we have learned proper lessons in each world, or will we have closed our hearts and minds?"

"Reacting initially to the story, it seems simple. It's diamonds, of course, that he should have brought back," Kahn said. "But after some thought, perhaps the people in the original world didn't value their fish highly enough."

"Either way, they probably didn't value the man's good intentions, which were important. There was a positive energy associated with his fish, because of his efforts. He must have spun off an angel or two with his intentions, which could have been of value to his family."

"You know, the story has much practical truth to it. I have traveled, as you have, to some pretty strange places," Kahn said, "and when you go to a place, and you see what seems to be ten thousand of the same type of objects, it seems like junk, because there is so much of it. But when you bring one or two of the objects home, all by themselves, they can look fantastic in a very different setting. And you then wish that you had brought more."

"Yes, so the setting, or background, is what is so often important to our thinking. We go along in this life, particularly in childhood, setting up a background of Jewish beliefs, morality, and learning—that is a perspective or viewpoint of our world. For the longest time we are perhaps wondering why. It may all seem like a lot of meaningless junk or clutter of information. Then one day, a person, event, idea, or object comes along, and our background is suddenly important—relevant and critical—because it sets off or accentuates the person or object. It organizes the reality of that person. The person, concept, or idea is the spark, which lights the match, which lights the room—or background—and brings it out of darkness and indistinguishableness, so that we may finally apply our discriminatory powers. But, it is as a direct result of the background, that we can truly identify and understand that person or concept.

"And you bring up another good point, Mr. Kahn. Is it not our challenge in life to see the unique value of a person, or soul, or concept, amidst all the jumble and litter of this world—to be able for example, to assess and react to a person, as if she were the only individual who mattered?" Prince said.

"But we have digressed again. To answer your question, when I came to this world from the previous one, I carried a strong feeling for G-d. I wanted nothing to do with the kelipah, and my soul longed for the previous world, where I felt closer to G-d. I felt imprisoned in this world, and unsuited for it in any sense. It would have been easier for me to be a Rebbe in a religious setting, where my followers would shield me from much of the obscenity and filth of the world. But this was not my destiny. I was specifically brought here to try to establish holiness in the most fetid of places."

"So you rebelled or fled. What brought you back?" Kahn said.

"Three gentlemen opened a door for me. Wherever I was physically located, wherever my consciousness lay, they were determined to meet me at my level, on my personal terms, in order to provide a gate, a portal, through which I could begin to return, to come back to G-d.

"This is why we must never prejudge a person's soul. Even a soul found at the lowest level of kelipah may make that turning. It's beginning the journey back that counts. And we as Jews have to be there to open that spiritual door at that critical moment, whether it is through the synagogue, through a class or a life cycle event, or assisting with a personal need. Absent the violation of Jewish law, we have to cast away our official rules, and go to where we are needed for each individual soul."

Kahn rose from his seat and began pacing while in deep thought. Then he turned to face Prince directly. "Rebbe, if you will, now think back specifically to that time before, and as you made that turning. What were your specific feelings, your specific emotions, at the time?"

Prince sat in contemplation for a moment. Then his eyes looked back at Kahn, flashing an intensity of emotion that made Kahn draw back. "Fate was tracking me, then stalking me. It was my own shadow coming toward by body all the time. At first, in the early morning—in my early childhood—it seemed far away, and it seemed as if I could possibly elude it. But as the years went by, and as I grew toward maturity, and the sun of my life moved close to overhead, my shadow condensed itself, became powerful, and drew closer to me. So I ran faster and faster, went further and further from my home, and closed my eyes to it, hoping that when I opened them again, it would be gone. But instead, when I carefully peered out again, it had drawn even closer to me, just as assuredly as the sun inevitably moves—or plots—its noon time summer solstice. And finally in that room, with those three gentlemen, it touched me with all of its force! There was no running away any more. The shadow, the possibilities of my soul, would necessarily become me. The only way to escape it was to deny the very life force in me. That was the only way to get rid of my shadow—my fate—to purge my soul from my body. In that moment I chose life over death."

Kahn sat back a bit dumbstruck. Then he recovered, to quickly continue. "You said that you began to return. What is the general process of development of the soul after it incarnates on this earth?"

"Every soul develops in its own way. But the ten sefirot in some ways express the soul's encounter with this world. The sefirot are organized into three columns. The right column is said to be 'long', while the left column is 'short'. The middle column is the result of the balance of the left and right."

"As I recall, the sefirot are attributes of G-d," Kahn said.

"Yes, and as our souls are our inheritance from G-d, so these attributes apply to our souls as well," Prince said. "The sefirot are made up of both 'lights' and 'vessels'. The light, known as 'or' in Hebrew, is designed to reveal, whereas the purpose of the vessels, or 'kellim', is to conceal—only allowing light to be revealed to the extent of the capacity of the finite beings. We humans are kellim, who hold a certain level of spirituality. But now this distinction between light and vessels—between the revealed and the hidden—is only in our eyes, so that we may regard ourselves as separate individuals with independent existences, and not be nullified in the presence of G-d.

To our Creator, there is no distinction between or and kellim. Just as a person cannot conceal his body by covering it with his hand, so the power of G-d to both reveal and conceal are limitless, and are unified as one and the same. Neither are there boundaries between revealed and concealed spirituality, which flow from one, back to the other.

"Now, returning to souls, each of course carries it own previous knowledge and memory into this world. Nevertheless, each soul must develop Chochmah, or wisdom, and Binah, or understanding, for the specific individual circumstances which it encounters. Chochmah, on the right column side, is the intuitive flash, wherein a person quickly knows something, for example an idea, but may not be sure exactly how. Binah, on the left side, is the development of the details, the elaboration, with all of its particulars, of the solution realized in an instant in Chochmah. Once a person possesses these, then she may obtain Daat, or knowledge. Daat is found in the middle column because it results from the interaction of Chochmah and Binah. In acquiring Daat, she has bound to the idea and knows how it may be applied to a situation. Now, a person can apply these three intellectual sefirot to a small concept or idea. But these sefirot can also be applied to the concept of intellectual and emotional maturity for a person in the course of her life. As a person moves from adolescence to adulthood, there is a process of self-actualization that should occur through Daat. In that process, the person integrates her wisdom and understanding, and decides how she will apply these to her life. This situation is what I personally faced when the three gentlemen met me.

"The truth is that Daat, when related to a person's own life, is quite challenging to possess. Many people, if not most, are unable to obtain the sufficient self-knowledge necessary to apply to their lives. Some never achieve the prerequisite wisdom and understanding. But even if they do, it is very hard to see oneself clearly. This is why it is necessary to have mentors, such as I have been fortunate to enjoy. Just as we may not be able to heal ourselves, even if we are doctors, so there is only so much self-knowledge which can be filtered through our individual consciousness. This is true, even though those individuals with more elevated souls are more successful at this endeavor, because they experience less interference with the ego and other personal desires, which are generated by the kelipah on this earth."

"So, now a person essentially knows who they are if they achieve Daat on a personal level?" Kahn said.

"Yes, it is important for all of us to specialize in ourselves, as selfish as that may sound, before we move on. You will see what appear to be a lot of selfish teenagers out there, whom their parents claim are self-absorbed and not focused on others' needs. But as these teenagers reach physical and intellectual maturity, particularly with regard to the capacity of their brains and their ability to do abstract thinking, it is only natural that they are doing what their souls need at that time. And for a while, this can make for some fairly unpredictable results. Of course, it's a problem if these youth are unable to pass through this stage, and then as a result, develop into self-indulgent adults, rather than giving people. The world has an oversupply of the former. But as a temporary phase, self-seeking is a normal and necessary stage of growth. Again, this is what I was doing when I selfishly left my uncle and wandered throughout the world. By the way, this uncompleted, but developing Daat in teenagers also explains why they are so sensitive to the opinions of their parents and especially to their peers. Because their self-concept is still developing, they have not fully constructed the boundaries between themselves and others."

"And then, let's say that a person is successful in knowing herself, what then?" Kahn said.

"Another very hard stage then ensues. Once a person has mastered herself, then there are complicated choices to consider about how she should live her life. If she really knows herself, then she has the capacity to make the right choices in order to fulfill her destiny, and may serve G-d in peace and contentment. Of course, she may flee, or deny that role, in which case her lot will be unhappiness. This was true in my case.

"Each stage, each sefirot, must lead to the next. If a person has insufficient Chochmah or Binah, then Daat will not develop properly. And without sufficient Daat to make the correct choices, it is hard to see how a person may live his life well. Likewise for the sefirot that follow. Without a personal knowledge of self through Daat, it is hard for a person to develop a free, frank, and open relationship with a mate."

Kahn sat with a complete look of engagement. "Could you go into more detail?" he said.

"Yes. After the three intellectual sefirot, just mentioned, the first two emotional sefirot are Chesed, or generosity and kindness, and Gevurah, which is restriction, discipline, and severity. Chesed, which is part of the right side column, is a flow and is outwardly directed, while Gevurah, on the left side, will act to constrict or limit Chesed, and is inwardly directed and focused. Chesed is associated with humility, while Gevurah is associated with strength. Both these qualities, Chesed and Gevurah, are needed to achieve balance in human relationships. The combination of these in a person gives rise to Tifferet, or compassion, beauty, and truth. Tifferet is necessary for a person to relate to another. Without Tifferet, it would be impossible for one person to step out of herself, and put herself in another person's shoes—see the truth about someone—in order to feel what that other person feels, whether it be pain or exhilaration. We exercise Tifferet when we do something for someone, whether giving or disciplining, which we would not otherwise do if we merely took our self-interest into account.

"Now this Tifferet can be no more in quality and quantity than the Daat possessed by a person. A person may only relate to another person to the extent to which he already knows himself. If a person is still working out his own inner conflicts, he will be responding to his own personal and pressing needs in a relationship, rather than doing the giving and taking, which would ideally strengthen his mate, merely for her own sake. When an individual has limited Daat, that is when he falls short of self-actualization, he may be unable to relate to his mate; thus, the lack of self-actualization is a major reason for the preponderance of divorces. How many times have you heard the phrase in a marriage, 'he just needs to grow up?' Alternatively, a person may find someone who is working through many of the same issues at the same level as he. In that case, the relationship will not be the best, but may be reciprocal, so that both parties can mutually benefit and grow together. We find in these cases many soul mates, who have lived many lifetimes together, assisting each other.

"And it doesn't end there. The natural progression of two people's relationship is procreation. This is symbolized by the next middle column sefira, which results from the balance of Netzach, which is endurance, and Hod, which is splendor. That sefira is Yesod, which means foundation. Yesod is the connector between the inner mind emotions and Malchut, the revealed world."

Kahn smiled. "That was an excellent exposition, Rebbe, or as you might phrase it: discourse. It was so good, that it jarred my memory for all of these terms."

Prince smiled. "Very good. I am very pleased."

"Rebbe, your Hebrew name is Joseph. You have lived up to that name in so many ways. But I keep discovering new ones," Kahn said. "And when you mentioned Yesod, it triggered another thought, from a long time ago; as you say, Rebbe, you never know how something Jewish you learn will apply, but nothing is an accident. I remember now that Joseph was the symbol of Yesod. He was the foundation of the survival of our people, just as you are now the foundation of our people, and of all this country.

"As I also recall, Joseph had another important characteristic. He was called the 'perfect master'—the tzaddik. At any one time, a special tzaddik lives among us in our world, and provides its spiritual foundation. Not only that, but a potential Moshiach, a Messiah, is available—who already lives in flesh and blood in our world now—in every generation, should G-d call upon him.

"This Moshiach will not be some mystery, or angel pulled down from heaven. We will not need to look for signs or miracles from heaven. As Rambam, Maimonides said, we will be able to identify him by his personality and actions. We will all know of his great saintly status. Rebbe, it is abundantly clear to me the identity of this human being in this generation."

27

The interview did not end there. For hours more, into the night, the two men talked. Before Kahn left, he thanked Prince not so much for the interview, but for his personal guidance. He requested the minyan hours of the synagogue and a contact for further information. Finally, he asked Prince to bless him, to draw down the Divine Light upon him. And he again asked for forgiveness from Prince, and stated that what he most desired of his future life now was an enduring friendship with this spiritual leader. Prince had responded by saying, "My friend, we have mended fences, not just between us, but between all the souls who have been connected to us through all these generations. We have repaired ancient ruins, and rebuilt the foundations of previous generations; we have corrected and healed the rupture."

The Prince interview had been one of the longest that Kahn had ever conducted. He had carried dozens of pages of shorthand notes home, as well as long tape recorded pieces. This first hand detailed information was certainly enough for him to write the biggest story of his career. It would have been accepted with enthusiasm, and gratitude, by any publication. And virtually all other writers would have quickly written it and rushed it to press, with the logical reasoning that this was big news, which immediately needed to reach the public. This would have made all the more sense in Kahn's case, since he had lost his professional stature and rapidly needed to return to his career.

But Kahn held back. He wasn't writing for glory anymore. He was writing with a mission in mind. Instead of immediately composing a rough draft, he spent several weeks, which turned into months, researching Prince's activities. This had never worked before, even when Kahn had dug deeply and tenaciously into the material.

People who had supposedly known Prince, particularly from his youth, before he had reached Oklahoma City, had been very reluctant to talk about him. Kahn had always felt that he was close to a revelation, that he was really talking to someone who had known him well, only to have a curtain suddenly come down across the stage. When that had happened on other stories, he had been able to find someone who would talk; he had always figured out the facts of the case. In contrast, he had never been able to go any where with Prince.

But this time, his intuition told him that what formerly had been a dead end investigation would turn out to be different. And it was. He found dozens of people who not only would talk, but wanted to tell their stories, and inquired how they might contribute to Prince's efforts. He wondered what the difference was this time. When he reflected upon it, he thought that he was an entirely different person asking the questions. Perhaps he had made a turning. And as Prince had said, he was no longer trying to bulldoze his way through the process; he was trying to follow a G-d given path.

Kahn had been as impressed with Prince as anyone could possibly be. And that was saying everything, because he was still at heart a skeptical reporter. Nevertheless, what he found surprised him, actually shocked him, because as much as he now respected Prince, he had never seen anything like it. All who had had contact with Prince, even those who had fought against him—for example in the merchant marine—had spoken highly of him. Many did not understand him intellectually, but in matters of the heart, they sang his praises. Clubs of former acquaintances—Prince had had no friends in the early years—had sprung up to watch him together on the nightly news and to follow his work. These citizens knew by their association with this special person that they too were exceptional and living in an extraordinary time. They reveled in his successes, cheering for him as they would their favorite football team. And each bonded closely with the others in the group.

Meanwhile, as the months of the third year of the drought slowly elapsed, and the nation had sunk even deeper into economic depression and a deflationary spiral, and had endured an unremitting despair, the nation's debate regarding Prince and the Messianic Age had grown more vociferous. Both sides had become increasingly frustrated by the deteriorating condition of the nation, and each was convinced that dramatic change was necessary. But this was the only idea upon which they could agree. The Prince advocates had not only coalesced around the core of his policies, but were expressing an exceptional loyalty to their leader; some of them had stated that America must rally behind such a strong person in uncertain times, or the nation would split apart. Some fringe political elements, seeing the popularity of Prince's forces, and trying to tap into his success, by associating with his movement, had even proudly proclaimed that they were willing to sign on to any of his policies; Prince's Independent Party had disavowed their participation, but it had had little effect. On the other hand, the opponents of Prince desired a restoration, a return to the America which they had previously enjoyed. They focused on Prince as their problem, because they claimed that he had been the agent of change, and as time passed, they increasingly blamed all of their difficulties on him. Some of these opponents could not contain their hatred of him and actually spoke of him as a source of evil in public forums. As each side had rejected almost all aspects of the other's viewpoint, the country had become increasingly polarized; after a while, there had been virtually no commonality of language or mutually understood concepts between the two, which would allow any dialogue to continue. On the talk shows, normally calm and apparently reasonable commentators, who otherwise rejected emotional involvement in their work, had been observed screaming at each other. One respected veteran had had to be restrained and removed in the middle of a show.

Then widespread demonstrations had begun in the streets. Each demonstration by a side had led to a counter demonstration by the other. The Prince advocates pridefully carried pictures of a smiling Prince. Their opponents carried pictures of the same man, but all of these had been defiled or dressed in various derogatory poses; a portion even garbed him in Nazi dress. As each side had become further enflamed by the other's representations, each had attempted to disrupt the other's public displays. Then violence had erupted and the National Guard had been called in to hold the peace. When Prince had appealed for calm, the violence had become even more strident; both his supporters and opponents had only seen the truth of their own message in his statements. As the violence spread to all fifty states, historians compared the period of division to the years before the Civil War. Eventually they openly talked about what previously had been unmentionable—the possibility of that devastating event occurring once again. This time, however, they noted that the civil war would not be fought over constitutional, slavery, racial, regional, and economic causes. And it wouldn't be fought over traditional religious disputes—there were plenty of those throughout world history that had divided mankind. It would instead be fought over something much more abstract: spirituality. The battles would go to the heart of every home in America and no one would be able to find any temporary safety in geography or physical distance.

As Prince's Independent Party gained strength, and the fortunes of the Democratic and Republican parties waned, a new fourth party, the Opposition Party, had quickly arisen, and seized upon the zeal of opponents demonstrating against Prince. Its sole stated purpose in its mission statement was to counteract Prince and neutralize all of his efforts. This party was primarily funded by formerly wealthy citizens, who under Prince's leadership in the Senate had lost much of their power to influence government and industry, but still retained enough resources to strike back at him. But there were many other disparate elements of the society who had affixed themselves to the cause. Many who had decided to affiliate with the party were afraid, if not repulsed, by the idea of bringing an observant religious person, with his own nascent religious movement, into the highest part of government. Others were specifically opposed to an observant Jew in all his aspects. Other groups, having been formerly rejected for a long time by the general society, saw an opportunity to finally have a voice in a political party. The Ku Klux Klan, White Supremacists, America Party National Committee, Nazi Party, and World Church of the Creator, among many other sects and persuasions, had now all made the party their home. And as the party grew and brought increased strength to its street demonstrations, the National Guard was an insufficient protector of people and property. For the first time since the Reconstruction in the south, the President of the United States had stationed the American army in civilian areas to keep the peace.

"This Independent Party is an odious thing. Its one purpose is to hate us, no matter what we do," Richard had said. "It will also be a magnet that will bring all of our detractors together. They are already organizing against us with more efficiency."

"Yes, this is true," Prince said. "We do indeed now see evil in all of its manifestation, parasitically feeding on the good in society. But this is what we have expected. Evil cannot exist by itself. It must depend upon man to feed it and sustain it. Not only that, but man must exile the Divine Light, so that it can grow. Just as a fungus, it must grow in darkness, on the refuse of society. And wherever there is transformation, and a turning in society, there will be waste, abandonment, discard, scrap, and junk generated upon which it can feed. So this natural development must happen. And furthermore, it is not all bad for us."

"Why is that?" Richard said.

"As we have manifested ourselves as a religious movement and a political party, and consequently attracted the yetzer hara, so they too will be flushed out and face renewed opposition to their goals. Every action will have a reaction in the universe. As a result, potential supporters of ours will be horrified by their agenda and join our ranks," Prince said.

"Furthermore, because evil must depend upon good for its very existence, and possesses no independent reality, entity, or presence of its own, it cannot get along with itself for any substantial period of time. Cooperation can only take place between independent beings. Parasitic substances, if necessary, will try to turn on each other for energy; this is particularly true if the forces of good are strong enough to reject the evil. Consequently, all the factions will eventually fight with each other, just as Hitler turned on Stalin.

"And there is another point too. These people were always against us, plotting against us by e-mail. But now we will know better their identities and their activities. We will know what they are saying to each other, and who is supporting them."

"Yes, and I also assume that it will much easier for the FBI to keep their activities in check," Richard said.

As the demonstrations continued, Prince still appeared to be gaining the upper hand. He continued to be on the news every night and his rational, unemotional explanations amid the violence were convincing wavering Americans that he was up to the job of the Presidency. Most people not already polarized to one side or the other, continued to find him charming, and those who were still indifferent to him, preferred the honest politician they knew to an alternative.

All this while, Kahn had continued work on his piece about Prince. In the media, he had been a source of continued speculation. Many rumors had circulated about his exit from the *Los Angeles Times*, and he had become as big a private topic of conversation among the media, as Prince was a public topic. After the apology printed in the *Times*, it had been concluded by all in the business that he had been summarily fired because of his last piece. But in a profession that was accustomed to finding out all the details, there seemed to be nothing but an information void that followed. Almost always, a person in Kahn's position in the world was interested in telling his side of the story to the press, in order to immediately restore some personal and professional credibility. This was particularly true in the case of media employment controversies, in which the fallen party not only knew how to use the press for his benefit, but could employ contacts and friends in the occupation for his purpose; after so many years, Kahn certainly had many debts to call in from allies and acquaintances.

But Kahn had said nothing. And no one had even seen him for sure. The most reliable rumor—and it was only that—maintained that he had been seen a few times shortly after his dismissal, walking the streets near his apartment, aimlessly like a drunkard, with his shirttail out, and his thick, wiry gray hair fixed in a wild Albert Einstein configuration. But this had seemed so out of character for him that it had been immediately discounted by those who knew him best. What everyone wondered was what this man was now doing. They knew he hadn't gone away. Whatever he was, Daniel Kahn was not the type to quit. As one who knew him well said, "He's not gone from us forever. He's gone away to prove a point. And you can bet, with what's happened, that he won't be back until he proves it beyond a doubt. But when he does come back, whatever he writes will be the best piece of his life." Virtually everyone in the media had concluded that Kahn would get the goods on Prince, if he could. And if he couldn't, no one would. They were waiting.

When Kahn finished his piece, he e-mailed his former editor Graves a message. He purposely did not say that he had been able to interview Prince, but merely stated that, "I have a piece that you would like to publish, Ken. Out of respect to you, I am offering this piece to the *Times* first."

When Graves had received his note, he had scuffed at it, and had written in reply, "Daniel, I told you that the only way I would publish a piece of yours again was if you had first obtained an interview with Senator Reed. If you now insist on sending your work without that interview, then I shall read it out of a respect for our former relationship. But I shall not publish it, nor will I ever read anything that you ever submit again, even if it is based on a future interview." Then as he came out of his e-mail, he muttered to himself, "offering to me first out of respect—who does he think he is now?"

The next day a huge package arrived over night. Kahn had previously been famous for his lengthy and thorough dissertations on subjects, but Graves had never seen an article of that size submitted by anyone. On the top of the article, Kahn had scribbled, "If you like this Ken, then you'll need to discuss a price with me before I give you permission to publish it. As you know, our old agreements are now void." Graves' face had turned beet red, as one of his assistants had entered the office.

"Are you okay, Ken?" the assistant said.

"Yeah," Graves said. "Before you came into the room, I was just about to throw this article by our old friend, Daniel Kahn, all away across the room, and then when it was good and torn up, it was going to hit the shredder. What chutzpah, sending me this incredibly long piece of junk to read on Prince Reed—another diatribe I'm sure—without his even getting an interview. And then he has the audacity to write on here that he needs to negotiate a price. He's really lost it now."

"Well, sir, if it's all the same to you, I'd really like to read it," the assistant said. "We don't have to publish it, but Daniel Kahn is news to the news organizations. All this time, no one has had any idea of his whereabouts and everyone is curious. And if someone should decide to publish it, maybe just to get an edge up on us, it sure would be nice to know in advance what he's saying."

"Oh, all right," Graves said. "You're right. I'd better take a look at it first. But I'm not putting up with his trash. He's still finished with me."

It was then late in the afternoon and Graves had an appointment across town in less than an hour. He figured that he would spend at most a few minutes sampling the piece and then pass it on to his assistants merely to satisfy their curiosity. But when he read the first paragraph he was unable to force himself to skip around to any other sections. And after fifteen minutes, he called his wife and said that he would be indefinitely detained at the office because of a big news story.

It was midnight before he left his office and he had not even thought to eat. His wife took one look at him when he entered their bedroom and said, "Ken, I've never seen you look like that before on any news story. It must be a very big one."

"Carol," he said, "it's the best story of my career, the quintessential reason for publishing, and I am ashamed of myself. I almost missed it. I didn't have faith in an old friend. He was testing me, and if it hadn't been for one of my assistants walking in at the right moment, I would have flunked the test. I would never have forgiven myself."

"It has to do with Kahn, doesn't it?" she said. "I told you that it took one great person to be so fixated on another."

When Kahn entered Graves' office, he quietly motioned to him to have a seat. "Daniel, I've misjudged you. For that, I apologize."

Kahn smiled at him, but his voice broke. "Ken, you don't owe me any apology, particularly after what I have done. And if you do, we're even now. Can we just be friends again?"

"Yes, that is what I would like too," Graves said. "Daniel, this is the best piece that I have ever seen, bar none. It will be the most influential and outstanding published work of this generation. You already have enough material for a book. How did you do this in such a short period of time?"

Kahn broke into a smile once again. "You know how I work when I get onto something, Ken. As for the quality of the piece, and the stardom, it is true, I know. But the strange thing after all this time is that I don't care any more. I'll win the prize I sought, but ..."

"I know," Graves said. "You've changed. That's why the piece is so good. It's unaffected. It's pure journalism. There's bias—not the kind I expected of course—but there's balance. You're not trying to score points or prove anything, any more. How in the blazes did you get all those people to talk?"

"When I stopped trying to extract it," Kahn said, "it flowed. The universe wanted me to have it this time."

With Joseph "Prince" Reed, Kahn wrote, *also known as Senator, Rebbe, and Tzaddik, among other respected names, we are extremely fortunate to be experiencing not just an exceptional historical phenomenon, but a rare metaphysical event on this earth.*

For a number of years, I have savaged Prince Reed. I railed against those who were taken by his presence. I said that no one could be that good, that wonderful of a public servant, much less such a dedicated servant of G-d. I was wrong. I was so wrong that I wrung the goodness out of my own soul. This man is everything that I have said that he's not.

Those who have read my work in previous years know that I have been a hard hitting, mistrustful, disbelieving, and often irreverent reporter. Unfortunately, my lack of faith in human action and affairs had always been proven correct. That view of human nature had made me very successful. That is until I met Prince Reed.

No, my mind hasn't suddenly gone soft, in the manner that I had falsely judged, even accused others, who have known the Senator. I am in possession of all my faculties. I have not changed. I have just finally met this man in person. And I am extremely grateful for that experience.

In any secular written piece about a person, the personal religion of that individual might be duly noted, particularly if this were a major part of his life. But a certain dispassionate objectivity would be strictly maintained by the author. And it would be further possible to clearly segregate the political or business parts of that person's life from the religious. That is what would occur with a normal person, who might be newsworthy, like you or me. But after interacting with the exceptional soul of Prince Reed, I believe that neither of these is conceivable in this article. It is not possible to talk about him and not always mix all the ingredients of his life, from politics to religion. His accomplishments interlock like pieces in a puzzle. And I cannot imagine anyone being in his presence without losing his impartiality.

In every generation, the sages of my Jewish faith—and to know the Senator is to want to return to your faith, whatever it might be—have said that there is one man who provides the spiritual foundation for the world. G-d sends one prophet down to this earth, and it is said, that if the people will only listen to him and follow the path that he sets forth toward G-d, then the world will be transformed. Jews such as myself refer to such a metamorphosis as the Messianic Age.

In that time, evil will be no more. The lion shall lie down with the lamb. Nations shall lay down their swords. The pain, suffering, and sickness of mankind shall end. The World to Come shall arrive on earth. And the spirituality underlying everything shall no longer be hidden to our eyes. Everyone shall come to know G-d. All this shall come to pass in the course of the natural order of the world.

I am absolutely convinced that Prince Reed is G-d's representative on earth. He has been sent to lead us into the Messianic Age. If we will only welcome him, he will be our Messiah.

All of the above small excerpts were taken from Kahn's introduction and conclusion to his article. If this had been all that Daniel Kahn had written, then he too would have been consigned by others to his previously designated pool of crazies, who had been strangely taken with Prince. But except for a few other allusions, this was all of the personal opinion that Kahn had offered on Prince. True, the opinion had been unusually controversial and highly unorthodox. But the rest of the extremely long series—more than ninety-nine percent—was something else. It was a detailed discussion of Prince's early life and times, specifically his early upbringing, his movement throughout the world, his time at the Jones' ranch, as well as his days at Stanford. After that, Kahn had analyzed his previous and current policies. He had talked frankly not just about Prince's admirable human qualities, but his early rejection of the world, and his running away from home. And he had not minced words regarding Prince's potential mixture of religion and politics, skillfully bringing in differing viewpoints, and giving historical examples for comparison and reference. He had even tutored his readers in the Jewish Messianic concept. He had shrewdly presented as much information as possible, and then allowed the reader to reach his own judgment. As he had said in his conclusion,

This matter is far too important for one person, or several people, a few million, or even a couple of billion people to decide. All human inhabitants on this earth, together, not separately, but together, must decide whether they shall follow this man. The fate of our world hangs in the balance. So I have earnestly and sincerely tried to present the material in as fair and impartial manner—with all viewpoints represented—as I can. I hope that you will draw your own conclusions. Yet, since this matter is so critical for all of us now, and since unfortunately only a tiny fraction of the world can personally meet this exceptional man, I feel that I would be remiss if I did not offer my own opinion.

Excerpts from Kahn's dissertation on Prince ran for a solid two weeks in the *Los Angeles Times.* The newspaper had carefully planned for substantially increased circulation. But it had not realized that it would be deluged by so many requests for newspapers, as souvenirs, from all parts of the country. And early on, before it became fully aware of the demand for the story, it found it necessary to reprint several editions of the newspaper. Readers were not just attracted by the story's topic; they were intrigued by Kahn's transformation, and even more by the rumors of his new friendship with Prince. The story became a national pastime for some, and an obsession, preoccupation, or compulsion for others. But it seemed that everyone had read some of it and was discussing it. For decades to come, many would even reminisce about where they had been, and what they had been doing, when the story broke.

28

If everyone was focused on the Prince Reed story, the reactions to it were incredibly varied. Of course, the hard core Prince advocates and detractors had reacted in predictable ways; they had continued to demonstrate and try to undermine their opponents. But for the "average" people in the middle, who had diligently tried to avoid the increasingly violent confrontations on the streets, this story had finally made Prince seem both human and understandable. They could now follow his life's path and identify with his pain and suffering. They could see underneath his surface and appreciate his kindness, concern for people, dedication, and drive. He was no longer some Adonis, some idol, but a real person. He had not been awarded his lot in life, as so many had assumed; instead, he had reluctantly accepted his role in the service of G-d, because he loved G-d more than himself. Kahn had made all this abundantly clear, as well as many other aspects of Prince's character, and the reverberations of his words kept ringing true to the public. Prince was not only competent and charming, he was likable. He was the best of both worlds; he not only excelled, but he was one of them. They knew him. And they would now root for him, just as they would cheer for the home town boy.

If many of the "average" people were turning outward to accept Prince, many groups had focused inward. For them Prince was not so much a story, as an opportunity. The end of the world theology had caught fire, particularly around many southern pulpits. These parishioners were concerned with their personal souls and how they would fare on Judgment Day. And now these people were sure that such a time was fast approaching. They saw it in the cataclysmic nature of the drought, the moral and economic decay which had followed, and now in the demonstrations, which were pitting neighbor against neighbor, and even spouses against each other. Now a new, strong leader had arisen to lead them to a better world. And it did not hurt that the person who had emerged was both Jewish and mysterious. Jews were still G-d's chosen people, and the ways of G-d were mysterious. One only had to pick up a copy of the *Old Testament* to see that. And it could be expected, as the mystery unfolded, that Jesus would once again return to earth, or reveal his presence—just maybe, it was said, through, or as, Prince Reed.

So now preachers across all parts of the land, but particularly in the devastated rural communities, rose up in front of their congregations and proclaimed that all this suffering had been preordained from the beginning of time, and that finally the time of redemption was nearing. When that time came, the righteous among the peoples of the earth would no longer suffer, but would be exalted before G-d. Some loosely cited from Isaiah, Ch. 2, to explain the distress and hurting to their Sunday flocks: "The L-rd of hosts will have His day, upon all who are proud and arrogant, and upon all who consider themselves high, and they shall be brought low...And man in his high place shall be bowed down, and his haughtiness brought low; And in that day the L-rd alone shall be exalted." Others paraphrased Amos Ch. 8: "And I will turn your great feasts into mourning, and all of your songs into lamentations...The days will come that I the L-rd, will send a famine into the land—not a famine of bread, nor one's thirst for water, but one that involves hearing the words of our L-rd." Regardless of the Biblical passage cited, the ultimate message remained the same to their audiences. All must repent now before it was too late. And all must pray to G-d now and accept His dominion over the earth.

In response, many individuals were preparing for the end of the world, by ending financial obligations, selling property, and gathering their families together to say good-bye. Some were taking all of their last resources and moving into isolated enclaves on pieces of land, where they would do subsistence farming in order to survive. Others were fasting and beginning lives of asceticism. With all the economic turmoil created in the depression, it was hard to know who was transferring property and abruptly not purchasing in the stores for religious reasons, as contrasted to those who had been forced to take the same measures as a result of economic hardship.

Still others who had read the article on Prince had become infatuated by the man, and were determined to follow every step he took. Many of these were young, idealistic women, and their passion was stirred more by their observation that Prince was still an unattached, very eligible bachelor—in fact voted the world's most eligible in the latest, most widely circulated, celebrity magazine. Each fantasized that she would one day meet the Prince Charming at a party, and he would be taken by her, and would then sweep her off her feet. Some of these ladies, as well as others who viewed Prince as the Messiah, had begun flooding into cities where Prince lived and traveled, in order to surround him, shake his hand, or throw kisses at him. Day or night, Prince could go nowhere without a crowd surrounding him; neither could he reside anywhere without masses of people encircling his residence. There was a constant vigil. Some wished to be close to Prince's presence. Some were waiting for the end of the world. Others knew not what they were awaiting. And a portion was attracted by the idea of being part of the crowd, and associating with something real which was happening. And the press felt compelled to cover it all.

Left out of these groups were the media and the so called intelligentsia of American society. As far as public expression, this segment of the society was now suddenly, and surprisingly, the most subdued. Most had been stunned—some said betrayed—by Kahn's switch to the other side. Prior to the article, these groups had been split in their view of Prince. Most it seemed, like Kahn, had questioned his authenticity and motives, and had made implied critical remarks about him. Others, particularly the environmental movement, had aligned themselves with Prince's goals, if not necessarily his personage. But no matter what role they had previously chosen to play regarding Prince, almost all were disturbed by Kahn's conversion. Deep down, virtually all of these people had been highly suspicious of the motives of politicians, businessmen—especially tycoons—and the religious, in part because they simply did not understand them. Prince was all of these, plus a lot more which had been unexplainable to them. For example, they had always been distrustful of his exceptional skills and moral character, since they had been unable to compare these to any other living soul. There were simply no models to study. Therefore, unlike the "average" person, this class of people could never truly love Prince. So, even those who prior to the article had been allied with Prince among this group were stupefied by its conclusions; they had counted on Kahn to at least tell them the worst about Prince. And now they were worried that there would be no checks in the press on Prince's authority; who would take his place they wondered? As this class of professionals sat back in astonishment from reading the article, events in the street and public domain were moving so fast that they were overtaking their ability to think things through. So for the first time in their professional lives, they were relatively quiet.

In this new atmosphere, the board of the central union of American Rabbis scheduled a special meeting to discuss Prince. Representatives of all the older Jewish movements in America—Orthodox, Conservative, Reform, and Reconstructionist—were all represented. Prince's new Jewish movement, now estimated at 1.5 million adherents, was not. It had not yet been admitted.

"The purpose of this meeting is to decide what kind of relationship American Rabbis will have with Prince Reed's movement," the Rabbi chairing the meeting said. "In preparation for this meeting, I asked a subcommittee of Rabbis to discuss this issue, and write a proposed document for our discussion. Everyone here should have received that document before this meeting. If we can agree on it, or modifications to it, then we shall present it to the full conference for a vote of approval."

"Could someone explain to me why we are even considering this issue?" a second Rabbi said. "I'm not aware that this movement has even applied for membership in our organization."

"They haven't. We are considering it because several Rabbis on this board have asked us to do so," the chairman said.

"For what purpose?" the second Rabbi said.

"I'll tell you why," a third Rabbi said. "You sit over there in academia, sheltered from the storm. But I've got congregants coming to me in throngs every day asking what Prince Reed's movement is all about, what they believe, and what our position is on their movement. That's not to even mention that recently I've had several members leave our synagogue, to join their new one across town, which was just built."

"But this paper we're writing, this infamous white paper, is not going to make him go away," the second Rabbi said. "No matter what we say about him, he's going to go on doing what he's been doing."

"I just want some structure. I want to hear what everyone else thinks. Maybe I'm trying to work this out for myself," the third Rabbi said.

"Okay, why don't we actually move onto the paper itself?" the chairman said. "Mark, why don't I give you a minute to discuss your subcommittee's conclusions in this document?"

"Thank you, Elliot," Mark said. "It is true that Prince Reed's movement has not yet applied for membership in our organization, but we thought it wise to anticipate that request, since they have established dozens of congregations already. But when we looked at what they are doing, we concluded that at this point in time, the conference should not offer them membership, even if they should make such a request.

"I know that you've all read the document, so I won't go into a lot of detail. But just let me say that their form of organization is so different from our synagogues, that we do not think that they would fit in comfortably here."

"I saw this," the third Rabbi said. "But is this all? Are you not proposing anything? Are we just supposed to have a non-relationship with them?"

"Well, this just describes our proposed official relationship, as an organization," Mark said. "You're all free to develop unofficial relationships, though I'm not recommending it."

"So, our official policy will be that we are just ignoring them, closing our eyes," the third Rabbi said. "What do we stand for, anyway?"

"Look," a fifth Rabbi said, "what else could we have done on this subcommittee? This organization, representing thousands of Rabbis, all spread out across America, means something. We are a board of Rabbis with certain standards. Prince Reed may be wealthy, and a Senator, but he's not a Rabbi. So their whole movement is not even headed by a Rabbi. And they have trained no Rabbis; they do not have a Rabbinic school, nor do we see that they have plans for one. The few Rabbis they do have, have been stolen from our movements. What kind of Jewish movement primarily has lay leaders running it? What else could we have done?"

"And what do they stand for?" a sixth Rabbi said. "All of our movements have a specific philosophy and kind of worship, as well as specific theologies, say for example, concerning whether the Torah is Divinely given, or inspired. Their main dictum is that all Jewish souls matter. What's that all about anyway? It's certainly not a subject that was part of my Rabbinical training."

A seventh Rabbi sat smiling and nodding his head in agreement. "We all have charters, organizational charts, and mission statements. What do they have? A spiritual advisory committee. Reminds me of some ragtag group gathering in the shtetl. If Prince Reed left them today, their whole movement would fall apart. It's based on one man. He controls everything."

"In modern Judaism, we've thankfully long since moved away from one man controlling everything," the sixth Rabbi said. "Rebbe...really! Does he really think he's our personal guru in this modern world? Would he have us go back to Eastern Europe, where we were oppressed for our behavior?"

"I'm not sure how we'd even collect dues from them," Mark said. "They just do not have an organization yet. They don't even know how many members they have, because they do not assess dues in the traditional manner of our synagogues. They raise money from participants, but their finances are hidden from us."

"But does this justify no formal relationship with them at all? Should we not be talking to them?" the third Rabbi said.

"Frankly," an eighth Rabbi said, "it wouldn't bother me if we didn't have anything to do with them. What do they have to offer us? I wish they'd go away."

"So, all of you say that we will have nothing to do with Prince Reed?" A ninth Rabbi, who had never said anything in dozens of previous board meetings, had suddenly spoken up in a booming voice. There was such surprise by his entry that all heads in the room immediately turned toward him. "So," he continued, "you all think that we should just officially ignore 1.5 million Jews in America, and pretend that they just don't exist?"

"Frank, we're not ignoring those Jews," a tenth Rabbi said. "They're free to join us in synagogue at any time. Our doors are open."

"I wonder," Frank said, "if our doors are so open, why has Prince Reed's movement been so successful, so quickly? Might we not learn something from him?"

"I have nothing to learn from that man," an eleventh Rabbi said. "What are you suggesting? That we go out there and pretend that we're the Messiah, just as he's done? Anyone can do that, and get attention."

Frank angrily turned to face the eleventh Rabbi. "What do you know about Prince Reed? Have you ever met him? And when has he ever claimed that he was the Messiah? How can you sit in judgment of a man whom you've never met?"

"Well, he's not denying the rumors about him," the eleventh Rabbi said.

"Well, just what if he were the Messiah?" Frank said.

The eleventh Rabbi laughed heartily. "He's not the Messiah," he said with incredulity.

"How do you know?" Frank said. "I mean, what would tell you if he were the Messiah?"

"This is truly an absurd conversation," the eleventh Rabbi said.

"What's so incredible about it?" Frank said. "Do you not believe in a Messiah, and a Messianic Age?"

"No, as a matter of fact, I don't," the eleventh Rabbi said. "I don't believe that G-d sits up there, and sends angels and messiahs down here from heaven, in some kind of fairy tale world."

"Well, what do you believe? Do you believe that G-d gave us the Ten Commandments at Mt. Sinai?" Frank said.

"Not the way you do," the eleventh Rabbi said. "They didn't just arrive on some stone tablets out of the sky. At best they were Divinely inspired."

"Well, tell me, just what do you believe? What caused you to join the Rabbinate? You must have believed in something. Or was it just a good income, and you didn't have anything else to do with your life?" Frank said.

"Gentlemen, this has gone too far," the chairman said. "Let's get back to our document here."

"We were on a point," a twelfth Rabbi said. "Let's be honest with ourselves, rather than hiding behind some legalistic document here. Most of us in this room, including me, do not like Prince Reed. And because we don't like him, we don't want to associate with him in any form. That is our prerogative."

"And what don't you like about him?" the third Rabbi said.

"He's a charlatan," the twelfth Rabbi said. "And if you don't believe me, then consider history. How many pretenders to the Messianic crown have we experienced throughout all these years? Consider just one of them, Shabbatai Zevi. He led our people to ruin, and ended up converting to Islam. These events have always happened during periods of grave uncertainty and inner questioning. Now, during another period of darkness, we have another impostor—not even an ordained Rabbi— taking advantage of our people. Woe to us—especially when our gentile neighbors figure out later that they've been had too."

"Not later. Woe to us now, as he flagrantly attracts Christians now to his Messianic aims, and makes the Jews sitting targets," the sixth Rabbi said. "They will surely strike back at us for proselytizing, just as they did in previous times."

"Wait a minute, you two," Frank said. "Just when do you think that the Messiah should come? During a period of light, or darkness? And just how is Prince Reed taking advantage of the Jews or anyone else? The guy's the top Senator, in charge of the crucial food program. He headed the biggest corporation in the world before that, and did some wonderful things. What has he done wrong? Attract Jews to synagogues? I thought that was what we all wanted. And if

Christians approach us by their own initiative, and express an interest in our religion, should we just shut them out?"

"I'll be frank again," the eighth Rabbi said. "It doesn't matter to me all the good things he's done, though one could question that. He's upset the apple cart, stirred everything up, when he didn't have to." Then he leaned over to his neighbor, and purposely whispered loudly enough so it could be heard, "he's an outsider, a stranger with no credentials, who thinks he's such hot stuff. A prima donna. We don't have to let him in here, and it can be just because we don't like him."

Then a thirteenth Rabbi, a young woman, arose from her seat and began pacing around the room as she spoke. "If I may say so, this is a disgusting conversation. Some of us here are not fit to be Rabbis. We're down on this man because he's stirred everything up? Our Jewish tradition was built on the prophets. What were they saying about the prophets, Isaiah, Hosea, Amos, Samuel, when they were preaching? Were the people saying that they were crazy and self-interested too? 'Cause they sure weren't preaching to keep the status quo. The questions of craziness and self-interest are fair to raise, but we'd better answer them honestly. And I have not heard one salient argument in this room today, by the promoters of this document, which truly tries to address who Prince is, other than saying he's different from us, and not part of our fraternity. Should we not be talking to him to find out? Should we not be talking to the Jews who are flocking to his movement? What's bad about Jews finding spiritual fulfillment in their tradition? Who are we rooting for, anyway? Sounds like ourselves. The self-interest we see is ours."

"You should not put down the Rabbis in this room! You've embarrassed me. And now I'm sorry I nominated you to be on the Board," a fourteenth Rabbi said directly to her.

"Just maybe you did it, because you thought I was a person of principle," the woman said. "Maybe I can live up to that. Maybe I can do what G-d would want here. Does anyone wonder what G-d would want in this situation? Or do we not care?"

"Thank you Rachel," a fifteenth Rabbi said. "It doesn't matter what we think with our little minds, haughtily contriving this and that, as if we had authority over all the Jews, and knew what we were doing. It matters what G-d thinks.

"The fact is that Prince Reed is the best thing that ever happened to Judaism in this country. Whether he is the Messiah, or not, doesn't matter, as far as our general position today. The fact that our people are returning in droves, pursuing their Jewish roots, does. Judaism is vibrant and growing because of Prince Reed.

"Why should Prince's movement be like ours? Have we done such a good job? Were our synagogues successfully attracting Jews before he came? Is our formal bureaucracy so effective compared to their spontaneous, informal approach?

"Tell the truth. Does he not aggravate you because some of your members have woken up to his spirituality? Is he not causing you to work harder than you did before? Be more creative, when you'd rather have done last year's program all over again? Answer questions that you previously didn't have to answer? Do you not in reality envy his talent?"

"I do not envy anything about him," the eighth Rabbi said. "I would like to crush him."

"Then a sixteenth Rabbi spoke. "We became a great people, because we believed. Abraham, Isaac, Jacob, and all of the matriarchs believed in G-d, and the power of His presence in our lives. If we will not believe in a better world, and allow change to occur, if we will not believe in the possibility of a Messianic Age, then how can we ever expect it to happen? If we as Rabbis will not believe, then how can we possibly expect our congregants to do so? And if we will not believe, then what is our purpose for being here? How can we bring down G-d's presence to this earth, if we have no faith in Him?

"And what about our people? What about the Jews in this country, in Israel, and throughout the world? Do they not deserve a better answer from us than this? We are talking about Jewish souls.

"We are also talking about the direction of American Jews, now that most have fully assimilated after at least a century here. If we wish to repudiate this man, we should not only have a very good reason, but we should set forth some kind of alternative vision for our life in America. Otherwise, in America, we shall likely go the way of all other minority peoples who have disappeared throughout history."

"Yes, and we have spoken about this man as if he were some kind of alien. This man may not be a Rabbi, but at a minimum, he is a person, with a soul imparted from G-d. At least, we should grant him that," a seventeenth Rabbi said, as he tried to catch everyone's vision around the large table. He sat next to the previous speaker.

"But in reality, he seems to be a great teacher," the seventeenth Rabbi continued. "Why would we then pass up an opportunity to speak to him? Are we afraid that we will suddenly be taken in and converted like the masses out there? Do we distrust ourselves? If we distrust ourselves, then we can have no trust in G-d. That's because if our motives are pure here, then we must believe that G-d will guide us to the correct conclusion.

"We all say we're Rabbis here, foremost, and why do we say that? It's because our training and faith hopefully has elevated us. Should we not therefore be making this critical choice at this critical time? If as many of you believe, he is a quack and a fraud, then should we not determine that immediately by first hand observation? G-d would want us to help make this choice for our people. Not to do so, is at best to remain blind and rigid and trivialize our roles here. At worst, it could be to allow our people to be victimized by another phony person."

Then the sixteenth Rabbi spoke once again, to support his colleague. "Some here today have implied that believing in a person, or a Messianic Age, is akin to going off the deep end, that it's just short of insanity. But those who feel that way may not really understand the concept of the Messianic Age. The Messianic Age is not something that will arise unnaturally. Likewise, I'm not advocating that we blindly believe in some miraculous jolt from heaven here. I'm recommending that we skeptically look at this fellow. Only if we are totally satisfied with his goals and vision, with his ethical behavior, should we associate with him. But, if we refuse to look at him, with all that he has truly already performed and accomplished well in this world, then we in effect say that we shall never follow a Messiah, that no Jewish leader will, or can arise, at any time, and lead us to a Messianic Age, no matter how exemplary his behavior is."

"They say that the spiritual advisory committee has members hidden in all types of important places," the eighth Rabbi said. "And it sounds like we have several present at this time."

"Well, actually, I am a member. And I am very proud of it. But if I hadn't been, I surely would be now, after this discussion," the sixteenth Rabbi said. "I believe that I have both served my congregation and this conference well at the same time. I know that many of you do not think that this is possible. But in my heart, there is no contradiction. And most importantly, I am not afraid to face my Maker when He decides that my time has come. You must all consider this to be the ultimate question, which you must answer for yourself, when you decide about this document."

"And what other deceptive ones do we have in our midst? You too, Brutus," the eighth Rabbi said, as he looked at the seventeenth Rabbi.

"No, I haven't been. But I would now be honored to be a member," the seventeenth Rabbi said. "But I don't imagine that you could nominate me," as he shook his head in disbelief.

An eighteenth Rabbi looked over at the sixteenth and seventeenth Rabbis, and said, "I don't agree with your conclusions. You haven't convinced me that we should deal with this Prince Reed, but I do respect your beliefs. I truly wish that I could believe as you do. It would give me peace of mind."

"You can," the sixteenth Rabbi said. "But you have to give yourself permission to do it. You have to give your mind the space and the freedom. Your heart must be open to receive. G-d gives us this potential, but we take it away from ourselves. We erect barriers around ourselves, and close ourselves out from the spiritual movement of the world.

"You see, the world was formed by G-d through many great and powerful contractions, which by their nature conceal the Supernal Countenance, or the inner aspect of the Divine Countenance, so that even unclean things—we call them kelipot and sitra achra—could come into being in this physical existence. We see right before our eyes, every day, these kelipot, these 'other gods', which draw their energy from the hinder-part of holiness. And consequently, we fail to perceive the holiness, which despite being veiled in this world, supports all life. We are constantly fooled in this world, as we are fooled here today. It is just like man to stare goodness in its face, and deny it. We live in a world of illusions."

"Your Rebbe has obviously taught you well," the eighteenth Rabbi said.

"He is of the greatest comfort to me too," the sixteenth Rabbi said. "I wish that all of you could feel this."

Then after a brief silence the fifth Rabbi spoke once again. "I feel violated by my colleague on my right here," he said, motioning to his side, but not turning to meet his gaze. "He should have let us know of his predilections."

"That is a fair statement, "the sixteenth Rabbi said, "but only in a certain context. If I had disclosed what you would call my bias, would you have been spiritually capable of seeing me for whom I am, or would your own prejudice have clouded your judgment, blinded you, and caused you to discount me as a person? Could we have continued to respect each other and could we have continued our deep friendship—you know well that I'm not just a colleague—in our disagreement? Could we have continued to exchange ideas and to challenge each other in our relationship, so that we could both grow from it? Or would our attachment to each other, which was previously moist, supple, yielding, tolerant, and forgiving, calcify into a rigid and inflexible, motionless chain, locking us in a death embrace? This is the question that you must ask yourself. And if I have misjudged you in any way, then I am very sorry and I shall do Teshuvah."

The fifth Rabbi's gaze had fallen to the tablet in front of him. He said nothing.

After another brief silence, Rachel spoke. "You know, when the Jews turned against each other in the Temple, when we lost our unity, the Jewish people lost their Temple, and their Land. If we cannot unite here today, then what hope is there for all the Jews to come together? And without that single vision of purpose, what hope is there for the Messianic Age?"

Then a nineteenth Rabbi—the last one—spoke. "You know, I too haven't liked Prince Reed. He just wasn't my taste. I don't care for fads either. His worship is also Orthodox." He smiled and shrugged his shoulders. "Perhaps he reminds me too much of the Eastern European model. I hate to see anyone idolizing him, and all the crowds in the street drive me just a little mad. Really, I had thought we Jews were past that point in this country. I was hoping that we had grown up to be a little more elegant, not so emotional—or irrational—with our religion. I guess it's my Reform pulpit.

"But I've been listening to the conversation here today. And I'm struggling a little right now. I've known I'm intolerant all along, but I've tried to rationalize it to myself. But the more I think about it, I can't. The spirit of Reform is change. The Reform movement was the first one in this country. Those Jews, the German Jews, wanted a new way, a new system, which fit their lifestyle and aspirations, and their new homeland. They changed the service; they changed the way they prayed. We've always said change is good, that growth is good—for the Jews of America.

"Now the path of American Jews has come full cycle. Funny, it always does. The change that is occurring is coming out of the Orthodox tradition in part. And we—the Reform, the largest movement in America, are fighting it. We are the established institution now. This Board is now more than half Reform, and the Conference even more so. The Reform movement always said that choice was very important, and that each Jew should decide how he should pray. We always said that each individual should do what was meaningful for him, whether it was traditional, or creative. We've always said that Jews should pull from all parts of our tradition for their prayers and observances, and often experiment with different means of expression. Now, that Prince Reed's movement is doing much of what we've preached all along—and attracting great numbers of Jews as well by doing it—we don't want to have anything to do with him. We need to stop to consider."

The arguments went on for some time. When everything was said, a vote was called. Not including the chairman, the paper had been approved by a margin of twelve to six. The committee had voted against establishing any formal relationship with Prince, or even inviting him to speak with them.

The angels had watched this event, along with many of the other recent occurrences concerning Prince, with rapt attention. There had been much anticipation of the board meeting, and its possibility of eventually uniting all the Jews in America into a single group. But after the meeting had begun, it had been like watching a football game, in which the other, stronger team had jumped out to an early lead, and merely had to be careful enough to hold onto it. In the later quarters, their home team had rallied, but it had not been enough.

"It is very sad," Ophan said.

"Yes, very true," Seraph said, "because I do believe this is the beginning of the end."

"What do you mean?" Ophan said.

"Well down there, they have Presidential watchers and Federal Reserve watchers," Seraph said. "Up here we watch G-d. They should be watching G-d more down there on earth too, but they get caught up in the banality of the physical world, which doesn't afflict us as much here. Anyway, if you watch G-d throughout human and Jewish history, it doesn't seem likely that He is going to allow Prince to establish a Messianic World."

"Why?" Ophan said.

"It is just what Rabbi Rachel said. If the Jews cannot get along, then there is no possibility of a Messianic Age. In fact there is the possibility of catastrophe instead. We saw it in the time of the Temple, but we've seen it in modern times with Israel and other issues," Seraph said.

"But I thought that G-d was leaving the choice of a Messianic Age up to the humans. Surely, everything is not played out yet," Ophan said, in a desperate voice. "There are still possibilities, and humans haven't risen up yet against Prince."

Seraph sadly shook his head in disagreement. "The die is cast, I think. You can't go there without structure. The Jewish people are the structure. Prince cannot unite all the peoples of the world, without first uniting the Jews. And while it seems that the world has not rejected him yet, the world is full of illusions, until the truth finally manifests itself. Just as Prince was doing better than we thought early on, so now his recent successes are moving forward on shaky ground. And at some point, once the die is cast, I believe that G-d will step forward to protect his servant Prince, before harm is done to him."

"Gee, I wonder if Prince senses what has happened today?" Ophan said.

"If he is aware of the meeting, and thinks about it, he shall realize," Seraph said. "The Rabbi on the spiritual advisory committee will report back. Whether they are in daily contact with Prince, or even think it necessary to tell him, as preoccupied as he is, I do not know—though some of the other angels might. But it doesn't matter. Prince is a chariot of G-d. He has complete faith in G-d, and goes in service where ever G-d wishes. Life or death will not bother him. And time does not have the same meaning to him as other humans. He knows that if the Messianic World does not succeed in this life, it will eventually prevail on another occasion, after humans learn sufficient lessons."

"But I'm still bothered by all this," Ophan said. I don't necessarily agree that G-d should pull the rug on this episode. Look at how far the humans have come. Look at what his servant Prince has achieved. You just can't expect movement that fast. It's not easy down there, after the expulsion from Gan Eden. Life is a struggle. Most of the humans are concerned with whether they are going to eat at night, especially during this drought and depression, and hardly have any time to attend to their spirituality. And then G-d comes along and insensitively says, 'Well folks, it just wasn't good enough for Me.' Is that fair? Don't they deserve more chances than that? Just what is He trying to prove anyway?"

Seraph smiled. "This whole thing has you stirred up my friend. I haven't heard you get so involved in a long time. But as the humans say, the ways of G-d are mysterious, and He is what He is. G-d has His reasons, and they are beyond our, or their, understanding. But G-d listens to human prayers, and they do make a difference. I understand that several of the board members from the central union of American Rabbis have already appealed to G-d."

"It must include the one from the spiritual advisory committee," Ophan said.

"Yes, it does," Seraph said, "and several of the other Rabbis who spoke up against the document, including Rachel. There were some very important souls in that meeting. That group has seen each other before, in other lives, when crucial decisions facing Jews were necessary. And though it may be hard to believe, they did better unifying today as a group than ever before. So that counts for something too. And it is important to G-d that those who stood up for Him and His prophet today, have chosen to pray for the redemption of all their people."

"It is ironic that the severely criticized in the meeting are doing the spiritual heavy lifting," Ophan said.

"Yes," Seraph said, "but that's life, isn't it."

29

The Prince Reed story was not dying down. Rather, its intensity was increasing. Every day it seemed to dominate more of the news. It wasn't as much the coverage of what Prince was doing any more. It was down home coverage of people reacting to him, changing their lives in preparation to follow him. It was stories of people having personal revelations and epiphanies. And it was the recording of personal change attributed to his example. Some prominent people had publicly converted to Judaism; others had rededicated their lives to the religion of their birth, whatever that might be. It was estimated that in just a few months time, the size of Prince's movement had attracted several hundred thousand more Jews, and was now approaching two million. Like a news pandemic, each story seemed to inspire many new souls' search for meaning, which in turn led to more news coverage. But, as with all news coverage, after a while some of it seemed rather mundane and a constant repetition of the usual. Still, amid the many accounts, several were truly astonishing, immediately making the national news, stirring the people's imagination, and shaking the national psyche. Two head turning stories occurred within just a few days of each other. One of them was a scene which occurred in Prince's office.

Jane was a highly respected and intelligent legislative staff person in her twenties, who had personally written or overseen much of Prince's Senate legislation. Her reputed character was beyond compare; she was also extraordinarily beautiful, with an allure that was said to be almost other worldly. She was single and had no known personal relationships with anyone on Capital Hill. In fact, there was no knowledge on the Hill of what she did after she left work, or even where she lived. Strangely, no one in her work environment had ever been with her after work, not even for a meal.

Jane had worked very closely with Prince. Their relationship had not only been cordial, but had involved many discussions about legislative details and the lobbying of Senators and Representatives on issues. At times, they had joked about their work predicaments. It was said that while Prince and Jane were not an item, they certainly had the potential to be so. It was whispered in the legislative corridors that she might even be his match in intellect and moral character. Here were two very mysterious characters of unusual ability, origin, and handsomeness, working closely together.

One night Jane had scheduled a meeting with Prince in his office. This was not unusual in any previous sense. Prince often worked late in the middle of the week, and he had met with Jane privately on many occasions. There was indeed new legislation to discuss.

"You know that you have a seven o'clock meeting with Jane—in about fifteen minutes," Richard said.

"Yes," Prince said, dropping what he was reading at his desk and looking up.

"Well, I figure I don't need to be here for the meeting," Richard said. "Though I planned to work a little longer, it's getting late, and I know you can catch me up on the details tomorrow. Would that be okay?"

Prince sat there quietly for a moment. He had a strange look on his face.

"I was wondering Prince, if you needed me any longer," Richard said.

"Ah, yes, Richard, I think I shall tonight. And I will also need Joyce to be with us too. She can come off that front desk and come in here. Perhaps for about an hour. I'm sorry about that."

"I wish I'd known," Richard said. "What's happening of so much importance?"

"I didn't know myself Richard, until just now. You know that hidden viewing area we have behind my office. It's still functional isn't it?"

"Of course," Richard said. "No one's used it, and I checked it out myself, just yesterday, as you told me to periodically do. I never understood why we put that in. We've never used it. I never thought we'd use it. In fact, as you will recall, I questioned the ethics of spying on anyone. And you specifically told me that it would not be used for that. In fact, you said that it would be used very rarely, if at all."

"Well, before Jane gets here, I'd like you and Joyce to go back there and carefully watch what happens between us tonight. I want that video recorder going on our interaction as well," Prince said. "So, you better get to work immediately."

"Oh, okay," Richard said, as he began to mobilize. "We obviously don't have time to talk about this right now, but I want to record my strong dissent before hand, especially in light of our conversations before we put this thing in. What could you possibly have to fear from Jane, after all this time?"

"It's not fear, Richard," Prince said. "But I'll have to explain it to you later. Better just trust me right now."

When Jane arrived, Joyce had her sit in the lobby, saying that Prince was detained for the moment. Joyce apologized that she was in a hurry that night, and would have to leave before Prince came out to greet her. "Jane, that's a fabulous outfit," she said.

Jane had actually seemed more pleased by Joyce's statement that she would be quickly leaving, than by her comment on her appearance. But she responded in her normally polite manner. "Well thank you, Joyce. That's such a kind thing to say."

Joyce shook her head. "I just wish that I could look a fraction that good, at any time. But you, you manage it at this time of day, after a long day at work. I just don't know how you do it."

Joyce then left through the public entrance, and reentered Prince's office through a private one.

When Prince had gone out to greet Jane, they had exchanged friendly banter as they had entered his office. At first, the conversation had gone expectantly. There was a bill which was finally expected to come out of committee and they were discussing the proposed amendments to it, and the possibility of a filibuster.

But if the conversation seemed normal, Prince knew that her personal cues were not. She was watching every move of his, trying to catch his eyesight. As they had looked at a list of amendments, she had moved her seat very close to him. And her hands were inching closer to his, never touching yet, but trying to move in parallel. He was an animal being tracked in the woods, and when he moved into a clearing, and he was finally in her scope, she would try to take him down.

"Oh my, what's she doing?" Richard whispered, as he watched from the viewing area."

"I don't know," Joyce said. "I'm worried for him, Richard. And I've never felt that way before."

"So am I Joyce," Richard said. "But understand that Prince is no ordinary man, which is probably why he faces an adversary like that. And he knows. That's why he's got us back here." Then he sighed. "It's never a dull moment with my friend Prince."

Prince knew that he must break away. So as he talked, he rose from his seat in order to retreat behind his desk.

Sensing his withdrawal, she rose quickly, and circled around him to cut off his escape. Now within a few inches of him, she fixed her determined eyes on his face. "Marry me, Senator," she softly whispered. Prince turned away from her.

"Please look at me Senator. You know that it's a relationship we both want," she said.

Prince said nothing.

"Senator, our relationship doesn't even have to be public. And there is nothing even questionably wrong with what I am proposing here. We are both unattached."

Prince remained silent. He did not move from his standing position.

"Senator, you know of my intelligence and beauty. You know my moral standing. Why will you not let me into your heart? Look at me, Senator. Look at me. I am yours."

She carefully observed Prince for a moment. "Senator, with our intelligence and persuasive abilities joined together, you know we will surely dominate Washington. No one will stop us. And your legislation will prevail. You will have ultimate power to effect the positive changes in the world that you desire.

Prince still had not moved. Inside the viewing booth, Richard and Joyce could barely breathe.

"You're scared Senator, aren't you?" she said. "Why not face me like a man? A real man would look at me!"

"I am not afraid," Prince said. "G-d is with me now. And I no longer have any fear now, or ever."

"I don't believe that," she said. "Why won't you look at me then?"

"Out of respect for you and your soul," Prince said. "Out of respect for Jane's soul."

"No, it's because you cannot look at me," she said. "You know that your soul cannot face me and survive your mission on earth."

"I now know who you are," Prince said, as he now turned toward her. He stared directly at her. She smiled in anticipated victory, expecting him to quickly embrace her. But instead of feeling his desire, she felt only disdain and retreated from him. After a minute, she no longer could take his direct gaze, and cast her eyes to the floor. The bloom of her beauty suddenly faded as energy drained from her form. Her elegance transformed to an ordinariness as the power she projected diminished.

"Who are you?" she said. "I've never been refused by anyone. You must have some superhuman powers."

"No," Prince said, "I am just a man. It's no power at all."

"But every man has wanted me. I exemplify what each wants: beauty, intelligence, charm, mystery, moral character, and a singular focus on that person, to the exclusion of all else."

"Everything, but what G-d wants," Prince said. "Who sent you?"

"You knew about this in advance, didn't you? How did you know from the beginning?" she said.

"Because I see the heart and the motivation of the heart. Everything that you offered before tonight appeared to be correct on the surface. But I could detect that your heart had evil lurking in it," Prince said.

"But then why didn't you stop me, earlier?" she said.

"Because most of humanity has the evil of the animal soul in the left side of their hearts, where the blood flows. It is a matter of whether that person acts on that motivation, or instead, intellectually chooses to do the correct action. Every human is given such a choice, and not presumed guilty before the deed. Every human is given the chance to do the proper action."

"And you were not afraid that you would be overpowered by me? Why?"

"No," Prince said. "G-d protects me."

"He must protect you, alone. No one else has the power to do what you have done tonight. Believe me, I know," she said. Then she looked directly at Prince until he nodded, to fully acknowledge the meaning of her last words.

"We all have that power," Prince said. "Some souls are more elevated than others. But G-d protects us all, if we will only receive Him, and keep our faith in Him and His majesty."

Then, she had disappeared into the night.

Richard and Joyce burst out of the viewing area, not even remembering to turn off the video first. "Why didn't you keep her here?" Richard said. "Shall we not immediately track her down?"

"No," Prince said. "Call the FBI immediately. She shall first lead us to those who hired her. Then she shall disappear. That is her destiny."

After the FBI had been called, and a team immediately put on her trail, and a copy of the video made, Prince sat down with Richard and Joyce. They had been composed earlier, but were trembling in shock now.

"I just can't believe it," Richard said. "Who would have thought that about her? But we've had so many other incidences of corruption. Why then am I so wired about another shameless person in this Capital? I thought I had gotten over the novelty of that a very long time ago."

"Because," Prince said, "it is novel. You were witnessing something truly different tonight."

"That makes me feel a little bit better," Richard said. "Because I was really fooled by her. I thought of all people..."

"I knew when she came in tonight," Joyce said, "that something was different. Her beauty was almost supernatural."

"Exactly," Prince said. "My opponents sent her. In their desperation, they wished to gravely embarrass me and totally neutralize my mission on this earth. They chose the strongest form of enticement they believed that they could find, in order to lure me toward evil.

"Evil, in whatever form it occurs, is almost always tempting; we just recognize it more when it is in certain forms, for example, tonight, or in the Adam and Eve story. But sometimes when we recognize evil, we are even more charmed by its form. We strangely think that because it temporally makes us feel better, that it is okay. Very few souls set out to do evil; they merely find it attractive, and because they associate attractiveness with good, they are misled.

"But even though man will perform evil, as occurred here tonight—even though man is evil's agent—G-d has purposes, which G-d will play out through man at the same time. So another noteworthy story was playing out tonight. Like a chess game, she told me the motivation of her moves. You know it well, Richard, from one of my classes."

"Yes, at one point, when you turned to face her again, you said that you knew who she was," Richard said. "And then she later said, 'Believe me, I know,' when she was referring to your powers. You both seemed to know who each other was, but not until you had clearly refused her charms, Prince. It was like you were in a contest with a very worthy opponent. I can see that she had a special reason for being here. Could it be like the parable about the King and his son?"

"Yes, very good. Why don't you tell Joyce this story," Prince said.

"There was once a king who desired to test the moral character of his only son," Richard said. "So he had a very clever and enticing woman brought in front of his son. She was instructed to expend all efforts to seduce the crown prince, using everything at her personal disposal, but without betraying the secret purpose of her mission. To betray that mission, would mean its failure. But the woman, while fulfilling her mission, secretly desired that the son would not succumb to her."

"So this is the nature of kelipah," Prince said. "We are drawn to the evil of kelipah in this physical existence, but it does not really desire to fool us. It is here strictly for man's benefit, so that he may have a choice and be able to prove himself."

"That explains why she was so attractive tonight," Joyce said. "She was fulfilling her mission all too well. And that explains why we knew her for so long before she struck tonight. Prince would never fall for a woman he did not know well."

"And that explains why no one here knows where she resides, or how she lives. She was sent here for a purpose," Richard said. "And why she will disappear again into the night, when she fulfills her purpose."

Just as Prince had predicted, the FBI had apparently been able to follow the woman to the group which had hired her. When they checked the address of the building that she had entered, they had found out that it had been rented by the Opposition Party. The FBI had quickly obtained a court order to wiretap the place, but just as Prince had said, they had been unable to follow the woman any further.

"You've apparently bungled this mission," the supervisor of the FBI team said to his subordinates. "How could she disappear like that? We need that witness."

"I swear to you, that we had that building surrounded from the time she entered," the leader of the team said. "She's either still there, and we now know that's not true, or she found a tunnel out of that place, and we now know that's impossible, or she transformed into a different body, and managed to leave in some kind of metamorphosed form. I'm sorry. You'll have to take your pick."

"This just fits with the rest of this case," the supervisor said, throwing up his hands. "We can't even track her identity. We don't have a record of where she lived."

Within a few days, another seemingly surreal incident had occurred. During that year, a number of ministers, as well as Rabbis, had stood before their congregations and endorsed Prince Reed for President, and as a moral leader of the world. Some of the ministers had now even taken the course of endorsing him spiritually, even though—and perhaps because—he was Jewish. In their eyes, Prince had come to lead the world as a Messiah, and the sooner the world recognized that reality, the sooner all people could receive the World to Come. As strange as this had initially seemed, it had been occurring more frequently, until it no longer was such a big news event. Then something else happened, which jolted the world even more.

In the middle of an Easter morning service in New York City, Cardinal Davis, the very popular, relatively young, and highest ranking Catholic clergyman in America, who was rumored to be favored to be the first American born Pope, rose before his congregation to speak. This morning he spoke in an ecumenical spirit, discussing the origin of Easter and how their Jewish brothers in turn celebrated Passover. Then he paused and took a very deep breath.

"Now, my friends, I have a confession of my own to make. If you feel that I have betrayed you, I hope that you will forgive me.

"I have served as your priest all these years, but in reality, I've been something else. Oh, it wasn't intentional, in a conscious sort of way. I had illusions that I really was a Catholic servant. But I'm not."

Then he slowly pulled off his robe. On his head was a kippah. He raised up both of his hands. One hand held a mezuzah and in another was a pair of tefillin. "These my friends are what guide me now," he said. Gasps could be heard from those who were paying attention at that moment, and they craned their heads to make sure they had heard him correctly.

"I am a Jew. My soul is Jewish. I tried to ignore it all this time, but when Prince Reed came before this country, I could do it no longer.

"No, it's really not that he converted me, or led me to think differently. It is otherwise with me. The truth is that my family was always Jewish. These are my grandfather's possessions," he said, once again lifting his arms.

A huge roar was building rapidly and rising up off the huge floor, but Cardinal Davis ignored it. "We were a family of secret Jews. For more than five-hundred years, we kept our tradition intact, secretly passing on our religion and spirituality in one country after another, after we left Spain in 1492. I was the last secret Jew of my line. So many others had assimilated, until they had forgotten their origins. A few had found their public Judaism. Then there was I. And thanks to Prince, I have remembered my G-d, as the Jewish soul that I really am. I have not cut the link, after more than five-hundred years. I have honored my ancestors, Abraham, Isaac, and Jacob. Hallelujah.

"Now, please join with me, as the Jews and Catholics go forward to meet G-d with Prince as our..."

By this point, the stunned fellow Catholic clergy had had time to reach Cardinal Davis and begin escorting him away. The crowds were surging toward the front of the room. In a scene reminiscent of the floor when Prince had announced his prediction of the drought, some people had fainted, while others had been trampled from the confusion. Only the pews prevented more injuries. Again, the police were forced to call for reinforcements, to evacuate the building—not an easy matter on that holiday Sunday.

The two back to back incidences, with Jane and Cardinal Davis, broke in the news at the same time, and had shocked the press. The *New York Times* would normally have carried one of them in huge bold headlines on the front page. This time, the whole front page was two huge headlines, with subheadings which referred the readers to the stories within. On that day the *Times* looked like other dailies in town.

The hysteria surrounding Prince swelled. Twenty-four hour news programs seemed to talk about nothing else. More news stories arose about people's conversions and the dramatic changes in their lives. To many observers, it really did feel like the end of the world. Many people were very overjoyed by the prospect. Even the skeptics were beginning to nod their heads and come around. Then to top the excitement off, Prince stated that he would be making an important announcement in a month in San Francisco. He had invited all who had helped him throughout the years, including Judy and John Jones, to be on stage with him. But in the Opposition Party headquarters, the politicos were desperately conducting an emergency meeting, with the explicit purpose of counteracting him.

30

When Jeff and Richard had brought him the news about Cardinal Davis, Prince smiled subtly and said, "Some things never change. Souls move from one life to another, continuing to accomplish their purposes, but under different circumstances. We are tested and retested at different levels, to see whether we have really repented. Each time, if there is progress, we are able to succeed to a higher level of repentance and spirituality.

"What do you mean?" Jeff said.

"Allow me to tell a story from the Baal Shem Tov," Prince said.

The Baal Shem Tov told all his students of their specific missions in life. Some of his disciples became teachers, some became hidden tzaddikim. But of all things, Yankele was informed that he should travel around the world and tell stories about the Baal Shem Tov. Yankele was certainly not excited by the prospect of leaving his family and asking for money to tell stories, but he did as he was instructed. The Baal Shem Tov had told him that he would know when his purpose was fulfilled.

So Yankele went from town to town, telling stories about his rebbe. Eventually, he heard that in a town nearby a wealthy Jewish merchant would pay a considerable amount for each story. Since Yankele knew thousands of stories about the Bal Shem Tov, he went to meet the gentleman. "I can tell you all the stories ever known," he said.

The Jewish man was very pleased. "It is now Thursday night," he said. "You can stay with me tonight and rest until Shabbat. At our first meal of Shabbat, you can tell your stories."

Yankele rested Friday. But when he wanted to tell his first story on Friday night, he could not remember even one! His mind was blank. "I really do know many stories about the Baal Shem Tov," he said, "but for some unexplainable reason, I can't think of even one right now." Yankele's host was encouraging. "Tomorrow, you shall do better," he said.

But the same thing happened during the next meal, then the third meal, and then the fourth feast. Yankele apologized repeatedly to his host for his bewildering loss of memory. The merchant nevertheless thanked him and paid him for his efforts.

On Sunday morning, Yankele left for a different city. But he was no longer a confident storyteller. He wondered how he could have forgotten every story about his Master. Then leaving town he saw a house where the shutters were drawn. It reminded him of a story he had never told before. He rushed back to the merchant. The merchant's eyes were red from crying.

"I don't know that much of this story," he said. "The story starts in the middle, and there is no ending. This is the best I can do." He was happy to finally return some of the kindness of the merchant.

"We were once traveling with the Baal Shem Tov," he said, "and as he often did, he suddenly had us turn the horses around and go to a large city of another region. When we arrived, the streets around the houses of the Jews were strangely deserted and the shutters drawn. The doors were locked. After we had knocked at one of the houses for a long time, someone finally cracked the door open. When he realized that it was the Baal Shem Tov, he quickly brought us inside the home. 'What are you doing?' the person asked. 'The bishop is calling for a pogrom today in the market place; we will all be killed!' But the Baal Shem Tov instead opened the shutters; huge crowds of gentiles were now gathering in the square. While his hosts pleaded with him to close the shutters, the Besht said to me, 'Yankele, go to the bishop, and tell him that I wish to talk to him.'

"I said, 'Rebbe, that is insane. I shall never get through those crowds to him.' But he assured me that I would. So, somehow I was miraculously able to move through all the people and reach the bishop, who was just about to step up on the platform. 'Bishop, the Baal Shem Tov wants to speak to you,' I said. The Bishop turned pale. He replied, 'Tell him that I will be with him soon.'

"So I ran back to the Baal Shem Tov and reported the bishop's message. The Baal Shem Tov said firmly to me, 'Tell him now, Yankele. He must come now.' So I made my way back through the crowd. Just as the bishop was being introduced, I interrupted him, 'The holy Baal Shem Tov says now.'

"The bishop got up. He said, 'Go, and I will follow you from a distance.' The bishop told his parishioners that he had an emergency, and went to meet with the Baal Shem Tov. For hours, the bishop met with the Baal Shem Tov behind a closed door. When the bishop left the room, he had changed. He had been crying. He

never returned to the platform, and there was no pogrom. I'm sorry but that's all I know."

The merchant was now crying. "Yankele, can you not tell who I am?" While the merchant's face seemed familiar to him, Yankele was puzzled.

"I am the bishop in the story," the merchant said.

"But you are Jewish," Yankele said.

"I was born a Jew," the merchant said, "but because I was poor, I entered the Church. Eventually I rose to become a bishop. But like many other converts, I was ashamed of my background. To prove my loyalty as a Christian, I decided to kill Jews. But the Baal Shem Tov knew the truth about my soul. He made me do teshuvah, to repent.

"I knew that my sin was so terrible that it would not be easy to repent. So I begged the holy Bal Shem Tov to let me know when my repentance would be accepted in Heaven.

"'On the day that someone comes and tells you this exact story,' the Baal Shem Tov said.

"When you first arrived," the merchant said, "I recognized you, and was so hopeful, because you are the only other person besides the Baal Shem Tov who knew this story. But when you couldn't remember even one story, I realized that my repentance had not been accepted. I began praying. But when you did no better at each meal, there seemed to be no hope that I would be forgiven. Today, G-d had compassion upon me."

There was a silence after Prince finished the story. And then Jeff spoke. "So this is the meaning of the Cardinal Davis incident, which will seem so flagrantly outrageous to many Christians."

"Yes," Prince said. "It seems on the surface, as if this is all a matter between Jews and Christians. But in reality, just as in the story, it is a matter between Jews and Jews, and Jews and G-d. The Jewish souls have their issues with G-d, and the Christian souls have their own separate issues with G-d."

"But I am afraid that the Christians will not understand that and will be offended," Jeff said.

"As with so many other issues in life that Jewish souls must face," Prince said, "this is undoubtedly true. What the Jews do to fulfill their covenant with G-d is often misinterpreted, and thought to be offensive. But we do not see our gentile neighbors in any less light than we see ourselves. We do not see their purpose as any less than ours. But just because we will be misinterpreted as Jews, does not mean that we can turn back from our G-d given mission."

More than a week later, the Attorney General of the United States walked into his meeting with the President of the United States. "We are scheduled for a 4:30 appointment to review some of the department's briefs, but first I have a short tape that I think that you should hear. As you may recall, Mr. President, this matter with this Jane person in Senator Reed's office was traced by the Bureau to a Washington site of the Opposition Party, which we wiretapped with a court order. It's hard to believe that they were that stupid and sloppy. But here's a piece of what turned up. The taped conversation is referencing Reed." He placed the tape recorder on the corner of the desk and turned it on.

"That ..., every time we think we're making progress against him, he turns around and gets one up on us. First the drought prediction, then the economic depression—the media every night. Then Kahn turned on us—the Jews always end up siding with their own. Now this hysteria over the woman we sent—and the Cardinal, too. This guy's got the luck. What won't happen next?"

"He's as good as President in the next election. He's unstoppable."

"Darn Jew. I wish he'd take his filthy religion to Israel, where he belongs."

"It's what I've been saying all along. We've run out of options. There's only one way to stop this guy."

"Hey, I told you I'm not funding that."

"We don't need your funding. We've already got enough in the till. It won't take that much."

"What's he referring to anyway?"

"He's a Jew, isn't he? They want to crucify him. It would be payback for what happened to another Jew two thousand years ago."

"I told you, I'm not having anything to do with this."

"Don't go soft on me. We cannot allow him to become President! I've already got it arranged. We'll be able to pick him off at the big rally in San Francisco in a couple of weeks. There's no way for them to have enough security there."

The Attorney General switched the tape recorder off. "There's much more. Much more detail about their intent. But unfortunately, we don't know a lot of the specifics—who they've hired, and exactly how they will do it. Do I need to play any more of it?"

"No." The President shook his head.

"Well, what are you going to do about it?" the Attorney General said.

"What you would normally do," the President said. "You've just recently got secret service protection assigned to him."

"With all due respect Jim, that's not enough," the Attorney General said. "The man's expected to announce for President. He's invited a ton of dignitaries. So everybody and his mother will be there. The preliminary estimate is more than a hundred thousand in that field. And Prince Reed always turns up with a lot more supporters than we think he's going to. It's even going to be televised live. I cannot enforce security with some secret service protection."

"Well, then you'll get some more Bureau agents and a lot of local police out there," the President said.

"Let's get real. San Francisco doesn't have those kind of resources. You'll have to spend some bucks and give me more than that," the Attorney General said.

"You don't have the details of anything here. No defined plan. And what's so special about this guy? I'm not doing more for him than I would do for anybody else—well myself," the President said. "You know I'm running for reelection too. You wouldn't be planning to do the same for me, would you?"

"You don't have the hysteria surrounding you that this man does. There's no tape that records a contract on your life. I am the Attorney General in this country, and I am sworn to uphold the law." Then after a pause, he added. "Come on. This is the Opposition Party we're talking about here. These people are truly evil. They aren't just talking. They're absolutely serious. And they have the money and the connections to do it."

The President shook his head. "No." Then he looked back at the document that he had been reading.

The Attorney General always knew that this meant that there would be absolutely no further discussion. But this time he went on. "I tell you, Mr. President, that I can no longer perform my duties like this."

The President lifted his gaze back to the Attorney General. There was a surprise on his face. "Goldstein, I made you in this position. I brought you up here. The least you can do is be loyal to me. Have you gone soft, like the rest of them out there? Are you suddenly finding your Judaism, like that Cardinal? I thought you were a different kind of Jew."

"What kind of Jew was that?" the Attorney General said. "One that wouldn't follow an ethical path and do his duty? If that's what you wanted from me, then you should have picked a different religion—or no religion at all. I may not be a practicing Jew, and I may have been aligned with you up to this point in time, but make no mistake about it, I'm proud of what that man's been doing for America, and I'm proud to be a Jew now too. And for heaven's sake, at the very least, he's a freaking human being. Don't you care?"

The President's jaws tightened and he stared at the Attorney General. "You'll turn your resignation in, effective tomorrow morning."

As he packed up his briefcase, the Attorney General said, "Mr. President, realize the political, if not ethical absurdity of what you do here today. One way or another, you are already finished. If Prince survives, he shall be President. And if he doesn't, well I've already recorded a tape with enough information to incriminate you, should I not survive either. Needless to say, that tape's already in a safe place."

31

Judy Jones noticed the whistle of the wind lessen, as the door of her ranch house was opened to the outside. She felt a huge rush of dusty wind and heard the boots of her husband rhythmically tapping the wooden floors.

"You got up even before I did," she said.

"Yes," he said. "You've been crying. Why?"

The tears began to stream down Judy's face once again. "I had a dream, John."

"Omigosh, so did I. That's why I was up. I just wanted to walk my land, one more time. But first tell me yours."

She thought he had a strange look on his face, and wondered what he was thinking. But she felt even more compelled to talk first. "John, it's about Joseph."

"So was mine," he said.

"John, he's in grave danger. I saw someone very clearly take a shot at him. It was from a field, with a lot of people. I'm sure that it's that rally that we're going to in a couple of days." Then she began sobbing as she struggled to get out the words. "John, you know that in all matters except Joseph, I am brave. But I don't believe I can go on living without his presence on earth."

John nodded his head. He pulled up his chair in front of hers and picked up both of her hands in his. "Judy, I thought a lot about this, since three in the morning, when I had this dream. It's going to be all right."

"How, John? That's what Joseph said two years ago, when I saw him in his Senate office."

"My dream was a continuation of yours. I was sitting on the stage close to him, as he's invited us to do. And I took that bullet."

"John, no! You can't do that!" She shook her head furiously.

"Now, you see why I've been up so long. For a while, my whole system was in shock. But then, I got to thinking about it."

"It's a choice, John. G-d doesn't make us do this. That's why you received the dream. It's a choice. We don't have to leave for San Francisco tonight. You can stay here."

"I know, but as you've always said, Judy, when you don't follow your destiny, there's the likelihood of unhappiness."

"Noooo, John! It doesn't have to be this way. I do not want you to get hurt."

He shook his head. "I'm going to die instantly. It's clear that there's no pain."

"Let someone else take that bullet. Maybe we can reach Joseph, though it's so close to the event that he's virtually unreachable. And if you take that bullet, they'll have another one. Where can Joseph run?"

"Judy, I'm not happy here any more. The drought has destroyed everything that I ever valued. We won't even see a hazy sun today, until ten at the earliest, because of the dust. And yet you know, I'm not willing to move. I know that Joseph will take good care of you." As he said the last part, he began to weep, and Judy reached over to hug him. "I owe that man everything, and this I can do. If I don't do it, I'll worry about him. I'll never forgive myself, if anything happens to him. There may be several bullets, and I will take the one which really matters. And Joseph is the one person on this planet, who knows souls well enough, to realize and appreciate what I've done."

She searched his face and then she knew that he would not change his mind. She had nevertheless tried repeatedly that morning to bring him back into her life, but it had been useless.

Finally, she had searched her computer. She knew that others, in touch with the Divine Light, would also know what was happening. But she first wondered about Joseph. What would G-d inform Joseph in these circumstances? She had never received an e-mail from him before, but she knew that this time, he would contact her, if he knew. He would know that she was likely to know. And her first message had indeed been from him.

"If circumstances in our lives should suddenly change," Prince had written, "and we should by fate be parted, and not see each other again, know that I love both you and John very much, and that I am so grateful for our association. Also know, that wherever I go, I shall see your souls, and extend my protection over them—Joseph"

"No, Joseph, no," she had yelled. "I cannot lose both of you." For the longest time, she had wept over the machine. Then she had thought to pick up the second message, from some unrecognizable e-mail address.

"You have not met me in this life. But I indeed know well who you are. By now, I believe that you are aware of certain events, which are likely to happen, and affect you greatly. When you reach the platform in San Francisco, I will be there, to direct you to the proper spiritual and physical place. You will know who I am. Do not worry. G-d shall protect you and His servant." The message was unsigned.

32

The turnout for Prince's announcement was phenomenal. The weather had even cleared after a major storm, which had sunk two rather large boats in the harbor, very near the shore. It was estimated, but not known for sure, that more than two-hundred thousand people had turned out for the event. The crowd was expecting the ultimate announcement—a bid for the Presidency of the United States. And the affair seemed like more of a victory party, than a traditional, low odds, uphill battle, which every other contender for that office was usually faced with fighting. The polls—and there had been many taken prior to this occurrence—showed Prince around fifteen percentage points ahead of his closest rival in a four way race.

When Prince stepped up to the platform and greeted the crowd, the roar was greater than any Super Bowl football game. But he modestly declined to receive the adulation. This made the crowd even more enthusiastic, so that the cheering went on continuously for approximately twenty minutes. Prince had worn a bullet proof vest, which he had made sure he could slip off immediately, and he spoke behind a bullet proof glass. There were plain clothes policemen all around him. But this still was insufficient for certain moments, when Prince might turn away from the podium, or move across the platform. The security that night was tight, but its managers knew that with the crowd size, it was not invincible for a well planned assault. Those who were after Prince would not hesitate to first kill anyone who stood between Prince and them.

When Prince was finally able to speak, he began to charm his audience. He spoke not only of issues which had been important to him, but also about his personal mission in life, about the future of America, and yes—about a Messianic World. He said, "It's a magical outcome, but it's not a mysterious route there. It's one good deed after another. It's one step after another. This is not fantasy, but a world which humans are able to accomplish on this planet now. It is within our grasp. Help us to accomplish it." By this point, the crowd was so wrapped up in his speech that there was almost complete quiet on the field. Then Prince turned to acknowledge and praise several people who had helped him, and a series of shots rang out.

The attack was obviously professionally planned. Many shots had come from several areas on the massive field, creating considerable confusion, and making an escape for Prince difficult. He threw his vest off, so that he could run. Through the secret service men, who moved in front of him, past John who lay bleeding next to the podium, pushing with great might around people, he ran. Observers, who were able to see him for only an instant, said that he seemed to run as fast as he had at the Olympics, when he had won his gold medals.

Now, Prince was remembering his own dream, reading it like a road map. It had been so clear in his sleep, the same night that Judy and John had experienced theirs. He had dreamed it three times in succession, each time recording more detail in his brain than the last. In the first one, he had understood the events as they would occur, starting with the shooting. In the second one he had looked at street names and landmarks along the way. And in the third, he had recorded significant tiny details which would be crucial to maintain his lightning speed. The repetition of the dreams—three times—the clarity, and the subject matter, had told him of their great significance. When he had awoken, he had written down all the details, and had rehearsed the route the night before.

His attackers had anticipated not only his athletic ability, but his uncanny capacity to outfox his foes. At several exit points, along corners, and in abandoned or currently occupied buildings, they had planted snipers and observers. They were in constant communication with each other and were prepared to circle around him, should they find him. But Prince had tried to take all this into account. He had headed toward the harbor, as his dream had instructed him, and as he ran, he had thrown off most of his clothes. By the time that he had reached the water, he had eluded all of his pursuers. But several of the observers hired by the attackers had seen him dive in the water and radioed their companions. Some of the killers were there in less than three minutes, but they could find absolutely no trace of him. There was never any trace of him in public society again.

Epilogue

The boy looked up. "Grandfather, you've spent three days of your visit here, from one meal to the next, telling me this story. And I've listened to it all this time. Is that the way you're going to end it—that he just dived into the water and disappeared? I don't think that's all there is. Please tell me it's not."

The grandfather chuckled. "No, you know I wouldn't do that to you. You've been very patient."

"Well, what happened to him then?"

"Well, you remember that Prince was not only an incredible runner, but he was a fantastic swimmer too. That unusual combination of athletic abilities had allowed him to win the world championships and the Olympic competition in the decathlon. Everyone always wondered about Prince's great athletic ability. 'Why did a tzaddik need athletic ability? Tzaddiks need special souls and superior intelligence, but athletic ability?' they said. But that ability not only critically enhanced his reputation in a society that highly valued sports, but allowed him to escape that night. G-d plans for everything, and all contingencies, and we never know how a skill or opportunity will be used. But you can bet there's a purpose."

"Come on grandfather. Tell me. Where did he go, and how did he survive, if he lived?"

"Patience. I'm getting there. It's just a few more minutes. Remember at the beginning of the last scene, I had casually mentioned that a couple of rather large boats had sunk in the harbor, just before this event. Well, as I told you, G-d takes care of everything. He was not going to permit His servant Prince to be hurt in any way. Prince had been instructed in his dream to find one of those two boats, enter the boat, and find a major air pocket which could sustain him for days. After a few days, at a certain appointed time during the night, he would swim to the surface, where members of the spiritual advisory committee would meet him. And that is how he survived. Incredible, isn't it? But Prince was an incredible man."

"And he did all this because of his dream?" the boy said. "Wasn't he scared—scared that he wouldn't get to the boat, or that it wouldn't be there, with enough air?"

"You and I would be scared," the grandfather said, "because we feel such a separation from G-d. But not Prince. In life or death, he had faith that G-d would be with him."

"And where did Prince go? And what did he do? What about Judy and John? And what did everyone say after he disappeared? And how is he my namesake?"

"One question at a time. I'll do my best. John died quickly that night. As he had predicted from his dream, he was in no pain. And Prince had thanked and hugged him immediately before the event had started. This had meant more to John than anything else in his life.

"As for Judy, she was met by the Hasidic Rabbi who had been Prince's mentor since Oklahoma City. When you adopt a soul, as this Rabbi and others did with Prince, it is like adopting or birthing a child. You have him, and feel responsibility for him for the rest of your life. So it was with the Hasidic Rabbi who had sent the e-mail to Judy. He had sat beside her at the event, and just before the tragic event occurred, he had taken her aside and showed her the e-mail, to establish his identity. He took her to a secure place."

"Come on grandfather. What really happened to Judy?"

The grandfather smiled. "I'm sorry. I just don't want to let go of a good story. But for your sake, we'll finish it now...Well Prince was picked up as planned, and then secretly flown to Israel. To escape detection, the spiritual advisory committee used a private plane owned by one of its members, and left from an unusual location. They brought him to the property that Judy had bought, where the two of them reunited after many years."

"Yeah, then what?"

"Well, the two of them were married under a huppah as soon as possible. And they both enjoyed that very green part of Israel. Prince's importance to the world was not diminished. He could no longer play a public role. But he became a tzaddik nistar, a hidden tzaddik. Not only was he a Lamed-Vov, one of the thirty-six Just Men who hold up the world, but the world in that generation depended solely upon his presence for certain attributes."

"Even though he was not seen, and very few even knew where he lived, or that he was even alive?"

"Exactly," the grandfather said. "In his generation, he was the spiritual entity which brought G-dliness onto this earth, even to those who had opposed him. And there's one more thing—both Prince and Judy are your ancestors. What a pair of illustrious great great...whatever grandparents to have. It'll be hard filling those great shoes, especially as your Bar Mitzvah comes up. But I know you'll be able to do it."

"Wow... that is something." Then after a pause, the boy said, "But there are a few things I don't get, grandfather. Like, why didn't Prince stop what was happening, if he knew about it? And why did he run that night? He could have tried to stay and continue to run for President."

"Those are very good questions, but the answers are not simple," the grandfather said. "First, Prince was a servant of G-d, so that he did as he was destined. He read the dreams the same way that John did. This was what was supposed to happen; this was his destiny. He could not know the exact reasons why. Even to a prophet like Prince, who towered over others in his generation, G-d is incomprehensible. No finite person can have any idea of the infinite nature of G-d."

"But why do you personally think that G-d did not let Prince become President? He was so close," the boy said. "And the world was getting much closer to a Messianic Age."

"I think," the grandfather said, "that America had become so radicalized in the short time before they tried to kill Prince, that it was impossible at that point in time for the Messianic Age to occur. Prince had accomplished a lot. Look at what he did for the world—if nothing else to get the world to seriously consider the idea of a Messianic Age and work toward it. He was also very much responsible for beginning the political and social processes that led to the better world we now have. We are much closer to the Messianic Age. If you look at history, very few nations are fighting each other any more, and we have worked hard on our environmental and population issues. In his time, many problems looked hopeless and appeared to be worsening. He was responsible for turning that around."

"So is that why he ran that night? Because he knew that this is what G-d wanted?

"Partially," the grandfather said. "His dream told him to do so. But Prince was also a tactician, down to the very end. He was a tzaddik, who could have commanded an army in the field. So he always knew the power of his opposition. As brilliant as he was, he was humble and not arrogant, as so many others would have been in his position. So that he never underestimated who went after him. That was the reason that they never defeated him. And that night, he knew that they had so many guns aimed at him, from all corners of the field. He also knew that they were absolutely ruthless, and would stop at nothing before they captured, tortured, and killed him. We would call him a brave man, but as he would say, he didn't have to be brave, if he fully trusted in G-d. Anyway, Prince knew that they would maul everyone around that platform until they reached him. The only solution was to flee, so others could escape."

"Well, what did the media say?" the boy said. "And if this was such a big deal, why haven't I heard of this from my American history courses?"

"Well, as you might expect, the media couldn't get off of it. The news coverage would have been long and dramatic enough, if Prince had died, and they had found his body. The coverage for a notable figure like that, who then becomes even more of a celebrity, and an icon, as a result of untimely death—not to mention his incredibly handsome figure—is nonstop, to the point of sickening. But in Prince's case, it was a lot more than that. You see, they never found his body."

"So?"

"So the speculation started. Some people thought that he had never died, which ironically was true in the real sense. But what I mean to say is that they thought that he must have left this world, and have been raised up to Heaven in a supernatural way. You see, they had caught those who had observed him going in the water, and the others who had arrived shortly after that, and the public knew that these guys were killers and trackers, and that they would have certainly found him, or his body, if he were to be found. And to many people's minds, this model of his disappearance fit the rumors regarding his Messianic purposes and prophecies.

"But that wasn't all, by any means. Some groups, who had been claiming that he was the second coming of Jesus all along, seized upon this whole episode as proof. To them, he had risen from the dead. How else to explain no body? They quoted from the *New Testament* in order to prove their case. And they also pointed out another twist to this whole matter. Like Jesus, he was thirty-three years old, when this happened. Another Jew, crucified by the world—or as some of course claimed in the Opposition Party—killed by the Jews once again.

"Oh, and we almost forgot Kahn. He was one of the few voices of reason through this period of hysteria. As irrational as he had once been regarding Prince, this was how lucid and logical he now became. In commentary subsequent to Prince's disappearance, Kahn maintained that aside from being a tzaddik and the most impressive man of his generation, Prince was still only an ordinary, mortal man. In his interview, Prince had specifically told him so. And if Prince's body was nowhere to be found, then, with his superior intelligence and athletic prowess, and the Will of G-d, he had surely escaped detection. Prince lived on, he said, supporting the spiritual wholeness of the world. It was Kahn who set up and promoted a well known center to further Prince's work, and it was Kahn who preached in print till his dying days the Messianic truths that Prince had embraced. With his superior knowledge and dedication, Kahn even became associated with the spiritual advisory committee, which, with the Hassidic Rabbi at its head, continued to vigorously work toward a Messianic Age. But that is another story."

"Wow," the boy said, shaking his head in disbelief. "But why haven't I heard of this story in school, or somewhere?"

"You probably have," the grandfather said. "Think about it. You're the history buff. You already know a lot more of the details than I do."

"Well, I think I remember a Senator Reed mentioned somewhere in our American history book—but it was only a sentence or two, about a period in our history when there were more than two major political parties."

"Very good," the grandfather said. "He's the one."

"But, there was nothing about this or anything else that..."

"That really told this story?" the grandfather said.

"Yes," the boy said. "I mean who cares about some stupid political parties when the world's at stake?"

The grandfather nodded his agreement. "There's so much the history books don't know, and can't cover because of space. First, there's only so much that's really transmitted to us in the public realm. And whatever is available for use, must of course be filtered through the consciousness of the historian, who chooses, from his very limited perspective, what he thinks is important. And in the course of human affairs, it seems that we get stuck on the physical things of this world, the wealth, the power, the movement of armies, because these are the things that we can see and track. The important hidden, spiritual movement—and this is the only critical reality for man—is lost to the 'official' record. It must be chronicled in stories like this.

"Some will say, of course, that this story is not really true, that it is merely folklore, unsubstantiated—even that it is only a fairy tale, built around an insignificant historical figure. But how little they know about what really operates human affairs! How little they know about G-d and His Kingdom!"

The boy was silent now. He was gently massaging his head, while he mulled over the story. The grandfather smiled at him, while he patiently waited. Finally, a look of recognition flashed across the boy's face and he said, "I never thought of it like that, grandfather. You know, we have this kind of artificial scale, by which we measure things. If Prince had become President—like he almost did—then in the history books, we would know all kinds of things about him. We supposedly would know if he chopped down a cherry tree, or whatever—not that any of that is for sure true, is it? But, in our history books, he's like all these Vice Presidents, or other Senatorial leaders, or community leaders, who really influenced our country and the world, but disappeared into thin air."

"But there's lessons to be taken from this, very Jewish ones," the grandfather said. "Each of us is a world. Each life is a world, which opens to many more worlds. Each of us has the power to bring G-d's love and Wisdom upon this earth, just as Prince did. We have the power to influence many people, not by necessarily leading movements, or getting in front of crowds and the media, as Prince did, but by doing mitzvot—that is by teaching, healing, or helping—just one person at a time. We have the power to be partners with G-d. The recipient of our Divinely inspired work, whether a child, a patient, or a friend, is then able to assist someone else, probably in ways in which we never could have originally done. And so on. That is how we can personally create the Messianic Age. We may not have the elevated soul that Prince did, but that does not matter to G-d. What matters to G-d, is that we do what is within our power to do—that we do our best. Recognition by others, while critical for the advent of the Messianic Age, is not important for each of our souls. Recognition by G-d is what counts. Of all the smoke and fame around Prince at the time of his life, the only thing that really counted was that he was a humble servant of G-d. We all can be humble servants of G-d."

"Wow!" the boy said. "Grandfather, do you have any more stories that you'd like to tell me?"

"On that day, Death shall be swallowed up forever, and G-d shall wipe the tears from every face with the coming of the righteous Moshiach. May it be speedily in our days! Amen!"

Glossary

Abram going forth from the land–Abram was Abraham's original name before G-d renamed him, in recognition of his covenant with G-d. This phrase refers to Abraham leaving his original home, Ur of Chaldees.

Aleinu–the part of the Jewish service called the Adoration, whereupon Jews bow down to G-d.

Amidah—one of the traditional prayers in which the Jew makes specific requests   of G-d.

Apikoris, Apikorsim (pl.) –heretics. Often these heretics were learned men, but they chose not to believe.

Asiyah–the lowest of the four created Worlds, the World of Action, which resulted from G-d's powerful contraction of the World of Yetzirah. This is our present world.

Atzilut–the highest of the four created Worlds, the World of emanation, which resulted from G-d's contractions in creating our present World.

Ayin–nothingness. G-d created yesh, something from ayin, nothing. This is beyond our understanding. Man can create by recombination, but G-d provides the primary materials.

Baal Shem Tov–literally Master of the Good Name. (Born 1698 or 1700–Died 1760) The mystical teacher and progenitor of all Chassidism. He had many disciples who continue to this day. There are many spiritual stories associated with him.

B'al Teshuvah–returnee to Judaism.   Often refers to a person whose religious observance previously lapsed, or whose observance was formerly relatively minimal, who then begins to observe the 613 Jewish commandments.

Beriah—the second highest of four created Worlds, the World of creation, which resulted from the powerful contraction of the World of Atzilut.

Binah—one of the ten sefirot (see definition) known as understanding. It is the development and elaboration of the details of the idea or concept which arrives through Chochmah. Also known as the mother for this reason.

B'nei aliyah—literally "man of ascent". Generally refers to a tzaddik, who converts darkness on earth into light and holiness.

Chesed—kindness, generosity. One of the ten sefirot (see definition). Chesed is a flow which is restricted by the attribute of gevurah.

Chochmah—one of the ten sefirot (see definition) known as wisdom. It also refers to an intuitive flash, an idea which suddenly pops into one's mind. It is our mind's connection to G-d. Also known as the father for these reasons.

Cohen—a priest in the Temples, or a descendent of a priest, all who were descended from Moses' brother, Aaron. Aaron and Moses were from the tribe of Levi. If a person was spiritually fit, the privilege of being a priest was hereditary and was passed down from father to son. Those of this lineage still give the priestly blessings in Conservative and Orthodox synagogues, which bless the entire congregation.

Daat—one of the ten sefirot (see definition) known as knowledge. After a person has Chochmah and Binah, he may then develop Daat, which is a middle column sefira. Daat refers to applying Chochmah and Binah to a situation.

Ein Sof—literally Infinite One. G-d is unknowable to man, whose body is finite.

Elul—the month on the Hebrew calendar which precedes Tishrai. Rosh Hashanah, the Jewish New Year, is the first day of Tishrai, while Yom Kippur follows on the tenth day of Tishrai. These ten days of spiritual questioning are referred to as the "Days of Awe". The month of Elul is spiritually important because it precedes the critical Ten Days of Awe, as well as other major Jewish holidays. It is thus a month of spiritual preparation and Kabbalists say that during this period "the King is in the field" {on the way to His palace}—in other words during that time G-d is accessible to ordinary people in ways that He normally isn't.

Galut—exile, referencing the Jewish dispossession of the Land of Israel and the resulting Diaspora of the Jewish people.

Gan Eden—Hebrew for Garden of Eden.

Gevurah—Might. One of the ten sefirot (see definition) which encompasses the qualities of constraint, restriction, and severity.

Hashem—name for G-d, literally the name.

Hillel—a Jewish Rabbi and Talmudic scholar in Judea during the Roman period. Hillel said, "If I am not for myself, then who will be for me? If I am only for myself, then what am I? If not now, when?"

Hod—splendor. One of the ten sefirot (see definition).

Huppah–a canopy used in a traditional Jewish wedding ceremony.

Kabbalah–literally to receive. Esoteric wisdom of the Torah.

Kabbalists–those who study Kabbalah.

Kavanah–spiritual intent and motivation. This is critical in prayer to G-d, which to be effective, must truly come from the heart.

Kelipah, Kelipot(pl) –the shell in this world which veils the hidden spiritual world. May be used in speech to refer to something which is the antithesis of something spiritual, such as money, fame, praise, which distract our attention from G-d.

Kellim–Vessels.

Kippah–skull cap which many Jews wear in synagogue, and which observant Jews will wear outside synagogue as well.

Lamed-Vov–means literally thirty-six from the numbers assigned to the Hebrew letters. Refers to one of the thirty-six Just men who hold up the world through their actions and presence.

Lashon Hara—Evil speech. The contents of lashon hara are actually true, as opposed to a worse kind of speech, which is slander. But even though lashon hara is true, it is unnecessary speech or gossip, which serves no functional purpose (other than perhaps to gratify the ego of the speaker), and therefore often hurts those to which it refers.

Levite–a member of the tribe of Levi, who assists the Cohen, by washing his hands (and sometimes feet) prior to the Cohen giving the priestly blessing to the congregation.

Love of Delights–a tzaddik's love of G-d. This love is not possible in the common man who remains at a spiritually lower level.

Madreigah–degrees or levels. Often references a spiritual context.

Mahd–acronym for masculine waters, which descend to earth, as a result of a tzaddik's elevation of mahn.

Mahn–acronym for feminine waters. The tzaddik, or "man of ascent", by his love of G-d, converts evil to good, and thereby causes the feminine waters to rise, which creates a corresponding descent of mahd.

Malchut–lowest of the sefirot, meaning kingdom. It unifies all the flows of the Sefira into our present every day revealed world existence.

Medeber–man. Refers to one who talks, as opposed to the animals, plants, or inanimate matter. Also refers to the idea that man has the spiritual capacity to make a choice.

Mezuzah–Hebrew for doorpost. A metal or wooden box with prayers affixed to a Jew's home.

Minyan(s) —refers in a traditional Jewish setting to a minimum of ten men for a prayer service, which brings down the presence of G-d, and permits the reading of the Torah, and the saying of other important prayers. Women now make up a minyan in non-Orthodox settings.

Misnagdin—opponents. Historically, the Chassidim had their opponents.

Mitzvah, Mitzvot(pl) —literally commandment. The Torah sets forth 613 positive and negative commandments that an observant Jew shall fulfill.

Moshiach—Hebrew for Messiah. There is a long Messianic tradition within Judaism.

Neshamah—the most common of the five Hebrew names which refers to soul. The other names for soul refer to two higher levels of souls, as well as two lower levels.

Netzach—Endurance. One of the ten sefirot (see definition).

Oath—This refers to the Talmudic Kabbalistic teaching that before we enter this earthly world, we all take an oath to be righteous and not be wicked, and even if the world regards us as righteous, to regard ourselves as wicked. With this oath, the soul is invested with the power to fulfill its destiny in its life on earth.

Ophan—one of the traditional angels in the Jewish liturgy.

Or—light

Rambam—Maimonides. A Jewish doctor, philosopher, and Talmudist born in Spain in the Middle Ages.

Rashas—wicked people of the world. Rashas follow the evil of their animal souls found in their hearts, rather than the 613 commandments.

Rav—a Rabbi who leads a community of Jews. Also know as an authority in Jewish law.

Rebbe—an acronym meaning Head of the Jewish People, but also known as a wise person who spiritually leads a group of Jews. Just as the head of a body feels even the joy or pain in the feet, a Rebbe feels the joy and pain of his people.

Rosh Hashanah—the Jewish New Year. Means literally head of the year. Also the world's birthday.

Sefira, Sefirot(pl) —ten attributes or windows, expressing qualities of G-d. The sefirot can be organized in three columns, left, right, and middle. The qualities of each of the sefirot affect and influence the others.

Seraph—one of the traditional angels in the Jewish liturgy.

Shabbat or Shabbos—the Hebrew word for the Jewish Sabbath, which begins Friday night at sunset, and ends Saturday night one hour after sunset.

Shabbatai Zevi—a Messianic impostor in the seventeenth century. He was able to prey upon the spiritual suffering of Jews after the huge Chmielnicki massacre of Jews in 1648.

Shtetl—Yiddish for small Eastern European Jewish settlement.

Sh'ma—the most important Jewish prayer expressing a Jew's faith in G-d and His unity in all creation.

Shoah—Hebrew word for Holocaust that killed six million Jews during World War II.

Shomer Shabbos—refers to a person who is fully observant in Jewish laws.

Sitra Achra—literally other side. Something which is not separated from normal existence and specifically devoted to the holiness of G-d is sitra achra. Something from the permitted part of the sitra achra may be made holy by observance of the 613 commandments.

Tefillin—phylacteries. A pair of square leather boxes worn by observant Jews, one on the arm, the other on the forehead. They contain prayers including two parts of the Sh'ma.

Ten Days of Awe—the ten days between Rosh Hashanah and Yom Kippur in which Jews spiritually question their relationship with G-d and the quality of their deeds in the past year.

Teshuvah—repentence, literally return to G-d. Coming back to G-d after one has strayed from the proper spiritual path. Literally means turning toward G-d's presence.

Tifferet—beauty, compassion. One of the ten sefirot (see definition). It is a middle column sefira which results from the interaction of Chesed and Gevurah.

Tzaddik—literally righteous one. A tzaddik has been used in many historic and religious contexts. The specific designation here is one used by the *Tanya*, written more than two hundred years ago by Rabbi Schneur Zalman. In this context, a tzaddik is a special person who has expelled the evil of the animal soul from his heart and has no conflict between his Divine soul and the animal soul; such conflict exists within the ordinary person. This is a simplified description, and one should glean information from Chapters 9 and 10 of the *Tanya*, and from the rest of the book, to help understand in part this special type of soul.

Tzaddik nistar—hidden tzaddik. Even though we can no longer see this person, he still has hidden powers over the world, by bringing G-d's presence into this world. This is critical for all of mankind.

Tzimtzumim—contractions. Because G-d is infinite, and created beings with form and physicality would be nullified by His Divine Light, His Light was contracted from one level to another, during creation.

Yesh—literally something. But can also be used in a mildly derogatory sense: You are nothing, a yesh.

Yesod—foundation. One of the ten sefirot (see definition). Yesod is a middle column sefira which results from the interaction of Hod and Netzach. It is a connector between the inner mind emotions and Malchut.

Yetzer Hara—literally evil inclination. Has a number of meanings and ways of use. The yetzer hara is the quality that opposes our Divine souls. It is that feeling that tries to lead us astray when we have resolved to do right.

Yetzirah—the third highest World of the four created Worlds, the World of Formation, which resulted from the powerful contraction of the World of Beriah.

Yom Kippur—the Jewish Day of Atonement. Jews fast and repent for their sins. G-d forgives true repentance, whereupon a person is truly sorry for his sins, and resolves with all of his heart and might, never to do such an act again. But forgiveness between one person and another must be granted by the person wronged.